There Are... Were No...

The Polovets w... river, tearing off his clothes as he ran.

He wasn't the only one. Polovtsi swatted, punched and clawed at themselves, making their ragged clothes even more so. Some drew their knives and started slashing at their garments or even stabbing at themselves, although Shea noted that none of those seemed to hit a vital spot.

In what must have been less than five minutes, the camp area was completely empty of live, or at least conscious, Polovtsi. A couple lay staring at the sky, after stabbing themselves or perhaps knocking themselves silly falling off their horses.

"By God's Holy Mother, Egorov Andreivich!" Igor exclaimed. "That was like something out of a tale. What did they see?" There was more than a touch of awe in the look Igor gave Shea, but also more than a touch of comradeship.

"Rurik Vasilyevich and I gave them a good look at their lice, Your Highness. Ah, does Your Highness know what a louse looks like?"

"Monsters," Igor said.

Shea nodded. "Exactly. The Polovtsi saw themselves covered with monsters, and panicked."

The prince's look was now one of complete amazement. "No *bogatyr* in any tale ever did a thing like that."

Also by L. Sprague de Camp & Christopher Stasheff:
The Enchanter Reborn

Also by L. Sprague de Camp:
Rivers of Time
The Fallible Fiend
The Incorporated Knight
(with Catherine Crook de Camp)
The Undesired Princess & The Enchanted Bunny
(with David Drake)
The Complete Compleat Enchanter
(with Fletcher Pratt)

Also by Christopher Stasheff:
Dragon's Eye
The Gods of War
Wing Commander: End Run
(with William R. Forstchen)

THE EXOTIC ENCHANTER

L. SPRAGUE de CAMP

CHRISTOPHER STASHEFF

THE EXOTIC ENCHANTER

A Baen Books Original

Baen Publishing Enterprises
P.O. Box 1403
Riverdale, N.Y. 10471

ISBN: 0-671-87666-X

Cover art by Ruth Sanderson

First printing, June 1995

Distributed by
SIMON & SCHUSTER
1230 Avenue of the Americas
New York, N.Y. 10020

Printed in the United States of America

CONTENTS

Part I
ENCHANTER KIEV

ROLAND J. GREEN
AND
FRIEDA A. MURRAY

I

The kaleidoscope of colored dots had slowed to an occasional swirl of green and purple ones. Now that their eyes could focus again, Sir Reed Chalmers, Ph.D, etc., etc., and Sir Harold Shea, Ph.D, took a good look at the country in front of them. It was virgin forest, some willow but mostly birch and oak, with the hint of yellow in the leaves that heralds autumn. The ground cover was thick brush, with an occasional wildflower.

There was only enough wind to stir the leaves, but the temperature said "autumn" even more than the yellow-tinged leaves. It was brisk enough to stimulate minds fogged by their transition from the world of the *Aeneid*.

"We'll need something heavier than these tunics and cloaks," Shea remarked, pulling his cloak tight and his tunic down. "This is *not* a Mediterranean climate."

"Obviously, my boy," Chalmers replied. "Have you any speculation as to where we might be?"

"In a temperate-zone forest," Shea suggested. "They all look alike to me, and they turn up in mythology and literature from all over the world."

He looked around, trying to wave away the flies that sought the blood on his clothes and hands. They had left mythological Carthage shortly after attending a sacrifice, with no chance to wash.

They were in a sort of clearing, but otherwise Shea

3

saw nothing but forest in all directions. He heard rustles and chirpings, but except for the flies and an occasional flash of wings, no animal life was visible.

The sky was a pale blue, almost cloudless. By the sun it was somewhat past noon. Far off in the eastern sky Shea could make out what must be a large bird, the colour of a gaudy sunset. No clues there.

The land was fairly level, but sloped downward a trifle toward the south. As Shea watched, the previously motionless forest began to stir from that direction. Rabbits hopped, squirrels ran, and he caught a glimpse of a fox slinking by. A few minutes later they heard shouts and curses; the voices sounded human.

"Let's get under cover," Chalmers said.

They crouched behind a waist-high clump of bushes, thick enough to scratch skin, which only encouraged the flies. Presently two men jogged into the clearing, both carrying long spears with barbed iron heads. They wore wide-skirted, knee-length coats, embroidered around the sleeves and hems, baggy trousers, and calf-length boots. They had bushy beards, and wore large round fur caps.

Two others followed, similarly armed and dressed. All appeared to be short of breath. They also appeared to be of normal proportions, not the outsized heroes of the *Aeneid*.

More cries and curses, and a full-grown brown bear, at least five hundred pounds, loped into the clearing. Its muzzle was wet and its temper obviously foul. To Shea, whose head was about two feet above the ground, its stained yellow claws looked as long as butcher knives.

Four more men followed the bear, and three of them flung their spears. One glanced off the bear's shoulder. A second struck the animal's side, but the third, badly aimed, landed beside the watchers in the thicket, a little too close to Shea for comfort.

Remembering his lessons as Aeneas's spear-bearer, Shea seized the six-foot shaft. Muttering:

"Backward, turn backward, O spear, in thy flight,
  Speed to thy target and dim the bear's light,"

he aimed a yard from a spearless man, and threw.

The spear arced down just close enough to the hunter
for him to snatch at it, then somersaulted on its point
before he could grip it and hurled itself butt-first at the
bear. It struck a skull-cracking blow to the bear's head,
then dropped to the ground.

Seven of the eight hunters hastily made gestures of
aversion, but the eighth, the leader by his elaborate coat
and high embroidered cap, thrust his spear through the
bear's eye. They all waited a few minutes, but the bear
stayed dead.

The leader glanced around the clearing. "Greetings
and thanks to he who has helped us," he said in a strong,
resonant voice. "I am Igor Sviatoslavich, Prince of Seversk. Pray join us. You have my word that you will not
be harmed."

In the thicket Chalmers looked a little dubious.

"They know we're here, and they can always prod us
out with those spears," Shea reminded him, and rose.

At eye level, the prince was a good six feet tall, with
a stern, noble face. Approaching, Shea swept a respectful
bow—he'd certainly had enough practice—and Chalmers followed.

"I am honored to have been of service to the noble
prince of Seversk," Shea began, trying to figure out
where and when Seversk might be. Seven spears at his
back didn't help. "This is Sir Reed Chalmers, and I am
Sir Harold Shea."

The prince hesitated, then asked in a tone that con-
veyed more suspicion than courtesy, "Ah, have you no
patronymic?"

"Andre—ivich," Shea said, tacking on the Slavic suffix
at the last minute. "And my colleague is Reed, uh—"

"My father's name was William," said Chalmers.

"Rurik Vasilyevich! A name of good omen!" the prince

said. The thumps behind them told Shea that spears were being grounded. "How do you come to be in the forest?" Igor continued. "You have not the aspect of hunters."

"We are, um, scholars, from the West," Chalmers answered. "I fear we, ah, lost our way, and wound up here."

"What was your destination?"

"We were trying to reach the Silk Empire," Shea said, taking inspiration from Igor's cap as Chalmers's inventiveness ran out.

"Was there trouble along your way, that you did not go south, to Constantinople? Any merchant could have told you that eastbound caravans start from there, not the lands of the Rus."

"Merchants in the west are very secretive, Your Highness. They tell so many fabulous tales about the lands to the east that our—superiors—have sent us to seek the truth."

The prince looked dubious. "You carry no books or paper," he said.

With a sigh for his library in Ohio, Shea began a polite precis of the difficulties of carrying valuable and fragile objects through unsettled lands—

"Therefore, Your Highness, we keep them safely, and pull them out only when necessary." Gesturing, he recited:

"Who hath a book hath friends at hand,
　And gold and gear at his command;
　And rich estates if he but look,
　Are held by him who hath a book."

A leather-bound, gold-stamped edition of the *Almanach de Gotha* popped out of thin air. Shea grabbed for it, caught it with one hand just before it hit the ground, and nearly dropped it from the weight. Carefully using both hands, he presented the stout volume to Prince Igor. The prince looked, but did not touch.

"The Rus honor learning, Egorov Andreivich, and I would know more of you, and yours," the prince said. "You and Rurik Vasilyevich will dine with me tonight."

"We are honored to be your guests," Chalmers said.

Leaving all but two of his men to skin the bear and haul the meat, Prince Igor led the way out of the clearing. Once out there was a suggestion of a path to the south, very easy to miss.

"Do you have any ideas about who these people are?" Shea asked, as they trailed the rest of the party.

"None, except that they are Slavs. I cannot recall any mythology or work of literature with this background." Chalmers' frustration was evident. "Your small magics have worked well, so far."

"Literally, I should say."

"What led you to try those in particular?"

Shea considered. "With the spear, it was a little insurance for something I was pretty sure I could do. The book—well, I had to do something. Prince Igor sounded pretty suspicious. We don't want to get locked up for spies, or something."

"At least we know we shall have to be careful in our phrasing here. Even a wish might produce something inappropriate."

"That's nothing new, Doc. But I'll keep 'em small and precise for the time being." He looked ahead; the forest was thinning out. "Maybe dinner will tell us something about this place." Then he looked at the *Almanach de Gotha*, which he didn't know how to return. "We need some sort of reference spell, Doc, for places like this."

"I'll think about it," Chalmers said.

On the edge of the forest they passed a rough two-wheeled cart to which a shaggy pony was hitched. A peasant lounged nearby. Igor sent them back up the forest trail.

After leaving the trees, Igor led the party along a small river through a logged-off stretch, then up a steepish incline to a walled compound set against another stand of forest. Inside were about six one-story log huts, with thatched or shingled roofs.

Prince Igor entered the largest of these. He came back to the doorway just as the psychologists, beginning to pant from the hike and the climb, reached it. The prince offered a flat basket to Chalmers. It contained two small loaves on a coarse linen napkin, and some large gray nuggets on another.

"Bread and salt, Doc," Shea muttered. "Can't refuse."

Dr. Chalmers looked annoyed, but bowed, took a loaf, dipped it in the salt, and chewed—carefully. To judge from his reaction it was dry but edible. Shea followed suit.

"Enter my house," Igor said with a slight bow, moving back from the threshold. "Although perhaps you would care to visit the bathhouse first," he added.

The psychologists accepted this evidence of civilization with exclamations of gratitude. A servant appeared in the doorway, and led them to one of the smaller buildings in the compound.

At the doorway he asked for their clothes, saying that clean ones would be provided. Stripped to the skin, the two entered.

Inside the steam was so thick they could scarcely see each other, and so hot that Shea's sinuses, which had behaved well in other universes, gave him a painful reminder of their existence. An imprecation from Chalmers clued Shea to his partner's whereabouts.

"The Russian bath has a long way to go," the younger man agreed.

Groping about, they found benches, and wooden trays holding a greasy soap and bundles of reeds. These primitive substitutes for Ivory and washcloths actually got rid of blood and dirt.

They also got rid of aches and pains, and produced a wonderful feeling of lassitude. Shea found himself drowsing on a bench, unsure how long he'd been sitting there.

Eventually they heard the servant ask if they were ready to come out. When they answered yes, the other door of the bathhouse opened. They exited onto an open porch, where two large and well-aimed buckets of cold water were splashed over each of them.

Chalmers yelped, but the cold water had shocked a memory into Shea's conscious mind.

"Doc," Shea said, "I think I know where we are."

Chalmers looked out inquiringly from the coarse linen towel with which he was drying himself, as Shea reached into the pile of trousers, shirts, coats, and low boots the servant had brought.

"Remember that cocktail party for the new faculty last fall?"

Chalmers nodded. A wealthy alumnus who had never outgrown an adolescent passion for Tolstoy had recently endowed a chair of Russian literature. The new incumbent was an emigre who said he had taught at the Imperial Academy of St. Petersburg. It might even have been true, and he was certainly the lion of the party.

Everyone was following the elephantine choreography prescribed for such occasions when Professor Zerensky's path intersected that of Vaclav Polacek, the bad boy of the Garaden Institute. Polite introductions had degenerated into a *katzenjammer* conducted in Russian, and at one point Polacek started to take off his jacket. Shea elbowed him out of danger, and after threatening to allow him nothing but water until he cooled off, asked what the fuss was all about.

"That (Slavic epithet) had the gall to say that Borodin was a better composer than Smetana!" (More Slavic that Shea didn't really want to have translated.)

Shea had learned, from occasional dealings with colleagues at Notre Dame, never to argue with nationalist fanatics. He suggested that the Rubber Czech solace himself by sticking to Pilsner and boycotting the vodka.

"I will!" Polacek said, and stuck to it.

"It's too bad Polacek isn't here," Shea concluded. "This cold water would be just the thing for him."

"I do not consider the theoretical virtues of the cold bath to be demonstrated in practice," Chalmers replied. "As Florimel is not here, the impulse it is supposed to quench does not arise. If she were, there would be even less need for one."

"Ah, right, Doc. But this Borodin character Professor Zerensky insulted Votsy with at that party—well, his last work was an opera called *Prince Igor*. He died before he finished it."

"You mean we're in an opera?" Chalmers cried, in the tone of someone who expects the overture to *Tristan und Isolde* to begin any second—and who can't escape. "And it's incomplete? Ah—are we expected to finish it?"

"I hope not," Shea said, with a shudder. "Anyway, someone else did, after his death. But it was based on legends of early Russian heroes, so we're probably in those."

"How early?" Chalmers asked.

"I dunno. A long time before Peter the Great made the Russians shave their beards, anyway."

"Peter the Great accomplished a great deal more than that, my boy. He founded the Russian navy, reorganized the military and civil administrations, and established the Imperial capital of St. Petersburg."

"Well, it's neither Imperial, the capital, nor St. Petersburg anymore."

The footcloths provided with the boots were puzzling to men accustomed to socks.

"Uh, Doc," Shea said, struggling with his, "about Florimel. Do you think she's . . . here?" Their departure from the world of the *Aeneid* had been made in haste and disorder, thanks to a vengeful god.

Chalmers' face was almost as stern as Igor's—his version of the stiff upper lip. "If she isn't . . ." was all he said.

Shea laced up his second boot, then rose and clapped

Chalmers on the shoulder. "Let's start looking. If nothing else, we can join up with one of those merchants Igor mentioned. Meanwhile, we've eaten his bread and salt, so let's see what else he has to offer.

"Ready, Doc?"

"Quite, my boy," Chalmers replied, steadily enough.

The servant led them back to the main building. Shea recognized the big, beehive-shaped stove in the corner; according to *National Geographic*, it was still used in the Russia of his own day. The benches and tables were of finely planed wood, and there was an icon on the east wall.

The building was well chinked and had only one window. Though warm, by Harold Shea's standards it wanted a good airing.

Dinner was smoked venison, more of the coarse bread, and plenty of mead, kvass, and weak ale. The cups and bowls were finely finished wood, and steel knives were provided. Shea had tasted worse mead, but this was much too sweet for his taste, so he only sipped.

While they were eating, the huntsmen trailed in, by way of the bathhouse. Each bowed to the icon and the prince before sitting down. Two joined the psychologists at Igor's table; they were introduced as Oleg Nikolaivich and Mikhail Sergeivich.

Apparently it was considered bad manners to speak with one's mouth full, but worse manners to have an empty cup. The room became loud with the sounds of cheerful drunkenness, the scurrying feet of servants and the stumbling ones of men seeking the privy.

Igor, and Mikhail, and Oleg after they sat down, watched the two visitors closely. As Shea and Chalmers did nothing more alarming than eat, the atmosphere at the table soon relaxed.

After the edge was off, Igor asked a number of shrewd questions about their origins. Shea left the answers to

Chalmers, who said quite honestly that they were adventurers who had seen many a strange land.

"Indeed, Your Highness, we have seen the hippogriff, ridden a flying carpet, and drunk the wine of the gods! May I tell you about—?"

"Another cup, and you will have battled sorcerers and tamed werewolves," Igor interrupted. "Doubtless you also saw the firebird, and the Yaga in her hut, while you were in the forest. But tell me—by what road did you enter the lands of the Rus? Did you come from Galich, or by way of Polotsk?"

"Ah, we came the long way round, Your Highness. We were trying to avoid trouble."

"Wise of you. But this is not trouble; you have yet to meet that. Now, to get to the forest, you must have passed Velikaya Klyucheva. How fared the harvest there?"

"Really, I am not a farmer, Your Highness. I could see nothing wrong."

"Well, then, have you seen any burned or abandoned villages?"

"No, Your Highness."

"Any men mounted on small, shaggy ponies, riding without stirrups and often without saddles? They would be wearing ragged coats and trousers, caps and boots, and many layers of filth. Their weapons would be long knives and curved bows."

"They sound like folk one would not care to meet. Bandits?"

"Polovtsi. You saw none?"

"No, Your Highness."

"Did you even pass by any of their campsites? They are hard to overlook, for one can smell them three days' ride downwind."

"I am sure we passed nothing of the kind, Your Highness."

"Hippogriffs and flying carpets you have seen, but not the scourge of the steppes! And you call yourselves scholars! You did not need to come so far just to learn new tales to spin for your supper! So perhaps—"

At this point, to the psychologists' relief, someone struck up a *gusla*, an instrument that looked like a near ancestor of the balalaika. Then he started a song that had everyone lifting their cups.

As more of the men joined in the newcomers were able to hear that it was a listing of heroes; at every name a cup was drained. Igor and the rest drank to Sviatoslav of Kiev, Yaroslav the Wise, Mstislav the Brave, another Sviatoslav of Kiev, Vsevolod of Suzdal, and Yaroslav of Galich. But when a certain Oleg was named, Igor looked morose, and his cup lost its rhythm. Nor did he drink again, and the song faltered as others followed the prince. The player ended with a roaring paen to Vladimir the Great, then called for the singer's due. No few cups were set before him.

Igor muttered curses against another list, starting with Boris and Oleg. "They will do anything for silver," he growled. "And you, who have come so far, and seen so little, tell me—are you for hire also?"

Shea couldn't tell if they were being insulted or recruited. "We are pledged to return to our own lands if we live, but on a journey such as this, it is no disgrace to earn some extra silver."

Further aminadversions were interrupted by a servant who hastily passed the prince's table on his way to the door. "Your Highness, the princess' personal guard is here!"

The sound of hoofbeats and jingling harness now penetrated the noisy room. Igor woke up and so did Harold's curiosity. He had seen a princess or two in his travels, and wondered how this one would measure up.

When Euphrosinia Yaroslavna entered the room, all heads turned in her direction. Every man got to his feet and bowed as she saluted the icon. Igor left the table and embraced her warmly.

She and her escort wore the boots, trousers, and coats

of hunters; the escort carried longswords and shields instead of spears, and wore mail. All had grim faces.

"The Polovtsi attacked Yuri the Red's estate at Nizhni Charinsk two days ago," she announced. "They were rebuilding the palisade after it burned last month, and were caught completely off guard."

From the curses that rent the air, the psychologists drew two conclusions: the Polovtsi had raided a "safe" location, and they had no business knowing that the palisade was down. Sure enough, the word "spies" came up.

"Yuri's son Boris rode to Seversk to report," the princess continued. "The raiders took the entire household, including that young woman who is neither Rus nor Polovets nor Greek nor anything else we have been able to discover."

Chalmers' face suddenly matched Euphrosinia's for grimness. "Is she a small woman, Your Highness?" His voice didn't break. "Good-looking, very fair skin and brown hair?"

"It seems that you know her," Euphrosinia replied. "What is her name?"

"Lady Florimel, Your Highness."

"So is she named."

"What—?" Chalmers' voice did break.

"Can she—they—be ransomed or rescued?" Shea asked, noting that many far from friendly looks were now aimed their way.

"Perhaps," the prince said. "What is she to you?"

"She is Sir Reed's wife, Your Highness."

Shea didn't notice any warming of the atmosphere, but Igor suddenly gave a bark of laughter.

"So that is why you said so little! 'Reports to your superiors.' Pig swill! You're trying to find her! But how did you—what happened?"

"She was stolen by a powerful enemy, Your Highness."

"He must have been. You don't look it, but I'm thinking you are *bogatyri* yourselves." He grinned. "Perhaps you really have seen hippogriffs and the rest of it.

"Regardless, we now have a common foe. We must rescue your wife and Yuri's family before they go to the Krasni Podok slave market." He filled his cup with an unsteady but practiced hand and rose on still more unsteady legs.

"By Our Lord who saved us, His Mother who bore Him, the Saints who followed Him, the honor of Seversk, and my own honor as its prince, I swear that I will do all that may be needed, yea unto holding my own life as naught, until the Lady Florimel is rescued from her captivity among the Polovtsi."

Then he fell forward on the table and began to snore.

Chalmers looked stricken, but the other Rus at the table, after hearing the snores, paid no heed to the fallen prince. Shea took a close look and a strong sniff. "Just drunk," he reassured his colleague.

Euphrosinia Yaroslavna's handsome face looked thoughtfully at Reed Chalmers' hopeful one. "You should know," she said, "that by both the laws and customs of the Rus, no man may be held to anything he promises while drunk."

Shea thought that spoke well for the good sense of the Rus, but wasn't about to say so. "What says the law?" he asked, covering for Chalmers.

"'If two men, both being drunk, come to an agreement, and after, when they have both slept their drunkenness off, one of them is not satisfied with the agreement, it shall be void.'" Her fluent quotation gave Shea some notion of how often it was cited. "By custom, no vow, contract, or promise is valid unless all parties are sober."

"There is reason to go after them," Chalmers said, his voice showing that he'd bounced back, for the moment. "Folk of the Rus were captured too."

The princess shrugged her elegant shoulders. She couldn't hold a candle to Belphebe were that lady present, Shea decided, but she definitely held the eye on her own. "There are boyars of princely houses in the tents of the Polovtsi at this moment. Yuri was a *muzh*, yes, but a border lord."

She looked directly at them; her words might give pain, but she didn't turn away from her victims. "Done is done. For now, it is more important to prevent further raids. The Polovtsi should not have been able to strike this close to Seversk."

In an academic setting, Dr. Shea might have appreciated her *realpolitik*. She showed more logic than most political commentators in the twentieth-century U.S. But thinking of Belphebe had triggered a gut reaction: if she were in a mess, politics could take a bath until she was out of it. And Reed Chalmers would back him up.

Ergo, since Florimel is in a mess, politics can take that same bath, and I will back Reed. QED.

Time for my realpolitik, *Your Highness.*

Shea's gut had also generated an inspiration. He looked in the kindling box (the prince's table was close to the stove). Good, it held unpeeled willow branches as well as birchbark. Now to unruffle the princess' feathers . . .

"If I may, Your Highness, I would like to return His Highness' hospitality by giving him a healing draught. He needs to be able to ride tomorrow, no matter where he goes."

"I will watch you prepare it, and you will drink it yourself before you give him any of it."

Shea had no problem with that, although he wished the samovar wasn't still a few centuries in the future. "Please ask your servant to boil water in a clean pot."

While that was being prepared, Shea stripped the bark from the willow branches, and cut about two dozen small pieces.

"What are you doing?" Chalmers murmured.

"Using your synthesis spell to make aspirin, Doc. Mark these, please; the formula is $C_9H_8O_4$."

Chalmers perked up and set to work with his knife, while Shea shredded the rest of the bark. The Rus were quiet, but Shea knew that if this didn't work, the trouble Igor had mentioned would come, with a vengeance.

A servant, his hands muffled in rawhide, brought in a pot of water. Shea indicated where it should go on the table, a fair distance from Igor. Then he arranged the marked pieces of bark around it, and dropped the rest of the bark into the pot.

Finally, he and Chalmers stood on either side of the pot, Shea reciting, the older man gesturing.

"When I consider how my life is spent,
   The time ill-used, the wealth I fling askance
   On fleeting follies tuned to my own bent,
   Or joined with others, dance delusion's dance;
   O Willow! Emblem of the soul's own tears,
   O weep with me, a-pent in mine own snare,
   Yet healing bring, lest prey to mine own fears,
   I fall into the pit of black despair.
   Although thy leaves our dreary truths bespeak,
   Thy bark, now shredded,'s balm to make us whole,
   This bitter draught gives strength, unlike the sweet
   Taste of the mead, to which our strength pays toll.
   Come, prince of drugs! Thy powers unleash, restore
   To all who drink, sobriety once more."

The atmosphere in the lodge was anything but salubrious, but the spears remained stacked and the swords sheathed. Shea checked the pot; the bark had steeped. He wiped his cup and dipped some out.

Yeech!! It tasted vile, but warmed his stomach very nicely. In a few minutes he felt his incipient stomachache go away. His head felt clearer than ever.

He held out the cup to the princess. "The draught, Your Highness."

All heads turned to her again. She didn't hesitate. "Give him the draught," she ordered. "If he is harmed, you will both be flogged and your eyes burnt out with hot irons before you lose your heads."

She gestured, and Mikhail Sergeivich raised the prince.

Shea was relieved to see that he was not unconscious, just asleep. He put the cup to Igor's lips; the prince swallowed by reflex. By the time it was empty he had opened his eyes.

"Gaaaah!" was his first sound, and "Water!" his first word. The water was hastily brought, and the hands which had tightened on swordhilts relaxed a trifle, but did not move. Igor downed a pitcher and part of a second, then looked around, cold sober.

The hands fell away from the swordhilts. The princess stared.

"Did you prepare this draught?" Igor asked the psychologists.

"Yes, Your Highness."

"It tastes like rotten maresmilk. You *bogatyri* have stomachs of iron." He smiled broadly. "Mine is only that of a prince, but I owe you a boon. Ask what you will."

"Only that my wife be rescued, Your Highness," Chalmers said, before the princess could recover.

Igor repeated his previous vow, not as loudly but with more dignity, as well as several embellishments. By the time he had finished, half the room was cheering.

The prince was also beginning to find company in sobriety. Three or four of the men came up to the table and dipped their cups, and many a respectful, even awed, look was aimed at the strangers.

Princess Euphrosinia gave them a respectful nod, then turned to the prince. "Let us go to bed, my lord. The morning is wiser than the evening, and there will be much to do."

Igor offered his arm. "Gladly, my lady," he said, with more than a suggestion of a leer. He escorted her out.

Two days later, Harold Shea and Reed Chalmers were riding with Prince Igor's party eastward to the Don country. It was a fine day for riding, clear and neither too hot nor too cold. The trails, the occasional wide trail that deserved to be called a road, and the stretches of grassland they frequently had to cross were all firm beneath the horses' hooves.

"Just as well we're riding now," Oleg Nikolaivich remarked. "In another month, two at the most, this will all be mud."

Shea paraphrased an old description of a swamp. " 'Too thin to ride on, too thick to row through.' "

Oleg Nikolaevich grinned.

Shea found the high-cantled saddle comfortable enough, and was grateful to be in a dimension that had invented stirrups. The Rus were clearly equipped to press home a charge with lance or sword, as well as fight from a distance with a three-foot bow. Some of them also carried battle-axes; Shea had yet to see a mace.

They all wore mail shirts, of varying lengths, some ring mail and some made of metal discs sewn to leather backing, or strips of metal and leather woven together. Their helmets were iron, open-faced, and pointed, with mail attachments to protect neck and throat. Their shields were kite-shaped, and the whole effect reminded Shea somewhat of the Bayeux Tapestry.

Except that no self-respecting Norman knight ever used a bow. The Rus might have equally grand notions of honor, but that didn't keep them from riding out equipped to pay horse archers back in their own coin.

Shea himself wore only a helmet and a knee-length mail shirt. He'd buckled on his basket-hilted saber and borrowed a dagger, but refused a shield.

"I am accustomed to fighting without one," he said, and his status as a *bogatyr* rose. So had Chalmers'; he wore a shorter mail shirt and a helmet, but carried only a dagger.

They were not actually headed for the Polovtsi camp—no prince of the Rus would do that unless he led a full war party. It would be prudent, Princess Euphrosinia reminded Igor, to see if the captives could be ransomed. So a negotiating party of forty men was headed for a neutral spot on the west bank of the Don, where the Polovtsi occasionally did some legitimate trading.

They stayed in the shadow of the trees as long as they could, and Igor deployed scouts a couple of hours' ride ahead. He feared treachery, it seemed.

"Some of the boyars and even the princes have fought with the Polovtsi," he explained. "You seldom know who's turned his coat until they attack."

Shea wished he knew more of this continuum. He vaguely recalled that in the opera, Prince Igor had been a Polovets captive.

"What is worse," Igor continued, "is the way the Rus fight each other. If we put our joint strength against the Polovtsi we could crush them. By Saint Vladimir! My grandfather Oleg Sviatoslavich, curse his name, fought against the last Great Prince of Kiev. Now I must negotiate new alliances each time I face peril, instead of being sure of support from all the princes of the Rus."

"If the Polovtsi are such bad neighbors," Shea asked, "why will any of the Rus deal with them?"

"They want Polovtsi slaves," Igor said shortly.

Shea and Chalmers discussed this later in the day.

"It sounds as if the Rus never learned about hanging together or hanging separately," Shea said.

"They didn't," Chalmers replied. "Russia was never united until the Grand Dukes of Moscow took a hand. That's why they styled themselves the 'Czar of all the Russias.' Plural."

"But no one's mentioned Moscow, Doc. Does it even exist here?"

"I don't know. But I'm pretty sure about the slaves.

"Russia's always been huge, Harold. Until the railroad and telegraph were invented, its eastern frontier was just like our west—dangerous, but a place to run away and not be found if you didn't want to be.

"To prevent the farmers, the peasants, from doing just that, Russia stuck with serfdom a lot longer than most countries. It wasn't officially ended until the reign of Czar Alexander II, well into the nineteenth century."

"Yeah, but what does that have to do with Polovtsi slaves?"

"It sounds as if these boyars and princes are trying to ensure a labor supply, and are not too scrupulous about its source."

There was silence, as both men remembered that the supply included Florimel.

They journeyed for nearly ten days, sleeping in their cloaks and existing for the most part on smoked meat and journeybread. They made fires and did some hunting while in the shelter of the forest, but once on the steppe, the dry grass and the chance of being seen made for cold meats and nights.

Shea occasionally visited his family in St. Louis by way of Chicago, and he was all too familiar with the hypnotizing sameness of Route 66. Mile after interchangeable mile of field and sky made the trip seem like three thousand miles, not three hundred. He was truly grateful for the succession of towns and country crossroads, which proved he was not just sitting in the same spot, and could even muster up some gratitude for the farm machinery ambling along. Having to watch for tractors did focus his attention.

I hope no one ever builds one of those German auto-bahns down here, he remembered thinking. *No one could stay awake long enough to reach St. Louis.*

Once out of the forest, the journey to the Don was Route 66 cubed and squared. The grass was turning pale as autumn came on, but was dotted with wildflowers. Sky and grass, grass and sky—the occasional rustle of rabbit in the grass or outline of bird against the sky did nothing to disturb their eternal immensity.

"I'm glad I'm not scouting," Shea told Chalmers as they made camp one night. "I'd have to spend so much time on antihypnotic techniques that I'd never spot anything."

As the sun rose on the tenth day, they saw the glint of the Don in the distance. The wind blew from the east, and the Ohioans discovered that Igor had been right about one thing. You could smell a Polovtsi camp a *long* way downwind.

The prince raised the trade-truce banner, a yellow trumpet on a field that must have been intended to be white, then slowed the pace of the advance to an amble. Easing into the smell made it no easier to get used to.

"Anything in your repertoire for this, Doc?" Shea asked.

"Unfortunately, this stink interferes with one's logical faculties. Moreover, I suspect that since the odor has entirely natural causes, the only way to overcome it would be to plant a posthypnotic love of cleanliness in every Polovets."

About three hours after sunrise Shea sensed that his mount was walking on softer ground, and he began to hear the cry of marshbirds. By the time they stopped for noon rations, they could all see where stands of brush and tall grass broke the steppe and marked the banks of

the Don. The air had grown more humid as they made
their way east, but the increased moisture did nothing
to blunt the smell.

That afternoon, Shea got his first look at the river.
The Don was broad and placid, seemingly untouched by
humans. It was totally unlike the Mississippi at St. Louis,
fringed with piers, spanned by bridges loaded with trains,
carrying squadrons of barges and towboats. *But this river
can still flood*, Shea reminded himself, *though it looks to
be at low water now.* The psychologist had done his share
of sandbagging before leaving St. Louis.

They finally ambled into the Polovets camp about two
hours before sunset. At that particular spot the Don
curved into a miniature bay, which made it easier to
water horses. There were no permanent structures, but
the grass was crushed, and the ground dimpled here and
there with firepits.

Some thirty Polovtsi were waiting, mostly mounted.
They looked remarkably similar, all with dark shaggy hair
and moustaches. Their riding coats and breeches were
similar to those of the Rus, and those who didn't wear
the caps Igor had described wore long pointed hoods
that tied under the chin.

Polovets saddles, when they were used, were leather
pads dangling ragged stirrups of the same material. Few
of the riders wore mail, and all they carried besides bows
and quivers was either long knives or short swords.

Looking at the Polovtsi, Shea realized the variety of
physical appearance among the Rus. There was a bushy
though well-groomed beard on every chin, but their hair
ranged from dark to blond and they showed a wide range
of heights and builds. This might look normal to an
American, but not to a tribal people.

Multiply this lot, the psychologist thought, *and you
understand what starts the legends about enemies where
two spring up for every one slain.*

The Polovets leader, who wore a riding coat stiff with
enough dirt to be half-decent armor, and lots of tarnished

gold and silver jewelry, rode out on a shaggy steppe pony. Beside him on another pony rode a figure, recognizable in spite of his dirty robe, that the Ohioans hoped they'd seen the last of a dimension or two ago.

Recognizing Malambroso was all they had time for, because the Polovets chieftain hailed them.

"What brings the noble prince of Seversk to my tents?" he said.

To Shea's surprise, Igor kept his temper. "It seems, chieftain, that some of my goods found their way to your tents."

Suavity was not the chief's strong point. "Dare you claim anything of mine, you self-gelded eunuch of a Rus? Your tongue will be next!"

Igor ignored this. "Those who steal rather than fighting for their booty are bandits, not warriors. Those who lead bandits are not chiefs. Can one be sure they are even warriors?"

"Ask the spirits of your dead about the Polovtsi, oh prince of windy words! Warriors and free men are we all, and we stand by each other against all enemies."

"So? Well, if one snake can speak for all, then I need not look for a particular thief. I may demand the return of my goods from any."

"The goods of our foes are ours to plunder at will. But as you have come under the truce banner, I will not refuse outright. You ask me to put myself to some trouble, and for that trouble I want twice eighty *grivnas*."

"That's twice the blood price of my bailiff! Twenty *grivnas* for the return, alive and uninjured, of all the captives taken at Nizhni Cherinsk."

"You ask for the ones from a particular raid? We are warriors, not scribes who sit about scribbling lists! Only a fool would expect us to tell one lot from another! You ask of me a long journey, many slaves come in each day, and the day we meet the traders approaches.

"A Greek trader would pay one hundred, for what you

ask. You say the Rus are better than the Greeks. So pay me twice sixty."

"Forty, you son of a she-ass."

From Igor's slightly relaxed seat and wandering attention among men on both sides, Shea gathered that the two leaders expected to be at it for a while. The figure at the chieftain's side backed his horse and dismounted, as if to relieve himself. The psychologists drew off a little, for privacy.

"At least we know where he is, Doc," Shea said. Chalmers' thoughts appeared to be inexpressible, but deadly.

Florimel's abductor, the wizard Malambroso, disappeared into a clump of brush. When he had not come out after the next three exchanges between the prince and the chieftain, Shea decided to follow.

"What if he's setting a trap?" Chalmers asked.

"He can't trap us without trapping all the Rus. If that costs the chieftain a profitable deal, the chieftain will be angry. He doesn't look like like somebody I would want mad at me, and Malambroso's not an idiot."

Chalmers looked mollified. Shea turned his horse and urged it to a walk, toward the clump. "One for all and all for one, Doc!" he called back over his shoulder.

Maneuvering the horse between tangles of tall grass, Shea felt a sensation, as if he were entering an invisible tent. Everything seemed quiet. He grasped the hilt of his sword and looked around.

Malambroso was twenty feet away, pacing restlessly. Shea saw that some of the dirt on the wizard's skin was mobile, and hastily backed his horse.

"I knew you'd be coming, so I put up a see-the-expected spell," Malambroso said. "All anyone on either side will see is this clump." He shook his head vigorously. "That iron bathrobe you're wearing does not become you."

"That cootie sark doesn't do much for you," Shea replied, releasing his grip on the hilt. "What are you doing in such company? Come to think of it, how did you get here in the first place?"

Malambroso gave the grandfather of all sighs, but continued pacing. "You remember Freston's, ah, unfortunate demise?"

"I do," Shea said.

Freston was a demon who, tricked by Reed Chalmers into committing good, suffered the ultimate penalty. The demon wasn't the only one who suffered; Chalmers and Shea, Florimel, and Malambroso were flung separately from a world in which Don Quixote *was* its greatest knight and not a madman's delusion, to that of the *Aeneid*.

"Well, I wound up in Troy also, and shipped out with a chief named Agamemnon. I jumped ship in Egypt with a bunch of the loot; I figured it was a good place to hole up."

Shea regretted that Malambroso had not continued to Mycenae with Agamemnon. If he had, Clytemnestra might have disposed of him permanently. According to the Greek legends, she'd made a pretty thorough sweep of her late husband's cronies.

Malambroso smirked. "Then I bargained with Hermes the Lightfingered. Ten percent of everything I took in exchange for news of visitors from other continua. I bargained him down to five when I hinted that they might be the advance party for new gods.

"But you can't depend on those Olympians. By the time I found out what you'd been up to you'd already left, although Hermes did drop me off in the same universe.

"I wound up on the edge of the steppe, and started looking for Florimel. I found her at Yuri Dimitrivich's estate, but I couldn't afford to have her recognize me. She was established enough to have me imprisoned. And I didn't, ah, want to try amnesia spells before practicing with the magic of this world."

"You don't seem to have learned much," Shea said, increasing his distance as the wizard took a step forward.

"Magic among the Rus is complicated," Malambroso

replied. "Many of them are strongly pious, which can cause spells to have, um, unintended results. Things are easier among these Polovtsi. Their old customs and taboos are breaking down, thanks to the wealth gained from raiding settled areas and providing slaves for the trade. They want spells for spying and battle-luck, things like that."

"Why didn't you just grab Florimel and run?" Shea asked. "Or are you a slave, too?"

"No, no. I am the chieftain's counselor, and expected to attend him at all times. After I was, er, captured, and happened to mention the, er, burned palisade, I am considered to bring good luck."

"Were you there when she was captured?"

"Of course. I had some idea of running off with her during the raid, but I had not then worked out a spell for leaving this world. Nor have I been able to persuade the chief to give her to me. These people are quite mercenary; they insist on cash down."

"Ah, has she been hurt in any way?"

"No, no. The chieftain, at least, understands the market value of undamaged merchandise. The captives are guarded by eunuchs. And—I have not been able to get her away. She and the other women get together and take turns calling on the saints to keep them safe." Malambroso looked sour. "Besides, she has developed much skill in biting, kicking, and screaming."

Shea wondered just how he had found that out.

"Why are you telling me all this?"

"Because Florimel has a most unfortunate habit of loyalty. She won't desert those she considers her comrades. And once she's sold—do you know how hard it is to rescue a slave around here? Nowhere to run, nowhere to hide, and everybody so solicitous of everyone else's property rights."

"Yeah, these bastards sure are."

"Well, they are among themselves, and—confound it!" (although that wasn't exactly what Malambroso said).

The wizard slapped himself in a sensitive spot, and the tent effect disappeared. Shea could hear normal background noises again, and the bargaining had risen to bellowing. With a last glance at Malambroso, who definitely had ants, if not something bigger, in his pants, Shea rode back to the Rus.

Igor's men had pulled their helms low over their eyes, so that might have been the only reason they seemed to look suspiciously at Shea.

Minus the infestation, Chalmers was as uneasy as his enemy. "This looks more like a challenge than a trade," he whispered.

"Or a trap," Shea noted. Everyone who had been riding with bows unstrung had now started stringing them. Those whose bows were already strung seemed to be displaying great interest in the number of arrows in their quivers.

"A lousy son of a mangy she-goat, am I?" the chieftain bellowed. "I'll show you, you dung-weaned boar's get of a Rus!"

Shea braced for an arrow in his mail or in him, but nothing happened—yet. Instead the chieftain shouted something loud but wordless. All the Polovtsi who hadn't mounted now did so. The ones already mounted started shifting outward, to the flanks. The Polovtsi would be stretched thin, but they would be able to hit the Rus with archery from three sides, and disperse rapidly if the Rus charged in any of the three directions.

The psychologist looked behind him. The Rus also knew what they were doing. Several bowshots away, the scouts who'd led the way toward the camp and then stopped were spreading out. They would be able to cover the retreat.

Except that Igor didn't look like a man planning to retreat. Lances were coming out of their slings and the fading daylight sparked ruddy fire from steel points. If the Rus could get to close quarters without losing too many men to archery, their armor and longer reach

would give them an advantage. The Polovtsi were going
to have to fight their way off this battlefield.

Shea scratched his sunburned nose. He was going to
have to fight his way *into* the ranks of the Polovtsi, or
lose his useful reputation as a *bogatyr*. He wished for
a helmet with a nasal, to keep his nose from leading
the way.

Hell, he wished (as he had done at other times) that
he'd given up syllogismobiling across the continua after
he'd married Belphebe! He wanted to see her. He
wanted to see their child, other children, their
grandchildren.

Not to mention that an all-out fight now would probably end any chances of rescuing Florimel. He could see
what that thought was doing to Chalmers; the older
man's face was even grimmer than before.

Shea looked at his colleague. "Doc, make your passes!"

Shea hastily began reciting:

> "O would some power the giftie gie them
> To see themselves as others see them!
> From many a hurtful notion free them!
> The truth make known:
> The sight o' vermin carried wi' them
> To them be shown!

A Polovets bowman, stretched to the limit, sighted
along his arm. It might have just been Shea's imagination, but he seemed to be aiming at Igor.

Then the man seemed to turn to stone, except for his
eyes, which grew very wide. A moment later, he reani-
mated himself—and let out the scream of a banshee with
a migraine headache.

The scream was only the first of many, not to mention
shouts and curses. All the Polovtsi grew bug-eyed, and
some of them leaped from their horses to roll frantically
on the ground. One of them rolled into a campfire and
out the other side, jumping up with his clothes on fire.

He threw himself down again, rolled until the flames were out, then ran off toward the river, tearing off his clothes as he ran.

He wasn't the only one. Polovtsi swatted, punched, and clawed at themselves, making their ragged clothes even more so. Some drew their knives and started slashing at their garments or even stabbing at themselves, although Shea noted that none of those seemed to hit a vital spot.

Hardly any of the Polovtsi paid any attention to their horses, and it would have been a waste of time to do so. Their riders apparently going mad had thoroughly spooked all the ponies, and they were running off as fast as the Polovtsi themselves. Some of the ponies threw their uncaring riders off; others didn't bother with that courtesy and ran away with them.

Shea took a firm grip on his own mount's reins, thrust his own feet even more firmly into the stirrups, and tried not to laugh.

In what must have been less than five minutes, the camp area was completely empty of live, or at least conscious, Polovtsi. A couple lay staring at the sky, after stabbing themselves or perhaps knocking themselves silly falling off their horses.

The chieftain and all the rest of his band were either heading toward the river or already in it. Shea saw heads bobbing around and clouds of spray as Polovtsi warriors tried to scrub themselves clean of what they'd seen. Some of the horses had run clear out of sight; others were winded and quietly grazing, waiting for their riders to return.

Seeing all the Polovtsi out of bowshot, Shea dismounted and walked over to the sprawled rearguard. Neither of them seemed to be bleeding, and both were breathing regularly. He did not stay long; even a couple of Polovtsi were ripe enough to force a hasty retreat.

At this point Shea realized that he and Chalmers were alone in the camp. The Rus had galloped away from the

Don as fast as the Polovtsi had dashed toward it. None of them seemed to have fallen off, but quite a few had dismounted, and were holding reins with one hand while busily crossing themselves with the other.

Shea let out a long gusty sigh of relief, at having changed the pronoun in the adaptation of Burns from "us" to "them." Otherwise he might have routed the Rus as well, which Igor would not have appreciated.

Igor had not dismounted, and now he rode back, accompanied by Mikhail Sergeivich and two or three others. All, Shea noted, were keeping their hands very close to their sword hilts, except for one who had a bow in one hand and an arrow in the other.

"By God's Holy Mother, Egorov Andreivich!" Igor exclaimed. "That was like something out of a tale. What did they see?" There was more than a touch of awe in the look Igor gave Shea, but also more than a touch of comradeship.

"Rurik Vasilyevich and I gave them a good look at their lice, Your Highness. Ah, does Your Highness know what a louse looks like?"

Prince Igor's eloquent look told the psychologist he'd made a major blunder.

"Um, well, in the Silk Empire they make, uh, crystals, and these crystals let us see things like bugs, or flaws in jewels, that are too small to see with just our eyes.

"If you looked at a louse through one of these crystals, you'd see that it has a small head and huge stomach, three pairs of legs, large jaws, and each of its eyes is made of millions of other eyes."

"Monsters," Igor said.

Shea nodded. "Exactly. The Polovtsi saw themselves covered with monsters, and panicked."

The prince's look was now one of complete amazement. "No *bogatyr* in any tale ever did a thing like that."

"One other thing, Your Highness. The Polovtsi have a sorcerer with them. He may send more after us than arrows."

Shea was relieved to see Igor shift back to the practical. He rose in his stirrups and called to the trumpeters and banner-bearers to signal the rally, then beckoned Shea and Chalmers.

Igor's men rallied around the banner, except for the scouts, who rode out at once to open the distance between themselves and the main body. Igor also set out a rearguard, in case some of the Polovtsi regained their wits and courage.

Shea offered to join the rearguard, in case the pursuit took magical form. Igor thanked him all over again and accepted the offer.

As they rode into the fading light, Shea wished this dimension had a bookmaker to take his bet that the bath-house was now as sacred as the church in the eyes of a good many men of the Rus. He could have made a pile.

They rode night and day until they were all away from the Don, and even after that set double guards around each encampment. The two psychologists agreed that one of them should be awake at all times, although Shea didn't care for Chalmers' remark:

"I can hardly sleep anyway, so why shouldn't I keep watch?"

The return trip seemed to take even longer than the trip out, without hope of Florimel's quick recovery to spur them along. One night Chalmers commented that everything seemed to take longer, cost more, and smell worse in this continuum than in any of the others they'd visited.

"I've been thinking about that," Shea replied. "Remember what you said about the peculiarities in the world of the *Aeneid*?"

"There were a great many such," Chalmers said. "Which ones were you thinking of in particular?"

"All of them, and your explanation," Shea said. "Homer lived four hundred years after the Trojan War, and Virgil lived eight hundred years after Homer, besides being a Roman with a political axe to grind."

"So?"

"Suppose whatever Borodin used for his opera—an old Russian epic, I suppose—was written by one of Igor's contemporaries. Maybe one of his nobles. It would be favorable to Igor, but it might leave in a lot of the details."

"Such as lice and smells and taking forever to get any-where?" Chalmers snapped. "I suppose that could be an explanation. It is hardly an excuse."

Shea decided that Chalmers was in no mood for aca-demic analysis, and turned away to take the first watch.

By the evening of the third day, Chalmers was feeling more reconciled to the realism of Igor's world and the absence of Florimel.

"Did that chief have any intention of negotiating at all?" he asked Igor as they made camp.

"They still respect the truce banner, though not as much as they used to," the prince replied.

"The wizard said that their rules, even among them-selves, are breaking down," Shea added.

Igor frowned, and Shea gave a thought to one of the virtues of being a Hero—what would be a grimace on an ordinary man was an earnest, noble expression on the prince's face. "I wouldn't mind seeing them fight among themselves, but if they no longer keep trade-truce ... Curse them for the Devil's own spawn and fools as well!

"Trade law holds that no one may be attacked at a neutral trade site, or for three days' journey before or after. In the lands of the Rus, of course, the princes punish theft, three days or no three days. But trade law holds even for the steppe, or has until now."

"Does that mean, Your Highness, that if we find Flori-mel ... ?" Reed's voice faltered. "If we find Florimel— for sale—that we couldn't challenge it there, or for three days after?"

"In the lands of the Rus you could," Igor replied with a touch of pride. "No one may be enslaved among us except according to the provisions of the law, and before witnesses. And the wise man will register his slaves, whether Rus or foreign, with the chiliarch's clerk, so that if they flee, or are stolen, their ownership will not be in question.

"But those who buy slaves on the steppe, by trade-truce, do not question their origins. And if they go to the chiliarch's clerk and say, 'I bought this slave on the steppe,' the clerk has to accept it. If it turns out that the slave belonged to someone else, or was not a slave at all, well, under the law, Polovtsi raids are treated as fire and shipwreck, a natural loss."

"I can see room for all kinds of corruption," Shea muttered.

"I have seen it, Egorov Andreivich."

"But how do we get my wife back?" Chalmers pursued.

"I could see about having her purchased by one of my agents," Igor replied. "That's risky; you never know how the bidding will go. A counterraid would be risky too, with that sorcerer among the steppe tribes. The only man I could count on would be my brother Vsevolod, but we might be enough, if we can catch them before they reach the truce area."

The psychologists could see that Igor was now the warrior-prince, considering options. They said no more, nor, as he walked off to his own campfire, did he.

III

Harold Shea sipped cautiously from the silver goblet in his hand. The mead in it was strong and sweet. Already he found himself unable to focus on the frieze of Olga's revenge, that marked the point where the walls of this chamber arched up to form its dome.

The inside of the dome was painted gold, and the afternoon sunlight gilded it further. How many more sips before it was too bright to look at?

His companions at the table were also hard to see, but not because of what he'd been drinking. Despite the long embroidered robe of fine green wool that Reed Chalmers wore, and the brighter silks and brocades that clad the Rus, they were all lost against the paint and gilding of the walls. Bright reds, blues, and greens patterned with gold—the prince, princess, and Mikhail Sergeivich fit right in.

"Vsevolod will ride," Igor said. "The bards don't call him a fierce aurochs just to flatter him. He maintains a full band at Kursk, so they can start at once."

"The prince your brother needs to get his harvest in, as do you," Euphrosinia pointed out.

"Who needs warriors for that? We could be over the Don and back before threshing is over!"

"And who will collect your taxes if your men are over the Don? Besides, if the rains come early, you'll do well to return before butchering is over."

"Hm ... Can the two of you control the weather, Egorov Andreivich?"

"I'm afraid not, Your Highness."

"Someone needs to keep an eye on young Sviatoslav Borisovich," Mikhail Sergeivich commented. "He's been talking too loudly and too long, of late."

"The ambitions of the young," Igor said. "Boris Vsevolodovich, God rest his soul, is a year dead. With the old stallion gone, the young one is kicking up his heels."

"Unless God brings Sviatoslav to a better mind, he'll be in your court before another year's out," Mikhail Sergeivich replied.

"Perhaps I should require his services on this expedition."

"Would you trust him at your back?" Both Euphrosinia and Mikhail Sergeivich seemed to speak at once.

"Ah, well . . ."

"And what is that sorcerer likely to do?" Mikhail asked.

"Probably set a trap with an illusion spell," Chalmers answered. "He'll be aching for the chance to pay us back."

"So will that chief," Euphrosinia said. "Will he even keep trade-truce?"

The talk turned to boyars and princes willing and able to ride. There was no question that the Polovtsi had numbers on their side, and it was obvious that the raid on Nizhni Charinsk had shaken many of the Rus.

"The raid may have been fortuitous, but no one wants to ride against a sorcerer," Euphrosinia concluded.

"They will if I order them, and I will if I must," Igor growled. "I have sworn to free those captives."

"They will ride more willingly after harvest," the princess said.

The meeting broke up shortly afterward. Chalmers and Shea took a turn in the palace yard to stretch their legs, then returned to their room. "The last thing I expected here was a Board of Directors meeting," Shea groused. "If I had taken a few more sips I would have sworn I was back at Garaden."

Chalmers did not respond, and Shea looked closely at his colleague. They'd survived some nasty spots in various dimensions, but this was the first time Shea had seen Reed Chalmers so close to the breaking point.

"*My wife* . . . is a *slave*, and I can't cut the bastards' throats!" Shea could hear the tears, but they didn't—quite—show.

"Reed," Shea said, and then no more for a while. When Chalmers seemed more in command of himself, Shea continued.

"Igor's doing the best he can, but we shouldn't depend on him. There's magic in this universe, so what can we do with it?"

They tried to recall verses on freedom and emancipation, but their harvest was meager. Slavery was also a part of this universe, so they doubted the effectiveness of any spell based on its immorality. The few spirituals that Shea remembered emphasized freedom in the next world.

"I don't think it would be any use trying to freeze the Don so she could walk across it, even if we could get there," Shea concluded, looking out at the sunset. "Maybe my subconscious will trigger something tonight. The morning is wiser than the evening, even if the Rus do say it all the time. Coming to dinner, Doc?"

"Not tonight. I really have no appetite."

Physician, heal thyself, Shea thought as he took another look at Chalmers, but he seemed safe to leave for an hour or so.

The Ohioan was not that enthusiastic about Kievan cooking, which, like that in the *Faerie Queen*, emphasized elaborate, highly spiced dishes. (A sturgeon stuffed with a carp stuffed with a mullet stuffed with a trout stuffed with something Shea couldn't identify stuffed with an egg stuffed with a pea was one main dish he remembered without pleasure.) But he wished to keep on the good side of the Patriarch, whose profession naturally required him to deplore the presence of sorcerers in the prince's domain.

So Shea put on his best robe and a seemly mien, and went down to his place at a table near the prince's. Shea was surprised when the Patriarch sat down with him, instead of taking his seat at the high table.

"May God smile on you and your house in all their lawful undertakings," the Patriarch murmured.

"May we always deserve His favor," Shea replied, wondering where this was leading.

As dinner progressed, it turned out that the Patriarch, who was near Shea's own age, wanted to hear about his travels. The psychologist edited these a bit, thinking that he'd better not admit to encountering demons and living to tell about it.

"I always loved tales, so I badgered my father into having me taught to read," the Patriarch said wistfully. "Naturally, he thought I had a desire for the religious life."

"Being able to read lets a man pursue all kinds of wisdom," Shea said, hoping he couldn't go wrong with that response.

"Or unwisdom," the Patriarch replied. Original vocation or not, he was a churchman now.

The Patriarch left right after dinner, and so did Shea. Reed Chalmers was dozing in their chamber, and Shea went quietly to bed himself.

Chalmers and Shea spent the next few days thinking up potential spells and wishing there were some way to test a few of them. After what Malambroso had said about the piety of the Rus, they would not have cared to test many in the shadow of the basilica, even if the Patriarch had been friendlier. Chalmers avoided company, and seldom left their chamber. Shea did not press him to socialize; Chalmers was in no mood to be diplomatic.

But there were times when Chalmers wanted no company at all, and Shea spent those in the practice yard. Regular dimension-hopping meant regular sword practice, even back in Ohio. Shea worried about leaving his colleague at these times, but there was nothing he could do, and as a psychologist, he knew when to leave well enough alone.

I never thought to play shrink to Doc Chalmers, Shea thought. *He's supposed to be* my *mentor.*

"Contagion and Similarity should work in this universe," Chalmers summarized one morning, "and you proved that Synthesis will. There's a strong literal element to the magic here. Your willow-bark analgesic might not have been so bitter if you hadn't insisted on that in your spell."

"There's also that strong element of reality we discussed," Shea replied. "Willow-bark tea is naturally bitter. It might not have worked otherwise."

"Malambroso seems to have found a way around any limitations of this world's magic," Chalmers said bitterly. "His see-the-expected spell would be just the thing for rescuing Florimel."

"We'll be expected to defeat such spells. Igor doesn't want his men confused when they have to fight."

"He is still planning to ride, then?" Chalmers asked.

"Oh, yes. He thinks it will discourage further raids, and besides, he just can't stand Polovtsi."

"When is he leaving?"

"He hasn't said."

The next day Shea was returning from arms practice when he met Igor. The prince wore old riding clothes and invited the psychologist to take a turn on the ramparts with him.

Igor's fortress—Shea couldn't quite use the Rus word *kremlin* with a straight face—was a good deal less imposing than its later Muscovite counterpart. It covered a considerable area on a rise of ground near the western edge of Seversk, but most of it was built of wood, including the walls.

A stout railed platform ran around the ramparts. The upper part had archery slits, and there was a deep ditch clear around the castle. The ditch served (from its smell) as the fortress' garbage dump, and also (Shea suspected) as a firebreak. Seversk was nine-tenths wood, and from where he stood beside the prince Shea could see three burned-out blocks without looking hard.

Inside the ramparts were two outer courtyards and an inner one. The larger of the outer ones held the storehouses, kitchens, and servants' quarters. It was also the place where taxes collected in kind were deposited, in sacks, barrels, chests, carts, or whatever else they came in.

The other courtyard had an outer gate guarded by two stone towers and an inner gate that led to the inner courtyard. Here were stables, smithies (one recently rebuilt, judging from the mixture of smoke-blackened and new wood Shea saw), and more storehouses. Shea didn't know precisely where the kitchen was; from the temperature of the food it had to be some ways from the dining hall.

Inside were the quarters for the prince's household troops, the family quarters, the basilica, the treasury, and (noises in the night hinted) the dungeon. The place would not last long against medieval or even Roman siege engines, but this did not seem to be an era, or an area, where sieges were feared. The fortress walls kept thieves out of Igor's treasury and fires out of his bedchamber, and that was enough.

The sun was crawling down toward the horizon; Shea had been here long enough for the days to shorten. He thought of everything the term "Russian winter" conjured up and hoped that he, Reed, and Florimel could be back in Ohio before the days grew much shorter.

"It seems we have less to fear than Mikhail Sergeivich thought, from my cousin Sviatoslav Borisovich," the prince said. "The first three carts of his taxes are in the lesser courtyard, together with a pack train. They are being unloaded now."

A party of men with Igor's colors on their shields came tramping up to the main gate. Shea counted twenty-five or thirty, all on foot but armed with everything but lances. Igor saw them too.

"Ah, those must be the men I bade Oleg Nikolaevich send out, returning. There was a small tax matter that is no concern of yours that I wished to see settled peacefully before we left. We shall have to—"

He broke off, as one of the approaching men nocked an arrow. "The fool—" Igor began.

The "fool's" arrow picked off a guard on top of the tower. Several more arrows soared up, then whistled down on the heads of the remaining guards and the men on the ramparts to either side of the towers. On the ground, the men not wielding bows drew their swords, except for a few who pulled axes from under their cloaks.

"By the Holy Mother—!" Igor exclaimed. He didn't get to finish this remark either. A din broke out in the other courtyard, among the storehouses. Shea heard shouts, screams, and the clash of weapons.

So did Igor. He spoke no more, but dashed back along the ramparts, heading for the family quarters. His expression reminded Shea somewhat of Chalmers', but this was a warrior prince of the Rus, not an American academic. Igor was in a berserker's fury, and Shea sincerely hoped that nothing would happen in the next hour to turn that fury against him.

First, though, he had to stay alive for the next hour.

Moving as fast as Igor, Shea dashed for the nearest stairway. He was too late. The inner gate to the courtyard flew open, knocking several defenders sprawling. What seemed like an army of men in Igor's colors swarmed in.

Shea whirled and headed for the other stairway on his side of the courtyard. Whoever the new arrivals were, they weren't friendly. Had Oleg Nikolaevich turned traitor?

As Shea took the stairs two at a time, an arrow whistled across the courtyard from the far wall. It stuck in his mail and only pricked his skin. He came down even faster after that, knowing that jumping down like Errol Flynn made a great movie shot but would probably sprain his ankle.

Several more arrows passed close enough to Shea for him to hear the whistle. Then the archer gave up, as if he couldn't tell friend from foe.

Shea sympathized. He had the same problem. Everyone was in Igor's colors, although one side was closer to the inner gate and one closer to the outer. Shea decided to assume the inner group was Igor's men, the good guys. He also saw that they were outnumbered at least two to one.

He hurried toward them, joining their ranks just as the other group charged. None of the defenders turned to fight him, and he suspected why. With only a mail shirt, and no surcoat, he had no place to show colors, and his basket-hilted saber was now fairly well known.

What bothered him about the next couple of minutes was that none of the attackers seemed to bother with him either. Did they expect to find somebody dressed like him on their side, and if so, how?

Shea decided to settle that point right now.

"Forward, for Igor of Seversk!" he shouted. Several men around him took up the cry. Several others decided that he'd proclaimed himself an enemy, and charged.

The two groups collided. Shea found himself ducking under the swing of an axe. The axeman thought he was inside Shea's sword's reach and drew a dagger. Shea thrust clumsily but effectively upward, catching the axeman under the chin. The wound made quite a mess and put the man out of the fight, even if it might take a while to kill him.

Shea slashed and thrust his way back and forth across the courtyard, as vigorously as he dared. The two lines were breaking up and it was almost impossible to tell friend from foe even down on the ground. Everybody was now shouting Igor of Seversk!" or some other battle cry; Shea began to think he might have made the confusion worse rather than better.

He got through several encounters with no damage to himself and some to his opponents, although he didn't think he'd actually put anybody down for good except the first man. The saber wasn't the world's best armor-chopper, but it gave him a useful advantage against anyone who didn't think of swords having points.

Working on that *bogatyr* reputation was all very well, but something smelled wrong. Something smelled magical.

Had someone put the see-the-expected spell on the gate and courtyard? And if they had could Shea break it in about two seconds, which was the longest interval he'd had between opponents? Otherwise he'd be the latest sorcerer to be run through for poor spelling.

Here came another man. Shea thought he saw Mikhail Sergeivich under the helm, but he'd already fought a couple of men who had the appearance of ones he'd sparred with in the practice yard.

"Wizard! This is your doing!" Mikhail's voice, too—but the swordcut he launched at Shea wasn't aimed at a friend.

Shea parried, the swords slammed together hilt to hilt, then the psychologist disengaged and opened the distance. He had reach and a point, and a fat lot of good either would do if they killed one of Igor's captains!

Sparks flew twice more, before realization flickered on Mikhail's face. He sprang back; Shea let him go; they both lowered their points and stood, staring and breathing hard.

"What's happening? Who's fighting whom?" Shea panted. He took another step backward and brought his heel up against a fallen body. It wasn't the first one.

"Our men have gone mad! They fight each other!" From the dazed way he spoke, Mikhail Sergeivich hadn't had time to think much.

Suspicion turned to blazing certainty in Shea's gut and burned its way to his brain. "Mount guard," he told the Rus. "I can stop it."

He didn't dare sheathe his sword, but kept his guard down. Gesturing with the sword in his right hand, he recited:

"O would some power the giftie gie us
    To see the truth the spell hides frae us!
What friends, what foes do battle wi' us
    To us be shown!"

Shea could detect no change in the fading sun or clouds, but everything looked a bit brighter. He could see small differences in the appearance and the armor of the fallen. As he caught his breath and looked around, he saw the living change also. Some still bore Igor's device on their shields, but others had their shields covered.

Mikhail Sergeivich looked a trifle less hostile. Before he could say anything a scuffle on the ramparts made them both look up. Euphrosinia Yaroslavna and a boy of about twelve, daggers in hand, grinned triumphantly at a prisoner between two guards.

Mikhail Sergeivich smiled too, or at least moved his lips. All around them the strange swordsmen were drawing back toward the outer gate.

A door in the wall between the two courtyards burst open. Igor charged through it at the head of bloodstained men moving too fast to be counted. The prince still wore his riding clothes, but carried his sword and wore a helmet at least two sizes too large for him. All were stained with blood.

The attackers recoiled from Igor. That left the prince a clear path to the gate. In a moment the last avenue of retreat was blocked—and a moment after that the strange men were dropping their weapons and lowering their shields.

Igor followed everyone's glance at the ramparts.

"Glory to God!" Igor exclaimed. A smile split his face. Then it vanished as he recognized the prisoner.

"Bring him down."

While the guards did so, the prince looked around the court, apparently counting the dead. His own men cordoned off the prisoners. Shea wiped and sheathed his saber, but Mikhail Sergeivich stayed at his elbow, his longsword still in his hand.

The guards shoved the prisoner, his hands bound behind him, through the archway. The princess and

Vladimir Igorovich followed. Igor hugged Euphrosinia tightly, and she didn't seem to mind the blood.

Igor smiled at his son. "Did you capture him?"

"Well, I helped," Vladimir said. "I was in Mother's outer chamber when he broke in. He kept trying to grab Mother, and I kept trying to stab him, and finally the guards came. If I'd had my own sword . . ." His voice trailed off.

"You shall have one, of the finest Frankish steel." The pleasure vanished from Igor's voice as he stared at the prisoner. "Sviatoslav Borisovich! Rebellion? From you, cousin?"

The prisoner stared at his cousin and prince with a corpse's eyes. "I thought to take Seversk by guile." He stopped.

Prince Igor looked at the prisoners, then gestured at one. The guards brought him over. "What were your orders?" Igor asked.

"To seize the castle, most especially the inner parts and the armory, slay you and Prince Vladimir, and take the Princess Euphrosinia alive," the soldier answered dully.

"You knew that this was treason," the prince stated.

"He was our lord."

Oleg Nikolaivich now entered the court, accompanying a man with a bloody bandage on his arm. "Sergei Ivanovich is one of the scribes assisting—who assisted—your steward, Your Highness. You should hear him." Oleg's voice was soft with tightly leashed anger.

In a low voice that grew stronger as he continued, Sergei Ivanovich told how the wagons supposedly bringing Sviatoslav's taxes contained weapons and armed men. They had slain the steward, seized the storehouses, and opened the gate to the inner *kremlin*.

"I lay as if dead from a wound," the scribe said. "The boyar ordered that word be brought to him when Your Highness, Prince Vladimir, and the princess were taken.

But he also said, 'Make sure it's Prince Igor's men you're fighting.'"

Murmurs and gestures of aversion followed this, but Igor paid no heed. "What demon possessed you, cousin? Even if you had succeeded, do you think the boyars of Seversk would have accepted you as prince? Or Vsevolod, or the Prince of Kiev?"

"I was told there was a man of power here, a *bogatyr*, who hated you. He would have given me your semblance until all enemies to my rule were either slain or won over."

A good many stares showing both understanding and hostility turned in Shea's direction.

"Not this man," Mikhail Sergeivich said. "He fought our enemies and broke the spell. I saw him." He looked at Shea. "Where is Rurik Vasilyevich?"

"In our chamber, the last I saw of him."

"Bring him down," Igor ordered.

"May I go up, Your Highness?" Shea spoke low, to keep his voice from shaking with the knowledge of what Chalmers had done. But Harold Shea would not desert him. Neither of them was Igor's man, after all.

Igor considered. "Disarm and bind him," he ordered. "Let neither of them speak or act, and bring them both back."

Mikhail Sergeivich unbuckled Shea's swordbelt and tossed it to a guard. He gestured, and another guard came over, bound Shea's hands with a rawhide thong, and gagged him with another. The two marched him off.

At the door of their chamber Mikhail marched him in, barely two seconds after his, "Open in the prince's name!" Fortunately, the door was not latched.

Chalmers was sitting calmly, but he was obviously shocked at the spectacle of Shea in bonds. "Take them off!" he ordered.

Then he recognized Mikhail Sergeivich, and Prince Igor's device. His shoulders slumped just a trifle.

That was enough to convince Mikhail Sergeivich. He

grabbed Chalmers and tied his hands. Being out of raw-hide, he took the gag off Shea and used it on Chalmers.

"Just cut that one's throat if he squeaks," Mikhail told the guard.

The augmented party returned to the courtyard, where, in addition to those they'd left, they found the Patriarch and a man who had to be an executioner; he held a huge two-handed sword.

Chalmers and Shea were shoved to the front rank of the prisoners. Mikhail Sergeivich exchanged a few words with Igor.

"Sviatoslav Borisovich," Igor said, "do you know either of these men?"

"No, Your Highness."

"Rurik Vasilyevich, do you know this man?"

The guard removed Chalmers' gag. "No, Your Highness," he practically spat.

"Do you, Egorov Andreivich?"

"No, Your Highness."

"Who told you then, that there was one here who would work with you?"

Sviatoslav was silent.

"Sviatoslav Borisovich, boyar of Seversk," Igor pronounced. "You did not pay the tax due the prince of Seversk. For that, triple taxes will be collected from your estate.

"You caused the death of my steward, and thirteen of my guards. For that you owe a blood price of eighty *grivnas* for the steward, and forty for each guard. You also owe a blood price for every wounded man.

"Finally, you attempted to slay the prince of Seversk and his family. For this, your estates are forfeit, as is your life, if I see fit to take it.

"I shall not take your life, Sviatoslav Borisovich. Instead, you shall be blinded. Before you are blinded, you will see the deaths of the men you led into treason. That is the last thing you will ever see."

The Patriarch said a prayer for those about to be

executed, and two guards flung several bales' worth of
straw at the executioner's feet. Fifteen times a man was
forced to the straw, and fifteen times the executioner
struck. He turned his blade and honed the other edge
after the eighth man, but never missed his stroke.

Shea did not enjoy his front-row view of this expertise.
The only things he could be grateful for were that this
brawl had started well before dinnertime, so he had
nothing in his stomach to lose, and that Mikhail Sergeivich was holding him upright. He got one look at Chalmers, obliquely away from him, and did not risk what
composure he had left by looking again. He found an
angle of the rampart he could focus on, and kept his
attention there.

The blinding was worse. The bodies were removed,
and the straw swept up and fired, along with some wood.
Irons were heated, then taken out—

Shea kept his attention firmly on the rampart. He
heard a gasp, then a throat-tearing scream that echoed
around the courtyard and died away to whimpering. The
smell of burned flesh joined the reek of blood. Mikhail
Sergeivich's hand trembled on his arm.

Sviatoslav was led out of the yard, still whimpering.
Igor turned to Reed Chalmers.

"Fifteen men are dead, and one is blind, for which
you bear some blame. Confess your part in this."

Underneath his caution, Chalmers had courage. "A
man, none of these, approached me and offered to return
the Lady Florimel to me if I helped him. If not, he said
she would be sold beyond the Volga and I would never
get her back."

Had Reed actually watched the executions?

"How do you know he was none of these?" Igor asked.

"He looked to have Polovets blood, Your Highness."

"And you believed him?"

"I couldn't take the chance that he was lying, Your
Highness."

"What did you agree to do?"

"To cast a spell, so that strangers could enter the palace without being questioned. Further orders would have been given me when the palace was taken."

"You knew, then, that you were dealing with my enemies?"

"It was for my wife, Your Highness."

From the look on Igor's face, Shea knew he had better say something before the prince pronounced sentence.

"Your Highness," Shea managed, hoping that Mikhail Sergeivich would keep his dagger sheathed, "I swear to you that Rurik Vasilyevich has done nothing out of malice to you, but only for the sake of his wife. Among us, the marriage bond is strong. A man who will not risk his honor to rescue his wife has no honor at all."

"A man who will take the word of a Polovets also has no sense," Igor said. "And with thirteen dead and more wounded men, it will be harder for me to rescue Yuri Dimitrivich's household."

Shea knelt, awkwardly because of his hands. "I beg you to spare his life, Your Highness. We can't pay your blood price in *grivnas*, only in service. When we work together, we can do much more than either of us can alone. Won't you spare him to recover your losses, if nothing else?"

George Raft could not have improved on the smile Igor's face wore. "He stands condemned, but I will pardon him if you defeat the Polovtsi for me without more loss of men. Or, if men are lost, if you pay their blood price—in *grivnas*.

"I place no punishment on you, Egorov Andreivich. Mikhail Sergeivich bears witness that you fought for me, and you are free to accept or refuse for your comrade's sake. If you succeed, he is free. If you do not succeed, and die in the attempt, his punishment stands but you shall have a warrior's grave. If you do not succeed, and live, I can think of no punishment greater than that you watch your comrade quartered on the execution ground.

"Do you accept?"

"Yes, Your Highness."

"Free him." Mikhail Sergeivich hauled Shea to his feet, and cut his bonds. "Take Rurik Vasilyevich to the penitents' cells beneath the basilica. Keep him guarded, but I doubt he can work sorcery there. And Egorov Andreivich," Igor concluded, "you will go to the barracks, where you can be watched."

The royal trio swept off, and the rest began to carry out their orders.

IV

Harold Shea swore as his horse shied from yet another balky mule. He had been in the saddle for what seemed like weeks, certainly long enough to learn the difference between riding with a war party stripped for action, and riding herd on a cavalcade of merchants. The dust from a long line of horses, pack and riding mules, carts and wagons, and a fair bit of foot traffic kept his throat constantly dry. He was reaching for his waterskin just as Mikhail Sergeivich rode by.

"Drink up. We'll reach a spring before noon," Mikhail said. Like Shea, the Rus soldier wore the plain armor of mercenaries rather than anything with Prince Igor's device.

"I swear, we seem to add more merchants every day," Shea said.

"That ruse of yours worked a little too well," Mikhail replied. "But I must admit it was clever."

To get Reed Chalmers out from under Prince Igor's death sentence, Shea had improvised a fairly desperate plan: hit the Polovtsi while they're drunk. The prince had

laughed aloud when the psychologist explained it, then
had come close to him and sniffed.

"No, you are sober," he'd said. "Eh, well, with you in
charge it might work. But how will we get them drunk?"

That was the difficult part. They needed thirty or forty
wagonloads of wine and mead, more if all they could
find was ale and kvass. They also needed an excuse for
the Polovtsi to all be drinking at a particular spot. Finally,
Shea needed to spare Seversk's treasury, or the plan
would never go anywhere.

Remembering tales of moonshiners in both the old
and new worlds of his own universe, Shea suggested that
a rumor be circulated that the prince was planning to
raise the liquor tax in kind, and that his agents would be
starting their collections in the west very soon. He hoped
that would put liquor merchants on the roads east, trying
to dispose of their stocks before the tax collectors caught
up with them.

The rumor succeeded far better than Shea, or Igor,
could have believed. It was compounded by an even less
pleasant one, that Seversk would face more frequent
Polovets raids shortly. It was possible that some of the
merchants were trying to turn goods into more easily
hidden coin. Most of them, though, were probably just
trying to evade their taxes.

The vintners and brewers were soon joined by all kinds
of other vendors. Not the purveyors of luxury goods: silk,
fine glass, gold and silverware, anything whose primary
market was in the city itself was not put at risk on the
roads. But woodwork, cheap iron and tinware, woolens,
rough-cured hides—everything that could be taxed in
kind found a market on the roads and added to the sights
(and smells) of the cavalcade.

The merchants were being delicately herded to a spot
on the border of the principality of Seversk. The area
was hardly settled at all, thanks to Polovtsi raids as much
as anything, and the actual border was somewhat

disputed. Shea's plan required, however, that Igor claim the spot in question.

It was the logistics of getting the merchants there and no further, protecting them from raids along the way, and pretending all the time to have no connection with the prince, that was making Shea and the other men Igor had sent curse, sweat, and ache. The strain of holding back the "in the prince's name" they were accustomed to use soon had the soldiers beginning every sentence with an obscenity.

A few of the merchants, too poor to afford horses or mules, tried to make do with oxen. They held everyone back so much that Mikhail Sergeivich finally ordered them to the rear, to keep up as best they could, for the caravan could not be held to their pace. The merchants howled, they offered bribes, they threatened to protest to the prince.

Mikhail Sergeivich and Shea ignored them.

They couldn't ignore one peddler who'd been too poor even to buy an ox for his cartload of hides. He'd stolen two, and the owner came after them.

The guards couldn't formally arrest him, but Shea gave him a persuasive lecture about mercenaries needing to stay on terms with Igor much more than they did with thieving peddlers. Igor's arm was long and his justice swift and stern. The thief already owed fine of a *grivna* apiece for stealing the oxen. What else was he prepared to risk?

The oxen were returned, leaving the peddler sitting disconsolately on top of his cart in the middle of the steppe.

Then there were the merchants with expensive horses who needed cut fodder and few scruples about where they cut it when their bagged supply ran out. There were the merchants who didn't hobble their ponies and mules properly when they turned them loose to graze, so that Mikhail Sergeivich had to send out search parties for the strays, risking warhorses breaking legs in rabbit holes and lurking bandits picking off the riders. There was the cart that broke down so that it blocked the only strip of dry ground for half the caravan; it eventually ended in the bog.

There was enough trouble so that Shea was actually glad Reed Chalmers was not with him. The older psychologist was not the world's most easygoing traveler, and on a journey such as this they'd have given each other migraines, if not ulcers.

It surprised Shea that men who supposedly traveled for a living would make so many simple mistakes on the march. Shea wondered if most of the merchants were actually accustomed to selling their wares locally. If they were traveling now to avoid paying taxes later, they were certainly paying the penalty.

The biggest problem, of course, was keeping *everybody* from too much sampling of the main cargo. Shea didn't want to place aversion spells on it, not when his plan depended on free swilling by the right people. He had to fall back on persuasion.

By itself, that would not have been too demanding a job. Mikhail Sergeivich, and Shea as his nominal second-in-command put on a convincing mean captain/nice lieutenant act, which kept the soldiers and most of the merchants in line, most of the time. Once Shea had to draw his sword on a merchant's servant, and a few other times it took Mikhail Sergeivich and his biggest men cracking a few thick heads to quiet things down.

Fortunately that happened after they were far enough out on the steppe that deserting the caravan wasn't a good idea. The owners of the cracked heads stayed in the ranks. But Shea and the soldiers walked with eyes in the backs of their heads and their hands close to their sword hilts for a day or two, and went about in pairs after dark.

And everything from sweet reason to cracking heads had to be done during and after days in the saddle, short of sleep and struggling with thirst. As the days dragged on, Shea began to dream about adventuring in a world based on a work written by some cloistered nun a thousand years and a thousand miles away from the actual events. No long trips, no saddle sores, no reeking horse-barbarian camps, no subtler reek of blood from executed traitors!

"How far have we come today?" Shea asked Mikhail.

"A third less than we should have, so far."

"The devil fly away with this steppe!"

"Speedily a tale is spun, with much less speed a deed is done, eh? Well, by midafternoon tomorrow we'll have to send out scouts, anyway—and messengers."

The messengers would be riding to Igor's column, well to the rear. Chalmers was traveling with it as a closely watched prisoner, doubtless in no great comfort. But there was nothing Shea could do for his colleague except bring this off.

Over the next few days, Shea found that, this trip anyway, the steppe had no power to hypnotize him. The merchants were settling down for the most part, but the steppe made trouble on its own. A wolfpack stampeded some mules one night, and on another morning, short of water, they reached a spring only to find a dead aurochs in it. That was the longest day of the journey, it seemed, and before they reached the next water source, boredom was the least of Shea's worries.

They saw no Polovtsi, but endured enough else to test everyone's alertness to the limit. Even Shea's dreams of Belphebe grew faint, which he soon realized was just as well. Seeing Belphebe again depended on getting Doc Chalmers out of this jam, and if he'd stopped to think about it, instead of just doing it, he might have convinced himself that it was impossible.

The scouts had gone out as planned, and they brought the good news that the Polovtsi were approximately where they were expected to be, and in about the right numbers—several bands of various sizes. It was another two days before the scouts could, without being detected, pass between the Polovets bands and find the slave caravan.

"Good smiles," Mikhail Sergeivich said on the ninth day, after hearing the latest report. "The slave train's heading for Krasni Podok at about the pace we expected. But the two largest bands are coming our way. We'd best have the trade-truce banner up before dawn tomorrow. Oh, and send word back to our friends—*they* also have to move the way we planned, or they'll miss the party."

"The party" was crippling the Polovtsi by getting most of them incapably drunk. That was Shea's job, with Mikhail Sergeivich to lead the mopping-up operations. Another column was to drive through to round up the unprotected slave train before it reached neutral territory, and a third was a reserve.

Thanks to their care in not mentioning Igor's name, no one had yet connected them with Seversk's ruler. Some merchants thought the mercenaries might be the last of Sviatoslav Borisovich's household, fleeing an appointment with the headsman.

"Better hope the weather holds," Mikhail concluded. "The autumn rains have been known to come this early."

"I told you, I have no weather magic," Shea said irritably. "We'll just have to hope that the water doesn't come until the wine is gone."

At dawn the next day they raised the trade-truce banner. At noon a party of eighty to a hundred Polovtsi rode in. The smell was as overpowering as ever, even though this time it was only the men, not the campsite as well. Shea briefly imagined conjuring up a gigantic bathhouse, large enough to clean the whole Polovtsi nation—or deal with them permanently, as Olga had done with her husband's murderers.

Mikhail Sergeivich left the negotiations with the Polovtsi to a senior member of the vintners' guild. They came to terms with a minimum of insults, and half the Polovtsi rode away. The merchants started setting up booths and stands, but kept looking nervously over their shoulders at the Polovtsi wandering about.

"These sons-of-bitches," Mikhail told Shea, "are bad enough when sober. How do you plan to control them when they're drunk?"

"That's the point, to get them drunk," Shea replied. "I've been meaning to ask: what does trade law require them to do?"

"To pay for anything they want or break, and to observe the three-day limit. And even then one band once claimed they'd spent a whole day drunk before they looted a border household, so they'd forgotten where they were.

"That only involved maybe fifty Polovtsi. By the time all our friends' friends get wind of the party and come, we'll have half the steppe on our hands!"

"What happens when they have something to sell?" Shea asked.

"They stay sober then, and haggle like everyone else. They generally insist on selling first. Then, as often as not, they've been known to claim that the coin was bad, or the trade-goods worthless, so they can steal instead of buying in turn."

"If this works, they'll actually be falling down. Tell the soldiers to stick to water tomorrow. There's nothing we can do about the merchants."

"True," said Mikhail, and went off to give the orders.

Shea was up before dawn the next morning. Sure enough, one of the Polovtsi had made a nuisance of himself last night, insisting on having his cup filled again and again and never offering to pay. The merchant involved seemed more resigned than angry, and Mikhail told Shea (after saying "I told you so") that the guild would cover his losses out of total profits, if any.

The rider had thrown the cup away after emptying it the seventh time, and Shea had retrieved the leather vessel. The Polovets had been satisfyingly drunk, too, but in this matter of life or death Shea intended to hedge his bets.

Concealed among the wagons, and as close to the sleeping Polovtsi as he could stand, Shea held the cup in one hand and gestured with the other. He didn't quite sing, but a melody lurked under his intonation.

"They're Polovets riders who've lost their way,
Da! Da! Da!
Smelly steppe goats who have gone astray,
Da! Da! Da!
Lousy barbarians out on a spree,
Doomed to get drunk until they can't see,
And the Rus will make prey out of all they see,
Da! Da! Da!"

Then he crept back to the trade area proper, and unstoppered a leather flask. It was filled with a mixture of ale, kvass, mead, and wine, and the thought of drinking the concoction was enough to make Shea turn Prohibitionist. Again holding the flask in one hand, and gesturing with the other, Shea chanted:

"All liquor in the cask and tun
And every barrel on this ground,
You mighty waters old and young
In which our senses oft are drowned;

From strength to strength let every drop
Proceed, nor let that power fail,
Let kvass be strong, the limbs to stop,
Nor be there weak nor watery ale.

Let mead o'ercome the will to move,
And wine be poured that blood not flow,
And every drop a Samson prove
And twenty men or more o'erthrow."

They've been warned, he thought, as he curled up under the nearest wagon and tried to get a nap in before the action started. He wasn't sure just what the strengthening spell had done, but he wouldn't have touched a drop of liquor in the camp.

As dawn lightened the eastern sky, the camp began to stir. The night guards came in, the day guards went out, the merchants lit fires and prepared meals. The wiser ones, Shea noticed, had all the old men and young boys

out of sight and were offering food to the soldiers. The
soldiers ate, and repeated their warnings about drinking
only water today.

Mikhail added, "Put the best drink out first, to put
them in a mood to pay."

Shea didn't really care if the Polovtsi were in a mood
to pay. All he needed was Polovtsi in a mood to drink.

The first Polovtsi rode in shortly after sunrise, and they
kept coming steadily after that. By midmorning the camp
was surrounded by the steppe horsemen, and the stench
was something one could almost reach out and pluck
from the air in handfuls.

The riders needed no encouragement to drink, and
some of them even had the courtesy to pay—at first.
After the fourth or fifth cup, they seemed to forget that
there was such a thing as money. Shea could see the
merchants gritting their teeth as they watched their
stocks disappear, without any reasonable amount of silver
appearing in return.

There was also a little trading in dry goods. The psychologist saw an occasional Polovets festooned with wooden
trinkets or woolen cloth. But balancing debits and credits
(Shea was the son of a bookkeeper), he doubted that the
merchants' guilds would show a profit today.

Shea was starting to wonder if his strengthening spell
had worked at all, and if instead he should have tried
turning the mead to whiskey. The amount the steppemen
could get through, on empty stomachs too, gave him the
feeling of lice in his pants (at least he hoped it was only
the *feeling*).

But by noon, Polovtsi were falling down and crawling
around like cockroaches. They couldn't walk, but they
could still drink. If they couldn't get to the barrels, they
could send friends who were still stumbling instead of
crawling.

Shea watched one Polovets give friends his short
sword, his metal cap (it looked like something captured

from a long-dead Rus), his shirt (complete with lice), and his trousers, all to trade for more wine. They came back with the wine, all except one man.

The last friend came back empty-handed, just as the now practically-naked warrior was finishing off the wine. He glared at his friend.

"No friend of mine you are. Buy wine—with my trousersh—then drink it yourshelf."

"Ho, I did—"

"You did."

"Did not."

"Did!"

"Did not!"

"I'll take—your trousersh—"

"No, you won't!"

The warrior on the ground suddenly developed the ability of a leopard. He gripped his friend by the ankles, tumbled him off his feet, and began pulling at his trousers. The other struggled, kicking at the first man's face.

A foot connected with the first man's jaw. His head snapped back and to the side. He rolled over on his side, then onto his back. A moment later he began to snore.

His friend lurched to his feet and staggered off. He staggered straight into the wheel of a cart, then reeled back, rubbing his nose.

"No brawl, my chief," he said. "Nothing—like that. Just a bet between friendsh. Jusht a . . ." His voice trailed off. Having lost his vision, the Polovets now lost his balance. He gripped the iron rim of the cartwheel, but that only slowed his fall. In another moment he was as soundly asleep as his friend, the only difference being that the second man was facedown.

Those two were the first Shea saw go down from drinking too much breakfast, but they weren't the last. Between them, breakfast and lunch took out a good half of the visitors.

By early afternoon, they were coming in dribs and drabs instead of whole bands. Some bought drink and rode off with it; Shea hoped it would at least knock the fight out of them.

A Polovets lurched up, his arm around a merchant's apprentice and brandishing an empty cup in his free hand.

"More wine! This—hish mastersh a pig. Won't—no more."

"You've had enough, friend," the young man said.

From his voice and breath, Shea thought that the apprentice could also skip the next few cups. But the spell was working on both of them; they were going to drink themselves under the table, under the wagon, or wherever else the drunks were ending up.

Shea personally refilled their cups. They emptied those cups twice before reeling off, thanking Shea with embraces that left him badly wanting a bath. Drunken Polovtsi were adding assorted stinks to a camp already ripe from the horde of sober ones.

Good thing I didn't turn the mead to whiskey, Shea thought. *I wasn't planning to kill the Polovtsi from alcohol poisoning. Now, if the drink just holds out—*

It did. A few Polovtsi seemed to realize what was happening, and tried to mount and ride off. Most of them fell right back off, and none of them got more than five hundred paces from the camp.

A few also didn't survive the afternoon—brawls, falling into streams and drowning, breaking necks falling off horses or wagons, and so on. Even that didn't sober up their surviving comrades.

Shea had seen alcoholics, people who couldn't stop drinking, and they weren't a pretty sight. Neither were the Polovtsi, as his spell drove them to pour more and more down their throats.

He reminded himself that Chalmers being executed or Florimel spending her life in some potentate's harem would be a much uglier sight.

By the time the sun was halfway down the sky, the work was done. Mikhail Sergeivich leaped on a wagon and waved his sword over his head three times, the

agreed-on signal for the soldiers to set on the Polovtsi.
Then he jumped down, joined Shea in pulling a sheaf of
rawhide thongs from their baggage, and went to work.

Not all of the soldiers had obeyed orders to avoid the
liquor, and those the two leaders left lying where they'd
fallen. A few drunken soldiers didn't make much difference, anyway. The Polovtsi were either sprawled flat or
sitting slumped against something, and none of them
could have stood unless tied to a tree. As for fighting,
they were so obviously past it that in a few minutes the
sober merchants came out and began helping the soldiers
bind the prisoners.

A few of the Polovtsi who'd been sleeping off their
breakfast woke up before they were bound. They only
stared dim-eyed at their captors; Shea wondered how
many of them (especially the ones who'd drunk kvass or
mead) would be paralyzed by hangovers.

They'd run out of thongs and were raiding the leather
merchants' stores for more material, when Igor rode up
at the head of his warriors. The prince stared at the acres
of helpless Polovtsi, and laughed so hard that anyone but
a Hero would have fallen off his horse. Then he dismounted and embraced Shea.

"You are a *bogatyr* like none ever named in song or
story! The Polovtsi are finished and Rurik Vasilyevich has
his life, by all the saints!"

"Did you capture the slave train, Your Highness? And
what of that other wizard? And Yuri Dimitrivich's family?
And—?" Shea hoped his day's victory entitled him to a
few straight answers.

"We captured it, all right," the prince interrupted.
"Word of your drinking party reached the guards, and
half of them rode off to join it. They are out there," he
added, waving a hand at the field of drunks.

"The rest seemed to suspect something, but we had a
scout who knew a ford across a little stream that they
counted on to protect one flank. We had our men on foot
right into the camp before the guards knew anything. Then

the horsemen charged before the Polovtsi could so much as draw a sword!

"We had the camp and the caravan under our hands in less time than it took one of those wretches to drain a cup. Yuri Dimitrivich's family and household, those who survived, are free."

"What did you do with the rest, Your Highness?"

The prince replied cheerfully, "They are on their way to Krasni Podok, and this vermin will join them. Don't worry about any blood prices, Egorov. The *grivnas* from that sale will more than cover the price of a few wounds."

Igor lowered his voice. "I think I really will raise the liquor tax. If these merchants will go to so much trouble to supply drink to Polovtsi, perhaps I can persuade them to take as much trouble for their prince. Speaking of which, I could use a drink right now."

"Ah, Your Highness, if anything is left, it would leave you flat alongside your enemies. In fact, I'd not offer anything here to anyone but an enemy."

The prince looked around, then headed for the spring. He gestured for Shea to follow, which the psychologist did, telling himself that his dreams of freeing all the slaves in the train had been a few centuries too early. But what about—

"Florimel, Your Highness! Was she freed?"

"I gave Rurik Vasilyevich permission to look for her, once we'd taken the caravan," Igor replied. "He will be coming in with the rest of my band. Oleg Nikolaivich will take the caravan to Krasni Podok and bring back my profits." His smile grew a trifle cruel. "I will also find out who has been depending on Krasni Podok to supply his needs, at the expense of his fellow Rus."

That should help a bit, Shea thought.

Near sunset the rest of the party rode in, including Reed Chalmers. Never was there a more truly named Knight of the Woeful Countenance.

He was still guarded, but Shea could see that the

guards were now superfluous. Reed slumped in the saddle so that it was a wonder he didn't fall. There was no
sign of Florimel.

Shea helped his comrade down, and wished he had a
drink to offer him. The best he could do was privacy, so
he took Chalmers to the outskirts of the camp.

"What happened?"

Shea was relieved to see a trace of life in Chalmers'
eyes, even if it was only frustration. "I—I don't know."

"Can you tell me what you saw, at least?"

"What—how can that help?"

Florimel is gone again, Shea thought. Aloud, he said,
"We never know what *won't* help. Besides, we kept our
promise to Igor. He owes us something. Even if I can't
help—"

"All right."

Chalmers described a search of the slave caravan,
wagon by wagon and tent by tent, him and four guards.
(Not just to keep an eye on him, either; suicidal last-
ditch attacks were a Polovtsi specialty.) There'd been
hundreds of slaves, some more wretched then others, but
none of them as happy as Chalmers had expected to find
them, now that they were free.

"One man was bold enough to explain that Yuri the
Red's household had been freed but no others," Chal-
mers said. "He asked if this was a true prince's justice.
One of my guards knocked him senseless."

Chalmers kept his anger on a tight rein until they came
to the last tent. It had some sort of warding at the entrance,
that kept Chalmers and his guards from going in.

The warding did not keep the psychologist from seeing
Florimel, standing with Malambroso in the far corner of
the tent.

"It should not have kept her from seeing me, either,
but perhaps it did. Certainly she showed no signs of
recognition. She looked like a sleepwalker."

Then Malambroso began making passes with his

hands. Chalmers knew there was only one thing to do: break the ward, then negate Malambroso's spell.

He tried three times to enter the tent, using three different verses (and Shea couldn't have remembered what they were to save his life). The warding stayed firm, which was more than could be said of the guards. Igor's orders or no, two of them ran off.

The other two remained in sight, but at a safe distance, as if fearing Chalmers might burst into flames at any moment, like a pot of Greek fire.

In the middle of Chalmers' fourth attempt, Malambroso and Florimel vanished.

"I'm sure I did everything correctly," Chalmers concluded. "Any one of those spells should have stopped him." His voice was tight with rage and grief. "And what has he done with my wife?" His voice rose to a shout. "Where has he taken her?"

Shea mentally cursed the whole continuum, starting with Malambroso, going on to the Polovtsi, and not stopping there. He didn't dare curse out loud, but right now he would knowingly have accepted a drink from the caravan's remaining stores.

The day was ending even worse than it had begun, and Shea hoped that Chalmers didn't want any company, because he himself certainly didn't. With a farewell grunt to Chalmers, he stumbled, half-blindly, back toward the center, where fires were beginning to glow.

Shea had to swing wide before he'd gone more than a few yards. The sober merchants had pulled their wagons into a tight circle, in case any sober Polovtsi wandered by. The drunken Polovtsi covered as much ground as ever, although some of them were awake enough to groan and a few were struggling against their bonds.

The psychologist was passing a wagon with a cover of smelly furs tied to poles, when one of the furs flew out and hit him in the face. Before he could react, a human figure leaped after the fur.

The attacker landed on Shea's back, and the Ohioan felt

the pressure of a knife seeking to pierce his armor. He tried to keep his balance and draw his sword, but did neither. He went down, his sword caught under him and the attacker on top of him. Shea felt another stab, this time higher up. He tried to free one arm to draw his dagger, because he had the feeling that the third time his attacker stabbed, the knife wasn't going to hit armor—

Something cracked, something else thumped, and a third something went *wssssh*. The attacker let out a scream and released Shea. The psychologist rolled clear, drawing his sword as soon as his right arm was free, then leaping up ready to go into action.

He didn't have to. The attacker, a thickset man with a Rus robe and a scarf over his face, was sprawled on the trampled grass. Reed Chalmers stood over him, with a long pole from the wagon's cover in one hand.

Shea took a deep breath. "Thanks, Doc. You're improving."

"I thought of killing him, but I suspect he may have something to tell us."

Definitely improving, thought Shea.

The scuffle had drawn the attention of the guards, and the prisoner was soon dragged to the center of camp and stripped of his scarf and headdress. In the light of fires and torches, it could be seen that in spite of his Rus merchant's dress, the prisoner had Polovets blood in him.

Chalmers looked closely at the man for a minute, then frowned.

"Do you know this man, Rurik Vasileyevich?"

Igor had come up, although both of the psychologists were too numb to notice. Chalmers stiffened like an icon. Those words were all too clearly etched in his mind.

"Yes, Your Highness," he said. "This is the man who approached me in Seversk."

"Doubtless a spy," Igor said. "But if I find out he had the cooperation of the merchants' guilds, they will pay."

He shouted for Mikhail Sergeivich. "Learn what you

can from this one," the prince told his captain. "If he survives, he goes to Krasni Podok."

The return to Seversk took as long as ever, and what seemed like the final failure to rescue Florimel raised neither of the Ohians' spirits. Chalmers was also frustrated and a little frightened at the failure of his spells. Shea did his best to help his mentor find an answer, but none of their speculation brought them any closer to Florimel or home and Belphebe, and chilly nights made it clear that winter was coming on fast.

They reached Seversk before the weather turned completely sour, and were promptly invited to the victory feast in the palace. Neither of the psychologists was in the mood for a party, but neither of them wanted to insult their host by refusing to celebrate his victory, particularly when he owed much of it to them and was not backward in saying so.

By the standards of his time, Shea realized, Igor probably *was* a great and noble warrior-prince. So they put on their best robes and new boots of the finest kidskin, and went to the party.

They might as well have gone in monk's robes, for all the attention they drew. Everyone had brought out their finest garments, some of which had obviously been in storage a bit too long. Shea wondered if Igor would appreciate a gift of mothballs.

Cloth of gold, brocades with half a dozen colors in them, fine wool and linen with borders of gold thread and jewels, a dozen kinds of fur, swords with jeweled hilts—for once the diners in the great hall were brighter than the painting on its walls. The food was just as lavish; the stuffed-sturgeon dish appeared again, this time with the innermost item some kind of shellfish, and a sauce poured over the whole thing that made Shea ask for more ale several times.

As authentic *bogatyri*, Shea and Chalmers were seated at the head table, one on either side of the Patriarch.

He listened with fascinated amusement to their account of the piles of Polovtsi.

"You never tasted *any* of it?" he asked Shea.

"I didn't dare. And if I had known what the effects would be—a soldier who drank the mead said that at first he felt as if he could carry the world on his shoulders, and then felt as if the world had fallen on him. There is a riddle in this, for all that I cast the spell myself."

"There is another riddle to be solved here, is there not?" the Patriarch said. He looked at Chalmers in a way that told both psychologists that someone had been talking. "You were not able to defeat a single Polovtsi sorcerer, while your comrade was able to defeat entire bands. It may be that warriors with no magic are no match for a wizard, my son, but there may be another answer. Cast a *small* spell for me. Now."

Both psychologists looked at the Patriarch as if he'd grown a second head.

He smiled. "I grant you absolution if they are harmless. But I think I see the answer to your riddle."

Shea recited:

"Who hath a book hath friends at hand,
  And gold and gear at his command."

Shea nearly dropped the small gold-stamped photo album into the sauce. It looked like—but it couldn't be. He opened it. Belphebe stared back at him from the photograph.

"Go back where you belong," he told the album. His voice nearly broke.

The album vanished.

Chalmers tried the same spell. The three waited expectantly for a minute. Chalmers tried again. Still no results.

Chalmers' face now showed stark horror. "Have I lost my ability?" His voice shook.

"You shouldn't have," Shea said. "Symbolic logic is a

constant, all across the continua. *It* hasn't stopped." Shea did stop, as he realized that he still had more questions than answers, which wasn't helping Chalmers.

"You took the prince's bread and salt the night you met," the Patriarch said. "You, Rurik Vasilyevich, betrayed that bread and salt. This has become far too common among the Rus, and it is never pleasing to God. Sooner or later a traitor's luck deserts him. And your magic was your luck—at least that is how I read this riddle."

"But it was for my wife's sake—I didn't betray her!"

"Were you able to help her, when she needed help?"

"What can we do?" Shea asked. Chalmers was past speech, apparently not knowing whether to curse or weep.

"If you wish to help your wife, you must do penance for the wrong you did the prince. But it must be true repentance," the Patriarch warned.

Chalmers was a good academic; "repentance" was a religious concept and more than a little alien to him. He hemmed and hawed and blustered longer than Shea cared for. At any moment he was afraid Chalmers would use the word "superstition" or even "nonsense," and he didn't want to think about the Patriarch's reply.

But Chalmers had no alternatives to offer. The Patriarch had the patience of those who take on the work of leading strayed sheep back into the flock. He listened calmly, until there was more grief than anger in Chalmers' voice. Finally, the older psychologist put his head in his hands for a moment, then looked at the Patriarch.

"What must I do?" he asked.

"You must fast tomorrow—that shouldn't be difficult, after tonight—and come to the basilica tomorrow night. I will meet you there."

The next night a thunderstorm raged as the Patriarch led Shea to the door of the basilica. Shea wore a heavy wool cloak with a hood that so far had kept him no worse than damp, but the mud underfoot was another matter. It kept trying to pull his boots off, and he wished paving wasn't another of those little conveniences this continuum hadn't developed.

The basilica was the snuggest building Shea had yet seen here, and one look at the sanctuary told him why. A vast iconostasis—a screen of icons—rose higher than Igor's head and spread out wider than most rooms in the palace. On the left were Old Testament scenes—Cain slaying Abel, Noah leading the animals aboard the Ark, Moses breaking the Golden Calf, Daniel in the lion's den.

On the right, Shea recognized other scenes, from the New Testament—Christ walking on the water, performing the miracle of the loaves and the fishes, and on the cross. Above the two wings was the Holy Trinity—and Shea couldn't tell if the Holy Spirit was intended to be incorporeal or if the artist hadn't known how to draw.

The whole iconostasis and many of the individual icons' frames were gold or silver or at least gilded or silvered wood. Elaborate carvings or castings, inlaid ivory and jewels, tapestry-work that made any formal-dress brocade look drab—the iconostasis outshone even the elaborately painted walls and ceiling of the basilica.

The only way to make that thing any brighter, Shea thought, *would be to set it on fire*. Then he hastily chased the irreverent thought out of his mind. This was a place that could almost make one believe in blasphemy.

It did make Shea remember Sunday school, and discreetly kneel.

The Patriarch returned, leading Chalmers, who was wearing a dun-colored penitent's robe. Facing the iconostasis, the Patriarch pointed out one just over halfway up the New Testament side. "Judas' kiss, the betrayal of Our Lord to His enemies. Meditate upon that, my erring son."

They watched Chalmers prostrate himself on the floor. The Patriarch turned to Shea.

"We must leave now."

The priest extinguished the basilica lamps and picked up their lantern. It penetrated the darkness but feebly, but it got them out, leaving Chalmers with only the sanctuary light.

"Let us pray that though he lie in darkness, God will lead him to the light," the Patriarch said. He began to pray, loudly enough not to notice that Shea was only mouthing words.

The problem wasn't that prayer might not work. Here the problem was that it *might*.

Shea had finally worked up an appetite for breakfast the next morning, when Chalmers entered their chamber. The older man still wore his penitent's robe, but he had the first smile on his face that Shea had seen in weeks.

"My penitence seems to have worked," he said. "I cast a small spell, and it worked. I changed wine into water."

Shea swallowed a chunk of dry bread. "I suppose the other way around might have been in bad taste."

Chalmers' smile turned into a grin. "Who cares about bad taste? Now that we can follow Florimel, all I want to do is leave this world. I have never been in one I shall be so happy to see the last of!"

His ending a sentence with a preposition told Shea just how excited his colleague was. Nor did he disagree—although there was no point in even thinking about returning to Ohio, not with Chalmers in this mood.

It took them barely ten minutes to dress and pack. Five minutes more and they were standing hand in hand, one on each side of a large puddle on the floor, the result of a leak opened by last night's storm.

"By the power of saints, and the might of princes, by the strength of men and the wit of women, may all the powers of the sky above, and the earth beneath, and the waters under the earth grant that if there is P, and there is Q, then P equals not-Q, and Q equals not-P. . . ."

They were off.

Part II
SIR HAROLD AND
THE HINDU KING

CHRISTOPHER STASHEFF

The lights faded, the ground jolted up under their feet, and Shea and Chalmers found themselves alone in the dark. Shea had a confused impression of single-story houses with curving adobe walls and thatched roofs, with bigger buildings of stone looming behind them in the moonlight. A world of aromas filled his head, sharp and pungent, some familiar, most not; the only one he could name was something that smelled like curry. The ground beneath him was just that—ground, the packed earth of an unpaved street. He seemed to be in a sort of expanded intersection, not big enough to call a plaza.

And hot. The heat beat all about him, stifling. By the time his head stopped spinning, Shea was already sweating. "Whew! If this is what it's like at night, I'd hate to be here at noon!"

"Brace yourself," Chalmers said grimly. "We probably will still be here."

"Where are we, Doc?"

"To judge by the heat, I would say it must be somewhere in the tropics." Chalmers swayed.

Sea caught his arm to steady him. "Only a minute, Doc—then you'll stabilize."

"I shall recover," Chalmers muttered. "Am I growing weaker, Harold? Syllogismobile travel has never struck me so hard before!"

73

But Chalmers lurched, bumping against Shea, who might have toppled himself, if it had not been just at that moment that someone bumped into him from the other side. "Oh, excuse me!" he said. Just to be on the safe side, he stepped quickly away, right hand dropping to his sword hilt—but with his left still holding to Chalmers just in case he was still woozy. He could have sworn the other party muttered something about a stupid beggar, but he must have been wrong, because the man said, softly but exuberantly, "Brother! Comrade in thievery! How are your pickings tonight?"

Shea stared, taken aback—and looked the man over in one quick glance. He wore a dark-colored cloth wrapped about his hips, sandals, a sword, and a forked beard with moustaches that curved up to the corners of his eyes. Besides that, he had a very flat nose—but the real distinguishing characteristic was the turban. They were in India!

No, wait a minute—there were other countries where people wore turbans, from Arabia through Persia. . . .

But they didn't eat curry.

Not exactly conclusive evidence, but the aroma, the heat, and the turban all added up, so Shea decided to operate as though this were India until proven otherwise. The syllogismobile had made him a natural speaker of the local language, so she he said, "Sorry, friend—the darkness must be deceiving you. We're not thieves, we're foreigners. We, uh, were traveling late—decided we were so close to the town that we might as well keep pushing until we arrived."

"Foreigners? Well, that does explain your outlandish clothing." Flat-nose eyed them suspiciously. "But how did you come into the city after the gates closed?"

A straight-line gleam caught Shea's eye and, looking more closely, he saw that the man had a thread tied over his nose and around his head. No wonder his nose was flat! For a wild second, he thought it was a fly-fishing leader, then realized that, in a pre-industrial town it must be something less exotic—horsehair, say, or catgut. But why the disguise? "After the gates closed? We didn't."

Chalmers nodded, muttering, "Quite true, quite true."

Shea hoped he was only indulging in irony, not shock. "We've, ah, just been wandering around, trying to find a good hotel."

"Wandering! Yes," Chalmers agreed.

Shea noticed he didn't commit himself to the questionable part of the statement. "Would you know of a good inn, kind sir?"

"An inn? Not if you have no money! And you do not, from the look of you."

Obviously, the man still thought they were thieves—or at the best, beggars. Unfortunately, his comment hit home—they *didn't* have any money, at least not in local currency. "What *can* you recommend, then?"

"To get out of sight! As quickly as possible! There is a gang of thieves plaguing this city, and if you run afoul of them, they may kill you rather than risk your bringing witness against them!" Flat-nose shouldered past them with a hasty, "May you have good fortune!" and disappeared into the night.

Shea's blood chilled; he had heard of such things, but had not thought they happened until the 1920s. "You don't think there really *is* a gang working the town, do you, Doc?"

"More to the point," said Chalmers, "is the possibility that we have just encountered a member of the band." He shuddered. "Who would know better of their existence—or have a better reason for wishing us to go indoors, where we cannot see what he does?"

He obviously didn't doubt the man for a second. "I guess you're right, Doc. After all, why else would he make such a clumsy attempt at disguise?"

"You mean the thread around his nose? Yes, quite so. Presumably, that tells us two things: that the thieves are ruthless, and that they are flat-nosed."

Shea stared in surprise. "You mean we just talked to a local cop?"

"It is a possibility," Chalmers said, "but more pertinent is his advice. Let us find a hole to hide in, Harold."

It was good advice indeed. Shea looked around, able to make out a bit more of their surroundings now that his eyes had adjusted to the moonlight. The larger buildings in the distance were elaborate and intricate—and he was sure he recognized the silhouette of a slim tower. "I think we're in India, Doc. More to the point, we're in a genuine city, not just a big town."

"I quite agree." Chalmers looked around, frowning. "Now, where do you hide in a city if you can't find a hotel?"

"A back alley is a good place." Shea drew his sword. "Of course, the local muggers might not have gone to bed yet, and they like alleys, too. Want to take a chance on it, Doc?"

"Let me consider the proposition." Chalmers steepled his fingers, resting his lips against them for a minute. Then he drew a circle in the dust with his toe, reciting,

". . . For knowledge if anyone burns,
  We're keeping a very small prophet,
  A prophet who brings us unbounded returns!"

There was a burst of light like a photographer's flash, and a two-foot-high man with a long beard and a longer gray robe stood before them, bald head gleaming in the moonlight. "Good evening, sir! May I help you?"

"Victorian," Chalmers muttered to Shea, and to the prophet, "You may indeed, O Wise One! Can you tell me where we are?"

"Where? Why summon me for such trivialities, sir? Well, it is your money. You are in India—the city of Chandradoya, to be precise."

"You guessed well, Harold," Chalmers observed. Then, to the diminiutive prophet, "Thank you, O Fount of

Wisdom. Can you also tell me the identity of that man whom we addressed but now?"

"He with the horsehair round his nose? To be sure, sir! That was Randhir, the rajah of this fair city! Will there be anything else?"

"The rajah himself, eh?" Chalmers mused. "Running about at night without a bodyguard, dressed as a peasant? Well, well! Quite eccentric . . . No, thank you, Esteemed One. I need no further information at this time."

"A pleasure to serve you, sir. That will be six shillings, please."

"Pay the man, Harold," Chalmers said.

Shea favored Chalmers with a quick glare, then fished in his purse. "I'm a little short on shillings at the moment. How about a Russian *grivna*?"

"I am sure that will be equal or better in value," the prophet said quickly. He took the coin and bowed. "Call upon us whenever you have need, sir!" With another flash, he disappeared.

As Shea blinked away afterimages, Chalmers told him, "So magic works in this universe—but not very well."

"Not well? Why?"

"Come now, Harold! Do you honestly believe the King himself would be going about at night dressed as a commoner, with a horsehair round his nose? This isn't the Arabian Nights, you know."

"Oh, isn't it? Any particular myth you recognize, Doc?"

Another flash, and there stood the miniature prophet again. "You are in the midst of a tale from the collection *Vikram and the Vampire*, compiled by the sage Bhavabhuti, and translated by Sir Richard Francis Burton—yes, the explorer who helped search for the headwaters of the Nile."

Shea goggled, but Chalmers said, completely unruffled, "Which tale exactly?"

"The fifth," the prophet said, and held out a cupped palm. "Two shillings, please."

Feeling numb, Shea handed over another Russian coin. The prophet took it and bowed. "Thank you, gentlemen! Call again, whenever you please!"

Shea found his voice. "But we didn't. Call again, I mean."

"True, but we make unbounded returns. Good evening." The prophet disappeared brilliantly.

"Don't ask any more questions," Chalmers advised, "or he'll be back in a flash."

"I won't," Shea promised. "I'm having trouble enough adjusting to the idea of a plainclothes rajah."

"Surely you do not believe the little man!"

"You mean the Prophet of Profit? Why not? We've run into stranger things," Shea sighed. "Besides, his being king would explain the attempt at disguise."

Chalmers frowned. "How so?"

"Because if his royal nose is of a size with his rank, of *course* he'd want to make it look shorter. Hadn't we better go looking for that alley now?"

"Yes, by all means." Chalmers followed Shea along the dusty street. "We must see to obtaining local clothing as soon as possible."

"I think we'll have to wait for daybreak, when the shops open. What caste do you think I should opt for?"

"Persian robes—a traveler from the West will be your best role here. That avoids the whole issue of caste as well as it can be avoided."

"But not too far to the west, hm?"

"Indeed. Our Medieval Russian garb must be quite incomprehensible to most of the local residents. We want to be believable as foreigners, not maniacs. For myself, a simple saffron robe will do nicely—I shall be a *sunnyasi*, a wandering holy man."

"With your Northern European complexion? Whom do you think you're fooling?"

"Philosophers can be of any breed, and still be credible," Chamers replied, with a loftiness that made Shea wonder about suppressed impulses toward asceticism. He decided a quick change of subject was in order. "I thought our little philosopher was Victorian English."

"He was—he came from John Wellington Wells' shop at Number Seventy, Simmery Axe."

"But we're speaking a Hindu dialect right now. How come we understood him?"

"He *is* magical, you know," Chalmers sighed, "unlimited knowledge, and all that sort of thing."

"Oh." Shea let that one sink in. Then he asked, "You mean he's apt to show up any time I ask a question now?" He glanced at the darkness about him with apprehension, realizing too late that he might have triggered another visit.

So did Chalmers; he let out a sigh of relief when nothing flashed. "Only if it's a matter of knowledge we do not have, or cannot gain locally, I would presume. Still, I would be careful what you asked for."

"I know—I might get it." Shea pointed. "There's a likely looking alley."

"What it's looking like, I will not say." Chalmers eyed the black space between buildings with misgiving. "Still, if it is our only hope of avoiding the gang of thieves, let us hie ourselves thither."

"Thither?" Shea echoed, but he headed for the mouth of the alley anyway.

Stepping in, they passed from bright moonlight into sudden shadow. "Where are you, Harold?" Chalmers whispered.

"Right beside you—or your voice, anyway. This place is as dark as the Black Hole of Calcutta." Then Shea remembered that they might not be all that far from Calcutta, and swallowed. Sweat would have sprung out all over his body, if it hadn't already. "Why are we whispering?"

"Because it's da-ah-uh-HO!" Chalmers stumbled, lurched, and reached out to catch hold of Shea, who braced himself just in time to keep both of them on their feet.

"Stupid fool!" hissed a voice that started below them, then rose quickly in both pitch and elevation. "Can you not see where you step?"

"N-no, actually, we can't." Shea huddled back against Chalmers, then remembered himself and stepped in front, hand going to his sword. He could only just make out the gleam of reflected light from eyes and an earring. "Can't see a thing." But his eyes were adjusting to the deeper darkness, and he could detect a vague, irregular circle low down in the wall opposite him, with another man coming out of it on hands and knees. Chalmers had tripped over their current conversationalist as he made his exit—but who came out of a building through a hole in the wall? Especially with a bagful of hard-looking lumpy objects over his shoulder?

Thieves—and ones who didn't pussyfoot around with such niceties as lockpicks or glass-cutters. But how did they knock a hole in a wall without making a racket that would bring down every policeman in the neighborhood?

Easy—no police. And the neighbors didn't bother the men because they were scared stiff. "Doc," Shea hissed, "I think we've found our gang of thieves."

"Not mine," Chalmers assured him, then forced a smile and stepped forward. "Greetings, O Man of Skill! We are strangers in your fair city, and . . ."

"Strangers indeed, not to know enough to keep within doors at night!" A knife suddenly appeared at Chalmers' throat—rough and homemade, by Shea's twentieth-century standards, but with a gleam of sharpness to its edge that showed it was quite functional. "What shall we do with these two, Chankoor?"

"Hold them a moment, Din," the other man said as he stood up. "When we are all out, we shall take him to the captain."

"Even as he says," Din told Chalmers and Shea. "Hold yourselves quite still now, or my hand might waver."

Chalmers swallowed convulsively, almost nicking his Adam's apple in the process, and stared at the man with bulging eyes. Behind his back, Shea stiffened a finger and let it relax, very slowly, as he began to mutter something about melting, but Chalmers clamped a hand onto his arm, and Shea decided that Doc hadn't quite given up hope of talking his way out of this.

"Take your hand from your sword-hilt, cow-eater," Din sneered, and twisted the knife for emphasis. Below him, a third man, then a fourth, crawled out of the hole, the last reaching back to drag out two more bags of plunder.

"Tell us who you are, completely and truthfully," Chankoor demanded.

"Tell him, Harold," Chalmers said out of the corner of his mouth, eyes never leaving Din's face.

"Harr-ld?" Chankooor scowled at Shea. "What manner of name is that?"

Shea tried to remember what the Hindus might have called Europeans, before the Portuguese opened up trade with their ports. "We are, uh, Frankish, uh . . . thieves! Yes, Frankish thieves, come to study the techniques of your so-excellent band, whose fame has reached even to . . ."

"The truth!" The knife twisted again, and Chalmers gasped.

Shea wondered on which part of his concoction the man had caught him out. "Oh, all right! We heard there were rich pickings here, and that no one could stop robbers in this city, so we came to . . . well . . ."

"Cut a slice of the haunch for yourself?" Chankoor grunted. "Foolish barbarian! Know that our captain will tolerate no band but his own in this city! However, if your gods bless you, perhaps he will allow you to join us. Come, then, and we will take you to him. Turn and go!"

The knife withdrew, and a hard hand turned Chalmers toward the mouth of the alley. His shoulders slumped with relief even as he stepped away, then stepped faster as the knife-point pricked the back of his neck and the hard hand tugged him along.

Another hand caught Shea's arm in a grip like a blood-pressure cuff and hauled him after Chalmers. He went, wondering why the thieves hadn't taken his sword. Could it be the design was so alien to them that they didn't recognize it for what it was? No, surely not! They must have been confident of being able to kill him before he could stab any of them. Talk about arrogance!

He fell in beside Chalmers, reflecting that, although the local dialect of Hindustani might be his native language now, and that he probably wouldn't even be able to remember a word of English, he should still be able to speak a language that had always been foreign to him. *"Qu'est-que nous faisons maintenant, Monsieur le Docteur?"* What do we do now, Doc?

"Nous irons encontre ce capitaine de voleurs," Chalmers replied. *"J'ai devient curieux."* We go meet this captain of thieves; I have become curious.

There were times when Shea could cheerfully have done without the inborn curiosity of the inquiring mind.

"Speak not in your bleating tongue!" Chankoor snarled right behind Shea, and a knife pricked the back of *his* neck. "Oh, all right," he grumbled, and followed the other two thieves out of the alley and into the night—where he virtually froze, staring about him in shock. The street swarmed with thieves, who didn't seem to be at all concerned about somebody's seeing them. A buzz of conversation filled his ears, and the moonlit gyrations of the thieves confused and dazzled him. He blinked, then rubbed his eyes. Had all this been going on before, and he just hadn't noticed it? Some of them must have just been starting the evening's work—apparently, he had fallen into the hands of the early birds that were out to get the golden worm—because they were still rubbing oil on their bodies between swigs from bottles that Shea was sure contained something more potent than fruit juice. Some had progressed beyond that point, rubbing lamp-black around their eyes and eyesockets, no doubt to make them less visible—between more swigs from bottles, of course.

Out of the corner of his eye, Shea saw a robed man hurrying along the street, apparently oblivious to the thieves, but apprehensive about them. A couple of foot-pads fell upon him and bore him down; a knife flashed, and the victim cried out, a cry that ended in a horrid gurgle. The footpads stood up holding a fat purse.

"Why didn't we see them before?" Shea asked Chalmers—and the knife was suddenly at his throat again. "You are not the thieves you claim to be," their captor growled, "or you would know the answer to that!"

"We do not practice the same skills as you do, in our benighted lands," Chalmers said quickly. "Indeed, we have come here to learn them! Pray tell us how we did not . . ."

He broke off, staring. So did Shea, for their captors had let go of their arms, and the street was suddenly empty again, except for the dead body—three dead bod-ies, now that he saw the view without the swarm of thieves. He could still hear them, but their voices seemed muted, distant.

Then, suddenly, a thief was there, crouching as he rubbed oil over his shoulders. He recited an incantation, and Shea and Chalmers stared, fascinated, recognizing only a few words here and there; obviously, the man was speaking in an old language, probably Sanskrit; Shea was mildly surprised that he didn't hear it as Latin.

Then the man disappeared.

Hard hands fell on their shoulders again, and the noise of the crowd was back in full force—and so was the gang, many of whom were now watching Shea and Chalmers, laughing with glee at their looks of surprise. "Do you understand now?" their captor asked from behind.

"Yes, I think so," Chalmers said slowly. "You have incantations to make yourselves invisible, but the effect does not last long."

"Yes, even as we have incantations to enable us to see in the darkness. Do you not have such?"

"No," Shea said, "but we'd love to learn them." He

pointed at a group of men who seemed to be practicing some sort of martial art, except that Shea could very clearly make out some movements that seemed to be those of cutting purse strings. "What are *they* doing?"

Chankoor seemed to puff himself up, grinning with self-importance. "They practice the lessons of the god with the golden spear."

"What god is that?" Chalmers asked.

Chankoor stared in surprise. "You are thieves, and do not know?"

"Thieves from lands far to the west, remember," Shea said quickly, "*very* far to the west."

Chankoor muttered something about ignorant barbarians, but explained, "He is Kartikeya, the god of thieves, who revealed to the master Yugacharya the Chauriya Vidya, the *Thieves' Manual*. Any who wish to succeed in theft must know its precepts by heart. Regard those men, now . . ." He pointed at two men who labored at the base of a wall. ". . . and those, those, and those!" He pointed out three other groups who were also at work on the walls of three other shops. "They carry out the four modes of breaching a house."

Shea peered through the darkness, and saw that the first pair were picking bricks out piece by piece. Shoddy material, no doubt—and Chankoor confirmed it. "Burnt bricks," he explained, but didn't say who had burned them. Another pair were at work with a cold chisel, cutting through. "Those bricks are unbaked, and old," Chankoor explained. "The monsoon winds softened them quite nicely—but exposure to sun or salt will do as well."

The third pair needed no explanation—they were splashing a mud wall with bucketfuls of water. Shea shuddered, feeling that he had never fully appreciated modern construction methods before. He also didn't need much explanation for the fourth pair—all he needed to see was the huge augur with which they were boring into the wall of a wooden house. "They're going to have to drill a lot of holes before they can make one big enough to crawl through."

"Not so many as you would think," Chankoor said offhandedly. "They have saws with slender blades with which they can join the holes. See with what artistry they practice their craft! These sons of Skanda make breaches in the shape of lotus blossoms, of the sun, the new moon, the lake, and the water jar!"

"They do seem to be enjoying their work," Chalmers said diplomatically. "I find it hard to believe that a group of such, ah, 'rugged individualists' would be willing to take orders from anyone."

"Ah, but you have not seen the captain yet!" Chankoor said with a grin. "Come, let us find him!"

Moonlight or not, they were caught in a maze of single-story mud-brick houses that was a tribute to a lack of city planning. Shea found himself growing dizzy with the turns and twists. He did notice that they seemed to avoid the big stone buildings carefully. As they went, other bands of three and four came out of side streets to join them, clanking bags on their backs, laughing and joking over their good luck. It made Shea's flesh crawl, especially since he was soon surrounded by them. Looking up, he happened to notice the disguised rajah only a few feet away; he had apparently been taken up by one of the other squadrons, just as Shea and Chalmers had. Shea nudged Chalmers and nodded at the rajah, ever so slightly; Chalmers looked, and his eyes widened. He exchanged a quick worried glance with Shea before they both turned back to the front, marching onward in the midst of a mob of muggers, feeling as though they walked under the Sword of Damocles.

Then they turned a corner and almost ran into the city wall. Shea jolted to a stop out of sheer surprise, but a knife-point in his back, and a snarl, motivated him to go forward again. "How are we going to get over it?" he whispered to one of his captors, but the man hissed back, "All shall become evident to the enterprising. Forward!"

Shea gulped and marched, Chalmers beside him. He could have sworn they were going to march right into the wall, and Shea found himself wondering if Chankoor were planning to have them grind their faces into it. "Doc, do you think they'll consider stopping?"

"The question has occurred to me, too," Chalmers admitted. "Perhaps they believe themselves to be invisible."

Shea remembered the incantation for invisibility. "But the guards won't open the gates for invisible men!"

"I do not think it will be the guards who open them," Chalmers returned. "After all, invisible men can still strike blows."

Shea remembered the Wells novel, and shuddered; after the random, senseless slayings he'd seen for no more than a few pieces of minted metal, he didn't doubt that the robbers would not hesitate to kill their way out every night. "Maybe they're just going to loiter around until the gates open at daybreak," he said hopefully. "They can mutter the spell over and over, after all." But the look of skepticism Chalmers gave him was all the comment the notion deserved.

Chankoor fooled them both. He simply walked up to the gate and knocked in what sounded like Morse code—three quick knocks, then two slow. For a moment, everything seemed frozen; Shea even held his breath. Then, slowly, the gate opened. "Magic?" he whispered.

"No," Chalmers said with disgust. "Bribed porters."

Shea stared, then felt a surge of self-anger at his own gullibility. He risked a glance about—and stared. He found himself gazing at the man with the horsehair over his nose! He couldn't see the horsehair in this dim light, of course—it was only a stray moonbeam that had showed it to him in the first place—but he certainly recognized the face. It was Rajah Randhir, and his eyes flared with anger at this betrayal by his own gate guards.

Din pricked Chalmers' neck again; he flinched and said, "I think we had better undertake our own transportation, before these fellows lose patience and leave us by the wayside."

"With our throats slit," Shea muttered. He started walking beside Chalmers, following the stocky moon-lighted figure before them.

Out they went, in the midst of a host of thieves and killers. They only walked for about ten minutes before they came to a knot of men milling about in the roadway, talking and laughing, with more joining them from foot-paths beside the way every minute. Shea stared. Could the thieves really be so bold, and so busy, that they had worn their own paths? If they were, how could there be anything left in the city worth stealing?

They certainly weren't worried about the sentries at the gate hearing them. The voices were loud, the laugh-ter louder, and here and there a snatch of song. Their guides led them to the center of the mob, which parted to let them through at a muttered, urgent demand from their captors. Looking about for any possible escape routes, Shea happened to catch the rajah's eye. Randhir gave a start of recognition, then gave him a furious glare that as much as promised instant death if Shea dared breathe a word about his not being a genuine thief—but Shea knew how he felt; he wasn't at his most relaxed, himself, surrounded by a pack of outlaws who would probably slip a knife between his ribs as easily as they would hiss him to silence. He tried to look reassuring before the thieves behind him hustled him along.

The crowd stopped parting at a man who was taller than the rest, and strikingly handsome, if you liked lots of beard and moustache. He had muscles, anyway, and his style of dress certainly let it show. After all, a loincloth and turban don't hide all that much.

"Captain Charya," said Chankoor, "we have here two strangers who stumbled upon us as we were leaving the shop of the goldsmith."

He didn't have to be so literal, Shea thought.

"Strangers indeed!" Charya said in a deep, amused voice. "I have never seen stranger!"

"Stranger strangers?" Shea murmured, but Chalmers kicked him in the shin, and he pinched his lips shut.

"They claim to be thieves from a foreign land," Chankoor explained.

"Are you truly?" Charya the captain eyed them keenly, as though he could spot a lie by sight—and maybe he could, if he was good enough at reading posture and attitude. "A high-toper, or a lully-prigger?"

"Uh-h-h-h ..." The terms caught Shea flat-footed. *When in doubt, stall,* he thought, and improvised. "Just another cove in the lorst, Captain."

"Ah! A *petty* thief!" Charya nodded, satisfied. "How if I told you to mind old Oliver?"

He might have been speaking Hindi, but the spell that gave Shea the ability to understand it, was doing a great job of translating it into English idioms. "Why, I'd keep an eye on the moon, to make sure I was done stealing and gone before it rose—but your coves don't seem to worry about that."

"Why should we care?" Charya's grin gleamed in the moonlight. "There's not a soldier in the city is not afraid of us—any, even the rajah himself!"

At the moment, Shea thought, that just might have been true. "If you have the town sewed up that tight, more power to you." After all, that was just a statement of fact. "But look sharp, Captain, or the lamb-skin man will have the pull of us, and as sure as eggs are eggs, we shall be scragged as soon as lagged."

"Then keep your red rag quiet," grumbled the thief beside him.

"Why should I be the only one?" Shea shot back.

Charya laughed. "Why indeed! All the Watch together would not dare accost us within the city—and outside of it, even less! Still, though, my lads are anxious to wet their whistles, so let us be off to the flash ken, where the morts are waiting. Come, join us!"

He turned away, beckoning, and what could Shea do but follow?

Chalmers paced beside him, muttering, "What manner of foreign language was *that*?"

"Thieves' jargon," Shea explained.

"And where did *you* learn it?"

"I've been doing some volunteer counseling," Shea explained, "unpaid—down at the county jail."

"Surely those terms were not American!"

"No, one of the thieves was English," Shea explained. "Besides, some of the language came over with the colonists and hasn't changed since. For example, if a pickpocket says a man carries his wallet on his left prat, that means his left hip pocket."

"Hence the term 'pratfall,' " Chalmers said thoughtfully. "Yes, I see."

Someone jostled Shea from the other side. Turning to protest, he found himself staring at an overly flattened nose with a horizontal groove across the tip. He shifted his focus up to the glaring eyes of the icognito rajah. "Do not whisper a word of our earlier meeting," he hissed, "or I shall see you scragged indeed."

Shea swallowed heavily, imagining the feel of a hempen noose tightening around his neck. "Don't worry, Your Ma ..." In the nick of time, he remembered that he wasn't supposed to know Randhir's real identity. "... your magic secret is safe with us. After all, if you wanted to drop us, all you'd have to do is tell them about our meeting yourself."

"You know I cannot do that without compromising myself!"

"Yes," Shea said, "exactly." He stared into the rajah's eyes until comprehension registered, and the royal lips parted in a grin. "Ah, a point well taken! We have both used the same ruse to keep our heads on our necks, have we not? Nonetheless, be sure you say nothing of me, or I shall bring down their wrath upon you!"

"It's a deal," Shea promised. "You don't betray us, and we won't betray you."

"Well enough." The rajah nodded, satisfied. "See that you keep to it." He drifted away from them.

"What was *that* all about?" Chalmers asked.

"Just a little mutual-silence pact," Shea told him. "Details later."

Chalmers took the hint, remembering the number of ears available to hear them, and changed the subject. He pointed to a large rodent that scuttled out of sight into a hole in the ground as they approached. "Reassuring sight, somehow."

Shea took his point—it was nice, sometimes, to remember who the *real* rats were—but Charya saw too, and exclaimed with satisfaction, "Ah! You recognize the rat-hole as a good omen! You must indeed be thieves!" He clapped Shea on the back, sending him staggering, and strode along, singing a merry tune.

As they went, Shea sneaked the occasional glance at the incognito rajah. The man was constantly glancing about him with an intentness that puzzled Shea. Was he memorizing faces for prosecution? Since that included Shea's and Chalmers' faces, the thought gave Shea a cold chill. He tried to ignore the rajah, and hoped he would return the courtesy.

The moon was setting, and Chalmers was beginning to stumble with fatigue, when Charya finally raised a hand to halt his gang. Shea stopped thankfully, leaning against Chalmers, who leaned against him—it had been a long day, starting in 10th Century Russia and finishing past midnight in India. No wonder he was tired, Shea reflected—that was a heck of a long hike. He looked up at the cliff that towered above them, then down at the rain forest at its foot, and shuddered. What else was he going to have to go through before he could rest?

High grass, for one thing; it was up to his knees in this meadow, and they had to hike across to reach the trees on the far side, which was apparently what the robber captain was planning on doing. Through the high grass they went, and Shea was just glad it wasn't late enough for the dew to have fallen—the grass seemed to drag at him badly enough as it was. He *was* really tired!

Charya put two fingers in his mouth, for all the world like an American schoolboy, and blew a whistle that Shea could have sworn must have blasted the feathers off every sleeping bird in the forest—but the only one that answered was an owl, who was very unlikely to have been sleeping. Charya shrieked back at it; Shea and Chalmers both jumped, but a voice near them murmured, "Be not afrighted; he imitates the jackal's cry—and very well, too."

Shea looked up, startled, and saw that Rajah Randhir had come up just behind them. He wasn't looking at them, though, but at Charya, and very keenly, too.

Half a dozen silhouettes rose from the long grass about them.

Shea couldn't help a start of apprehension, and for a minute, he thought he was seeing ghosts—anything could happen in a magical universe, after all—but he recovered from his surprise, and realized they were just men, though big ones, and armed to the teeth—literally; one of them was biting his spare knife, his hands being full with sword and shield. But he took the knife out without letting go of the shield—nice trick, that—and demanded, "What do we offer when Kali demands tribute?"

"A melon," Charya replied.

Chalmers stared, but behind them, Rajah Randhir hissed, "Ah! The password!"

It must have been, for the guard challenged again, "Then where is your melon?"

Charya tapped the side of his head.

The guard bowed. "Proceed, my captain." He stepped back, and the guards sank down into the grass again as smoothly as though they were sinking into the earth itself.

"They are cautious indeed," Randhir breathed.

"Yes, if they're going to check the password even with the captain himself," Shea agreed.

"They aren't really Thuggee, are they?" Chalmers asked nervously.

"Worshippers of Kali, who offer her human lives?" Randhir shook his head ever so slightly. "I think not. They are thieves, and though they may murder, it is only to gain the gold in their victims' purses. No, they worship Kartikeya."

Shea hoped he was right.

"You know a surprising amount, for foreigners," Randhir said, eyeing Chalmers narrowly—but the psychologist was saved from a reply because, just then, they passed in among the trees, and Randhir had to turn to chop secretly into the bark of a tree as they passed. The action triggered realization in Shea—the rajah was blazing his path! His constant scrutiny of his surroundings wasn't shiftiness or fear—he was memorizing landmarks! He was planning to escape, then come back with an army!

They walked for another ten minutes; then the trail opened out into a large clearing, but the light of the moon was blocked by a huge sheet of rock that reared up at the far side of the glade like a butte in the desert—or like a painter's canvas, because the bottom ten feet or so were decorated with vermillion handprints. Shea wondered what they signified, but the psychologist in him decided he didn't want to know.

Charya walked up to it and bowed low, then knelt and pulled up a tuft of grass. He beckoned, saying, "Come, new boy! Aid me here!"

Shea started to step forward, but Rajah Randhir brushed past him and stooped to help the robber captain. They heaved, and Shea saw they were both holding on to an iron ring.

"Replace your divots," Chalmers muttered.

As they heaved, a trapdoor opened in the ground. A shaft of light poured out, and a hubbub of voices drowned the night noises. Some of the voices were shouting, some singing loudly and off-key, and beneath them, Shea definitely heard the clink of glasses. Some of the voices, he was quite sure, were female.

"This is the ken," Charya said. He turned, stepping down into the hole, and commanded, "Follow me!"

Shea's hair stood on end, but the rajah very calmly stepped down into the hole as Charya sank from sight, and the robber behind Shea growled, "Hurry up! I thirst!"

"If they're eager for it," Chalmers murmured, "it can't be all that dangerous."

Shea nodded reluctantly and stepped forward. As he came to the hole, he saw a ladder stretching downward. It was made of bamboo and looked entirely too flimsy to hold him, but both the captain and Randhir looked to be heavier than he was, so he swallowed heavily, braced a hand against the trapdoor, and stepped down onto the ladder. It held—it didn't even sway—and he descended a rung at a time, Chalmers following him.

He stepped off and turned around to find himself in a large cave with troughs of water against the walls and suits of silk and fine cotton hanging on racks. Charya began to wash away his night makeup, and Shea's hair tried to stand up as he realized part of what was flowing off the man's hands was dried blood. Randhir started washing, too, then stood back and watched philosophically as the robbers filed down off the ladder and went to wash off the dirt and brick-dust of the night's work— and the dried blood. That done, they took off their turbans, and Shea found out why the fabric rose so high— it was concealing a heap of hair. The men started to comb out their long, disheveled, dusty locks, then to rearrange them and wind clean, colorful turbans around it. Recoiffured, they turned to annointing their clean skins with perfumed oil.

"Come, strangers! Refresh yourselves!" one man cried.

"A chance to acquire local dress, Harold," Chalmers

muttered, and Shea called, "Why, yes, thanks! Don't mind if I do!"

As he washed, Shea kept an eye on the men around him. Some had long, slender daggers hung to lanyards lashed around their waists, some had little bags slung under their left arms, and some, oddly, wore kerchiefs around their necks.

As they finished dressing, the gang members leaped through a curtained archway with whoops of delight. Charya took his time, though, robing himself in splendid brocade over silken trousers, and Shea wasn't about to go through the curtains ahead of him. Nether was Chalmers, of course, and it didn't surprise Shea to see that Randhir waited upon the robber-captain's pleasure, too. He began to suspect that Charya was dawdling, and sure enough, most of the gang had gone before he led the way through.

They came out into a huge cavern, lighted by torches fixed to the stone walls—and if they gave off light, they gave off smoke as well, but that didn't matter much, because the floor was crowded with men sitting cross-legged with water pipes before them and bumpers of something alcoholic by their sides. Carpets of every kind, from the choicest tapestry to the coarsest rug, were spread out under the smokers, and were strewn with bags, wallets, weapons, heaps of booty, and here and there, a grappling couple—for there were women among the men, carrying trays and mugs, and dispensing kisses as freely as food and drink. Here a thief made a ribald comment at a waitress, and she answered him back with both sauciness and earthiness. Here and there a waitress gave a shriek of delight—at least, Shea hoped it was delight—as one of her "customers" pulled her down from a contest of wits to a wrestling match.

A pretty young woman saw Charya and struck a gong beside the archway. At its brazen note, all the robbers stopped what they were doing and turned to him, clapping. The captain stood there with a glittering grin, drinking in the applause. As it slackened, he threw out an arm toward the Rajah—and, incidentally, Shea and Chalmers—and cried, "Make shantī to our new companions!"

"Shantī!" the robbers cried with one voice, and suited the action to the word. Randhir smiled and bowed to them. Watching him in the lamplight, Shea could only think it was lucky for him that the light was so dim—even this close, he couldn't make out the horsehair that flattened his nose.

"What of the score of the evening, Captain?" one man called out.

Charya grinned. "I've scarcely had time to count it all—but I have numbered the bags of loot. There are twenty, and at a guess, we have hauled more booty tonight than ever before!"

The robbers gave shouts of approval, applauding and hooting.

"Eat, drink, and be merry!" Charya cried. "You have earned it!"

The robbers answered with a shout of agreement and settled down to some serious debauchery.

But even the most decadent must grow sleepy, and these particular debauchers had put in a hard night's work before they began debauching. It took four or five hours, but the flaring torches began to burn out, and one by one, the robbers began to nod, then to lie down and pull up a cushion for a pillow. Some rolled themselves up in the rugs and covered their heads; all fell asleep right where they lay. They dropped off by twos and threes, until only the thieves right next to the wall were still sitting upright, and that was only because they were leaning back against it. Even they were nodding drowsily or leaning to one side; they might have been technically awake, but they were too stupefied with opium or hashish to really be aware of anything.

Shea and Chalmers still sat with the Rajah, not feeling at all safe, the more so because they were among the few still awake. "Feign drowsiness," Randhir muttered to them, "or our heads will be forfeit." He wrinkled his nose at the smell of the smoke coming from Shea's hookah. "What manner of hashish is that?"

"One that couldn't stupefy a mouse." Shea didn't bother telling the king that he had chanted a singing commercial for a brand of cigarettes while he was lighting up.

A servant woman strolled by them, looking about for anyone needing attention. She glanced at the rajah, then looked again, staring in alarm. Randhir tensed for action, but the woman gave a quick, furtive glance about her, then knelt down by the rajah and busied herself tidying up about him. "Majesty!" she hissed. "O Rajah! How came you with these wicked men?"

Shea looked up, affronted, but Chalmers murmured, "She means the thieves, Harold, not necessarily us."

"You, too!" the woman said. "If you are with the Rajah, you must be his guards, or at the least, men of goodwill. Do you run away as fast as you can, Majesty, or they will surely kill you when they awake."

"Many thanks for kind wishes, woman," Randhir answered, his voice as low as hers, "but I do not know the way; this cave is a veritable maze, and I could not say how to find the trapdoor. In which direction am I to go?"

"Follow me!" the woman hissed, and stood up, hands full of dirty goblets. She threaded her way through the confused mass of snorers. The Rajah followed, walking as lightly and deftly as a tiger. Shea followed, trying to put his feet exactly where Randhir had, with Chalmers behind him. An inch to the left or right, and he would have stepped on the sleepers, who were likely to resent being awakened so suddenly and unpleasantly. He had a notion that they would show their resentment with knives or clubs, and wasn't eager to try to reason with them about channeling their aggressions.

The woman pulled the curtain aside, and they stepped

into the robing-room again. There stood the ladder, rising up from the floor to lean against the foot-thick rim of the hole.

"Here stands your escape," the woman whispered. "Go now, my Rajah, and quickly!"

"I shall remember you for this," Randhir promised her. "You shall be rewarded."

"The only reward I crave is rebirth in a higher caste, my rajah, and to that I bend my efforts as well as I may. Forget your lowly handservant, and go!"

"May this good deed bring you great karma," Randhir said, and climbed up the ladder. Shea followed, reflecting that the woman was clearly a slave; she was doing the best she could to fulfill her *dharma*, her role in the order of the universe, but certainly had no choice in being maidservant to a gang of thieves.

Randhir crowded himself up against the trapdoor, hunched over; Shea wondered, but as the Rajah straightened with a grunt, heaving up, he saw the sense in the man's strategy; the heavy stone trapdoor swung up ever so slowly—but the ladder dipped and swayed, and Shea clung for dear life, thinking that the rung on which the rajah stood *had* to snap, it couldn't possibly hold against such pressure. . . .

It did hold, though, and with a final thrust, Randhir straightened. The door shot up, then fell open with a thud that made Chalmers wince. Randhir climbed up and out of the hole, then turned to heft the trapdoor closed . . .

. . . and saw Shea's head just above the opening. "What," he hissed, "are you still here?"

"And just as eager to get out of here as you are." Shea sidled over to the edge of the ladder, lifting one foot off to leave as much free room as possible, and beckoned to Chalmers, below the rim where Randhir couldn't see it. "We need to get out in a bad way, because if those bad men find out we're not bad too, then we're going to be in bad trouble."

Chalmers squirmed up past him.

"You put me in a dilemma," Randhir said, scowling. "If you are truly thieves, you could raise the alarm and bring down an ambush upon me, for surely there must still be guards about!"

"If I were a thief," Shea retorted, "I would have raised the alarm long ago, and they would have killed you while they had you in their hall."

"There is some sense in that," Randhir allowed. "Still, I cannot . . . Ho! Stop, you!"

But Chalmers threw himself over the rim of the hole and rolled out from beneath the trapdoor.

"Tricked!" Randhir snapped. "By Indra, if I suffer you to . . . Pah!"

The last was said in disgust as Shea rolled free, too, then rose, dusting off his hands. "Can I help you lower that thing? It won't do any of us any good if it goes 'boom' as it falls."

Randhir stood a moment, irresolute, Shea's offhanded offer taking him by surprise. Then he sighed and accepted the *fait accompli*. "Aye, it is well thought. Aid me, then, for the trap has grown heavy during this chatter."

Shea laid hold of the iron ring too, and together they lowered the trapdoor until it closed with a muffled thud. Then Randhir cast about him, doubled over, searching. Shea was just about to ask what was going on when the Rajah straightened with a soft exclamation of satisfaction, holding the plug of grass in his hand. He tamped it carefully back over the iron ring.

"He *does* replace his divots," Chalmers muttered to Shea.

"Sure he does," Shea whispered back. "He owns the whole golf course!"

"Come—away!" Randhir whispered, and turned to plunge back into the woods.

Shea hurried to catch up with him and said, keeping his voice low, "I think you said something about there maybe being guards still posted?"

"We shall deal with them when we must." Randhir drew his dagger. "If we are going to travel together, we must know one another. I am Matun."

Shea held his face neutral for a moment, thrown by the alias—then realized that a man in disguise certainly wasn't about to use his own name. "I'm Shea, and my friend is Chalmers."

"Shea and Chalmers—well met." Randhir gave them each a curt nod. "Let us hurry, now! We would be well advised to be clear of this wood while it is still dark!"

"And the sentries sleepy. You are very brave," Chalmers said, coming up on his other side, "but this very night, we have learned an incantation that makes people invisible."

Randhir halted. "Why, so we have! Indeed, I made shift to memorize it as soon as I heard it! But can I remember it now?"

"We should be able to, between the three of us," Shea said, "but will it work if we don't cover ourselves with oil?"

"The coconut oil was to aid the robbers in slipping through tight places," Randhir told him, "and to prevent a man of the Watch from gaining a hold on them. Still, you may be right; we can only attempt it."

"There were gestures that went with it," Chalmers informed him, "like this." He made a circle above his head, then drew his hand flat down in front of his face, palm toward his eyes, and on down along his whole body. "Do that as we recite!"

They all pantomimed as they chanted the words together. They were meaningless, incomprehensible, but Shea felt sure that if he had ever learned Sanskrit, they would be poetry of the highest order. He looked up at Chalmers and Randhir . . .

Just in time to see their forms waver, grow transparent, and disappear. "I can't see you at all!"

"Nor I you," Chalmers' voice answered out of thin air, "nor His Majesty."

Shea looked closely at the space where the rajah had been. Sure enough, he was completely invisible. No, wait . . . there was a gleam of light, a ray, a straight line. . . .

The horsehair. Randhir really ought to do something about that.

Dawn was breaking as they came to the city gate, so they didn't have to wait long until it opened. The invisibility spell had worn off after the first couple of hours, so Shea had no trouble seeing Randhir as he said, very casually, "It would be nice if there were somebody here who could simply command the porters to open the gate for us."

"It would," the Rajah agreed in a wooden tone.

"But there isn't, of course," Shea sighed. If the guards recognized the "thief" of the night before and heard him issue a royal command, they would run for their lives the second the king was through the gate—and probably keep on running all the way to the ken and warn all the other thieves, too. The king was out to capture them, not just inconvenience them.

So they waited until the gates opened, three travelers among the many who gathered, waiting. When the huge panels swung wide, they poured into the town—and Randhir led Shea and Chalmers unerringly toward the gleaming dome of the royal palace.

As they came up to the gates, Chalmers dropped behind Randhir a few steps and pulled Shea alongside. "He is going to reveal his lofty station to us, Harold. Be suitably impressed."

"Oh! Yes, of course." Shea smiled brightly.

Randhir marched right up to the gates, and the guards stared, amazed at the insolence of the "peasant." Then they clashed their spears together, blocking his way. The Rajah halted and told them, "Summon your captain."

The guards began to look angry, and the older of the two said, "We take no orders from ruffians!"

"You do not know me, then?"

"Know you?" the younger cried. "We have never seen you in our lives."

"That is reassuring." The Rajah took out his knife and cut the horsehair. His nose, freed, swelled back out to its royal proportions, somewhat resembling a cross between an eagle's beak and a seaside promontory. "Do you know me now?" he demanded.

The men stared, then bowed low. "My King and sovereign!"

"I am indeed. Now summon your captain."

One guard ran to call his boss, and Chalmers leaned over to mutter, "Most interesting. He made sure neither had been among the thieves last night, before he risked revealing his identity."

"Very wise," Shea agreed. "Of course, they might have been lying."

"Quite so, but I'm certain it was only double-checking; he would have recognized them if he had seen them last night."

"If he could have," Shea said. "He's got a much better memory for faces than I have."

"Well, yes," Chalmers agreed, "but that would not take much, would it now?"

Shea turned a look of indignation on him. "Well, thank *you*, Mr. Memory Wizard!"

Chalmers was saved from an answer by the arrival of the guard captain, who took one look at Randhir and blanched. "Seize him," the rajah commanded.

The captain reached for his sword, but the guards managed to react to their surprise fast enough so that it never cleared the scabbard. A spear-point touched his chest, and he froze; then a fist cracked into his jaw, and he folded.

"Chain him in the dungeon," the rajah commanded, "and bind his mouth; make sure he speaks to no one. He is a thief, and has betrayed us all."

As the guards carried the man away, Shea conceded, "I guess he does have a good memory for faces."

"Yes," Chalmers agreed, "but very poor recruiting procedures."

Finally, Randhir turned to Shea and Chalmers. "Now you know whom you have accompanied this evening."

Shea stared and took a step back—right into Chalmers, who muttered, "Pure ham." It was a good thing—Shea had been on the verge of sticking his hands in the air and crying, "I surrender, Sheriff!" Instead, he risked a glance at Chalmers, who was simply staring, pure and simple, then began to tremble ever so slightly.

Randhir saw and smiled, sure of his power and majesty. "Do not be afraid, for we have been comrades in danger. Come with me now, and refresh yourselves."

He turned and marched before them. As they passed through the gates, Shea suddenly became sure of safety, and felt himself go limp—limp with relief, but also weariness.

"Do not relax yet." Chalmers' voice was heavy with exhaustion. "One misstep, and we could still lose our heads."

"That's right—the Rajah has no reason to think we're *not* foreign thieves." Shea managed to muster a few grams of remaining strength, enough to imagine the Rajah's face swollen with anger and his voice shouting, "Off with their heads!" The result was remarkable— adrenaline surged through him, stiffening his backbone and brightening his eyes. He managed to keep his step brisk as he followed Randhir.

Into the palace they went, but by a side door that led into a room with long tables adorned with knives. For a moment, Shea thought the Rajah had led them to his torture chamber. Then he saw the garbage bins, and realized they were in the kitchens.

The light of dawn showed him an old woman who was snoring in a chair by the window. "Up!" Randhir commanded, but his voice was gentle. The woman's eyes snapped open; she saw the Rajah, and pushed herself painfully to her feet. "Water," Randhir commanded, and the woman hobbled away to dip water from a bucket into a silver bowl. She hung a clean cloth over her arm and brought both to her King. He peeled off false eyebrows and washed his face thoroughly, taking away some of the coloring, then dried it and began work on his moustaches, twisting them down from the corners of his eyes to blend in with his beard. The woman handed him a comb, then went to bring a richly brocaded robe. Randhir combed his parted beard back into one single, well-trimmed mass, then doffed his rough tunic and slipped into the robe the old woman held out for him. He tied a sash about it, then exchanged his black cotton turban for one of purple silk with a peacock's feather held by a golden brooch to the front and turned to face them, magically transformed into the very image of a Hindu king. "Come, friends of my night's adventure! You must tell me what you have seen, so that we have as full an account of this night's work as we may!" But he didn't give them a chance to talk, only led them out of the kitchen and through a narrow hallway into a broad one, then up a broad flight of steps and into a room floored with cool marble and roofed by an azure dome upheld by columns of alabaster. At the far end, on a dais surrounded by more columns, stood a great chair covered with gold. Randhir stepped up and sat in the throne as casually as Shea might sit in his office chair. "Now, my guests! Tell me what you have seen."

"You ... you're the Rajah!" Chalmers spluttered, and Shea took his cue, staring as though still stupefied. "*You?*"

Randhir permitted a slight smile to play over his lips. "Indeed. Your companion of the evening's search is truly the Rajah Randhir—and I gather, from your conduct and the strangeness of your garb, that you are no more thieves than I am."

"I assure Your Majesty that we most certainly are not!" Chalmers said. "But surely our observations can be of little value when we have seen only what so esteemed a personage as yourself has seen!"

Trust Doc, all right. When it came to knowing how to lay it on, he had no peer.

"Ah, but before our separate groups joined together, you saw what I did *not* see! Come, tell me of it!"

"We saw some men finishing the looting of a house," Shea said slowly. "Then we saw the rest of the gang gathered out in the street, getting ready for the night's work and practicing their skills. A few of them even practiced them on passersby, killing them for the few coins in their purses."

"It would seem you have indeed seen no more than I have myself," Randhir sighed, "for from that time on, we were together. However, you can join us when we march against them, to help me remember the way, and the means of entering."

Shea wasn't all that sure he liked that idea, so he changed the subject—quickly. "Your Majesty must have been willing to sacrifice your pride enormously, to consort with such low-lifes for a night!" He didn't say anything about aiding and abetting a burglary.

But the stroke seemed to please Rajah Randhir. He nodded, saying, "The good of my subjects demanded such a sacrifice, since the spies I sent on that errand did not return. I could see that if I wanted knowledge of the thieves' ways, I should have to go myself. Now I know why, and it is fortunate that I disguised myself so thoroughly, for a number of the thieves were my own people— watchmen and guards, patrolmen and spies."

Chalmers stared. "Surely not the spies you sent to ferret out information about the gang!"

"The very same, and a merry laugh they must have had at their assignment. I do not think they shall laugh tomorrow."

His tone chilled Shea, and reminded him of the cold-blooded killing he had witnessed. "Are you *sure* none of those men worshipped Kali? They seemed bloodthirsty enough to be genuine Thuggee." Even as he said the word, though, he realized that it only meant "rascals"— at least literally.

"Many of them were," Randhir admitted. "I lied to you at the time to prevent you from panicking, for I saw you knew of Kali, and that her worshippers sacrifice human lives to her. They whom you call Thuggee are more accurately termed Phansigars; you could tell them by the kerchiefs they wore round their necks—the kerchiefs with which they strangled women and men alike. Others worshipped Bhawani; those with little bags slung under the left arm were Dhaturiya-poisoners. Even some among Kartikeya's crew are dedicated to murder—for example, those who wore their poiniards at their waists; they are stabbers by profession."

Shea shuddered.

"But how is it," Chalmers asked, "that Your Majesty found this gang of low-lifes worth your own personal attention? Should that not have been left to hired spies?"

"It should," Randhir confirmed, "but as I have told you, my spies disappeared; I have no doubt the theives found them out and slew them."

"That leaves only one question," said Chalmers. "How did the thieves know who your spies were?"

"Because *they* had spies, Doc," Shea said, before the rajah could answer. "In fact, they had spies among the king's spies."

"It is true," said Randhir, "and the merchants of my city have become extremely upset over their constant losses, while the whole populace has begun to live in fear of the murderers. To make all worse, the kingdom to the east of mine has seen the weakness these thieves make in my land, and have begun to assemble armies near the border; I have no doubt their rajah means to invade. It became vital to find out these thieves, break up their gang, slaying the murderers and punishing the thieves."

"And since no one else could do it," Chalmers said slowly, "you undertook it yourself."

"That is a part of my *dharma*, the duty of the station in life to which I was born," the rajah confirmed. "Now, though, I know where they lair, and how many they are— so this night, I shall take my archers and my soldiers and set upon them."

"But what if their spies warn them you are coming?" Chalmers asked.

"Ah, but now I know who the men are that they managed to plant in my household," Randhir reminded him. "At last I have found the rats hidden in the walls of my palace, and can trap and exterminate them. First, though, I must find some cats. Will you be among them?" The look he gave assured them that if they weren't, they would swing with the rest of the thieves. Apparently he still wasn't entirely sure of their innocence.

Well, at least they had a chance to survive the raid. Shea glanced at Chalmers, caught his infinitesimal nod, and turned back to the Rajah. "Why, sure, Your Majesty! After all, we know where the rat-hole is." Then he remembered how the robber chieftain had thought such holes were good omens, and swallowed.

A guard stepped up behind them and bowed.

"What is your message?" Randhir snapped.

"My Rajah," said the man, "a deputation of merchants awaits to heap upon you their grief over this last night's losses."

Randhir sighed. "Let them enter." Then, to Shea and Chalmers, "Do you stand against the wall, and you shall see the agitation and misery these thieves have caused."

Shea started to protest that he already had a pretty good idea, but Chalmers beat him to it. "Of course, Your Majesty. We are honored by the privilege of observing your court." He bowed, and Randhir gave him a gracious nod, apparently pleased by his courtesy. Shea began to understand how Chalmers had become Director of the Garaden Institute.

They stepped over next to one of the guards, maintaining a discreet distance from his spear, and watched the merchants file in. They wore plain white pyjamas, but the robes they wore over were of silk or damask, as were their turbans. They lined up in front of Randhir and bowed.

"O Pearl of Equity!" said the one who was presumably oldest, to judge by his gray hairs and lined face. "Only yesterday, you consoled us with the promise of some contrivance by the blessing of which our houses and coffers would be made safe from theft—but our goods have never yet suffered so severely as during the last twelve hours."

"The Rajah hears; the Rajah's heart bleeds with your own," Randhir assured them, "and I do indeed speak of blood, for I know men were slain this night past. Still, an elephant grows not in a single night, nor by eating only one heap of hay—so it is not likely to be slain by a single arrow. Go back to your shops and guard your goods and your family as well as you may; let none go out on the streets after the sun has set, but let them stay within doors. Tomorrow, or surely in two days' time, I shall, with the blessing of the Bhagwan, relieve you of further anxiety."

"But what more can you do?" asked another merchant. "You have hired watchmen, you have changed your officers, and you have established patrols; nevertheless the thieves have not diminished, and plundering is constantly taking place."

"Indeed," said a third, "we have suffered more in this night past than ever before!"

"Be sure that you do not suffer more sorely yet," Randhir told them. "Read the *Thieves' Manual*, and guard against the methods it teaches! Close your shops and sleep today, then guard each the inside of his own shop this night, with sword and club—for if you are vigilant, it may be effort wasted, but if you are not, it will surely invite disaster!"

The merchants shuddered at the idea.

"The end of this seige is in sight," the Rajah said in a

consoling tone, "but that end may be long in coming— or short. Go now, each to his own house, and pray that disaster passes you by—but pray also to strengthen your Rajah's arm, for I will destroy these men of violence, or myself die in the attempt!"

His tone rang through the marble hall, and the merchants winced at the sound. They lost no time in bowing, then hurrying out, so quickly that they almost trod on each other's heels.

When the merchants had left, Randhir stared after them, looking grim. Suddenly he turned and said to a guard, "Bid a score of archers sleep long during the heat of the day, then hold themselves in readiness for service."

The man bowed and left the throne room on the run.

Randhir turned to another guard and said, "Bid ten come."

The man bowed and, like the first, left on the run. Randhir sat still in his chair, brows drawn down over glaring eyes, staring straight ahead, not moving a muscle. His face was so grim that even Shea and Chalmers held still, watching, feeling the tension building about the man, waiting for the storm to break.

The guard reappeared with ten soldiers behind him. "They are come, O Guardian of the Poor!"

"Follow!" Randhir snapped, and fairly leaped down off his throne. He darted a glance at Shea and Chalmers, snapping, "You, too!"

Under the circumstances, they weren't about to disagree.

Randhir led the way to a small gate in one wall at the rear of the palace. There he brusquely ordered the guard who stood by it, "To barracks with you!" and to two of the soldiers he had brought with him, "See that he talks to no one until tomorrow morning."

A sudden look of terror crossed the man's features, but he was smoothing them out even as his fellows marched him off.

"You don't *know* that he was one of the thieves," Shea objected.

"No," the Rajah agreed. "If I did, he would be dead. There is small doubt of his guilt—how could his fellow thieves have come and gone without his connivance?—but since I have no proof, he may live until I do."

The gate opened, and a guard's voice outside said, "The way is clear." A villainous-looking man in soldier's livery came through, not exactly sneaking, but certainly not making any unnecessary noise—not even when the Rajah himself clapped a hand over the man's mouth, holding him from behind, and commanding a soldier, "Slay him."

The sneak's eyes widened in horror for a few seconds before his fellow soldier plunged a dagger into his breast. The man's eyes rolled up and he went limp. The king let him fall, then nodded to the man who had slain him. "Well done. Lug him away to the burning-ghats. You, assist him!"

Another soldier helped the first pick up the dead one.

"Send more men," the Rajah told him.

The soldier nodded and went, carrying the body.

"Stand ready as sentry," the rajah told another man, "and when next a man comes through that gate, if I nod to you, like this . . ."—he gave a short, curt nod—". . . catch and gag him, as I did even now."

The man nodded, poker-faced, and took his station.

"Uh, Your Majesty," said Shea delicately, "isn't this a little drastic?"

"The dead," said the Rajah, "do not, like grandmothers, tell tales."

Shea stared, aghast, "You *killed* them to keep them from sending word to their gang? Wouldn't gags have worked just as well?"

"Gags, a dungeon, and many guards?" Randhir nodded. "But it would have come to the same fate in the end. They were guilty of robbery one and all, and many guilty also of murder—but without exception, since they were members of the Rajah's household and bore information to his enemies, their fellow thieves, they were guilty of treachery."

"You, uh, couldn't maybe have given them a little time to think things over and see the error of their ways?"

"To what end? I have set forth laws; they have broken those laws, and would still have to receive the punishment. The penalty for murder is death," the Rajah informed him, "and so is the penalty for treachery. Be sure he deserved his fate, for I recognized him from the robbers' ken."

"His Majesty *is* the Incarnation of Justice," Chalmers said, with a very meaningful look at Shea and a tone that clearly said, *Shut up!*

The Rajah nodded, with a thin smile. "What greater justice could he wish, when the Rajah himself is witness, and his judge is the highest in the land?"

It took Shea a second to realize the Rajah was talking about himself. With it came the realization that from Randhir's point of view, everything he had said was perfectly true. In a kingdom in which the Rajah was not only the executive and legislative power, but also the ultimate court of appeals, Randhir *was* the highest judge in the land, and surely the most reliable witness! He was sentencing men he had seen the night before with his own eyes, and was witness, prosecutor, judge, and jury all in his own right. All that was missing was the executioner.

Apparently he was willing to be that, too. As the next thief tiptoed in through the door wearing his civilian garb (a gardener), Randhir gave the guard the nod, and the man caught the thief in a wrestling lock, with his free hand over the thief's mouth. He barely had time to realize what was happening to him, and his eyes were just widening in the horror of that realization, before Randhir's dagger plunged into his heart.

Shea had to look away, feeling ill. Randhir noticed; his frown turned to concern. "You do not look well, friend Shea."

"It is your burning Hindi sun," Chalmers explained, ever glib. "We folk of the north are not used to its rays being so direct—so bright, and so hot."

"So that is why you were abroad at night! Well then, go into the palace, and tell a porter that I said to find you a chamber. Sleep well, for I shall need your vigilance tonight."

Shea took that as ominous, but since the Rajah turned away, obviously dismissing them from his thoughts, they turned away too. When the porter showed them the bed, Shea fell into it without undressing, without even taking off his swordbelt. It had been a long day followed by a sleepless night, and very, very stressful.

Under the circumstances, he wasn't surprised to see a torch flaming in a sconce on the wall when Chalmers shook him awake. "The Rajah summons us, Harold. There is time to wash and eat, though, before we join him."

Shea remembered the executions he had watched. "Don't know if I have much appetite, Doc."

"Nor have I, to judge by the odors wafting from the kitchens—I never have been partial to curry. But we shall have to find something palatable, for I do not doubt that we shall need all our energies tonight."

"Don't know if I'm up to watching any more cold-blooded killings," Shea said. "Do you suppose we could plead headaches?"

"Randhir's cure would probably be to cut off our heads, Harold. He is still somewhat suspicious of us, and would take any hesitation as evidence of guilt."

"I suppose so," Shea sighed, and pushed himself to his feet. "Doc, what about Florimel? So far, whenever a god or a magician has sent us out of his universe, we've wound up in the next one Malambroso has sent her to. It seems we've been following her magical trail, sort of."

"An interesting notion." Chalmers frowned. "Perhaps Malambroso's spell moving her on has weakened the barrier between universes, and the next spell ejecting us has hurtled us onward along the path of least resistance."

"But if that's so," said Shea, "where is she in *this* universe, Doc?"

Chalmers spread his hands in a shrug of helplessness. "She could be anywhere, Harold! It may have been only luck that led us to her before this."

"Or it may have been magic of her own! She has learned *something* about the art, Doc! Can't you sic a direction-finding spell on her?"

Chalmers' gaze became distant. "An interesting notion ..."

"But not immediately," Shea said quickly. He hadn't meant to distract Chalmers into an academic trance. "First we have to survive the night and prove we're not thieves."

That brought Chalmers back to the needs of the moment with a vengeance. "An excellent point, Harold. Come, let us find some chapattis."

"But we're already dressed!"

"No, chapattis are food," Chalmers sighed, "a sort of Hindu tortilla. They, at least, should not be too highly seasoned. Let us dine."

Fed and armed, they were ready when the guard appeared at their door and summoned them. They followed him through only two short corridors and down one flight of stairs—they were near the kitchens, only one step above servant quarters, though their room had been furnished with cushions and silken hangings. They came out into the courtyard into a darkness relieved only by starlight, to find a hundred archers and fifty spearmen milling about, conversing in very low voices. Suddenly they stilled and turned toward a doorway in the palace wall itself, for through it came Rajah Randhir, clad in steel helmet and breastplate, sword on his hip and small shield on his arm. A murmur of amazement ran through the troops, for Randhir had tied the horsehair round his nose again, and his waxed moustaches stood up to the corners of his eyes like the horns of a Brahma bull.

He looked about him, gave a single nod of satisfaction, and said, "Yes, I am Rajah Randhir, though I have disguised myself as a thief. Follow me and do not ask why. Shea and Chahmers! Stand by me!"

Shea swallowed with great difficulty and walked down an avenue that opened magically within the troops, Chalmers one step behind him. As they came up to the Rajah, he said, "If I mistake the route, you will correct me. Come!" He turned about and strode away into the darkness. Shea followed, grimly reflecting on the unspoken proviso—that if Shea or Chalmers betrayed him, they would be handy for instant execution by the Rajah himself. Somehow, Shea wasn't eager for the honor.

Through the darkened town they went, and Shea wondered at the quietness. Then, remembering that the moon was down, he realized that it was so late that the thieves had finished their bloody work and gone back to their ken. There was a singular lack of dead bodies, though. Apparently the merchants had heeded the Rajah's warning and passed on the advice, and everyone had stayed indoors.

He found out later that he'd been more right than he knew—not only had everyone stayed sensibly indoors for once, the merchants had hired bodyguards and patrolled their shops and houses on the inside. When they had heard scraping at one place, they had hurried to it, and when the first head had poked through the hole, they had brained it neatly with a cudgel. The thieves' partners had pulled him out at once, of course, but the bodyguards had stabbed through the hole with a spear. There had been an outcry on the other side, then silence, and after a while, the householder had taken up the patrol again, leaving one bodyguard at the hole. The only booty the thieves had taken that night had come from the few bodyguards who had been thieves themselves, and had knocked their employers senseless (or, in some cases, slain them), then let their fellows in—but there had been only two or three successful in such ruses. All in all, it had been a grumbling, dissatisfied band who had wended their way home that night—but it had included three fraudulent bodyguards who had overheard some very interesting gossip from their employers.

At the moment, though, neither the Rajah nor any of his men knew that. They padded through the unnatural hush of the night until the city wall rose up before them. There, the Rajah gave the rhythmical knock he had heard the robbers give. After a moment, the huge portal opened, and the porter stuck his head around, hissing, "What has kept you so late? The others have all gone on long before you, and . . ." He broke off, staring in horror at the array of armed men. Randhir clamped a hand over his mouth and yanked him through; one of his soldiers, apparently primed for the task, leaped past. Shea heard a howl of fright, suddenly cut off into a horrid gurgling, even as he saw a soldier transfix the captured porter with a spear.

Randhir dropped the body and dusted his hands. A soldier hauled the gate open, and the troop filed out after their Rajah.

"The term 'rough justice' comes to mind," Chalmers murmured.

"Rough, but legal," Shea reminded him. "You can't call him a vigilante when he *is* the government, can you?"

"Are you there, Shea?" Randhir called softly.

"Right behind you, O Lightning of Indra," Shea called. After that little display, he certainly didn't want to be in *front* of the rajah.

As they neared the meadow, Randhir called them to a halt, then murmured briefly with his soldiers. When he went on, Shea and Chalmers had followed him for a good ten paces before they realized that the soldiers had stayed behind. Chalmers' step faltered, but Randhir took him by the arm, saying, "The thief-sentries will recognize you two and think nothing amiss. As for me, you see I have disguised myself as I did last night. We three, at least, will hold the attention of the guards without alerting them. Come!"

Chalmers gave Shea a look that clearly said they had no choice. They really didn't—the Rajah had a grip of iron, and his men were watching.

Randhir whistled twice through his fingers, just as the robber captain had done the night before. There was a pause during which Shea's heartbeat seemed to him the loudest night sound of all; then he heard the hooting of an owl. The rajah replied with an excellent imitation of the robbers' jackal-scream, making Shea wonder if it was a standard part of the military training in this part of the world. The six robber-sentries rose from the grass like spectres, and their leader advanced to receive the password—but before he could, Shea found out why the soldiers had stayed behind.

They hadn't, really—they had just filed around the edges of the meadow, then wormed their way forward toward the Rajah. Now they rose from the grass and fell on the robbers, silencing them with clubs and knives, then tying up the ones who still lived.

"It is well done," the Rajah said, smiling at the sergeant who came forward, breathing heavily. "Are any hurt?"

"Only two of our own men," the sergeant answered. "Ramjit is wounded in the right arm and will be unable to fight more tonight. Kamal bleeds from a cut in the ribs, but protests that he can still fight."

"Then let him see Ramjit safely home," the Rajah said, "but not until we are done with this night's work. Bid Ramjit come with us, and wait while we assail the robbers—but see them bandaged first."

"We have done so." The sergeant glanced to the side, saw another soldier's wave. "They are tended; Ramjit bears the pain well. We can march, O Sword of Justice."

"Let us go, then." Randhir turned away into the night.

But as they came in sight of the sheer rock wall, a figure rose atop it against the light of the predawn sky, and a shrill whistle sounded. Instantly, a hail of arrows fell on the rajah and his men.

"Back!" the rajah cried. "The thieves lie in ambush! We have been betrayed!"

Soldiers cried out in pain, and more than a few fell to the earth, pierced through. The troops gave ground, but Randhir called out, "Turn and flee! We must find a place to make our stand! Run!"

At the command, the soldiers turned and ran.

"Never argue with legitimately constituted authority, Harold," Chalmers advised.

"No, Doc!" Shea protested. "Someone tipped off the thieves' captain! The Rajah obviously didn't kill off all the robbers' spies, but he *thinks* he did! If they don't win this fight, he'll blame it on us!"

"Why, so he will, won't he?" Chalmers stared, thunderstruck.

So did the Rajah—but as he ran, Charya came scrambling and sliding down the cliff-face, calling out, "Hola! What kind of Rajput are you, if you run away from combat?"

Randhir churned up the grass in his haste to stop and turn around. He whipped out his sword and waited for Charya to come up. "Strike at your king, and the penalty is death!" he bellowed.

"Hung for the lamb, hung for the sheep," Charya retorted. "If you take me alive, you will slay me for one reason or another. Why not regicide?" As he said it, he slashed with his scimitar.

It was a blow that would have done credit to the Lord High Executioner, but Randhir met it with a blow equally strong, that set both blades ringing.

"Doc," Shea said anxiously, "if that blow had landed, the next rajah would have tracked us down and tortured us to death!"

"Indeed! We must protect the Rajah, and quickly!" Chalmers ripped up handfuls of long grass and began weaving them into a very rough, very clumsy fabric as he chanted,

> "Weave a circle round him thrice,
> That turns all blades from heart and head!
> For he on royal food has fed,
> And is sent to rule by Paradise!"

"Coleridge will forgive you," Shea promised.

"Let us hope that it works." Chalmers watched the fight with anxious eyes.

Randhir slashed a stroke that would have opened Charya's chest wide, if it had landed. But the chieftain leaped back, and the Rajah staggered as his own blow pulled him off balance. The captain gave a shout of triumph and leaped in again, sword whirling straight toward the Rajah's head—but Randhir managed to swing his blade up in the nick of time. Shea gasped, thinking Chalmers' magic shield had failed—but Charya's blade glanced aside inches from Randhir's face. Shea relaxed with a sigh. "Your spell worked, Doc."

"Yes, but I don't think anyone else realizes that." Chalmers glanced nervously about him. "At least, I hope they do not; a reputation as a sorcerer is the last thing I need right now."

"Don't worry," Shea assured him. "To everyone else, I'm sure it looked as though Randhir parried the blow."

"I trust so," Chalmers agreed, "but I am certain that I saw Charya's sword glance off the rajah's blade and on toward his head, where the spell turned it aside scant centimeters from his skin."

"Don't tell," Shea advised.

Charya slashed another blow at Randhir, but this time the king really did catch it on his own blade. Charya shoved against it, jumping back, then advanced on the Rajah, whose sword whirled in a figure-eight that would have minced anything it met. Charya retreated and retreated, though, his own blade up and ready for the slightest opening in Randhir's guard.

Now came the real beginning of the fight; it seemed the opening rain of blows had been only a prelude. Having tested each other, the two swordsmen settled down to serious fencing. They withheld their steel and bent almost double, knees flexed, skipping in circles around each other, each keeping his eye well fixed upon the other, with frowning brows and contemptuous sneers. The battle stilled as soldiers and robbers alike stopped to watch their leaders battle.

"Ah! The king cuts a caper!" cried a soldier.

"But Charya answers with a measured leap!" cried a robber.

"Aye!" his mate cried in delight. "He springs forward like a frog!"

"And the king hops backward like a monkey!"

Then, incredibly, the king began striking his saber against his shield, a steady rhythmical beat—but Shea could see the blade never wavered much from readiness to strike. Charya, not to be outdone, began to beat on his shield, too—and Randhir stooped low with a loud cry, cutting at Charya's legs. Charya sprang into the air, though, and the blade whistled harmlessly under him. Even as he came down, though, the robber chief whirled his sword three times around his head and brought it down like lightning in a slant, toward the king's left shoulder—but the king snapped his shield up, and the sword clashed against it and bounced off. The rajah staggered back, thrown off balance by the strength of the blow. The captain followed closely, slashing and cutting, and for a moment, it was all the Rajah could do to block with his shield and parry with his sword. Then he rallied, suddenly leaping forward and striking, and Charya had to raise his shield in defense.

On and on they fought, till they were both rasping huge ragged gasps and the blows became rough and clumsy and slow. They were so well matched in courage, strength, and skill that neither could obtain the slightest advantage,

Of course, the Rajah *did* have Chalmers' magical shield—but Shea could see that Reed was watching the match far too intently, with drops of sweat starting on his brow, his whole body tense. "Somebody trying to cancel your spell?" he asked softly.

Chalmers gave a terse nod. "Our captain has some sort of supernatural help siding with him."

"Or against us," Shea pointed out. "Malambroso's probably in this universe too, after all, and if we can figure out that our lives depend on the Rajah's right now, so can he."

"A point well taken," Chalmers grunted. "Lend a hand, can you, Harold?"

"How?" Shea asked, at a loss.

"Something, anything, to throw that robber off balance!"

"Off balance?" Inspiration struck, and Shea dropped to one knee, patting the ground about him until one hand closed on a pebble in the darkness, an irregular lump about two inches across. Carefully, Shea stood up, lowering his foot onto the pebble and chanting,

"Beneath Charya's foot
Let this stone at once be put,
Rolling as it is discerned—
Never leave a stone unturned!"

Shea felt a sudden absence beneath his sole, and stepped down to feel nothing but grass. It was hard to tell in the half-light, but he thought he saw something small appear under the robber captain's instep—and sure enough, Charya stepped down and the stone revolved, sliding from under his foot. He cried out in rage, arms windmilling, and landed on his back so hard that it drove the breath out of him, leaving him helpless for a moment—and when he caught his breath, he found himself staring at the point of the Rajah's blade, six inches in front of his face, right between his eyes. "I am lost!" he cried. "Save yourselves! Flee!"

With a wail, the thieves disappeared into the forest. The soldiers shouted and ran after them.

"Bide, Shea and Chalmers," the Rajah grated. "Do you, O dexterous and cunning swordsman, now loose grasp from your hilt, or my point will pierce your brain."

"Strike, then!" Charya cried in defiance. "Better a clean death in battle than execution in shame!"

"While there's life, there's hope," Shea said. "Miracles have happened before."

"Not for one so guilty as I!" But even as he said it, that very hope wavered in Charya's eyes, and his hand loosened on the hilt. Shea knelt and tugged the sword away.

"You speak truly," Randhir told Charya, "for I shall do all in my power to see you executed for your crimes."

"Can you control the whims of the gods?" Chalmers challenged. "Can you read *dharma* so clearly as to be able to say there is no chance of this doughty knave living? For surely, he is most admirable in his skill and courage, no matter how despicable he may be in the ways in which he uses them."

"There is truth in that," the Rajah admitted. "However, though the race is not always to the swift, that is the way to place your wager. Bind this knave, then set him on his feet!"

So because of the shred of hope that Shea and Chalmers had raised within his heart, Charya of the robbers was taken alive for the Rajah's justice, not slain on the ground where the turned stone had stretched him.

The next morning, Shea and Chalmers presented themselves in the Rajah's private audience chamber. They found Randhir standing by the window, gazing moodily out over his kingdom.

"Your Majesty," Shea prompted, "you sent for us?"

"Indeed." Randhir turned to face them. "I wish to thank you."

Alarm shrilled in every fiber, but Shea forced a bland and uncomprehending smile. "Thank us? For what?"

"It *could* have been chance or fate that placed that stone under Charya's foot," Randhir said quietly, "even though we had been back and forth over the same ground before—but I doubt it. And I *know* his sword glanced off some invisible shield when I thought it would surely cleave my head open."

Chalmers protested, "Surely Your Majesty is . . ."

" 'My Majesty' knows what I saw, and knows magic when I see it!" Randhir snapped. "Since there was no magician there, I can only conclude that it was done by one of you foreigners—or both!"

"Surely we're not so foreign as *that*," Shea objected.

"Are you not? You do not even know the proper forms of address for a king! You can address me as nothing but 'majesty!' "

"Why, if that is so," Chalmers said quietly, "we could not be very powerful magicians, or we would have known those forms."

"Aye, if you deemed it worth your trouble! Do not deny what a Rajah knows—you are magi from Persia, are you not?"

Shea exchanged a glance with Chalmers, who sighed and turned back to the rajah. "Not from Persia, O Fount of Wisdom, but from much farther to the west."

"*Much* farther," Shea agreed.

"And we are not magi, for they are Zoroastrian priests," Chalmers went on. "Rather, we are scholars who study magic for its own sake."

"Then you *are* magicians!"

"Just so," Chalmers aid quietly, "magicians, nothing more—not sorcerers, nor necromancers, nor even magi, though the word 'magic' stems from that term."

"I knew it!" Randhir slapped his thigh in glee. "You

are indeed magi, and I thank you for your help—nay, for my life! But just how far-ranging are your powers?"

Shea stared, his mind racing. They had to say enough to make themselves look important, but not enough to make Randhir want to keep them as permanent assets. Before he could decide on the right balance, though, Chalmers said, "We can work defensive magic only, O Eye of Insight—spells to protect, and spells to aid. Slaying and other evil works, we are more than glad to leave to those who *are* sorcerers and necromancers."

"Good, good!" Randhir nodded energetically, and Shea breathed a secret sigh of relief. Once again, Chalmers' skill at the conference table had turned the tide.

Or maybe not. "The protection you gave me during the fight," the rajah said, "can you do that for a city? For an army perhaps?"

Chalmers let his shoulders slump with disappointment. "I fear not, O Gem of Rectitude. Magic on such a scale is simply beyond my strength—or even that of our combined powers, my friend and I. It would require a virtual corps of magicians, all working together in concert—and quite frankly, it is almost impossible to persuade so many of us to acknowledge any one of our number as leader, or to work together without arguing."

True enough, Shea reflected—at least, if you substituted the word "scholar" for "magician."

"I had feared as much," Randhir said, disappointed. "Still, I will trouble you to stay near me as we take Charya out to be executed. A dozen or more of his gang escaped, and I would not put it past them to try to rescue him at the last minute, even at the cost of slaying their Rajah."

"How horrendous!" Chalmers said, with just the right amount of horror. "Be certain we shall stay close by you, O Rajah!"

Shea listened to it all with foreboding. He didn't mind staying close to the Rajah—for a day or two, or even until they managed to locate Florimel. After that, though, the Rajah's possessiveness could become a serious problem.

"Why have you come to my city of Chandrodoya?" the rajah demanded.

"We have come seeking my wife," Chalmers explained. "She was kidnapped by a wicked enchanter named Malambroso. He is old, about my height, and lean, with a graying beard and moustache and long graying hair. She is perhaps the height of my ear, slender, brown-haired, and remarkably sweet-faced."

"I should hope you think the last, if you are her husband," Randhir said with a smile. "Well, I shall have my spies seek throughout the city for any word of such folk—but I am certain that if a woman with brown hair had appeared, word would already have come to me. They are not unknown, but they are rare in Chandrodoya."

"I shall be grateful for whatever boons you may bestow, O Ocean of Compassion."

The Rajah smiled with grim amusement. "Only remember that those boons require I remain alive, O Magus. Remember it well, and guard me closely."

Charya's last day began with a bath at the hands of servants who were guarded by vigilant soldiers. They dressed him in fine clothes, then turned him over to the soldiers, who mounted him on a camel and led him parading around the city, followed by the Rajah with Shea and Chalmers right behind him and in front of his bodyguard. In front of the thief marched a herald who proclaimed, "Who hears! Who hears! Who hears! The king commands! This is the thief who has robbed and plundered the city of Chandrodoya! Let all men therefore assemble themselves together this evening in the open space outside the gate leading toward the sea. And let them behold the penalty of evil deeds, and learn to be wise."

"What *is* the penalty, O Cleaver of Criminals?" Shea called to the monarch in front of him.

"He is to be nailed and tied to a scaffold, with his hands and feet stretched out at full length in an erect posture until death takes him," Randhir answered. "He shall have everything he wishes to eat, so that we may prolong his life and misery—but when death draws near, melted gold will be poured down his throat until it bursts from his neck and other parts of his body."

Shea shuddered. "Talk about royal treatment!"

"I would just as soon die by a more lowly, but faster, method," Chalmers said grimly. "It would seem the Romans were not the only ones who practiced crucifixion."

Shea stared. "Why, that *is* what he's talking about, isn't it?" He turned back to Randhir. "Is that the usual punishment, O . . ." He swallowed, thinking up an appropriate honorific that wouldn't be too insulting. ". . . O Hammer of Retribution?"

"Impalement is more common," the rajah replied, "but since this man has caused so much suffering, he should endure a longer death—and since he has slain so many, the manner of his own dying should be as painful as possible."

"But why so expensively?"

Now Randhir turned back to give Shea a wintry smile. "He wreaked misery upon his victims, and slew so many for no better reason than to gain gold, Shea. Now let him drink it."

Shea had to admit that the punishment did fit the crime. That, however, did not make it any less gruesome.

The evening was still hot when they led Charya out to his execution. Crowds lined the streets, jeering and making obscene gestures. Their jostling and stamping churned up an amazing amount of dust, and between that and the heat of the setting sun, Charya and those who followed him were soon stifling and coughing. The air was probably rich with the scents of curry and cardomoms, but all Shea could smell were the horses of the soldiers who mounted guard on the prisoner through his long march.

Now the procession turned into a broad boulevard, passing beneath the windows of some of the wealthiest merchants in town—and the ones who had lost the most to the thieves. Revilement and abuse poured from the windows above, turning into a chant:

This is the thief who has been robbing the whole city! Let him tremble now, for Randhir will surely crucify him!

Unfortunately, the man didn't look like the villain they described—anything but. Now that he was cleaned up and riding tall, straight and proud in the ruddy light of sunset, that light showed him to be handsome, very handsome, carrying himself with pride and bravery, meeting the jeers of the people with a faint sneer. Wicked or not, everyone knew of his strength and courage, and in the silks and satins the king had put on him, he looked like a prince himself. His gaze was calm and steady as he glared with disdain at the tormentors about him.

They saw, and redoubled in their rage. "Let him tremble now! Let him tremble now!"

But Charya did not tremble; instead, his lips quivered, his eyes flashed fire, and deep lines gathered between his eyebrows. Finally, his face creased into a sardonic smile.

A scream echoed above the clamor of the crowd, a scream that pierced their noise enough so that many of them broke off, staring upward at the window in the grand house that the procession was passing. There, at a second-story window, stood an unveiled woman, very young, who was staring straight into the robber's eyes, for on his camel, he was only a few feet below her, and not a dozen feet away. She went pale, and quivered as though his glance was a flash of lightning. Then she broke away from the fascination of his gaze and turned to the old man beside her, saying something with great force as she pointed at Charya. As the procession moved on, Shea came near, and heard her say, "... Go this moment and get that thief released!"

But Shea looked at the old man's face and gasped, "Malambroso!"

So it was, or his exact double. Shea grabbed Chalmers' shoulder with one hand and pointed with the other. "Look, Doc! Our kidnapper!"

"No," Chalmers said, his eyes on the woman, "my wife."

Shea stared at him, then whirled and looked again at the young woman. It *was* Florimel—except that she had black hair and a much darker complexion. But hair could be dyed, and so, for that matter, could skin—not that an enchanter of Malambroso's stature would need to resort to such crude techniques to change a person's appearance. "You're right, Doc! That's either Florimel's exact double, or Florimel herself in disguise! But why would Malambroso ..." His voice trailed off as the answer struck him.

"Yes," Chalmers said grimly. "How better to hide her from us? We would be seeking reports of a fair-skinned, brown-haired woman!"

"And, of course, that would be the only way to make her fit in with the local populace." Shea nodded. "Good hiding place, now that you think of it—but it seems to have backfired on him."

Malambroso was pleading with Florimel. "My darling Shobhani, that thief has been pilfering and plundering the whole city, and by his command scores of citizens were killed! Why, then, at my request, should our most gracious Rajah Randhir release him?"

Almost beside herself, Florimel exclaimed, "If by giving up your whole property, you can induce the Rajah to release him, then instantly do so—for if he does not come to me, I must give up my life!"

She turned away, covering her head with her veil, and sank down weeping, while Malambroso stared down at her, wounded to the core.

So was Chalmers, at seeing Florimel so obviously in love with another man.

"He called her 'Shobhani,' " Shea said quickly. "Maybe it's not Florimel after all, just her double!" Then inspiration struck. "Maybe each universe has analogs of the people in our universe! Maybe that old man is just an analog of Malambroso!"

"No," Chalmers said, his face turning wooden. "That is Malambroso, and the young woman is indeed my Florimel."

"Oh, yeah?" Shea, in another fit of inspiration, turned him and pointed at the thief, whose face was in profile to them as he stared at the young woman. "Think of him without the beard and the muscles! Think of him as a withdrawn young scholar! Who does he look like?"

Chalmers stared, and turned ashen. "He is me!"

"A younger analog of you," Shea said quickly. "The real you is still here! But this is what you would have looked like if you had been born a Hindu outlaw! No wonder she fell in love with him!"

Chalmers' face sagged. "I feel very old, Harold!"

"*You* feel old! How do you think Malambroso feels?"

"Very angry." Chalmers turned back to the window, suddenly afraid for Florimel—or Shobhani, whichever she was. Sure enough, Malambroso's face was suffused with rage—but even as they watched, all the fight went out of him as anger gave place to misery. He nodded with resignation and said, "I shall try to give you what you want, my child." He turned away from the window, and Shobhani looked up in sudden hope.

"He *does* love her," Chalmers said in surprise. "Her happiness means more to him than his own!"

"I never would have guessed it of him," Shea agreed.

Malambroso came running out into the midst of the parade and threw himself to his knees in front of Randhir's horse. The Rajah necessarily reined in—why lose a perfectly good taxpayer?—and Malambroso cried, "O great king, be pleased to receive four lakhs of rupees, and to release this thief!"

But the rajah replied, "He has been robbing the whole city, and by reason of him my guards have been destroyed. I cannot by any means release him."

"Alas!" Malambroso cried, and scuttled back into his house, his face in his hands.

"I never thought I would feel sorry for the man," Chalmers murmured.

The procession moved on, but Shea turned back in his saddle to watch the end of the domestic crisis. Malambroso appeared again in the window and explained, "Shobhani, I have said and done all that is possible, but it avails me naught with the Rajah. Now, then, we die— for I shall not outlive you!"

"Father, you must not!" Shobhani/Florimel cried, taking his hands.

"You are dearer to me than life itself, and I made plans weeks ago for the manner in which I would slay myself if anything brought about your death."

"You must not!" she cried again, "but I must! I must follow my husband and die when he dies!" And she darted away from the window. Malambroso stood a moment in shock, then ran after her, crying, "No, Shobhani! Stop!"

But Chalmers was trembling. "Husband? How can Florimel have another husband? Even if Shobhani is only Florimel's analog, how can she be married to a thief?"

Shobhani darted from the house to take up her place by the side of Charya's camel.

"Away!" snapped a guard, riding up beside her.

"I cannot," she replied. "I fell in love with him at first sight."

The guard drew back, aghast, and Randhir moaned faintly. "The poor child!"

Malambroso burst from the house to fall on his knees in front of Shobhani. "No, my child! Come back inside!"

"Away, old man!" The soldier raised his spear-butt,

threatening. "How dare you dissuade her from her pious duty!"

"Pious duty? What is he talking about?" Chalmers demanded, white showing all around his eyes; but Shea, more practical and less involved, leaned down to catch Malambroso by the arm and haul him up to his saddle. "Okay, Malambroso! Explain—and it better be good!"

The enchanter looked up at him, then stared in shock. "Harold Shea!"

"And Reed Chalmers." There was a note of incipient mayhem in Chalmers' voice, and Shea realized with a shock that even the gentle Reed might be capable of a crime of passion. "Explain what we have seen! Is that Florimel, or not?"

"She is, she is!" Malambroso yammered. "I enchanted her body into the coloring of the local people, I enchanted her mind into forgetting that she was Florimel, to believe instead that she was the maiden Shobhani, reared out of sight of men, never being allowed outside the high walls of the garden, because her old nurse, who died when she was only five, gave me, her father, a solemn warning—that Shobhani should be the admiration of the city, but should die a *sati*-widow before becoming a wife. A harmless piece of nonsense, surely— but reason enough for her father, who kept her as a pearl in a casket."

"*Sati*!" Chalmers stared in horror. "Ritual suicide when her husband dies? Letting herself be burned alive on his funeral pyre?"

Malambroso shuddered. "That is one of the ways, yes."

"You mean she's following that scoundrel to his execution because she's planning to die when he does?" Shea cried, aghast. "But how can she think he's her husband if you've got her hypnotized into believing she isn't even married?"

"It is this confounded belief in reincarnation," Malambroso groaned, "and in the events of one life affecting the next life! Having begun life anew in this universe, she is reincarnated in its terms—but the only previous life she has had was the one we all know, in which Reed Chalmers was her husband!"

"*Is* her husband," Reed said in an iron tone.

"Not in this universe! By its rules, this is a new life!"

"But she's been in half a dozen universes!" Shea protested. "Was each of them a previous life?"

"Yes, as far as this universe is concerned," Malambroso moaned, "and in each of them, Chalmers was her husband! But here in Chandrodoya, Chalmers' analog is the robber chieftain, so she fell in love the moment she set eyes upon him."

Shea stared. "You mean that, in Hindu terms, the robber chieftain was her predestined husband?"

"Yes, unless she had seen Chalmers first! Oh, how I wish I had not kept her so well hidden!"

"But why does she *have* to commit *sati*?" Shea demanded. "Nobody would have known if she had just kept quiet! She could even fly in the face of convention and stay alive even now! They weren't married—no one would blame her!"

"*She* would," Malambroso told him. "As a good Hindu maiden, sati is part of her *dharma*, the obligation of the role in life to which she was born; to refuse to commit sati would load her soul with bad *karma*—the wages of sin, in our terms—so when she did die, she would be reborn in a lower caste. But if she does commit *sati*, her soul will gain a great deal of good karma—I suppose the closest equivalent we have is grace—and she will be reborn in a higher caste. She even had the gall to recite Hindu proverbs at me—that there are thirty-five millions of hairs on the human body, and the woman who ascends the pyre with her husband will remain so many years in heaven before she's reborn—and that, as the snake-catcher draws the serpent from his hole, the wife who commits *sati* will rescue her husband from hell and will rejoice with him; though he may have sunk to a region of torment, be restrained in dreadful bonds, have reached the place of anguish, be exhausted and afflicted and tortured for his crimes, her act of self-sacrifice will save him."

Chalmers stared in horror. "And she really *believes* this?"

"No other effectual duty is known for virtuous women at any time after the death of their lords, except casting themselves into the same fire," Malambroso sighed. "As long as a woman in her reincarnation after reincarnation shall refuse *sati*, she shall not escape from being reborn in the body of some female animal. Her only road to rebirth in a higher caste, and to eventual nirvana, is to commit *sati* when her husband dies!"

Chalmers gave him a very black look. "You have a great deal to answer for, Malambroso, you and your in-depth hypnotic spell! Certainly you have placed entirely too much knowledge of Hindu dogma in her mind. Whatever possessed you to impose such an asinine scheme of disguise? Your daughter indeed! Oh, I will admit it was far easier than to believe that she was your wife, since you're such a relic—but how did you think you were going to be able to marry your own daughter?"

"When I was sure you had come and gone, I was going to remove the enchantment from her mind so that she would know I was not her father, then feed her a love phyltre," Malambroso snapped, "and who are you calling a relic, you antique?"

"Antique! I'll have you know . . ."

"I'll have you *both* know that we only have a few minutes," Shea interrupted. "We're almost to the city gate! If you don't nail down a solution to this dilemma before they nail down the robber, we're going to be dealing with a barbecue, not a woman!"

"Yes, quite so!" With a visible effort, Chalmers throttled his anger and wrenched his mind back into analytical mode. "So love at first sight was her recognition that the robber was her fated husband," he summarized, "and because he dies, she must die! Oh, blast and flay you,

Malambroso! You have really made a thorough mess of it this time!"

"I know, I know!" Malambroso groaned, "but curse me later if you must! For now, only aid me in finding some way to save her!"

By now, they had come out of the gate, and the robber chieftain saw the scaffold standing upright, waiting for him. His steps faltered, but the guards pricked him with their spears, and he gave them a look of disdain before he marched up proudly and firmly to stand before the giant wooden X. He lifted his arms, holding them out to his sides, and the executioners stepped up with hammer and nails.

"If you can do anything to prevent this, do it now!" Malambroso pleaded.

"The invisible shield we put over the rajah when they were fighting?" Shea suggested.

"I have no grass," Chalmers answered, watching the scene with narrowed eyes, "and Randhir would know in an instant who had done it. No, we must concoct an effect that could be mistaken for something valid, within their own religion."

The three men stood silent for a long moment as the executioners threw a rope around the thief's waist and tied him firmly to the middle of the X.

"Iron skin," Shea said suddenly.

"Of course! From the elbows to the fingers, and from the knees to the toes! Quickly, Malambroso! You take the arms! Harold, take the right leg! I will take the left!"

Malambroso cast a quick look of confusion at Chalmers, then shrugged and turned to business. He drew a few odd objects from beneath his robe, began to manipulate them, and muttered a verse in Arabic. Chalmers took a small knife from his thief's finery and leaned down to rub it against his shin, muttering. Shea, realizing how his boss was applying the Laws of Sympathy and Contagion, drew his own knife and stropped it against his thigh, muttering,

"Joe Magarac was born in Iron Mountain,
And therefore as he grew, he turned to steel.
Let our bandit chief bathe in his fountain;
Turn his skin to iron, so he'll no longer steal!"

Malambroso and Chalmers finished their verses in a dead heat with his—and just in time. The exectioner placed a huge spike against the bandit's wrist, drew back a hammer, then drove it forward with all his might.

The spike struck the robber's skin and glanced off, burying itself in the wood. The executioner stared in amazement, then shook himself, obviously thinking he had missed his stroke. He placed the spike again, struck again—and watched it skid again.

The robber, watching, grinned. "What is the difficulty? Is my skin too strong for your weak muscles?"

But the other executioner was having the same problem with the other wrist. The first firmed his lips into a straight line, placed the spike, and, with great determination, drove his hammer as hard as he could. The spike skidded again and flew out of his grasp.

The robber chieftain gave a low, mocking laugh.

The executioners each snatched up another nail and hammered at them with fury. They couldn't even dent the bandit's skin. His laughter grew louder and louder as their frustration mounted. Finally, they threw down their spikes, crying, "He is bewitched!"

At the word "bewitched," Randhir's eyes automatically swiveled to Shea and Chalmers—but Harold only returned a gaze of blank innocence, while Chalmers stood with head bowed. Of course, his head was bowed to keep the king from seeing his lips move as he chanted a verse while he pulled a thread from his cuff and stretched it between his hands until it snapped.

The rope fell from the robber's waist. He looked down in surprise, then grinned and stepped forward, holding up unmarked wrists in a gesture of triumph.

"The gods have spoken!" cried a woman in the crowd. "The God of the Golden Spear protects him!"

"Or perhaps the Goddess of Brides," another woman countered.

"Yes, it would seem that the gods have given their judgment, and that the thief is to live." Randhir looked as though he had bitten down on a rotten nut, but he managed to force the words out.

"Praise Heaven!" Malambroso cried, going limp—then straightening in alarm as Florimel gave a cry of delight and ran to throw her arms around the thief's neck. Grinning, he caught her up and whirled her about. "He cannot marry her!" Malambroso cried.

"I did not say that he would," Rajah Randhir grated, "for though he shall live, he shall not go unpunished. He shall be a common soldier in my army, and I shall send him to the border, so that when my greedy neighbor invades, this robber chieftain shall be the first whom arrows strike! If the gods still protect him then, if he comes home from the battle alive and well, I *may* permit him to pay court to the maiden—or I may find more tasks for him to do, many more, until he has proved his worth and made amends, at least in part, for all the misery he has caused."

The thief put down Shobhani and turned to salaam to the Rajah. "Whatsoever you wish, O Diamond of Justice, I shall do! Indeed, if I had known virtue might win me the hand of so beauteous a maiden as this, I would have forsaken my evil ways long ago!"

Shobhani threw her arms around him again, and the people cheered as Malambroso moaned—in harmony with Chalmers.

"Stand away, maiden!" the Rajah commanded. "He must go forthwith to the border, this very night! Soldiers! Take him to your barracks and equip him for the journey!"

The soldiers surrounded the bandit and marched him off, back into the city.

"I wonder how many beatings he will sustain between the city and the border?" Chalmers muttered.

"Accidents will happen," Shea said virtuously. "Hey, it's gotta be better than dying, Doc—and he's proved he can take it."

As the crowd moved off, cheering the same man they had cursed only an hour before, the Rajah turned on Shea and Chalmers. "Well enough, magicians! I cannot prove it, and I certainly do not know why you did it— but I could swear his escape was your doing, and not the work of the gods at all!" He gave Malambroso a narrow glance. "He is one of you too, is he not?"

"I assure you, O Gem of Insight," said Malambroso, "that I have no wish to see my daughter Shobhani marry a thief!"

"No, but you would rather that than see her commit *sati*, would you not? Come, Shea, admit it!"

"Okay, we're guilty," Shea sighed.

"Harold!" Chalmers snapped in alarm.

"Fear not," Randhir said grimly, "I have already spoken, and I shall not reverse my judgment again. However, it is not *my* judgment you need fear now, but that of Shiva—for it is with his justice that you have interfered!"

"Perhaps," Shea said slowly, "or perhaps I have been sent here by another god, whether I knew it or not. Who knows but that I may have been the instrument of Heaven?"

"Oh? And what god would choose a foreigner for his tool?" Randhir said, not quite sneering.

"Oh . . . one who likes to see handsome young men sporting with beautiful young women," Shea said slowly.

Randhir frowned. "Krishna, you mean?"

At that point, Shea was open to all suggestions. He shrugged. "He loved playing with the milkmaids himself, didn't he?"

The Rajah's eyes narrowed. "If you truly believe that," he said, "I challenge you to prove it by coming with me to Krishna's temple and standing before his statue. If you are not struck down by Krishna's anger, I may begin to believe you are sent by a god, and are not liable to punishment yourself, for interfering with the king's justice."

A look of alarm spread over Chalmers' features, but Shea felt only a wash of relief. Statues were only sculptures, after all—lumps of wood or rock fashioned into something resembling human form. He bowed. "As you wish, O Scale of Justice."

"But," Malambroso said hastily, "since the maiden Shobhani is the cause of this difficulty, should she not also stand by us before the statue?"

"She shall," the Rajah promised. "Come!" He turned away, and his soldiers stepped up behind the three enchanters, spears out to prod.

As they followed the King, Chalmers muttered to Malambroso, "You colossal idiot! Admittedly, a statue is only a statue, but you never know what tricks priests can work, especially in a magical universe! Do you want Florimel to be struck by lightning, too?"

"Come, Chalmers." Malambroso had regained his former aplomb. "You do not truly believe such a thing can happen, do you?"

"Well . . . no," Chalmers admitted, "and it does keep her from getting lost." But a gleam had come into his eye, and Shea wondered what he was planning.

He found out when they stood before the image of Krishna—wooden, apprently, for it was painted, and the blue face of the boy-god looked down upon them as Chalmers reached out to stroke Shobhani's black hair, muttering a verse. Alarmed, Malambroso spun to prevent him—but too late. The woman looked up, blinking in confusion, then saw Chalmers and cried, "Reed! Oh, thank Heaven! But where are we?"

Malambroso groaned, "I shall win her yet, Chalmers! You shall regret this!"

"Maybe sooner than you think." Shea eyed the statue nervously.

Chalmers turned to him with a frown. "Whatever can you mean?"

"Only that this universe has its own rules," Shea reminded him, "and Krishna might be more than a myth, here."

Chalmers stared, and alarm was just beginning to show in his face when a shaft of light burst from the statue, engulfing them all.

Shea flailed, catching Chalmers' hand, then stood, frozen by the glitter that dazzled him and filled all the universe about him. He could only hope Chalmers had been able to catch hold of Florimel. Then Shea found room to wonder if this was really what it was like to be hit by lightning, and if it was, it was odd, because he felt no pain.

Then the dazzle died, the ground seemed to push itself up under his feet, and he looked around him, blinking in confusion—Florimel, arms around her husband's neck, cried, "Oh, Reed, praise Heaven! We are home!"

Belphebe started to struggle up from the chair where she sat watching, but Shea reached her in two steps, dropped to one knee, and enfolded her in an ardent embrace. The room was very quiet for a few minutes, as the two married couples celebrated the travelers' safe return with a kiss and a promise—of more kisses to come.

Finally, Shea came up for air and turned to Chalmers to ask, "How did you do it, Doc?"

"I did not, really." Chalmers still looked rather dazed. "I only reached out for Florimel's hand—I remember thinking that if I were going to die by electrocution, I could at least die holding her. I reached out for your hand, too, but the hand I touched was quite bony—I am certain it was Malambroso's, and I let go at once. Even as I did, though, I felt his hand pulling away from mine, but even as I caught yours, I could swear I heard him cry out in fright." He shuddered. "I could wish the man many evils, but none so bad as that cry seemed to express."

"You don't think he ..." Shea couldn't finish the question.

"No, I do not." Chalmers collected himself with a visible effort. "I think it probable that Krishna—or his priests; they may have been magicians who resented the competition—sent our old adversary back to his home, as he seems to have sent us to ours. And oh, Harold, I am mightily glad he did!"

"You can say that for me, too." Shea turned to watch Belphebe and Florimel, chatting as merrily as though they had seen each other only last week. "So Florimel *didn't* get herself lost by trying to work a syllogismobile spell on her own?"

"It would seem not. Certainly Malambroso appeared in my house for the purpose of kidnapping her, but before he did, he no doubt took advantage of the opportunity to update himself on our researches. Thank Heaven he is so untidy that he did not bother to clean up the evidence, or we should never have been able to track him!"

"But we did, and we won Florimel back, and we're home. Just to be on the safe side, though, Doc—maybe you'd better give her the full syllogismobile course, so that if somebody kidnaps her again, she has a fair chance of escaping."

"An excellent thought." Chalmers gazed at his wife, but his face was grim. "I assure you, Harold, I intend to guard her very closely from now on! She shall never be stolen from me again!"

Shea glanced uneasily from husband to wife, and hoped Chalmers was right.

Part III
SIR HAROLD OF ZODANGA

L. Sprague de Camp

I

"So, Doctor Malambroso," said Professor Doctor Sir Harold Shea to the man who faced him across his desk at the Garaden Institute, "what do you want of me?"

The man facing Shea was a tall, lean person with a close-cut graying beard. His graying hair hung to his collar. He wore a cheap suit with a loud checked pattern and an eye-blinding cravat, tied in a way suggesting that Malambroso had never learned to tie a necktie. The last time Shea had seen Malambroso, in the universe of Hindu myth, he had worn white pyjamas embroidered with gold thread. Malambroso had, Shea thought, made a not altogether successful effort to adopt local coloration on the mundane plane.

"I want the Lady Florimel back!" said Malambroso in a rasping, growling voice, as if he hated asking any favor of anybody.

"Gods, what crust!" exclaimed Shea.

Malambroso frowned. "You puzzle me, Sir Harold. Methought 'crust' meant the hard covering or integument of something softer, such as the outer surface of a loaf of bread or a pie."

"Colloquially, 'crust' is also used for . . ." Shea paused to think. " 'Obtuse aggressiveness' is close to the colloquial meaning. That you should ask *my* help to regain possession of the Lady Florimel, who seems quite happy

141

to be back with her husband, my colleague Reed Chalmers! . . . If that be not a case of obtuse aggressiveness, I don't know what is."

"I can explain," growled Malambroso.

"Then pray do so, and I hope concisely. I need to get back to these term papers."

"The fact, Sir Harold, is that, for the first time in a long and active life, I am in love. Methought I was far beyond such petty, juvenile mortal sentiments; but in that, lo, I erred. I would never admit this, save that I know you for a man of exceptional ability, at least for a native of this stupid, brutish mundane plane."

"Thanks. But I always thought you hated everybody?"

"So I did, before the tender passion awakened a side of my nature that I did not know I possessed. Anyhow, the gist is that I must have the lady for mine own paramour. I must and shall have her!" Malambroso smote the desk with a bony fist.

"Don't be silly, Malambroso," said Shea. "For one thing, you're too old for her."

"No older than Doctor Chalmers. What reason have you to think that he can perform his connubial duties to the satisfaction of all concerned?"

"He's been giving himself magical rejuvenating treatments."

"How can he, when magic does not work in this continuum?"

"I didn't say he performed the treatments *here*, and it's none of your business anyway. What makes you think that, after he and I went to so much trouble and risk, surviving dangers both natural and supernatural, to reunite the lady with her lawful husband, that I would help you to snatch her again?"

"Because if you do not, I will turn you into an insect of an especially loathsome kind!"

"You can't. Spells don't work here."

"Think ye so?" Malambroso pointed bony fingers at

Shea and muttered an incantation, ending with a shout of: "... be thou a lowly *Geophilus!*"

Nothing happened. Malambroso's face took on expression of petulant frustration, muttering: "The Incantation of Sorax has always worked for me before! You should be a little crawler, on a hundred-odd legs."

Shea laughed. "Told you. Wrong universe. I seem to have only the two legs I started out with. Besides, if I had a hundred-odd, I couldn't be an insect. They all have exactly six."

"Oh, curse your silly pedantry!" snarled Malambroso.

"By the way," said Shea, "how did you get here from the world of Hindu myth?"

"By the Spell of the Tipulidae, which worked perfectly well in that universe. But think not that I failed to consider means of exit from this miserable, magicless world of yours. I read your publications in the Institute library anent the manipulation of symbolic logic. 'Twas right shrewd of you to have worked out your system. The papers revealed what a formidable fellow you could be, whether as foe or ally. I shall convince you that it were better for you to be mine ally rather than mine enemy. I know of universes where you could be a great man— belike an arch-wizard or an emperor. I could furnish you with mighty assistance towards those goals, Sir Harold."

"You may skip the 'Sir,' Malambroso. American citizens are not allowed titles of nobility, so it doesn't apply in this world. Anyway, I have no desire to be an emperor or even an archimage. I am quite satisfied to be a well-established academician, a fond husband, and a doting father. I've adventured enough on other planes to do me for the rest of my life."

Malambroso argued further, but Shea remained firm in his refusal, until Malambroso said: "Is this your final word? You refuse to discuss practical arrangements between us?"

"Yes and yes. Good afternoon, Doctor Malambroso."

The wizard rose. "You shall regret your contumacy, good my sir!"

"We shall see," said Shea.

Malambroso took a topcoat from the rack, picked up a cheap suitcase, gave Shea a stiff nod, and stalked out.

Some hours later, Shea looked at his watch and saw that it was nearly time to go home. Then the intercom said: "Doctor Shea? Call your wife, right away!"

"Darling!" said Belphebe, breathlessly. "That wizard Malambroso has kidnapped Voglinda!"

"Good God!" said Shea. "Have you called the cops?"

"First thing I did. Sergeant Brodsky's here now."

"I'll come right home."

"Fine, but drive carefully!"

"Pretty little thing," said Pete Brodsky, passing back the photographs. "About three, isn't she? Now, Belle, suppose you tell Harold what you told me, about how this Doctor Malefactor got away."

"Malambroso," Belphebe corrected. "He came to call, he said, ever so politely. When we sat down in the living room, he gave me a sales pitch, trying to get me to persuade you to throw in with him in an attempt to win Florimel away from Reed for his own—'paramour,' I think he said. When I said no, he tried to sway me with tales of the wonders of other universes he could take us to and make us big shots in, where I could have all the fancy clothes and jewels any girl could want. He didn't realize that my taste runs to simple, outdoorish garb, suitable for running through the greenwood.

"When I persisted in saying no, he seemed to give up. He said he wanted another look at Voglinda, who was having her nap. He stole up to her bedroom door and slithered in as quietly as a cockroach. I was right behind him; but he shut the door in my face and shot that little bolt we put in high up. I heard him reciting a sorites and called the emergency number. I couldn't break down the door myself, but Pete drove up and gave the door a good push with his shoulder, and away went the bolt. You'll have to do some carpentry, dear, to mend it.

"Well, there was nobody in the room, and the window was latched on the inside. So here we are."

Shea said: "Did you hear enough of the sorites to tell where Malambroso was going?"

"No. Sorry."

Brodsky growled: "Trouble with chasing you dimensional guys is, you can vanish into the goddam world of some jerk's imagination. Like that phony Finland and phony Ireland we visited together.

"See, if you want a guy and know he's somewhere along a line, say a railroad or a bus route, you can start at the beginning and go on to the end. Perps don't often make it that easy for us.

"If you know he's somewhere on a map, that's harder, because you got two dimensions to cover. Then, if he can go not only north-south and east-west but also up-down, it gets pretty goddam impossible, unless you get a tip from a snitch or stoolie. And I suppose chasing a perp through your alternative universes would be using the fourth dimension or something, eh?"

"You get the general idea, Pete," said Shea. "If I can examine Malambroso's personal room, I might find us a clue. Okay?"

"Sure, I can arrange it, if you promise not to touch anything."

Shea stood in Malambroso's rented room, staring at the bookcases. At last he said to Brodsky: "I think I know where he's taken our kid."

"Where's that?"

"To Barsoom."

"Huh?"

"Barsoom, Edgar Rice Burroughs' version of Mars."

"Aw, hell; I know there ain't enough air on Mars to keep a bug alive—"

"Not the real Mars, but the one Burroughs imagined for his John Carter stories—or, to put it another way, the Mars in another universe, which somehow got into Burroughs' mind and formed the basis for his stories. In fact, I suspect Malambroso's already made at least one trial there to test out our syllogismobile. You can see the books. For Barsoom, he's got a collection somebody would give real money for: the old McClurg hardbacks, the Methuen reprints, and the paperbacks: Ballantines from the sixties, the later Ace series, the Del Reys . . . I take it to mean he's a Barsoomian fan. So, knowing about Barsoom already, he'd naturally take off in that direction. Looks as though the only way to catch up with him is for me to go to Barsoom."

Brodsky sighed. "Wish I could go with you. But since I got promoted, seems like I'm buried under a daily blizzard of papers."

"Harold Shea!" said Belphebe in tones of exasperation. "If you think for one minute I would let you go off by yourself after Voglinda, you're as mad as some of your faculty colleagues think you are. She's my daughter, too, you know. From what I've heard of Barsoom, gunmaking there isn't so far advanced that a good longbow wouldn't be useful as a backup."

Shea sighed. "Oh, all right, darling. Get your stuff together."

"What do they wear on Barsoom?"

"Mostly they go naked, except for a kind of harness of straps with pockets and pouches dangling. It doesn't conceal anything."

"You mean—you mean real naked, with everything showing?"

"That's what I understand. They don't seem to have the ancient Hebrew tabu on nudity, inherited by Christianity and Islam. Maybe you'd best stay home—"

"No, sir! If I have to show the Barsoomians my personal anatomy to get our precious back, I'll do it! And if any Barsoomian makes a pass, I'll make him eat a clothyard shaft for breakfast! But then, you couldn't wear your mailshirt under your clothes, could you?"

"Not and pass myself off as a native Barsoomian, which we may have to do. According to Burroughs," said Shea in his classroom manner, "Barsoomians are pretty puritanical in matters of sex and theft. Where they go off the reservation, from our point of view, is in their permissive attitude towards homicide. If you want to kill somebody, you just up and do it, and nobody gives a damn. At least, so Burroughs says, and I don't know how accurate he was. I wouldn't very far trust any writer who put tigers and deer in Africa."

"Then I'd better pack an extra quiver!"

Shea made a slight face, knowing that it would fall to his lot to carry the extra weight on the portages, however short, that any extensive trip entailed. But he did not dissent, since the proposal made sense. He said:

"And I'll take the old six-shooter. It's not the most up-to-date firearm—everybody goes for automatics nowadays—but it's simple and rugged and has fewer things to go wrong with it."

"Is Barsoom a universe where firearms work?"

"According to Burroughs, yes; though I doubt his story of radium rifles that shoot fifty miles with radar sights."

Harold Shea and Belphebe sat cross-legged on the rug in the center of the Shea living room. Shea, in breeches and boots, with a cowboy hat on his head, sat with a scabbard containing a shortened nineteenth-century saber on his left, a sheath holding a bowie knife in front, and on his right a holster with a big Smith & Wesson .44 revolver.

Belphebe wore green slacks, a similar jacket, and the feathered hat of her home world. Her longbow, unstrung, was slung over her back by its bowstring, passing between her full, young-mother breasts. A laden quiver was also slung to her back, its strap forming an X with the longbow string.

"Okay," said Shea, "let's go!" He grasped her near hand and began: "If P equals not-Q, then Q implies not-P . . ."

II

Shea had been through these transitions before and so was ready for their effects. The living room dissolved into a whirl of colored spots. Momentarily he seemed to be suspended in nothing, as in a free-fall. Then, bit by bit, the world around him solidified. But this world was nothing like the one they had left.

The scene was of nighttime out-of-doors, lit by a brighter moonlight than Shea had ever seen on Earth. The source was a big, bright moon, even larger than Earth's Luna, passing overhead. Elsewhere sparkled a myriad stars, brighter and more numerous than they would appear to the naked eye anywhere on Earth.

Beside him, Belphebe said: "That moon is traveling so fast you can see its motion against the stars. Also, it seems to be going from west to east, unlike our Earthly moon."

"Quite right, darling," said Shea. "That's Thuria, the closer of Barsoom's two moons. It corresponds to Phobos in our own universe. I don't see the other satellite, Cluros as they call it here. If this were our Mars, you could only see Phobos from near the equator, and it's only a big boulder anyway."

"Why couldn't Phobos be seen from elsewhere?"

"The bulge of the planet would hide it, just as it hides

the Southern Cross from viewers in the northern parts of our world."

"How do you know what the Barsoomians call them, if you've never been here before?"

"I've read Burroughs. Besides, the advantage of the sorites is that, if you compose it right, you arrive in the other universe already knowing the local language. Otherwise we should have to spend months studying Barsoomian in order to get around, as Burroughs' John Carter did on his first arrival."

"Probably several different languages, as on Earth," said Belphebe.

"No; Burroughs says they have only one spoken language for the entire planet, though different nations have different ways of writing it. I daresay there are local dialects."

"How could that be? Since languages are always changing, what would prevent the speech of Barsoom from diverging into branches, like those of the Latin or the Slavic languages on Earth?"

Shea shrugged. "I don't know, darling. Perhaps some conqueror once brought the whole planet under his sway and ordained that his particular speech was the official one, which everyone had to use on pain of death. And it hasn't had time to split into different languages yet."

Thuria sank below the eastern horizon, whereupon a deeper darkness closed down, relieved by the pyrotechnic starlight.

"Oh, my!" said Belphebe. "Look at those stars! I've never seen them so bright on Earth—or in any other world I've visited."

"It's the thin atmosphere," said Shea, "sort of like that on top of the Rocky Mountains. But if I'm not mistaken, the sun is coming up soon."

The sky was visibly paling in a strip along the eastern horizon. Little by little, a small but very bright sun climbed into view.

"I hope it warms us up," said Belphebe. "I'm cold! And you tell me the Barsoomians go naked!"

"I think they usually put on some sort of wrap when they have to go out at night," said Shea, pulling her close for warmth. "Nudism isn't really comfortable for us Earthlings unless the air temperature is well over twenty-five Celsius. Hey!" He pointed. "I think we've landed near Lesser Helium!"

In the slowly waxing light, a few hundred meters distant rose a massive city wall, high enough to conceal any buildings within, with one exception. This was a tall, slim tower. As the light grew stronger, it lit up another tower, even taller but much farther away.

The Sheas were sitting on a flat surface covered by a pinkish-yellow mosslike growth, stretching away to the horizon in all directions, save where it ended at the foot of the city wall.

"Hurrah for us!" said Shea, rising. "I aimed for the twin cities of Helium, and that's what we got. The one in front of us is Lesser Helium; the one off in the distance, where you see the bigger tower, is Greater Helium." He gave Belphebe a hand up.

"Where next?" she asked.

"Walk around the wall till we come to the main gate. Remember, your weight is less than half what it would be on Earth. So it's easy to trip and fall if you don't step cautiously."

They set out briskly. As soon as they became used to their own reduced weights, they bounced along fast to warm their muscles. After a trot of a quarter to half an hour, they approached a road, whereon people and animals moved. The road led to a massive fortified gate, and the crowd looked like an assemblage of locals bringing in wagonloads of farm produce. They were massed around the gate, waiting, and more constantly arrived.

As the Sheas approached, Shea made out the distinctive features of these Barsoomians. They were black-haired men with bright-red skins—redder than that of any Native American, together with facial features much like those of Earthly Europeans. They shivered under blankets wrapped cloakwise around themselves. Shea recognized the beasts of burden harnessed to the wagons as thoats—hefty animals on eight slender legs apiece, with gaping jaws and massive tails ending in broad blades, usable as weapons.

As the Sheas came near the gate, a silvery trumpet sounded. With a screechy creaking, one valve of the gate swung outward. After a pause, the other valve did likewise. Several men, naked but for a harness of straps supporting swords and other personalia, bustled out. Their harness was all of one design, thus constituting the gate guards' uniform.

The gate guards talked among themselves and with members of the waiting crowd. Then two guards strode purposefully toward the Sheas. As they neared, the low sun flashed on large, bejeweled metal buckles and badges, where the straps of the harness crossed or joined.

"Who are you?" barked the nearer guard.

"From your garb," said the second guard, "you look like Jasoomians."

"So we are," said Shea. "In fact, we are—"

"You must come with us at once!" said the first guard, seizing Shea's arm in a firm grip, while his comrade took hold of Belphebe's arm.

"Unhand me, sir!" cried Belphebe.

"Orders are orders," said the first guard. "Come along, now!"

"What orders?" said Shea.

"To bring any Jasoomians before the Jed at once!"

"Harold!" cried Belphebe. "Will you let these knaves lay hands on me?"

"Best we go along with them, darling," said Shea, "since they're taking us where we want to go anyway."

Mors Kajak, Jed of Lesser Helium, sat behind a huge desk piled with scrolls. As Shea noted, the Barsoomians had not yet made the transition to the codex, the book of separate pages all bound together along one edge. The Jed was a big red Barsoomian of what, in an Earthman, would be called early middle age. He was stouter than most Barsoomians, with a few strands of gray in his bristling, crew-cut black hair.

Shea had read that Barsoomians kept the appearance of youth longer than Earthmen until, in the last century of their millennial lives, they rapidly aged. Like other Barsoomians, the Jed wore nothing save a harness of straps, whence dangled pouches, pockets, and a pair of swords in scabbards. At last he dropped the scroll he had studied and looked up.

"Well?"

"O Jed," said the senior guard, "we found these Jasoomians trying to sneak in the main gate. Mindful of our orders, we seized and brought them hither."

Belphebe looked ready to utter an angry outburst, when a gesture from Shea silenced her.

"You did right," said the Jed. "You may return to your duties, leaving the Jasoomians here. As you go out, tell the two door guards to step into my sanctum."

The senior gate guard saluted (a gesture that reminded Shea of the Roman salute made notorious by Mussolini and Hitler). Then he did a smart about-face and departed, followed by his comrade. The two door guards entered the room and took places at either end of the massive desk.

"Well, Jasoomians," said the Jed, "how explain you your presence on this world?"

"First, O Jed," said Shea, "permit me to protest the gate guard's referring to my wife's and my approach to the gate as 'sneaking.' We came peacefully and in plain sight." Shea then plunged into the tale of Malambroso's abduction of the infant Voglinda Shea.

The Jed judiciously put his fingertips together. "You say you are Professor Doctor Sir Harold Shea, and that the lady is your wife Belphebe?

"It may be that what you have told me is true. Pray ignore the manner whereby you were fetched hither. We have learned to be wary of Jasoomian visitors. They are such wild exaggerators and prevaricators, like my crazy son-in-law, Lord John Carter. When he bests one man in combat, he tells everyone that he has slain three. If he defeats three, they become a score.

"Moreover, Jasoomians are forever introducing subversive ideas, trying to upset our sound, stable, time-tried Barsoomian customs to make them more like those of their native world. Why, Carter has spoken of making it illegal to slay a man in fair fight!"

"You disagree, O Jed?" said Shea.

"Of course! Did we Barsoomians not kill one another off with such zest by duels and assassinations, the planet's population would soon exceed that at which its scanty resources could support its people.

"Another Jasoomian, Ulysses Paxton, goes under the Barsoomian name of Vad Varo. He urged that each Barsoomian nation adopt a written constitution, to be confirmed by popular vote. He persuaded the Zodangans to try it, with the result that the chief of the Zodangan assassins' guild, Ur Jan, won the Jedship.

"Paxton has even preached that slavery is wrong, if you can believe that an apparently intelligent being could entertain such a nonsensical idea, and an inhumane idea to boot."

"How is it inhumane?" asked Belphebe.

"Why, what else could you do with prisoners of war except to make slaves of them or kill them? If you turn them loose, they will return to their own land and come back to fight you again. The remaining alternative is to kill the lot, and Paxton deems that even more inhumane. But it is the only practical alternative to enslaving them.

"When Paxton took up residence in Zodanga, Ur Jan would have slain him for his subversive ideas had he not fled. Any such doctrine would utterly overthrow our social system and reduce the world to seething chaos!"

Shea said: "My own home world has struggled with similar difficulties. Where is Lord Carter now?"

"He has gone off to Ptarth to visit Thuvan Dinh, the Jed, and to promote some of his revolutionary ideas. It will be interesting to see how long Thuvan Dinh puts up with Carter's transgalactic nonsense."

"O Jed," said Shea, "could you tell me more about Lord Carter's mysterious arrival on Barsoom? Likewise with Paxton. Some of our wise men have speculated that they sent their astral bodies to Barsoom, leaving their Earthly ones on their native planet. But that leaves open the question of whence came the mass of their Barsoomian bodies.

"There is also a mystery about where Lord Carter was born and when. He seems to have appeared out of nowhere and to have spent several times the normal Earthly life span, earning his living on Earth as a mercenary soldier—an occupation that no longer commands the respect it once did. Truth to tell, it has fallen into disrepute."

"We have been puzzled, too," said the Jed. "Nor have questions to Lord Carter done much to enlighten us. He is a jovial man of action, with little interest in the whys and wherefores of his becoming a Barsoomian.

"Now the consensus is that he is really a Barsoomian, taken to Jasoom as a child or youth by some occult means, like that which brought you and your lady hither. It is surmised that his fair skin marks him as a descendant of the white race, so called, which dominated parts of Barsoom back when the oceans still washed the margins of the continents, before the races that then existed merged to form the present red race.

"But enough of this pleasant chatter, Sir Harold. Not for naught do some folk of Lesser Helium call me 'Mors Chatterbox'—albeit not to my face. But the man whose duty it is to stand beside me and stop me when I talk too much is on vacation. So, Doctor Shea, what mean you to do next in pursuit of your vanished offspring?"

"My first step," said Shea, "is obviously to find out whether Malambroso has actually come to Barsoom. Is that the sort of thing your Barsoomian mastermind, Ras Thavas, would know?"

"Of course! Had you not brought up the matter, I should have suggested him myself. He has his own system of keeping track of events in Barsoomian cities, which we have found useful in warning us of aggressions and revolutions." The Jed turned to one of his guardsmen. "Dator Thin, you shall send a message to Doctor Ras Thavas, respectfully requesting his presence here forthwith."

The guardsman saluted and departed. The Jed said: "Sir Harold, plan you to go about Barsoom searching for this miscreant on your own?"

"Yes, sir, unless you could furnish me with helpers."

The Jed shood his head. "Since this is a matter among Jasoomians, it concerns not the Empire of Helium. I will not, therefore, let my people become involved therein, aside from furnishing such information as you can elicit from Ras Thavas. It strikes me, however, that clad in those hideous and overheating garments, you could not hope to do aught by stealth. You are as conspicuous as an Otzian on a snowbank."

From his reading, Shea knew that by "Otzian" the Jed meant a member of the black-skinned race of Barsoom, who dwelt in Otz Valley at the South Pole. He continued:

"You will, therefore, wish to adopt Barsoomian garb and color of skin. I am sure that Ras Thavas can show you how to do that—unless you have that curious prejudice among Jasoomians, that it is shameful or improper to expose one's sexual parts to the view of one's fellow beings. You Jasoomians must be a singularly nasty-minded lot, forever thinking of copulation."

"We can overcome such feelings," said Shea. "Agreed, darling?"

"Not being a native Jasoomian," said Belphebe, "I have never suffered from this twitch. If my husband ever had it, he is cured."

The Jed rang a little bell on his desk. A red Barsoomian, with the usual harness of straps, came through a side door to the sanctum. Mors Kajak said:

"Dattok, lead these Jasoomians to one of the hospitality suites, third class. Farewell for the nonce, O Sheas. Pray hold yourselves in readiness to return hither when Ras Thavas appears."

The Jed picked up the scroll he had been reading when the Sheas arrived. He unrolled it again and hunted about his cluttered desk for weights to hold down the corners of the strip and prevent it from rolling itself up again.

The following morning, a flunkey summoned the Sheas to the executive chamber. There Shea and Belphebe found another red Barsoomian in converse with the Jed. The new arrival seemed to be in what to a Barsoomian would be youth—say, in his second or third century—of handsome aspect, but notably lean and starved-looking.

"Here," said the Jed Mors Kajak to the new Barsoomian, "are the Jasoomians whereof I have told you: Mr. and Mrs. Harold Shea, unless you prefer all the fancy titles titles they claim: Sir, Professor, Doctor, and so on. Sheas, this is Doctor Ras Thavas, with whom you asked to speak."

Shea raised his right hand in the Barsoomian greeting. "*Kaor*, Doctor."

"*Kaor*," grunted the young Barsoomian. "Where do you wish us to confer, O Jed?"

"Dattok will show you the way," said the Jed.

The secretary led them through a maze of hallways to a small conference room. Seated, Shea studied Ras Thavas. He asked:

"Doctor, is it true that you had your brain transferred to the body of a younger man?"

"It is true," rasped Ras Thavas. "But let us not dwell upon the circumstance of my brain transfer, since social pressures have forced me to give up that kind of neurosurgery. Nor am I a chatterbox like Mors Kajak, to waste precious research time in idle chatter. What would you of me? Pray make it brief."

Shea poured out the tale of Voglinda's abduction by Malambroso. He ended: "And so, knowing you for a far-sighted and well-informed man, I ask if your intelligence system has apprised you of the arrival of this pair on Barsoom?"

Ras Thavas chuckled. "You are a clever fellow, Doctor Shea, knowing that flattery is the surest means of procuring favors from your fellow man. But think not that it will work on a person of my superior intellect. I easily see through such childish sleights.

"Now, let us suppose that my informants have in fact told me of the arrival on Barsoom of your Doctor Malambroso and his captive infant. If I put you on this wizard's track, I shall expect a favor from you in return."

"Such as?" said Shea.

"That depends. By diligent investigation, Doctor Shea, I have learned a few things about you, if not enough to grasp all aspects of your personality."

"You mean you have a dossier on me? Where did you get your information, since I only arrived on Barsoom for the first time yesterday?"

Ras Thavas gave a lopsided grin. "Oh, I have ways; I have ways. The inventions of your fellow Jasoomian, the wireless pioneer Gridley, have been of substantial help. But to get down to cases, Doctor, what is your occupation on your native planet?"

"I am a professor of psychology at the Garaden Institute, in Garaden, Ohio."

"Just what I needed! I understand that, starting as a brash, hot-tempered, and emotionally volatile youth, you have learned by painful experience to bridle your natural impulses to as to avoid offense and disarm hostility. Your conduct here during the last few *xats* shows all the smoothness one would expect of you."

"And what has all that to do with you, Doctor?" asked Shea.

"I shall come to that forthwith. When Vad Varo—formerly Ulysses Paxton of your world—transferred my brain from the worn-out body it then occupied to the body you now see before you, he did an excellent job. That is no cause for surprise, since he had the greatest possible teacher of neurosurgery, namely me."

Shea asked. "What happened to the original brain of the body you are now using?"

"It was incinerated. That was no great loss to civilization, since it was a brain of a relatively primitive, stupid type, who had left school for good as a child. But when these facts came out, sentimentalists raised such an ebullition that I was forced to give up my practice of brain transfer.

"In one respect, however, Vad Varo was never able to complete his task. The original body retained a battery of glands, whose functions affect even my superior brain. Therefore mundane urges and desires that I thought I had long since cast aside as mere irrational sentimentalism arise to plague me.

"In fact, I seem to be turning into the very sort of creature I most despised: an emotional, irrational sentimentalist. Why, finding myself recently in the company of two of Mors Kajak's handsome nubile daughters, I found to my horror that I developed a hearty erection. Since on Barsoom we do not conceal the parts in question by those ridiculous costumes that Jasoomians wear, and since the phenomenon in question is, on Barsoom, accounted the worst possible breach of good manners, I was forced to mutter an excuse and beat a hasty retreat.

"So then, you may ask, why do I not simply mingle with others of my class and form such attachments as my glands dictate, as other mortals do? The difficulty is that, having steered my course for centuries by the ideal of a purely rational, objective, emotionless scientist, I find that I cannot freely mingle with the rabble. To be blunt, they do not like me and, further to aggravate matters, most of them bore me.

"In forming their personal relationships, they make no allowance for my obvious mental superiority. If I join a group happily chattering away about trivial matters, they fall silent at my approach. If I seek a social engagement with one of the more promising rabblites, of either sex, the object of my wish for good fellowship makes transparent excuses: he or she is unwell, or has a previous engagement, or has just lost a close relative, or some such fribbling pretext. Nobody ever invites me to anything! Intellectually I know that lonesomeness is just one more irrational sentiment, forced upon me by the primitive glands of the stupid previous owner of this body. But that fact does not make the emotion any less painful."

Shea, grinning, said aside to Belphebe: "He reminds me of Edgar Poe."

"Who or what is Edgar Poe?" snapped Ras Thavas.

"A crow I once knew."

"What is a crow?"

"A large black Earthly bird, omnivorous and relatively intelligent. Edgar was found by a couple as a fledgling who had fallen out of its nest before it was airworthy. They took him home and fed him up, so that he grew into a big, handsome adult crow. Then the couple decided it was a shame to keep Edgar penned up indoors. They took him to a place they knew a flock of wild crows frequented and turned him loose.

"A fortnight later, one of them opened the back door. There was Edgar, taking the begging attitude, like this." Shea squatted, half spread his arms, and looked up with his mouth open. "He was bald, because all the feathers had been pecked off the crown of his head.

"What had happened was that Edgar, having lived among human beings through his formative years, thought of himself as human and tried to behave accordingly. He had never learned proper crow manners and etiquette; so the other crows of the flock he tried to join set upon him. In the end, the couple had to take him back, although they confessed that the full-grown Edgar in the house was something of a nuisance. Now, what am I supposed to do about your problem?"

"You shall take me in hand and teach me the little sleights and dodges and mannerisms of friendly social intercourse—the details your Edgar failed to learn about his fellow crows. For centuries I have avoided learning such details with the rabble, lest they waste time that were better spent on my research. In other words, you shall teach me how to get along with people, even mere rabblites."

"Jeepers!" cried Shea. "That would take a lot of doing. What makes you think an alien like me would know how to tinker with your mental works? You need a Dale Carnegie type."

"A what type? Never mind; my superior telepathic powers convey the sense of your meaning. As a professional psychologist—an occupation entirely lacking on Barsoom, save for my own limited forays into that field—you are the best-qualified person on this planet. Psychologically, we Barsoomians are very close to you Jasoomians. The difference you will in due course discover and make allowances for. Your being an alien is an advantage, since it enables you to view Barsoomian society and customs with a coldly objective eye."

Shea objected: "Meanwhile, what happens to our daughter Voglinda? I can't chase after Malambroso and at the same time give you a crash course in human relations."

"That is my condition," said Ras Thavas. "Teach me the skills I have set forth, and I will do what I can to further your search for your daughter. Otherwise I will do naught, and with your ignorance of this world you will probably encompass your own speedy destruction."

"Be reasonable! What you ask is as feasable as jumping out the window and flying by flapping my arms!"

"I am always reasonable. You have my condition."

"May I make a suggestion?" asked Belphebe.

"By all means, do," said Shea. "Whenever we get really stuck, I know I can count on you to pull a rabbit out of the hat."

"What is a rabbit?" asked Ras Thavas.

"A mere figure of speech; ignore," said Shea. "What's your suggestion, darling?"

"Why don't we bring Doctor Ras with us in searching for Voglinda? You can coach him daily in polite social intercourse and scold him when he makes a gaffe. If he be half as brilliant as he thinks he is, he would be a valuable guide in this alien world."

"Depends on where we're going." Shea turned to Ras. "So, will you now tell us where we are going?"

"Do you agree to the lady's scheme?" said Ras Thavas. "I hate to lose the research time; but the cold logic of my superior mind dictates that I agree to the lady's scheme. Do you also agree?"

"Yes, I do. If you will guide and help us to our objective, I'll do my best to make you over into a suave Barsoomian-of-the-world. I can't guarantee success in changing your habits, fixed by a thousand years of conditioning; but I'll do my best. So, where are they?"

Ras Thavas replied: "One of my informants in the city of Zodanga has reported that a man of alien aspect arrived from another world with a small child a day or two ago. From such details as I could elicit by wireless, the pair agree with your descriptions of Malambroso and Voglinda."

"Where is Zodanga?"

"About three thousand *haads* from here, in a roughly northeasterly direction."

Belphebe asked: "What's that in Earthly measurements?"

Shea replied: "I don't remember the exact conversion factor; but it's something like two thousand miles. The *haad* comes close to the kilometer."

"Quite a distance," said Belphebe.

"One must get used to great distances on Barsoom.

Although the planet is smaller than our Earth, the fact of having no oceans makes the land area over twice ours."

"Then how do we get there?" she asked. "Borrow one of their flying machines?"

"That would not be practicable," said Ras Thavas. "If any Heliumite were willing to lend or rent such a machine, he would certainly not do it to an alien of whom he knows naught."

"How much would one cost?" asked Shea. "New or secondhand?"

"A new flier to carry three would run about ten thousand crowns."

Shea exchanged looks with his wife. "I doubt if we brought anything like that with us. And I don't suppose they accept credit cards."

"What is a credit card?" asked Ras Thavas. "Never mind. Anyway, who should pilot the craft? The Heliums, who like to think of themselves as thoroughly up-to-date, have installed a newfangled system of licenses for piloting fliers, and rules to govern air traffic. I do not have a pilot's license, so one of you Sheas would have to obtain one. That calls for a course of instructions and passing a flight test and a written examination."

"Oh-oh!" said Shea. "Looks as if bureaucracy has caught up with Barsoom at last!"

"There are reasons," said Ras Thavas. "Lord Carter was persuaded to start a course at the local university on Earthly capitalism. His praises of the free-market system proved so popular that the Jed was prevailed upon to abolish the former restrictions on free enterprise.

"Soon, enterprising Heliumites set up factories to make fliers, cheap enough for ordinary folk to buy. Some of these machines were hastily built and killed their occupants. That was only one example of the shortcomings of capitalism, which transpired little by little. So now a powerful faction is urging more regulations, which Lord Carter furiously opposes, calling such interference in business un-American, whatever that means.

"In any case, the air over the Heliums became too crowded for safety, especially when some of the younger and more reckless males began doing acrobatic stunts with their fliers. Aerial collisions became a daily occurrence. The rain of machines and bodies on roofs and streets led the Jeddak, following Lord Carter's advice, to impose a strict system of licensing."

Belphebe asked: "Isn't there any public transport on Barsoom? Say, an airline?"

Ras Thavas chuckled. "One Heliumite last year essayed to start a regular passenger service by flier to Zodanga and Zor. But it foundered on one of the weaknesses of human nature."

"How so?" asked Shea.

"You know our Barsoomian custom, of always going armed, at least with sword and dagger if not with a pistol as well? That is how we distinguish free men from slaves by sight. Thus I, being unarmed at the moment, could be mistaken for a slave, were not my repute so high that no Heliumite, at least, would commit that error. The Jed's secretary, Dattok, is a slave. I forgo sword wearing in the Heliums because the cursed things are a nuisance, forever tripping me up or hitting me in the shins.

"Well, it did not take long for the lawless element to reason out a way to turn the airline fares to their advantage. Suppose a criminal wished to fly to, say, Horz, which is halfway round the planet. So he would buy a ticket to Zor, which was vastly cheaper. Then, when the flier had taken off, he would draw sword and pistol and command the pilot to take him to Horz. This led to aerial fights and fatal crashes.

"First, the capitalist who launched the scheme tried to disarm his passengers, demanding that all weapons— swords, daggers, pistols, and so on—be handed in to the gate guards. But you must understand that, for Barsoomians, the sword has a mystical prestige. To ask a free Barsoomian to surrender his sword is like asking him to become a slave.

"Hence fights broke out, with gate guards and would-be passengers slain. Hence the passengers dropped off, and his company went bankrupt by the end of last year."

"What happens to one who goes bankrupt here?"

"He is auctioned off as a slave to his creditors. Of the money paid for him, most goes to the government's tax collectors, while the remainder is divided amongst the unsuccessful creditors. I am sure that your home world, being technologically more advanced than we are, has long since mastered such problems."

"I fear not," said Shea. "Among certain classes of Jasoomians, the pistol has acquired something of the same mystical glorification that here applies to the sword. A few centuries ago, the sword on my world had much the same status. Wearing a sword proved that one belonged to the gentleman class. Now that the sword is obsolete as a military weapon, the pistol has somewhat taken its place psychologically."

Belphebe: "That's all very well, but then how do we get to Zodanga? You don't seem to have railroads or buses."

Ras Thavas said: "I fear we must either walk or ride on the backs of thoats. Do you two ride any riding animal?"

"Yes," she replied. "We are both experienced riders of a Jasoomian beast called a 'horse.' How long would it take to get to Zodanga on thoat-back?"

"Three thousand *haads* . . ." Ras Thavas frowned in thought, twitching his fingers to do sums. "With good beasts, assuming no accidents or hostile encounters, forty to fifty days."

Shea grunted and Belphebe groaned. Shea said: "Is there no way to get us there faster?"

"Not that I know of, unless Sir Harold can work his symbolic-logic spell to move us to another part of the planet."

"I fear that won't work, either," said Shea. "An attempt would probably snap us back to the planet we started from."

"Then," said Belphebe, "we must make the best of it. It

might even have advantages. Harold can work on Doctor Ras to make him into the perfect Barsoomian gentleman."

Ras Thavas made a face of disgust.

"Yes," said Shea. "And, Doctor, have you been eating regularly? You look starved."

Ras Thavas waved a dismissing hand. "My body keeps signaling that it wants more to eat; but I cannot afford the time away from my research to indulge its primitive lusts. Its previous owner was an athlete, and his body doubtless wishes to continue in the gluttonous habits it formed in its previous life."

"For our scheme," said Shea, "you must be in top physical trim. So be prepared to eat what and when I tell you to."

"The body I now wear," said Ras Thavas haughtily, "was the physically finest among the hundreds of specimens that have passed through my laboratories. In fact its previous owner, if weak in intellect, had a repute as a champion wrestler or something of the sort."

"It may have been a perfect body then," said Shea, "but I can see where you've let it run down. Too much crouching over lab tables, not enough food, and not enough exercise. Daily workouts will soon fix that! Then I must try you out on some sword practice, since Barsoomians have such romantic ideas about the glory of the sword."

Ras Thavas groaned.

III.

Harold Shea said: "Seems to me we've ridden far enough for one day. What do you think, darling?"

"I think you're right," said Belphebe, mentally

commanding her thoat to halt. Hitching her longbow up out of the way, she slid off the animal.

Shea dismounted with a grunt. "I fear we shall have some sore muscles tomorrow."

"We haven't done enough riding lately to keep in shape," said Belphebe. "It's not as if I hadn't reminded you."

"I know," said Shea. "But there's always a meeting at the damned Institute, or a stack of papers to grade. At least, with all those legs, these critters give a smoother ride than a horse."

Ras Thavas had more difficulty in halting his thoat. The animal trotted on for several thoat-lengths before he brought it under mental control and circled back to join the others.

"Accursed beast," he growled, dismounting. "How comes it that you two aliens manage to guide your beasts as well as native Barsoomians; whereas I, despite being Barsoomian-born and having the most highly developed brain on this planet, find it difficult to do so?" It was plain to see that Ras Thavas had gained weight, compared to the starveling savant whom the Sheas had first met.

"My guess," said Belphebe, "is that you take a purely intellectual approach to your beast, whereas Harold and I make friends of ours."

"Mean you that these dumb brutes are motivated by irrational emotions, like human Barsoomians of the lowest kind?"

"That's one way of putting it," said Shea, rounding up the eight thoats—two for baggage and three as spare riding animals—and staking them out. Spreading their eight spindly legs apiece, the thoats fell to grubbing up mouthfuls of the salmon-pink moss that covered most of the Barsoomian surface.

Ras Thavas growled: "It is wrong that I, the greatest mind on Barsoom, should have to truckle to the irrational whims of these animals."

"No doubt," said Shea. "It is also wrong that I, if I fell off a pier into deep water on my native Earth, should have to give a bad imitation of an aquatic animal to escape death by drowning. But that's the choice that would face me." He turned to Belphebe. "Target practice?"

Belphebe was setting up a tripod to support an archery target. "Absolutely, love. Without practice, you soon lose any skill."

Having dug the legs of the tripod into the moss, she walked from the tripod, counting her paces as she went, and strung her bow. She and Shea, like Ras Thavas, were entirely naked save for footgear and a few straps supporting pockets and, in Shea's case, a large purse, a longsword, a shortsword, and a pistol. Both Sheas had been stained all over with bright-red pigment to match the Barsoomians. Belphebe's red-gold hair had been dyed black, not only on her scalp but also wherever else it grew.

"Time for your workout, Doctor," said Shea to Ras Thavas. "We'll start with deep-knee bends."

Ras Thavas groaned, but Shea bullied him into calisthenics. At the end Shea, sweating freely, said:

"Now for a whack with the sticks."

From the pile of gear removed from one of the baggage thoats, Shea pulled out a pair of padded jackets, of wire face masks, and of wooden singlesticks with basket guards. Soon the dry clatter of the sticks resounded. Shea said:

"You're coming along, Doctor; much better than when we left Helium—*unh!*"

Ras Thavas had feinted a lunge and, when Shea parried in sixte, competently doubled and poked Shea in the solar plexus with the blunt end of the singlestick.

"Hey!" said Shea. "That was good!"

"No problem to one of my intellect," said Ras Thavas. "I simply listened to your instructions and applied them intelligently."

"Okay," said Shea. "But, as I've told you over and over, you'll have to get out of the habit of telling everyone who'll listen about your superior mind."

"It is a simple statement of fact!" protested Ras Thavas.

"No doubt; but to get along with your fellow mortals, you'll find it more effective to keep quiet about your marvelous intellect. Remember poor Edgar the crow!"

Ras Thavas chewed on this unwelcome advice. At last he asked: "What should I say?"

"Pass off the victory with a light laugh and say you were merely lucky."

"Rank hypocrisy!" snorted Ras Thavas.

"True; but hypocrisy is one of the factors, like liquor and religion, that enables mortals to put up with one another, at least when they form masses larger than primitive foraging bands."

"Foraging bands? Kindly explain."

Shea gave a summary of current Earthly theory of human prehistory, from the time when Australopithecines in Africa adopted erect posture and bipedal walking down to the rise of civilization.

"That is not at all our Barsoomian view," said Ras Thavas. "Know you the story of the Tree of Life?"

"I know of it. Not having done scientific investigation here on Barsoom, I won't say anything against it. But we have had similar traditional stories on Earth—the Garden of Eden, the Red Sea crossing, and so forth—which turned out to be mere myths and legends. To get back to our last subject, if one of these thoats—" Shea gestured toward the eight animals "—took a grudge against you, do you think it would do any good to lecture it on your mental superiority?"

"I suppose not," grumbled Ras Thavas. Then he looked past Shea with a widening gaze. "Behind you, Shea!"

Shea whirled. Stealing up on the fencers were half a dozen wild calots, the Barsoomian equivalent of a pack of wolves. Each had eight lean legs, bent so that the animals slithered along with their bellies brushing the moss. Their heads, which reminded Shea of those of Earthly bulldogs, had gaping jaws full of fangs, whence the animals drooled on the moss.

Shea's instant thought was for his weapons, which lay with his harness in the direction whence the calots were coming. In fact, the leader of the pack now stood over their gear, gave it a brief sniff, and resumed its stalk, leaving the fencers to face the pack with singlesticks. Over his shoulder, Shea called:

"Hey, sweetheart!"

As he did so, Ras Thavas threw his singlestick at the leading calot, turned, and ran. Instantly the calot bounded erect from its crouch and sprinted after the fugitive, detouring past Shea.

Having eight legs to Ras Thavas' two, the calot, Shea could see, would overtake the savant in seconds. The rest of the pack ran after their leader.

Shea dashed to the pile of equipment that he and Ras Thavas had dumped on the moss. As he did so, he heard the snap of Belphebe's bowstring. The leading calot doubled up with a howl. A second shaft laid it, writhing, on the pinkish-yellow moss.

Ras Thavas continued his flight. The five other calots hesitated at the sight of their leader's throes, then resumed the chase.

Shea straightened up with pistol in hand. Holding it in a two-handed grip, he fired it at the calot closest to the fleeing Ras Thavas; missed, and fired again. The animal collapsed, just after another of Belphebe's arrows struck another calot. The latter beast began to turn in circles, trying to reach the shaft in its flank with its jaws. Shea fired again, and the calot fell.

The three remaining members of the pack ran away. Breathing hard, Ras Thavas came slowly toward Shea, unfastening his padded jacket. Shea said:

"Well, you're a fine one to have as an ally in a tight fix!"

"On the contrary," said Ras Thavas, "it was obvious to my superior mind that singlesticks were inadequate weapons for coping with beasts of prey. That was all we had, thanks to your stupidity in leaving our swords and things out of reach."

For a few seconds, Shea struggled with a primitive lust to beat the shit out of this mastermind. When he finally got his rage under control, he said: "On the other hand, if you hadn't panicked and run, we might well have faced them down until my wife got her bow into action. Jasoomian predators hesitate to attack any prey animal who boldly faces them; but when one runs away, they go after it instantly. From what I've seen, it's the same for Barsoom."

"I did but follow the logical course," said the scientist. "I knew that I could not outrun the calots. But if I led them close by you, they might attack you instead of me, affording me a chance to escape."

Shea snorted: "Any normal Barsoomian would call that the act of a son of a calot."

"That merely shows the primitive mental state wherein most of them dwell. Any thinking person could see that, between the two of us, my mind is infinitely the more valuable to the planet."

"And you wonder why people don't like you!" roared Shea. Ras Thavas held up a hand.

"Please, let us not continue this bootless argument further. Had we known of the incident in advance, we could doubtless have planned a more generally satisfactory course of action.

"To go to a more agreeable subject, I note that you fired three shots from your alien pistol without reloading. This must be one of those repeating Jasoomian firearms whereof Carter and Paxton have told us. Our Barsoomian smiths have tried to make them, but they always jam. Our smithery is not yet accurate enough. Of course that

Earthman who wrote about life on Barsoom said many
things that are simply untrue, like the number of legs on
some animals, and repeating firearms that shoot a distance of eighty *haads*."

Shea took off his jacket. Belphebe walked past him,
saying: "I missed one shot; help me to find it. I don't
see anything around here that we could use to make
more, such as wetlands with stands of cane or reeds. I'd
have done better with that Turkish composite bow, but
I was afraid I hadn't had enough practice with it."

"Next time we make arrows," said Shea, "let's paint
the shafts a color that contrasts with that of the moss. It
may take *zodes* to find this one. And then we must cut
the others out of the calots you hit. I could use some
pistol practice, too."

She said: "There's just not enough time to practice all
the skills we might find useful. Oh, there's my shaft, half
buried in the moss."

Ras Thavas said; "You will find plenty of plants of the
sort you mentioned in the Great Toonolian Marsh. But
count yourselves lucky if the pursuit of Malambroso lead
you not thither. Do you mean to cook and eat the
dead calots?"

"If you consider them edible, and our little oil stove
works." As Shea puttered with culinary preparations, he
asked:

"Tell me something, Doctor. Barsoom, being the
fourth planet from its sun, corresponds in a general way
to a planet called Mars in my universe. Yet it differs
from Mars in a number of striking respects. Mars, in the
words of an Earthly friend, lacks enough air to keep an
insect alive.

"Now, you call your sun's third planet Jasoom, and it
corresponds more or less to the Earth in my universe.
My question is, how much like Earth is Jasoom? Carter
and Paxton both thought they were going to our Mars
and landed on Barsoom instead. On our Mars they would

have died of anoxia in a matter of minutes. What is the Jasoom of your universe like?"

"I do not know," said Ras Thavas. "It appears to be inhabited by a species somewhat like yours, Doctor Shea. But our means of communication are not yet perfected enough to enable me to say more."

Shea flashed a grin at Belphebe. "We must learn not to confuse Jasoom with our own Earth. Any time we get restless, darling, we can crank up the old syllogismobile and set it for Jasoom."

She replied: "You forget, sweetheart, we're *parents* now. We can't any more just dash off on adventures whenever the whim takes us!"

The trio, trailed by the extra thoats, trotted through the Zodangan suburbs along a road that became smoother and better maintained with each passing *haad*. Ras Thavas explained:

"The reason the houses all look so new is that they *are* new. When the city fell to besiegers in the jedship of Than Kosis, the Heliumites and their Thark allies destroyed most of the old city. But thanks to its natural advantages, it has been rebuilt and is now almost as populous as the old Zodanga."

"What are its natural advantages?" asked Shea, staring about at the monotonous, featureless, pinkish-yellow, moss-covered Barsoomian plain. "It has none that I can see."

"Why," said Ras Thavas, "it lies at the crossing of the road from the Heliums to Ptarth and Phundahl, and the road from Zor to Duhor."

"I see," said Shea.

"That attack on Zodanga," said Ras Thavas, "was one more example of the incorrigible stupidity of most of my fellow Barsoomians. Since the last big war, guns had evolved from smoothbores to rifled muskets, far more accurate. Yet Tars Tarkas repeatedly led his Tharks in massed mounted frontal attacks on the Zodangan defenses. Naturally they took tremendous losses, whence the Thark nation has not yet recovered."

"I recall similar events on Earth," said Shea. "Battles in places called Fredericksburg and Gettysburg."

Ras Thavas sighed. "You must tell me more about your Earthly history, since your people seem capable of quite as egregious stupidities as ours. Sometimes one wonders whether it be worthwhile to try to do anything for the future of this planet at least, since anything good one accomplishes will soon be undone by the stupidity and shortsighted selfishness of individual Barsoomians."

"The same can be said of Earth," said Shea. "And if the dominant species on Jasoom is similar, I daresay it could be said of that world also."

They came to the main wall of the city, where their badges, identifying them as subjects of Jed Mors Kajak of Lesser Helium, got them past the gate guards without questioning.

"That was easier than I expected," said Shea.

"We are fortunate that Lord Carter be not off on one of his lunes, such as trying to abolish assassination," said Ras Thavas. "If he were, you can be sure that Ur Jan, the elected Jed and head of the local assassins, would subject every Heliumite to minute examination ere admitting him, if he let him in at all. Inside, he would be followed night and day by the Jed's police agents. Vad Varo thinks that Barsoom needs a system of passports like that of his native world. Belike it does, but that would make travel even more difficult than it now is."

"How long does Ur Jan's term of office run?"

"According to the newfangled constitution, it should have ended some time ago. But Ur Jan pronounced the constitution null and void and declared himself supreme and absolute ruler. Since his followers had the power, no other Zodangans dared to object."

"Sounds like one of our more backward Earthly nations," said Shea. "Time for another charm lesson. I meet you in the morning and say: 'Good morning. How do you do?' Then what do you say?"

Ras Thavas grumbled: "I say 'Good morning,' too, even though it be plainly a terrible morning. As for 'How do you do?' I am sure that you would not wish a detailed account of all my symptoms—the toothache, the constipation, the sore toe joint, and so on. So what say I?"

"You say: 'Fine, and you?' "

"Oh, very well. 'Fine. And you?' though I no more want to hear a list of his symptoms than he does mine."

"What next?"

"I forget, Tell me!"

Shea: " 'How nice to see you!' "

"Rubbish! Hypocrisy! Most of the people whom I meet, I do not find at all nice. Those who do not display obvious faults of intellect or character tend to be insufferable bores."

"You must say it anyway. Go on, say it!"

Ras Thavas complied, with the expression of one who has unexpectedly bitten into something sour. "What then?"

" 'How well you are looking!' "

"Even if the fellow looks as if he were about to drop dead?"

"One must exercise discretion. If he really looks all in, you say: 'Can I help you?' "

"Oh, Issus! What if I care naught what befalls the wretch?"

"Make the offer anyway. Go on, say it!"

Ras Thavas groaned but complied. A few blocks further on, Shea said:

"That looks like a respectable eatery. What do you think, Doctor?"

"I am no judge of such matters," said Ras Thavas. "For centuries I have devoted my superior mind to the solution of more recondite scientific problems, paying no more heed to the demands of my animal body than I must to keep the mechanism efficiently functioning."

"No *bon vivant*, you," muttered Shea. Belphebe, dismounting, said: "I'll take a quick look inside and report."

When she came out, she said: "At least it looks passably clean. Come on!"

The eatery served in automat style. Machines proffered dishes to patrons, who collected them on trays as they passed. Belphebe was ahead of her two men in the line, and next before her was a burly red Barsoomian. After her came Shea and Ras Thavas. The latter murmured:

"Have a care with that hoodlum in front of us, Doctor Shea. His metal says that he is one of Ur Jan's personal guards, an old comrade from the assassins' guild."

Shea loosened his pistol in its holster. The assassin meanwhile moved so that his naked skin brushed lightly against that of Belphebe. When she turned a frowning face toward him, he muttered:

"Hey, you pretty spear-shaft! How about a little quick fucky-fucky? As you can see, I have the equipment!" He glanced down to where he displayed the physical symptom of lust for all to see, since Barsoomian costume made no attempt to conceal the private parts. Angrily, Belphebe spat:

"Begone, sir! I am an honest wife!"

"Is that so?" said the assassin, loosening his longsword in its scabbard. "Is one of those two behind you, wearing Heliumite metal, your husband? Tell me which, and I'll make you an instant widow. Then I'll show you some lovemaking, the like of which you have never enjoyed!"

Shea tapped the man's shoulder, at the same time bringing up his revolver. He grated: "Sir, I am the husband in question. If you bother us, I shall shoot you dead!"

"Shea!" cried Ras Thavas. "Put that pistol away! You know not what you do! To use a gun is a capital offense, even in self-defense! I will take care of this jackanapes, and you must not interfere! Stand clear! The code does not permit you to help me." Ras Thavas drew his own longsword, saying:

"Sir guardsman, anyone who confronts my friend here must answer to me. He is a foreigner who does not fully understand local customs, whereas you are a mannerless *ulsio*. Draw, scoundrel!"

The guardsman's sword came out with a *wheep*. Slaves rushed out from behind the food counters and shooed people away to clear a space. The guardsman roared:

"Lay on!"

Ras Thavas and the guardsman crossed blades. In an instant they were at it, *zip-whisht-clang!*

Shea watched uncertainly, torn between a natural urge to help Ras Thavas and the command laid upon him not to interfere. He expected the guardsman to make mincemeat of the scientist, whom he persisted in viewing as elderly despite his youthful body. But to his surprise, after a few short passages, Ras Thavas nailed his opponent with a coupé and lunge, driving his sword through the guardsman's beefy chest and out his back. The guardsman folded upon the floor.

Ras Thavas wiped his blade with a napkin that someone handed him and sheathed his sword. A couple of slaves picked up the corpse by wrists and ankles and bore it out, while another cleaned up a small puddle of blood with a mop. Another staff member chivvied people back into line at the serving tables.

Shea paid for their meals and said: "Doctor, I never expected to see you such a swashbuckler!"

"That was nothing," said Ras Thavas. "I have listened to your words and practiced with you at singlesticks, and I simply put my knowledge to use. Now, I trust, there will be no more aspersions on my courage!"

Evidently, thought Shea, his remarks about the incident of the pack of wild calots had rankled. Otherwise Ras Thavas might not have been so ready to take up Shea's quarrel with the guardsman. Shea was tempted to twit Ras Thevas on displaying a common human weakness, despite his profession of lofty superiority to such sentiments, but thought better of it. Instead he said:

"You certainly picked up fencing skill in record time. On Earth it takes years of practice to attain that level."

Ras Thavas smiled thinly. "I would attribute that accomplishment to my superior mind, did I not know that allusions thereto displease you. Let us assume that my youthful athlete's body retains some reflexes from its former life."

"What will be done about the guardsman's death? Shall we be arrested?"

"Naught, since he met it in a fair fight. I have committed no legal offense. But if you had fired that gun, we should all have been in deep trouble."

"Kindly explain. Why is it all right to puncture a man with a sword but illegal to do the same thing to him with a bullet?"

"That requires thought to make clear. For many centuries, slaves have been forbidden, for obvious reasons, to wear weapons. So a sword has, as it were, become the symbol of a free man—what one of you aliens would call a 'gentleman.'

"At the same time, the tradition grew up that, to prove his free manhood, a man must be prepared to defend his honor with his sword. So sword fights to the death, like that between me and the late guardsman, were accepted as the normal order of things. Of course, there is an element of luck in the outcome of such a duel; but at least most Barsoomians accepted the notion that such a fight was mainly decided by the skill of the fighters.

"Then, a few centuries ago, they invented guns. This obviously enlarged the rôle of luck in the outcome. Hence death by shooting was no longer deemed a 'fair fight' and was considered illegal. I do not personally consider these fine distinctions logically sound. To me, courage is an irrational sentiment, even though my glands may force me betimes to attempt to display it. But that is how things now stand on Barsoom."

"Seems to me," said Shea, "that Barsoom has a strong case of class rule here: a majority of slaves, bossed around and bullied by a minority of sword-wearing free men."

"True, O Shea. But from what I hear of Jasoomian— or perhaps I should say Earthly—social systems, all embody a similar distinction betwixt the ruling minority and the subject majority. Laws are passed and constitutions adopted to enlarge the power of the ruled majority over their own destinies; but the ruling minority somehow keeps a grip on power, whether they pass under the name of counts, colonels, capitalists, or commissars. It must be a tendency built into the species' makeup.

"If the ruled revolt and expel or exterminate the ruling class, almost instantly the more aggressive and energetic members of the ruled class form a new ruling class, lording it over the rest. In theory, a free man is not supposed to use his sword on a slave, since that is obviously unfair. But every day we hear of cases where a free Barsoomian lost his temper with a slave and sworded him to death."

"Is anything ever done to the swording bully?"

"Not unless the slave's owner takes offense at the loss of his servitor and challenges the slayer. The result of the duel, of course, depends on the strength and skill of the combatants—and, inevitably, on luck."

"So justice has nothing to do with it," said Shea, rising to leave the eatery. Belphebe and Ras Thavas followed him out. The scientist said:

"What is justice? An ideal, which everyone interprets to his own advantage. Methinks the hostelry we are now passing might furnish us and our beasts with suitable accommodations."

Belphebe said: "Darling, your telling me what sexual puritans the Barsoomians were was a little premature."

Shea sighed. "Live and learn."

The following morning, Shea and Ras Thavas had to wait at the entrance to the hostelry for Belphebe to appear from the women's half of the building. Ras Thavas pestered the clerk to draw him a map showing how to find the house where dwelt Mar Vas, his local informant.

"Turn right as you leave," said the clerk, "and at the third street on the right, turn right again. Number fourteen is the last house at the end of a long block on your left. You cannot miss it."

Shea muttered: "I've had people tell me before that I couldn't miss the place I was looking for, and gotten as thoroughly lost as ever."

Ras Thavas: "I hear that on Jasoom, the streets all have names or numbers, shown by signposts; and the houses are numbered in regular order, with number fifteen following number fourteen and so forth."

"I don't know about Jasoom," said Shea, "but that's how we do it on Earth. It makes places much easier to find."

"You would never get Barsoomians to agree. Why, if anyone could be tracked down from the name of his street and the number of his house, any assassin or enemy could find and kill him! That is the reason that the costlier houses can be raised on telescoping pillars at night."

"Since Jed Ur Jan," said Shea in a lowered voice, "is himself an old assassin, I should think he'd want to make things easier for assassins."

Ras Thavas smiled crookedly. "A Jed soon discovers that he cannot rely solely upon one small part of the populace for support, especially in a world as much given to homicide as Barsoom. A ruler can keep his subjects under control for a while by terrifying penalties. But if he makes himself disliked enough, sooner or later a subject—even a mere slave—will try to shoot or stab him."

Belphebe appeared. As she and Shea exchanged a morning embrace, Ras Thavas said: "Lady Belphebe, had I met you a thousand years ago, my life might have followed a different pattern. I have watched with admiration how you and Doctor Shea act in concert, supporting each other. Even though you squabble occasionally, you always present a united front against the outside world. And I believe the building across the street is the one whereto the clerk directed us."

The building in question was a rooming house, run by a red Barsoomian landlady with four slaves. She informed them that Mar Vas had gone out earlier and had not returned. He had left word, however, that if Doctor Ras Thavas came, he was to be shown to Mar Vas' room.

The room turned out to be used as a home laboratory, with tables here and there bearing unfamiliar pieces of equipment and a tangle of wires everywhere.

"You behold Mar Vas' experiments in wireless communication," said Ras Thavas. "Do you understand this apparatus?"

"I'm afraid not," said Shea. "On Earth they used to sell do-it-yourself kits for making such apparatus, but in my time they sold complete sets, contained in a single compact box, so big." Shea illustrated with gestures. "I never mastered that skill, unfortunately."

In answer to further questions, the landlady said: "I remember his saying something about visiting the Arms Fair."

"Where is that?" asked Shea.

"Go *that* way along the nearest cross street till you come to the public fountain, then turn right. . . ."

Another hour found them before a circus-sized tent, with swarms of Barsoomians going in and out. To one side of the entrance, a stand bore a spacious sign. Shea could not read the writing; for, while Barsoom spoke essentially one language, each nation had evolved its own system of writing. He appealed to Ras Thavas for a translation. The latter studied the sign for some seconds, then spoke:

"It says; 'Down with the Restrictionists! They seek to deprive us honest men of means of defending our lives, property, and honor. They would reduce all free Barsoomians to the status of sniveling slaves! Smite the cowardly scoundrels!' "

"What's that all about?" asked Shea. "Who are the Restrictionists?"

"They are members of a movement to restrict the right of free Barsoomians to go armed. Since a sword is a symbol of being a free man, any threat to take away a man's sword incites him to furious resistance."

"How about guns?"

"Meseems they have not got around to considering guns yet, since guns are a fairly new feature of Barsoomian personal armament. The gun was invented in my own lifetime and has not yet acquired the status in Barsoomian culture that the sword has. You have already learned that, if threatened with a sword, it is deemed a dreadful crime to defend oneself with a gun, which is thought a cowardly, unmanly weapon. But, because of its ability to slay at a distance, in some places the gun is inching its way into the status that the sword has long enjoyed."

"Will the Barsoomians get around to forbidding guns in private hands?"

"They may." Ras Thavas gave a cynical smile. "But even if they manage to stop all carrying of weapons, the only result will be an increase in population, until numbers are again limited by lack of food and water."

Shea frowned at the sign. "What's that squiggle down at the bottom?"

"That, my good Doctor Shea, is the colophon of the Arms Makers Guild, who paid for the sign. I would not be so misanthropic as to accuse the Guild of erecting the sign purely from selfish motives, to stimulate the arms business." The scientist snickered. "But you may judge that matter for yourself. Here, Shea, it is up to you to pay for our admission. The entrance fee is small. I trust that you changed enough of your Jasoomian—excuse me; I meant Earthian—gold pieces into local currency?"

Shea said: "I think we shall manage. The kind of man

you claim you would like to be would say: 'Oh, let me pay for all the admissions!' Then I would argue the matter, and you would gradually let yourself be talked out of paying."

"Meseems a silly business, making an offer that I do not intend to keep. What if you then said: 'Thank you, Doctor; that is generous of you!'?"

"You would pay with a good grace, not even looking sour at the prospect. That is how things are done among human beings."

Shea handed in the required number of elliptical coins. Inside, they found long aisles between rows of tables, on which arms displayed by dealers were set out in lavish quantities: swords, daggers, muskets, pistols, and less usual arms such as battle-axes, pikes, halberds, maces, and fauchards. Shea remarked:

"Doctor, one thing about Barsoom puzzles me. For folk who make such a fetish of combat with hand weapons, nobody gives a thought to armor, or even shields. On Earth, at one time the art of making armor was highly developed, so that a fighter could go into battle completely encased in steel, so cleverly made that he could move about almost as freely as he could without any armor."

"The matter has been discussed on Barsoom," said Ras Thavas. "For centuries, the general opinion among the sword-wearing class has been that wearing armor is an open admission of cowardice. Most Barsoomian warriors would rather die bravely than survive by means deemed unmanly."

"Seems a little extreme," said Shea. "We Earthians admire courage, too, but not to the point of suicide."

Ras Thavas chuckled. "I know what you mean. As the philosopher Kong Dusar said, any virtue carried to an extreme becomes a vice. But the actual reason for the Barsoomian disdain of armor—albeit Barsoomians are loath to admit it—is that before guns appeared, during the first century or two of my former life, our smiths were too unskilled to make practical suits of the sort you speak of. They would have so weighed down the warrior that he could not make full use of his limbs.

"Then came the gun, and to make armor bullet-proof it would have to be even thicker and heavier. So sword wearers, unable to obtain suits of practical armor, made a virtue of fighting naked."

Shea said: "Some Earthian peoples, like the ancient Greeks and Celts, went through similar stages. When their smiths learned how to make good, practical armor, the warriors put it on. On Earth, the gun had an effect somewhat like that on Barsoom; it caused the virtual abandonment of armor."

"Doctor Ras Thavas!" cried a voice in the crowd. It was the informant Mar Vas, whom Ras Thavas introduced to the Sheas. Shea was in the midst of asking after the whereabouts of Malambroso and Voglinda, when an infantile shriek of "Mummee! Daddee!" cut through the background noise.

Between them and the front entrance stood Doctor Malambroso, in his gold-embroidered purple robe conspicuous amid the throng of naked Barsoomians. On his head he wore an obviously Earthly Panama hat. In one hand he held the end of a leash, the other end of which was affixed to a harness securing the small body of three-year-old Voglinda Shea.

"Laws or no," snarled Shea, "I'm not taking chances with that guy." He drew his revolver.

As he did so, Malambroso's free hand came out from his robe bearing an egglike object, which he tossed on the ground between himself and the Sheas. Shea began:

"Your spells are no damned good here! So hands—"

"No magic!" shouted Malambroso. "Just an ordinary smoke—"

The egglike object burst with a loud *pop*, emitting a vast cloud of smoke, which filled the area around them. Shea plunged into the cloud, while behind him Belphebe cried:

"Harold! Where are you?"

"Here!" shouted Shea, coughing. "Try to reach the front entrance!"

Shea ran full-tilt into the ticket taker's booth, upsetting the stand. He groped his way out the front entrance, cursing a bruised knee. Behind him the ticket taker, cursing even more vehemently, struggled to right his stand.

As Shea emerged from the tent, he saw Malambroso, carrying Voglinda, leap into the first of a row of taxi-carriages at the curb, each harnessed to a single thoat. Malambroso shouted orders to the driver, who vaulted into the saddle of his thoat. Off went thoat, postillion, gig, magician, Shea infant, and all.

Shea and Belphebe reached the second carriage in the row just as the first disappeared at a gallop around a corner. To the second driver, Shea shouted:

"Did you hear where that one was going?"

"To the airport, sir," said the second driver.

"Then we're going to the airport, right away! Catch up with that other rig if you can!"

He and Belphebe piled into the cab. Ras Thavas, breathing hard from his dash from the tent entrance, squeezed in between them, making three on a seat designed for two. Luckily, all three passengers were lean rather than stout.

Leisurely, the driver swung into his thoat saddle, and the carriage pulled out. They wove this way and that, rounding corners until Shea felt totally lost. He called:

"Can't you go faster?"

The driver replied: "No, sir. There are three of you, and I shall have to charge extra for the load. But I will not kill poor Blossom when she has all she can do to move the vehicle!"

Shea sat fuming until they came to a broad field on which a score of slaves were at work, filling holes and raking the ground level. Off to one side, several Barsoo-

mian fliers were parked before a row of sheds, evidently
the local version of hangars. Shea asked:

"Does one need a pilot's license or a series of examina-
tions here?"

"Not to my knowledge," said Ras Thavas. "Zodanga is
still a citadel of rugged individualism, with all its advantages and disadvantages. If one has money, one can buy
or rent a flier and take off whenever one wishes."

"Then we'll get a flier. Doctor, I'll let you dicker over
the fare, and I'll repay you. Do they tip here, and if so
how much?"

"I can manage," said Ras Thavas, pointing. "There go
your magician and his captive now!"

Across the field, a boat-shaped, wingless Barsoomian
aircraft was taking off on a long slant, impelled by a
single airscrew in the stern. Shea groaned, saying:

"We could never catch up with that machine on thoats.
We must obtain our own flier!"

"Could we rent one?" asked Belphebe.

"I daresay." Ras Thavas addressed the driver: "Put us
down at the big central building!"

The driver obeyed. He and Ras Thavas settled the
fare, while Shea jogged into the building and sought out
the rental desk.

The man at the desk proved a stout Zodangan with an
aggreesively commercial manner: "... Are you sure you
do not wish to buy a ship, sir? I have several repossessed
craft in excellent shape, every one a steal at its present
price. One was used by a former Jed of Zodanga...."

"I do not wish to buy," said Shea. "As I said, what I
want is to rent a ship for three or four passengers, for a
few days."

"... But sir, our easy-payment plan calls for payments
hardly larger than our rental fees, and you end up owning
the ship." He spread out a sheet of Barsoomian paper
bearing sketches of fliers. "Now here's a fine little ship,
with seats for five and a stern gun for emergencies...."

"I won't buy," said Shea with emphasis, "but I do wish to rent."

"But consider, sir! This one was owned by a former *dwar* of the Jed's guard. . . ."

By shouting, Shea finally convinced the salesman that his sales pitch went to waste. At long last he signed papers making him the renter of a five-seater named the *Banth*. He paid most of his remaining cash as a deposit to insure the return of the craft. He also insisted upon a receipt.

"Do you know how to work everything?" asked the clerk.

Shea nodded toward Ras Thavas. "I shall rely on our friend here, since he owns the finest intellect on Barsoom."

Ras Thavas explained: "You rise by dropping ballast—those bags of sand tied along the sides. This instrument tells you your altitude."

"How do you come down again?" asked Shea.

"This lever releases some of the—" Ras Thavas used an unfamiliar word, which sounded to Shea like *refufupizaidi* "—which causes the ship to descend. Be careful not to release too much at once, or we shall crash, or at best not be able to rise again."

Shea inferred that the mysterious *refufupizaidi* was some sort of lifting agent, comparable to the hydrogen and helium gases used in Earthly balloons. Burroughs, no scientist, had called it the English Barsoomian Ray. Ras Thavas continued:

"This is the motor control. Turn it to the right and the propellor revolves, the further the faster."

"What's the source of its power?"

Ras Thavas gave a technical explanation full of words that Shea did not know. Shea got the impression that the source was analogous to an Earthly storage battery, with a much higher capacity in proportion to its weight.

"How do I steer?" asked Shea. "I see no rudder or ailerons."

"The stern post holding the propellor swivels," explained the savant. "You turn this wheel, so. Here is the compass. You can set the machine to fly on instruments and stop at a predetermined time. This is the airspeed indicator. These gauges tell you how the charge of *refufupizaidi* is doing."

"Tell me," said Shea to the clerk, who stood around. "Was that little ship that just took off one rented from you? It flew that way—" he pointed "—but it's now out of sight."

"Mean you that alien in the weird costume, with a tuft of hair on his chin?"

"Yes. Did he say where he was going?"

"Yes, sir. He said he was taking his granddaughter to visit her kinfolks in Toonol."

"Where can I get a map, showing the landmarks between here and Toonol?"

"There should be one in the side pocket, sir. Here you are!"

They climbed aboard. Shea studied the map as the clerk walked off, back toward the administration building. Shea said:

"Are we all ready, despite the fact that this is one of the most amateurish, ill-planned expeditions of my long experience?"

Ras Thavas: "You snap the fittings on the ends of these harness straps to these cleats."

"Like Earthly seat belts," said Shea. Belphebe had already fastened hers.

"Watch me," Shea said to Ras Thavas, "and correct me if you see me doing anything wrong. Here goes!"

He released the sand in one of the ballast bags and turned the wheel controlling the motor. The *Banth* rose slowly, and the airscrew began to revolve in its protective cage. When it dissolved into a blur to the sight, the *Banth* began to move horizontally.

IV

The airscrew purred in its cage behind the passengers, whose hair fluttered in the wind. Belphebe spoke to Ras Thavas:

"What surprises me, Doctor, is the ease with which we took off. On Earth you'd need a pilot's license, like those they demand in the Heliums; and you'd have to file a flight plan with the Federal Aviation Administration, and so on. More and more paperwork."

"Things have not yet got to that stage here," said Ras Thavas. "But there have been so many accidents lately—people getting lost in strange parts of the planet, pilots flying drunk, and fliers running into one another—that there is a move to impose similar rules all over Barsoom. Of course, the move meets fierce resistance from those who think it a natural right of any free Barsoomian who can get his hands on a flier to fly it whensoever and whithersoever he pleases. Besides, each city-state has its own ideas of the right rules and would resist with arms any attempt to impose upon it rules written elsewhere."

Belphebe asked Shea: "Are you doing all right, darling?"

"It's not difficult, compared to flying an Earthly airplane," said Shea. "It feels much like the blimp of which I was once allowed to take the controls for a few minutes. Presently I'll give you your turn at the controls."

Ras Thavas asked: "How goes your navigation, Doctor Shea?"

"All right so far," grunted Shea, whose attention flickered back and forth from the terrain below to the flier's compass and to the map spread out on his lap. He said:

"This Barsoomian landscape is notably shy of landmarks, compared to Earth. You have to figure out where you are by dead reckoning, or you don't figure it. Nearly as I can guess, it should take us about ten *zodes* to reach Ptarth, which lies almost halfway from Zodanga to Toonol. Then another day's flight should take us to Toonol.

"Doctor, would Ptarth be a safe place to land, to get a bite to eat and maybe spend the night? Or is it one of those xenophobic cities where they kill strangers on sight?"

"Safe enough for us," said Ras Thavas. "Just put the Heliumite badges back on your harness. Jed Thuvan Dinh is an old ally of the Heliums."

"Harold," said Belphebe, "I'm cold! Nudism is one thing on a beach in Florida but something else up in the Barsoomian atmosphere."

Shea rummaged through the lockers until he found a pile of blankets and handed one to each of the others. Belphebe asked:

"Is there any way to catch up with Malambroso before he reaches Toonol—if that be where he is going?"

"Since I don't know the top speed of Malambroso's flier," said Shea, "I have no way of telling. I've already turned our motor control all the way to 'fast.'"

"Then," she continued, "what is that little speck in the sky ahead? Now and then it winks at us, as if the sun reflected from metal."

Shea stared. "I can't see it, darling; but then, your eyes were always better than mine at long distances."

"Too bad we don't have some sort of telescope or field glasses," she said.

"Now that you mention it," growled Ras Thavas, "I have something that may help." From a container dangling from his harness he produced a small monocular telescope, which he pulled out to full length and put to one eye.

"It is indeed a flier," he said at last. At Shea's request he handed him the scope.

The vibration from the whirring airscrew made it hard to get a fix on the target, and the magnification was so high that the scope could cover only a narrow field. After tracking back and forth, Shea finally fixed upon the image of a flier, stern-to and looking no bigger than a gnat. Belphebe asked:

"Would Malambroso follow the same route as ours, passing near Ptarth?"

"Probably," replied Ras Thavas. "Ptarth is only a slight detour, and navigation charts assume that, on a flight from Zodanga to Toonol, all ships would fly to or near Ptarth. The same would apply to Phundahl, if the Phundahlians did not shoot down any foreign flier that enters what they consider their airspace. So we give Phundahl a wide detour."

"What would happen if we landed there?" asked Shea.

"They would ask us whither we were going, and if we said 'Phundahl' without exactly using the local pronunciation, they would cut off our heads."

"Hospitable people," said Belphebe. "What is the official pronunciation?"

"It is neither 'Fundahl' nor 'Pfundahl,' but something like 'Pwhundahl.' It takes practice to say it just right."

Belphebe said: "Then let's not stop at Phundahl."

"No argument there," said Shea. "Reminds me of one of those Balkan countries, where using the wrong dialect of the national language can get your throat cut." Peering through the telescope again, he said: "Maybe it's wishful thinking, but I do believe we are gaining on them."

"Let me have a look," said Belphebe. "I can't see that they're getting any closer."

"You wouldn't," said Shea, "with a difference in our

speeds of only a few *haads* per *zode*. Let's have a look at that bow gun."

"Harold! Even if we catch up with them, you wouldn't dare shoot for fear of hitting Voglinda, or causing them to crash."

"I suppose you're right," sighed Shea. "If we get close enough, perhaps we can pick off Malambroso, either me with my pistol or you with your bow."

"Assuming he doesn't snatch up our child as a shield!"

"What should I do if he does? Jump from the *Banth* to his flier, sword in hand?"

Ras Thavas said: "That were too risky to be practicable. You would probably fall to the ground below, and at this altitude that were fatal. If we get close enough for any such leaps, I am sure that, with our gun, we could disable their ship sufficiently to let us take it in tow."

"Unless," said Belphebe, "he's holding a knife to Voglinda's throat, threatening to kill her if we make a hostile move."

"Sentimentalists!" snorted Ras Thavas.

Shea: "I've warned you not to use that word, Doctor. If you want to make people hostile, just sneer at their profoundest feelings!"

"Sorry; I forgot," said Ras Thavas.

Belphebe said: "And suppose he throws a magical spell at us?"

"Wouldn't work here," said Shea, "same as on Earth."

"How about that cloud of smoke he used to cover his flight from the Arms Fair?"

"That was just a plain, nonmagical smoke grenade, such as they make on Earth."

For hours the *Banth* purred along, now and then rising or falling with thermal air currents, while its three passengers argued over strategies. Malambroso's flier became larger with agonizing slowness. To Shea's naked vision it grew from a speck the size of an insect to that of a small bird.

The small, brilliant Barsoomian sun was nearing the flat horizon when Ras Thavas, telescope to eye, said: "Methinks our quarry has seen us, Doctor Shea. He is turning his flier. He has a bow gun like ours, and he cannot shoot straight aft for fear of hitting his own propellor."

"I'll take a converging course," said Shea. "When we get closer, you might fire a couple of shots to throw his aim off. Be careful to miss him!"

"I am no gunner," said Ras Thavas. "The last time I fired one of these things was centuries ago, in my other body. Methinks it better than you give me the helm whilst you do the shooting."

"Maybe so. But how do you work these guns?"

"Pull this bolt handle back, opening the chamber. Place the projectile, here, in the chamber and push it forward. Place behind it this cartridge of propellant. Close the bolt, and you are ready to fire by pulling this lanyard."

Shea followed instructions. Ras Thavas said: "Try to cripple his propellor."

As the fliers came closer, Shea saw Malambroso climb out on his foredeck and swing his bow gun around. Shea aimed low and jerked the lanyard. *Boom!*

The gun discharged a vast cloud of smoke, which for an instant hid Malambroso's flier. While Shea did not know the composition of Barsoomian gunpowder, he saw that its effects were much like those of Earthly black powder.

Boom! A similar cloud erupted from the other flier's gun. There was no sound of a projectile striking the *Banth*, so Shea inferred that Malambroso, too, had missed. But, he thought, Malambroso might not have missed on purpose.

Shea tried to imagine what went on in Malambroso's mind. The wizard had started out by demanding Florimel and, finding Shea uncoöperative, had kidnapped the Sheas' daughter in a daft attempt to compel Shea's help in the matter. But if he slew both Sheas, then what good would his possession of Voglinda Shea do him? It would hardly advance his suit for the body and soul of Florimel, who very much had a mind of her own. Altogether, Malambroso evidently did not have a well-worked-out plan. Ras Thavas might be an exasperating egotist, but at least he was smarter than that.

"Clean out your cartridge chamber before reloading," said Ras Thavas, reaching into the flier's tool chest and handing Shea a rag. "Otherwise a spark might set off your next charge of propellant."

Shea was working away on his chamber, and the ships were circling closer, when there came another *Boom!* followed by a loud *clank*. The *Banth* shuddered.

"Propellor," said Ras Thavas.

Boom! The Banth lurched. Ran Thavas said: "Hull, methinks. He is turning away."

Shea took back to the helm, but now the *Banth* vibrated violently. When he turned the motor control back to "slow," the vibrations eased. The other flier diminished swiftly into the evening sky.

"Guess we stop at Ptarth willy-nilly," said Shea. He brought the propellor to a halt. "How much damage, Doctor?"

"We shall have to get it repaired," said Ras Thavas, "before proceeding. One blade is badly bent."

"How about that hit on our hull?"

"Just a *sofad* whilst I look."

Ras Thavas shifted the ends of his safety straps to cleats on the sides of the hull. Then he climbed over the rail and lowered himself headfirst toward the keel. When he came back up, his naturally red face was further incarnadined by a suffusion of blood. Shea could not avoid a twinge of admiration for the scientist's courage. He, Shea, could not have undertaken such a human-fly stunt so casually.

"It looks like a mere graze, a glancing blow," said Ras Thavas. "Let us hope it did no damage to the interior."

"Damn, damn," said Shea.

"Be not too disturbed, Doctor Shea," said Ras Thavas. "It was luck that enabled Malambroso to fire three shots without cleaning his chamber between shots and without blowing up his flier, himself, and your infant. Perhaps luck will be on our side next time, though I am not so childish as to think that bad luck one time assures good the next."

Below, a shadow of night swept across the flat landscape toward the sinking sun. Soon the last bit of sun winked out, and darkness sharply fell. Stars blinked in. The moon Thuria was not in sight; Cluros was visible but no brighter than Venus appears at its maximum on Earth. Belphebe said:

"I see a distant patch of light off our port bow. Would that be Ptarth?"

"Bless your eyesight, darling," said Shea. "The map shows Ptarth in that direction."

Belphebe said: "Didn't Jed Mors Kajak tell us John Carter was off visiting the Jed of Ptarth? Why shouldn't we look him up? He might be glad to see an Earthian couple and lend his help against Malambroso. From what I've heard, he throws a lot of weight on Barsoom."

Shea thought before shaking his head. "I think not, darling. Malambroso could use the time to get far ahead of us. My guess is that the time is more precious to us right now than even the help of the great John Carter."

At the following sunrise, the *Banth* took off from Ptarth with Shea at the controls. He studied the map and set the course for Toonol.

"Aside from padding our hotel bill with a charge for wine we never drank," said Shea, "and overcharging us for straightening our bent propellor, the Ptarthians treated us nicely enough."

"Be fair, darling," said Belphebe. "They worked through the night on the propellor, and you know any

Earthly machine shop would charge overtime rates for that."

"True," said Shea, who then had to explain to Ras Thavas what he meant by "padding a hotel bill." "Do you think I am giving Phundahl a wide enough miss, Doctor?"

Ras Thavas looked at the chart. "Yes, I believe you have. A fellow named Fal Sivas in Zodanga is, I hear, working on a system for mental control of a flier. It were handy to whisk us out of danger if the Phundahlians should attack us in the air.

"This Fal Sivas, I am told, thinks all too well of himself. He goes about calling himself the Master Mind of Barsoom, when it is obvious that he is no such thing. If anyone deserves that title, it is I, not he.... Oop, sorry, Doctor Shea. I forgot again."

Shea grinned. "You're learning, old boy. With half a year of my training, you'd be so polite and tactful that Helium could use you as ambassador to negotiate sensitive issues."

"They tried that once," said Ras Thavas sadly. "They sent me with a delegation to Manator. But something I said so enraged the Jed there we almost had a war, although Manator is halfway round Barsoom from the Heliums."

The day passed uneventfully, save for the sight of a column of the nomadic green men of Barsoom, each with four arms and twice the stature of a red Barsoomian, crossing the yellow-pink, moss-covered plain below. One green man wheeled his oversized thoat, pulled a musket from a boot in his saddle, and fired upward at the *Banth*, with a cloud of smoke. A projectile whistled past.

Shea hauled the *Banth* into a turn and pulled the rope releasing sand from one of the bags of ballast. Below, the green warrior was reloading. Shea growled:

"I'm tempted to shoot back, to teach the bastard not

to take pot shots at harmless travelers just for the hell
of it. But I guess that wouldn't be smart under the circs."

Ras Thavas said: "I am happy to see that some members of your species, at least, can overcome their animal urges."

By the time the green warrior raised the gun to his
shoulder again, the *Banth* was out of range. Shea said:

"Doctor, I don't like the way the ship behaves. We
ought to have risen faster."

Ras Thavas said: "It is possible that the shot that struck
our hull has caused a small leak in one of the buoyancy tanks."

"We must watch our altitude," grumbled Shea, plotting
the course to Toonol again.

A glance over the side showed that they were entering
a widespread marshland, stretching to the horizon.
Below, small streams and lakes were interspersed with
patches of solid vegetation. Shea said:

"Looks like Barsoom's last wetland." Then he had to
explain the term "wetland." "Time was," he said, "when
it was considered the right, natural thing for any Earther
to kill any wild animal he came upon, and to drain and
ditch wetlands to turn them into farmland. But lately,
people have begun to see that wetlands have their essential function, too. Get rid of them and you'll be sorry."

"I understand," said Ras Thavas. "A few Barsoomians
have tried to agitate similar proposals to conserve natural
features. But so far the masses have taken the view that
these are mere busybodies seeking excuses to meddle in
others' affairs and to deprive them of their normal means
of making their livings. One might think that the length
of Barsoomian lives would lead the rabble to take a long
view, extending over centuries or millennia. But most
find a year as far ahead as they can or are willing to
think."

"Sounds like Earth," said Shea.

"How is your altitude holding, Doctor?" asked Ras Thavas.

"Losing, little by little. I don't like to empty our last bags of ballast, because that would leave us without vertical control."

"I can see that we are flying lower and lower," said Ras Thavas. "Perhaps we had better alight on the first good landing spot we find, rather than wait for the loss of *refufupizaidi* to bring us down on a spot not of our choosing."

"Sound thinking," said Shea.

"What else would you expect, from one of my superior intel—Sorry; there I go again." With a shamefaced grin, Ras Thavas got out his telescope and scanned the marshland below and ahead of them. "Methinks I see a patch flat enough, dry enough, and sufficiently unencumbered by plant life to serve our needs. About ten degrees to port, Doctor."

The *Banth* came down to a quiet landing on a patch of soil overgrown with the yellow-pink moss instead of the ubiquitous shrubs, trees, and swamp plants. Shea said:

"I don't think it's practical to try to walk to Toonol."

Belphebe said: "The understatement of the year, darling. Is there any chance you could find and repair the leak? You were always pretty fast with the wrench and the soldering iron with our car."

Scrutinizing the hull, Ras Thavas said: "I cannot see any holes in the tanks. But then, we should have to take the whole ship apart to find a mere pinhole, and all the remaining *refufupizaidi* would escape. Have we any lift left?"

Shea worked the controls. "I think there's a little; but not enough to raise us off the ground. So we might as well manhandle the *Banth* into the water. If the hull leaks, we can use those mugs we brought along for lunch to bail it out."

Belphebe: "Can this flier float?"

"It should," said Ras Thavas. "When, following discovery of the *refufupizaidi*, these machines were first devised, their design followed that of the smaller water craft, since remnants of Barsoom's oceans still existed. That was before my time. So fliers still look something like boats. Propose you to attempt the rest of our journey by water?"

"We can try," said Shea. "Even if the swamp watercourses wriggle like worms on a hook, I think I can figure out a route from this map."

"What are 'worms on a hook'?" inquired Ras Thavas.

Shea explained, adding: "What worries me more right now is how we shall ever get this contraption back to Lesser Helium, to recover our deposit. It took most of our liquid funds."

"I may be able to tide you over," said Ras Thavas.

"What, you?" said Shea in mock astonishment. "You being altruistic?"

Ras Thavas looked embarrassed. "I try to benefit from your pronouncements, Doctor. Since we are all in this together, it is the logical course to follow. And I am sure that we shall be able to have the ship repaired in Toonol."

"All right," said Shea, taking a grip on the stern of the *Banth*. "Let's see how that fine new body Vad Varo gave you works with loads. Take the bow, and grab the end of the painter."

"Grab what? Oh, you mean the rope at the bow. I fear my Barsoomian thews are not the equivalent of yours, since my body—either this one or its predecessor—lacked the advantage of growing up on a high-gravity planet. On your own world, are you classed as a man of exceptional strength?"

"Not at all," said Shea. "If anything, I rate as a rather skinny fellow."

"Fortunately for me," said Ras Thavas, "my superior

brain has made it unnecessary to develop musculature above that which I inherited, and the habits that I formed in the thousand years of my former life have remained with me. At least, in the *Banth*, you will not be able to force calisthenics upon me!"

With final grunts, they slid the ship into the stagnant water. Shea seized the painter, and the three boarded the craft, which rocked a little. Shea coiled the painter, studied his map, and bent to turn on the motor. The airscrew revolved in its case, slowly at first, then faster until it became a blur to the sight. Shea said:

"Doctor, please get up on the forward deck to watch for snags and shallows, so you can warn me off them."

"Can't we go faster?" said Belphebe.

"I don't dare, lest we run into an obstacle. So I have set the motor control to 'medium.' "

For hours, Shea navigated the flier cautiously through the countless creeks and sloughs of the Toonolian Marsh. In the bow, Ras Thavas called back warnings of snags and shallows. Once a half-submerged log turned out to be an animal of the crocodilian kind.

"I sure don't want to run into *him*," said Shea. "He might take it into his little reptilian brain to come aboard."

"Harold!" cried Belphebe. "Look at that thing over-head! We're going to pass right under it." She bent her efforts to stringing her bow.

"Where?" said Shea. "Oh, that! Looks like a tough customer. How about it, Doctor?"

"If you leave it alone, it will probably extend the same courtesy to you," said the savant.

The creature in question looked something like a man-sized lizard with six legs, each leg ending in formidable hooked claws. It was perched on a branch of a large tree that grew out of the water in midchannel. Belphebe shrieked:

"Watch out, Harold!"

Shea's attention had been distracted long enough for the *Banth* to run head-on into the tree. Ras Thavas slid off the bow into the muddy water. The tree shuddered, and the Barsoomian swamp lizard fell from its branch to land on the engine compartment of the flier, forward of the seat in which Shea sat handling the controls. Belphebe had occupied the other seat, but she had risen to string her bow. She seized one of the safety cleats to steady herself.

In falling off the bow, Ras Thavas had quick-wittedly grabbed the painter. He had scarcely emerged from the water when he began hauling himself up on the bow again.

"Don't shoot!" cried Belphebe, who had nocked an arrow but not drawn it. "If you missed, you'd hit Ras Thavas!"

Shea, trading stares with the swamp reptile at arm's length, returned his pistol to its holster and instead drew his short sword, saying:

"At such close quarters, I'd prefer this."

The reptile hissed and yawned, showing formidable fangs. Further forward, Ras Thavas called:

"Let it alone, Shea! I have it under control."

Shea could not see what sort of control the savant had over the swamp reptile. But after a few more seconds, the animal turned and dove over the side. It swam away with serpentine sweeps of its tail.

"How did you do that, Doctor?" asked Shea.

"All higher forms of Barsoomian life are more or less telepathic," said Ras Thavas. "I simply exerted my superior mental powers, and chide me not for referring to those powers. Without them, you and your lady might have sustained fatal wounds. These animals are difficult to kill. Is there a towel aboard, to wipe off this muck?"

Shea hunted through the lockers until he found a piece of suitable cloth. He said:

"At least, on Earth you'd be covered with clothes,

which would have to be washed before you wore them again."

"Perhaps you can explain this curious Earthian custom of covering oneself with textiles, even when the air is warm enough not to need them."

Shea sighed. "Some of the leading religions insist upon it. I suppose it goes back to primitive times, when our brutish ancestors, up to then as naked as you Barsoomians, first migrated out of Africa, a hot continent, to colder climes. . . ."

Shea was well into a lecture on the anthropological explanation of the nudity tabu prevalent in Judaism and its two offshoot religions, Christianity and Islam, when something flew past with a loud buzz. Ras Thavas uttered a shrill scream and threw himself down on the floorboards.

The flying organism whirled about in a circle and returned. Belphebe cried out and slapped at it. "It tried to sting me!"

"Keep it away from me!" shrilled Ras Thavas, cowering in the bottom of the flier.

Shea started to reach for his revolver, then changed his mind and drew his short sword. When he got a good look at the flying organism, he saw something resembling an Earthly hornet, but several times as large, with a length the span of his hand and a wingspread the length of Shea's foot.

"There's another!" yelled Ras Thavas. "Save me, Doctor Shea!"

The first intruder hovered, rising and falling with a bouncing motion. Shea swung his short sword. His blade struck the flier with a click and sent its body whirling away in two pieces. The second pseudo-hornet instantly swooped down and stung Shea in his right buttock.

Shea jumped with an angry yell and, with a backhand slash, slew this attacker also. A third buzzed up and was likewise bisected by Shea's blade.

"We must be near a nest!" wailed Ras Thavas. "Speed

up the motor! The smell of dead *stiths* will fetch more of them!"

Shea stuck the point of his short sword into the floorboards, leaving it standing upright and gently rocking back and forth. He advanced the motor control, and the *Banth* surged forward. Another *stith* circled the *Banth* and swooped toward its passengers, but it tried to fly through the propellor and was hurled away in pieces.

"Are they all gone?" quavered Ras Thavas.

"Seem to be," grunted Shea, running a hand over his swollen fundament. "Get up, Doctor; you're not hurt. I'm the one with a sore arse, who'll have to eat standing up for a while."

"I—I am sorry that you should behold me in such contemptible shape," said Ras Thavas. "It is my only weakness."

"You mean a phobia about creeping things?"

"Yes, I am shamed to say. The mere sight of even a harmless one sends me into a panic. I trust you will not regale the other Barsoomians, as a great joke, with the tale of the downfall of the mighty Ras Thavas."

"The story is safe with me," said Shea. "In my trade as psychologist, I come upon all sorts of phobias. Some I can cure, at least in my own species. Do you know how you came to have this phobia?"

"I have a vague notion that a *stith* must have stung me as a child. But it would have happened a thousand years ago, and I have no clear memory of the incident. Could you cure me?"

"Doubt if I had a chance to try, Doctor. It would take many days of conditioning."

"How would you do it?"

"By gradually habituating you to the sight of such a bug, let's say starting with a picture of one, then a mounted dead one, and so on, until you could handle a live one without a shudder."

"I must try such a cure on myself," mumbled Ras Thavas. "It were painful but better than the risk of

making a fool of myself in public." The savant cracked a
wintry smile. "At least, you can tell the folk back on your
Earth that the *stith* does not grow to the size of a thoat,
as that writer would have his readers believe."

"They couldn't," said Shea, "because of having to have
soft bodies during times of growth. That doesn't work
when you wear your skeleton on the outside. There are
also difficulties with increases in size in getting enough
oxygen to the muscles. . . ."

v

Vantos Vaz, the Chief Constable of Toonol, said: "Yes,
yes, Doctor Shea. I understand that you are an alien on
this world. But I must put you down on this form as of
a place on this world, not some other. Nobody's identifi-
cation is complete without it."

"All right," said Shea. "Call me Sir Harold Shea of
Zodanga; that's where we were a few nights ago. I could
say 'of Ptarth,' but I think Zodanga has a prettier name.
Now, how about our fugitive wizard and our daughter?"

"Yes, Doctor Shea, such a person did arrive in Toonol
a few days past. A tall, gray-bearded man of alien aspect,
with a light-tan skin, wrapped in a robe ornamented with
golden thread. He insists on retaining this robe, as if
Toonol were in the polar regions. He had with him an
unmistakable alien child with yellow hair, whom he kept
under control by means of a harness and leash. I must
get such an apparatus for my wife, to control our own
hatchlings. Why do you wish to know?"

Shea told of Malambroso's abduction of Voglinda. Ras
Thavas added:

"I have been traveling with Doctor and Mrs. Shea and have found them persons of exceptional faithworthyness."

The Chief Constable sighed. "If the world-famous Ras Thavas says it is so, it must be so. Mean you to slay this Malambroso person? I warn you, homicides are not permitted save in accordance with the code and through the licensed guild of assassins."

"No," said Shea. "While Malambroso's demise would not cause me inconsolable grief, our main objective is to get our daughter back, unharmed. All else is secondary."

Belphebe added: "If Malambroso would just go away and leave us alone, we should be satisfied. Where is the scoundrel now?"

"According to the last report from the officer assigned to watch him," said Vantos Vaz, "he and the little girl have put up at the Purple Apt. Were you going thither forthwith?"

"Not quite, sir," said Shea. "First we must make arrangements for the repair of our flier. Who gives first-class service in such matters, at reasonable prices?"

Vantos Vaz suggested a repair shop, adding: "Do not be surprised if I assign a man to watch you. Since a confrontation is likely betwixt you and this off-world magician, we must make sure that any slaying is done in accordance with the law. Undermanned as we are, we find it hard to make all killers follow the code. Had you a difficult trip through the Toonolian Marsh?"

"Not too hard," replied Shea, "except that we ran out of food and starved, although we killed and tried to cook a swamp lizard. We've been eating like pigs since we arrived to make up."

"What is a pig?" asked the Chief Constable.

Ras Thavas, Shea, and Belphebe returned to Van Larik's Inn after a fatiguing morning of hunting down the machine shop recommended and then waiting while the mechanics disassembled the *Banth* and examined the buoyancy tanks for signs of a leak.

Shea opened the door to his room and stepped aside to let Belphebe enter. He and Ras Thavas followed her in, when a sound caused all three to whirl.

For a closet, the room had a simple conservatory consisting of a rail curving out from the wall and back to the wall again. From this rail hung a curtain. Now the curtain had been thrust back on its curtain rings, revealing Malambroso in a purple robe, Voglinda in her harness, and a naked red Barsoomian in his caparison of straps and sheaths, longsword in hand. Malambroso trained on the Sheas a large black automatic pistol of a common Earthly make.

"Well!" grated Malambroso. "It seems that I am destined to encounter Doctor Sir Harold again! Reach not for your pistol, Doctor Shea. If you do, I shall shoot you dead. Or better yet . . ." Malambroso trained his gun on Voglinda. "Force me not to end the life of this winsome young lady. I have become quite fond of her in the short time that we have been traveling companions. Would you believe it, last night we stopped at a place where an orchestra was playing and couples were dancing. Voglinda insisted that I take her out on the dance floor, too. Imagine me, at my age, wheeling this tot around on the floor!

"I see that you and your wife, Doctor Shea, have adopted the local costume, or lack thereof. Thank Lucifer, I at least retain a civilized sense of decency, even though my robe causes the natives to stare!"

"And who, then, is the Barsoomian?" asked Shea. "I don't believe I have had the pleasure of meeting him."

"The pleasure, I am certain, will prove ephemeral," said Malambroso. "Know that this is the honorable Spor Mopus, a leading light of the local assassins' guild. He has come with me to kill you. Lady Belphebe, think not to string your bow, or you shall suffer the same fate as Doctor Shea."

"Now why," said Shea, "should the honorable Spor Mopus wish to kill me? I am too lean to make good eating."

"He will slay you because I have hired him to do so. But he insists that the killing must be done in accordance with the highest ethical principles. He will not even let me shoot you, unless you draw a gun on me first. It must be done with honest face-to-face swordplay. If you will kindly draw your sword, he will set out upon his task."

The red Barsoomian stepped forward, bringing his sword up to guard position.

"This is childish nonsense," grumbled Ras Thavas. "So is all the elaborate politeness betwixt you twain."

"Since," said Spor Mopus, "you disdain our ancient and honorable principles, I shall tend to you after I have finished off this alien. Have at you, Doctor Shea!"

The Barsoomian threw himself into a lunge that would have spitted Shea had he not, almost unconsciously, drawn his saber and parried. In an instant the twain were at it, *tzing, zip, clang!*

Shea found Spor Mopus good but not superlative. Unless he made a stupid mistake, Shea thought, he should be able to handle this assassin. Still, there was an element of luck in these encounters, and what right had he to leave Voglinda fatherless, assuming they rescued her from Malambroso?

Back and forth they went: double, one-two, beat, and coupé. Spor Mopus was only so-so on attack but very good on defense; Shea could not penetrate his guard. Shea began to fear that Spor Mopus would keep him in play until fatigue laid him open to attack. *Tzingg!*

Suddenly, Spor Mopus backed up and lowered his point, crying: "That is not fair! It is unethical, to bring a squad of supporters with you. Withdraw them, or I shall refuse to continue the fight!"

"What on Earth?" murmured Shea.

Spor Mopus sheathed his sword and stamped out the open door. At that instant, Belphebe's bow twanged. While Malambroso's eyes had been fixed on the combatants, she had stepped aside and quietly strung her bow. The arrow pierced Malambroso's body. Malambroso swung toward her, striving to bring the big pistol up to bear. The bow twanged again. Malambroso dropped his pistol, which struck the floor with a bright yellow flash and a deafening *boom*. The magician folded up, joint by joint, on the matting. Ras Thavas moved quickly to kneel over the wounded magician.

"Mummee!" screamed Voglinda, running to Belphebe.

"How did you do that?" Shea asked the scientist.

Ras Thavas looked up. "My mental superiority, that is all. I have told you that all the higher Barsoomian organisms are somewhat telepathic. I simply forced Spor Mopus and Malambroso to see, not one sword-wielding Shea, but six, all advancing upon them at once. Now, let us see about this fellow. He will soon be dead if I cannot render aid."

The innkeeper appeared at the door. "What goes on here? Did I not hear a gunshot?"

"You did," said Shea. "but it was an accidental discharge, when the magician dropped his pistol."

"Find a stretcher and a pair of slaves to carry it," snapped Ras Thavas, "and get this man to a lazaret!"

"Why try to save him?" asked Shea.

"Because I once swore an oath to John Carter himself," barked Ras Thavas, "that I would thenceforth try to help those who needed it. Besides, if he dies of the lady's arrows, you would be in trouble with the law, since he did not perish in a proper, legal sword duel.

"I know that he deserves to be let die, but my oath had no such qualifications. Ah, here come Master Van Larik with a stretcher and a pair of slaves. Be careful, boys. Slide him over; do not attempt to roll him!"

A man wearing the badges of the constabulary appeared, panting for breath. He said: "Is the fight already over? Was it conducted in proper accord with the laws on homicide? I must make out a report."

Ras Thavas assured the constable that all had been done in accordance with the code, and the cop went away satisfied.

* * *

Several days later, Shea and Belphebe, with little Voglinda in tow, visited the lazaret. They found Ras Thavas sitting by Malambroso's bed. On the other side stood a plump red Barsoomian nurse. Shea said:

"Doctor, the shop assures me that the *Banth* will be airworthy again tomorrow, with the buoyancy tanks full. From what I saw, I think they are right. Are you ready to go with us?"

"My patient is virtually ready for his discharge today," said Ras Thavas. "By tomorrow I am sure it will be safe for me to leave him."

"Either of those arrows ought to have killed him," said Belphebe. "Unless you Barsoomians are tougher than most civilized species."

"Either would probably have proved fatal," said Ras Thavas, "had my patient not had the luck to fall into the hands of the greatest physician and surgeon on Barsoom."

Shea cleared his throat meaningfully, at which Ras Thavas looked embarrassed. Shea said:

"But I can't go off leaving him loose so long as he pursues that crackpot idea of taking my colleague Chalmers' wife away from him."

"I do not think you need worry on that score," said Ras Thavas. "How about it, Doctor Malambroso?"

"Oh," said the magician in a weak voice, "I now have completely different plans." He rolled an eye at the Barsoomian nurse, who tittered.

"Yes," he said, "I have at last discovered true love. My attachment to Lady Chalmers was just a passing fancy, an infatuation. My affianced bride, here, is Mordalia, the widow of Jan Valos, who was slain last year in one of those ridiculous duels. She has promised to accompany me whithersoever I go. If you see Lady Chalmers, present her my respects and assure her that she has naught to fear from me."

"Daddee," said Voglinda, "when are we going home?"

"As soon as I can arrange it," said Shea. "Widow Mordalia, I am happy to have met you and wish you luck." He silently added, you'll need it!

"May our departure be soon," said Belphebe. "My hair's beginning to show its natural color at the roots. I should soon need another dye job."

Ras Thavas said: "Are you flying back to Zodanga? If so, I am going with you."

From his bed, Malambroso said: "Could you not save some time by working your sorites here and going directly back to Earth?"

Shea grinned. "No. I must return the *Banth* to its owners and get our deposit back. Also, we left eight riding thoats there, which I shall want to resell. Besides, we left our Earthside clothes in Zodanga. Can you imagine the sensation if Belphebe and I, nude as we are, materialized on the grounds of the Garaden Institute? We shall have to get used to clothes again, dear."

"They'll seem unnatural for a while," said Belphebe.

"Also," said Ras Thavas, "you promised me another lesson in making friends and influencing people. I have tried out your principles and have been agreeably surprised to find that they actually work. Why, even Malambroso here—whose ethics, I fear, are not up to Barsoomian standards—seems to like me. So let us get to it forthwith!"

Part IV
HAROLD SHEAKSPEARE

TOM WHAM

I

"Well, Doc, I'm ready for your lecture!" Vaclav Polacek said as he strolled into the room. "If I'm gonna be coming and going between parallel universes, I gotta bone up to be a good magician."

"It would help a lot, Votsy, if you could do something besides turn yourself into a werewolf every time there's trouble," Harold Shea muttered as he shifted in his chair.

"Gentlemen," interrupted the bushy-haired man behind the desk. "I'm in full agreement with Vaclav. It wouldn't hurt any of us to study the principles of 'magic' for they are, in reality, the physics of other universes. In my long stay in Faerie and the abortive trip to the *Furioso*, I believe I finally have a grasp of the measurable qualities of the fourth, fifth, and sixth dimensions. So, beginning tomorrow at this time, we shall commence daily discussions on the subject. There must be more method to our madness."

The man speaking was Reed Chalmers, once the director of the psychologists at the Garaden Institute, now in charge of the hush-hush, "Interplanar Project." He had recently returned from a rather protracted stay in several different, parallel universes. Gathered around him were the new director, Walter Bayard, and two psychologists, the outspoken Vaclav Polacek and Harold Shea. The fifth

213

man in the room was the most unlikely member of the group, a police sergeant named Pete Brodsky.

"As you know," Chalmers continued, "ever since Harold here, proved that our—uh—'syllogismobile' actually works, we've been involved in a series of willy-nilly chases from one universe to another, often narrowly escaping with our lives."

"I can't say that I found my stay in Xanadu either unpleasant or dangerous," added a sleepy-eyed Bayard. "Boann's settling down okay."

"That's beside the point, Walter," answered Chalmers. "Although I must admit it was all my fault. I never should have dragged you, Polacek, and Brodsky into that affair in the first place. It's a perfect example of imperfect science. We have to be aware of the disturbance that our various disappearances have caused here at the Institute. That with the police is something we dare not repeat."

"No need to thank me, boys, for squaring things between you guys and the law," Brodsky said, smiling broadly.

"Very reassuring, Mr. Brodsky, but we shall not be calling upon you to get us out of any further scrapes with the law. From now on . . . pure science!"

"So, it's time we started minding our extra-dimensional P's and Q's, eh, Doc?" said Polacek.

Chalmers leaned forward in his chair. "We've done enough playing swashbuckler . . . and I fear I must personally bear a large portion of the responsibility. But no more! Now we begin the application of serious and ordered scientific method. And since we're all back here safely in Ohio, there must be no more trips until we analyze the data we now possess."

"That's fine for you, Dr. Chalmers," Bayard said with annoyance, "you and Harold married dream girls you brought back from the land of Faerie. My Dumyazad was sent back to Xanadu quite without my consent. What about the rest of us?"

Shea remembered that Walter had actually been quite

relieved when the houri, Dumyazad, was accidentally sent back to her world of origin and wondered what old Walter Bayard was really complaining about. He had brought back the stunning red-haired quasi-celt, Boann Ni Colum. Did he want two women at once?

"Seems to me, you guys have got something here that's too hot to handle," said Brodsky. "If word of this gets out, every Tom, Dick, and Harry is gonna want to go off to the world of his dreams. Like some kind of magic carpet almost."

"Ahem," Chalmers cleared his throat meaningfully, "that is precisely the problem!" He turned to Bayard. "Walter, I'm not closing the door to the rest of you, I merely want a temporary halt to interdimensional travel. We're sitting on the greatest cosmological discovery in history. We must be very, very careful, until we are ready to publish our findings."

"I'll be as meticulous as you will," said Shea.

Chalmers stood up, resting his hands on his desk. "Then we all agree. No more trips will be made into parallel universes until further notice." He looked around the room and stared seriously into each man's eyes.

Polacek, who had stopped in a corner, resumed his pacing and opened his mouth to speak. Reed Chalmers beat the Czech to the punch and continued: "I want all of you, including Brodsky here, to prepare written reports on your recent—uh—experiences." There was a general groan from those present. "I want you to note every detail about the acts of magic you saw or experienced. We must leave no stone unturned. We must determine exactly what we have done to transport ourselves and others to parallel worlds. Our formulae must be refined and made more accurate."

"Not to mention the fact that we've seldom gotten back to this universe without help from the locals," added Shea.

There was a murmur of agreement. Chalmers continued. "Vaclav, I'm putting you in charge of correlating our experiences with the magic, or more accurately, the physics of the various worlds we have visited . . . with my assistance and guidance, of course." The Czech beamed with obvious pleasure.

"Don't look so smug, Votsy," Shea admonished, "the only way we'll ever be able to trust you with magic is to make you an expert on the subject."

The Czech shot Harold a hostile glance as Reed Chalmers closed the meeting. "Ahem. Yes, well, then, I think that will be enough for today. And remember, gentlemen, be careful what you say, and *no* experimenting on your own."

Harold Shea stopped typing and leaned back in his chair. Two weeks had passed since Doc Chalmers had asked for the reports which he had still not finished. Of course, some of his experiences were months old. . . . His eyes drifted across the room to his wife, Belphebe, seated at a table in the den, busily fletching arrows for her bow. Not everybody, he thought to himself, can be married to a red-haired, freckle-faced huntress. The main problem with being married to a huntress from the woods of Faerie was that she was not too happy with the city life of a modern American psychologist.

He had solved part of the problem by moving out of his town house in the city. Together, they had picked out a lovely place in the woods at the edge of the city limits. It wasn't perfect. Their backyard was a giant cornfield. But oaks and maples bordered them on both sides.

Harold and Belphebe had made a pact: if it wasn't raining and the babysitter was available, they would sleep outside in the trees on even dates. Otherwise, she would join him in the bedroom. He looked out the window into the gray drizzle and smiled. It had rained every day since they moved in.

He stared down at the page in his typewriter, and his mind drifted back to mythological Ireland and his adventure with the Sidhe of Connacht. Harold's conversations with the Druid Miach in Tir na n-Og, in mythical Ireland had seemed to explain a lot.

The old man had, in effect, said that it was not possible to be released from a world without doing something to alter the pattern of that world. It appeared to be Harold Shea's personal geas. Was it his own? Or had it applied to all of those from the Institute who had traveled to another continuum? He made a mental note to discuss this concept with Doc Chalmers.

The clock in the hall chimed six, and Shea was startled to see Belphebe standing before him.

"Harold, darling, is it not time we were leaving for this place you call the theater? Sir Reed and Lady Florimel will be awaiting."

"What . . . ? Oh, of course, dear," answered Shea. "Just give me a minute to change. Is the sitter here? You *are* going to wear the long green dress, aren't you?"

"Voglinda is in her care, and I shall wear the dress if you insist," his wife said reluctantly.

"I insist!" After he had lost her favorite dress in the frozen wastes of the Finnish *Kalevala*, Belphebe had accepted his gifts of twentieth-century clothing only with persuasion. Tonight was a special occasion—the psychologists had been given complimentary tickets to a Shakespeare festival and Shea had picked out a lovely formal dress and matching high-heeled shoes for his wife.

"Then I drive!" she stated flatly.

He hesitated, "Uh . . . yes, dearest." Belphebe at the wheel of their Chevrolet was something that required nerves of steel. But she had agreed to wear the dress.

They arrived at the theater intact. At no time was Shea ever in fear for his life; the lightning reflexes of his wife served her well on the streets of the city, though the driver of the Ford they passed on the hill would probably never be the same again. . . .

The first act of *The Tempest* had come to an end,

and now Harold stood in the crowded lobby talking to Reed Chalmers.

"Y'know, I hadn't really thought much about it before, but the world described in this play looks like a target for our explorations."

Chalmers frowned. "If it were based more on myth and legend, I should agree with you, but I do not believe it to be a systematic attainable universe. Shakespeare drew his material from a confusion of Greek and Roman mythology, sixteenth-century Italian pastoral drama, and God only knows what else."

"Think a minute, Doc! Spenser's *Faerie Queene* is the same sort of thing. It was based on Ariosto's *Orlando Furioso,* and we managed to travel to both places." Shea sensed that he had won his point and smiled. "A trip to Prospero's magical island shouldn't be difficult. It may be a Shakespearean romance, but it describes a valid parallel universe."

A worried expression came to Chalmers' face as he glanced furtively from side to side. "That, I fear, is exactly what worries me, Harold. In spite of my protestations, I'm sure it would be possible. Ever since the *Furioso,* Vaclav's been dropping little hints. I think he might be up to something. Did you notice what he's wearing tonight?"

"Is he here?" asked Shea.

"Indeed! Sitting two rows behind you. He looks like . . . uh . . . a fourteenth-century Italian courtier. We must have a talk with him."

Shea nodded in agreement.

Polacek had found his dream girl in the world of *Orlando Furioso,* all right. True to form, however, the Czech had found two of them. And one of them had a jealous innkeeper for a husband.

Just then the lights dimmed, and Florimel and Belphebe appeared before them, stunning in their strapless gowns. The matter of Vaclav Polacek and his medieval garb would have to wait.

When they had reached their seats, Shea turned to look at the audience. Almost directly behind him, dressed in a gaudy orange silk jacket with puffy brown shoulder pads, sat the Czech. Vaclav noticed him, nodded, and smiled. Harold was not sure he liked that smile.

The play resumed, and Shea allowed himself to become immersed in the trials and tribulations of the shipwrecked king of Naples. Alonso was just saying "Prithee peace" for the second time, when the hairs on the back of Shea's neck began to tingle.

Belphebe tugged at his arm and whispered, "My, how this play doth excite me."

Harold began to worry. The play wasn't that exciting, and he had felt this way before . . . Vaclav! Shea craned his neck to get a look at Polacek, but even as he turned, the crowd around him began to fade to a foggy gray. Desperately, he grabbed Belphebe's hand and—

Pmf!

Harold and Belphebe plopped to the ground in a field of green grass.

"Oof!" remarked Belphebe. Shea looked around. They were in a broad green field surrounded by low, tree-covered hills. A fresh breeze whispered past. He shook his head in disbelief. The characters had just been talking about this place in the play.

"Shea! Belphebe!" a distressed voice cried out behind them, "what are you guys doing here? I—I had no idea . . ."

Harold climbed to his feet. There, sprawled in the grass, was Vaclav Polacek in his ludicrous costume.

"Votsy, for two cents I'd—" Shea bellowed, with murder in his eyes. "You've dragged us into the play!" He started ominously toward the Czech, clenching his fists.

"Honest, Harold, I didn't mean to bring you two along." Polacek tried to scramble to his feet but Shea was on him in a flash, and the unfortunate Czech was wrestled to the ground.

"Guk, you're choging me!" gurgled Polacek.

"If you possessed even half a brain!" raged Shea, "you'd have trouble . . ."

Belphebe intervened, pulling her husband back, "Vaclav, Harold! Stop this foolishness. Have you not better things to do than fight among yourselves?"

The Czech sat up, rubbing his neck. "I really meant to come alone, honest!"

"It's that damn magicostatic charge," fumed Shea. "Belphebe and I are heavily charged. When you transported yourself here, you pulled us along with you. Doc Chalmers is lucky he wasn't sitting as close to you as we were."

Polacek picked up a book he had dropped, brushed himself off, and stood up, regarding Shea with a cautious gaze.

"So what's the big idea, Votsy?" Shea continued. "You know the Doc doesn't want us doing this till he's got it perfected."

"Look, I just figured I'd jump in here, grab the old man's daughter and some of his magic books, and beat it back to Ohio. It was no big deal!"

"Now that's a hell of a fine plan!" Shea said in disgust. "Prospero is one powerful magician, and he's got invisible spirits to help him. Besides which, didn't you think it might be a tad immoral to just kidnap someone? Just how did you propose to kidnap his daughter and steal his library anyway?"

"Hey, gimme some credit, will ya? While you guys were writing reports, I've been busy studying this magic business pretty seriously." Polacek held up the book. "This here is the Doc's latest symbolic magic textbook." He thumbed through a couple pages. "And I can still read the symbols even though we're in this continuum."

"That's all well and good, Votsy, but that book is full of untried theory as far as this place is concerned," grumbled Shea.

"All right, already," answered Vaclav, "how's about I

send you and the Mrs. back to Ohio?" He began flipping pages.

Harold recalled the geas laid upon him in the world of Irish myth—the requirement that he change things in this world before returning to his own and sighed. "It's no good, Votsy. We have to alter this place before we can leave."

"Nonsense." Vaclav nudged Belphebe closer to Shea. "You two hold hands and think Ohio thoughts." They did so and Polacek began motioning in the air with his free hand. "If either A or (B or C) is true, and C . . ."

"Wait a minute," Shea said after a moment of thought, "even if this would work, which it won't, because you don't have it right, I'm not leaving you here alone." He looked off into the hills.

Belphebe spoke: "We are indeed in a strange land, methinks the very one spoken of in the play." Suddenly she pointed up into the sky. "Look, there!"

Shea and Polacek gazed skyward but could see nothing.

" 'Tis some sort of creature slowly circling," she said quietly.

"Damn! That must be Ariel! We'd better find some cover," said Shea, "before that spirit reports us to Prospero. I don't think we'd be too welcome here." They hurried across the field, heading for the nearest trees.

Belphebe stumbled, catching her heel in a clump of grass. "These do me no good in this place!" She took off her heels and was about to toss them away.

"Better keep those, dear," said Shea, "even if you can't wear them, they're still high fashion. Maybe Miranda would like to have them." Actually, he was remembering just how much he had paid for those shoes only the day before. Belphebe shot him an angry look and continued barefoot, holding the shoes in her hand.

They soon came to a little stream and splashed across to a grove of trees on the far side. As they worked their way upstream, the sparse brush gave way to dense forest.

At length, Shea sat down on a rock. "Well, whatever

that was in the sky must not have seen us. Let's stop a moment and take stock of our situation. Votsy, did you bring anything besides the book?"

The Czech rummaged through his pockets and looked up rather sheepishly. "Sorry! Nothing but a pocket full of change, keys, and my wallet."

Shea looked at his wife. "Anything useful in your purse?" She frowned and dumped out a small pile of assorted cosmetics. He began to wish he had not tried quite so hard to convert her to twentieth-century fashion.

"Well, that's just great," Shea said heavily as he searched through his suit and produced a cigarette lighter and a pocketknife. "As you can see, we're well equipped for life in the wild."

Belphebe grabbed the knife. "With this I can fashion a bow and arrows, though 'tis a shame that I left such a fine one at home." So saying, she darted off into the woods.

"Say, Harold," said Vaclav, "you wouldn't happen to have a cigarette to go with that lighter, would you?"

Shea pulled a pack out of his breast pocket and tossed it to the Czech. "Here, I'm trying to quit."

Polacek put a cigarette in his mouth and flipped open the top of the lighter.

"You realize," said Shea, with a cynical smile, "that thing won't work here! Remember how Brodsky's gun wouldn't fire in Xanadu?"

Vaclav calmly flipped the wheel. A spark flew onto the wick and produced a flame. Shea stared in amazement, then grabbed the lighter and tried it himself. Again there was fire. Shea remembered with disgust how his matches would not work when he had tried to light a fire for Thor and Loki.

"Looks like some of our physical principles apply to this world," said Polacek, triumphantly. "At least flint and steel can make oil burn." He blew a puff of smoke into the air.

"Or maybe we're still somewhere in the U.S.A. Hand me that book and I'll try some magic," said Shea.

"Oh, no, you don't!" Vaclav said defensively. "I've been studying the art, you know. I'll do the magicking." He thought for a moment. "How's about I summon up some chow?"

Shea grimaced in disgust and reluctantly agreed. Two weeks with Reed Chalmers was definitely not enough training for Votsy, but what else could he do?

Harold was put to work gathering small twigs. Meanwhile, the Czech searched the nearby trees until he found a small blue caterpillar. He carefully built a framework of the twigs and placed the insect on top of it. Shea wondered just what kind of meal could be made from a blue caterpillar, then decided that he really did not want to know.

Polacek began waving his hands in the air. Then he recited:

> "I've never seen a purple cow.
> I've never hoped to see one.
> But I can tell you anyhow!
> I'd rather see than be one!"

Shea suddenly realized what was happening and, horrified, yelled: "No! Stop!" but it was too late. A sudden rush of air was followed by a dense cloud of purple smoke rising from the caterpillar. The smoke stung Shea's eyes—he rubbed them, and when he opened them, Vaclav Polacek was gone.

There, standing before Shea, was an immense, sad-eyed, purple cow. It mooed plaintively and began munching some grass by the edge of the stream.

"Well, Votsy, at least you proved we're not in Ohio," said Shea, "And, I might add, I'm not sure that I can change you back." The cow moaned and rolled its eyes. "It takes time to learn the nuances of the magic in the worlds we enter." Shea leaned over and picked the book up from under the purple cow.

He still preferred the cards he had made for his last set of adventures, but the book did have certain advantages . . . if it could be read. Shea studied the logic symbols and frowned. He was unable to decipher the notes scribbled in English around the edge of the page, but the pictograms showed how to summon a medium-sized animal. Since he could no longer read English, he wondered just what language they were speaking here; probably a mixture of Italian and Old English.

Suddenly, a sinister laugh seemed to float out of the treetops behind him. Shea turned to look but could see nothing unusual. The laugh came again, this time from a bush across the stream. Once again, he saw nothing.

"Hee, hee, hee," cackled the mysterious voice without form, this time originating behind the cow, who was now calmly munching the underbrush.

"Who's there?" cried Shea as he looked around desperately for something he could use as a weapon. He spotted a fallen branch, grabbed it, and began snapping off the twigs. Not much defense, he thought, but better than nothing. The laugh came again, this time from behind the tree nearest him. Shea lifted his makeshift staff.

"Some minister of magicks thou art," the voice said mockingly. "Wouldst change thyself into such a beast as well?" The air in front of Shea began to blur and ripple. In a flash, an enormous birdlike creature appeared before him. Its wings beat noisily back and forth, stirring up leaves. Atop its body was the head of a dark-haired woman. The entire creature was frazzled and dirty.

It rose into the air and hovered above Shea, extending an enormous clawed talon. "I'll thank thee for that tome," shrieked the creature. "My mistress would have't on her shelf." The purple cow let out a baleful moan and trotted off into the woods.

II

Shea threw his club in the general direction of the monster, grabbed the book, and made a dash for the woods. The fleeing cow had cleared a path which Harold followed, hoping the trees would interfere with the flying monster. There was little undergrowth to slow Shea down, but the ground was uneven and littered with fallen trees. He ran clumsily down the rude path and leaped over a dead tree trunk. He turned left abruptly and dodged behind a large bush. The harpy was hot on his trail, beating its wings and hissing loudly. It was having absolutely no trouble negotiating the tree branches.

Shea circled around the bush twice, with the harpy right behind him. Finally the creature wised up, flew over the top of the bush, and landed directly in front of him. Harold turned and ran back the way he had come. He bounded over a log and almost cleared another ... but his foot caught on a branch and he tumbled to the ground. The creature was directly above him now, hissing malevolently. Twigs and dirt clouded the air, stirred up by the beating of its great wings.

Shea crawled to his knees; escape seemed hopeless. And then, before him, almost in his hands, lay a large dead branch ... the club he had thrown away! In a flash he grabbed it and stood up to face the monster.

Shea had trouble keeping his eyes open against the

buffeting downdrafts created by the creature's beating wings. What he wouldn't have given for his trusty saber now! He mustered all his strength and swung the club at an outstretched claw. The monster pulled back at the last moment, and Shea whirled around like a baseball player who has just swung at a bad pitch.

The harpy cackled and before Shea could regain his balance, his face was buried in a mass of smelly feathers. Something whacked him on the back of his head, and the world became a shower of stars.

Harold Shea dreamed he was packed in a snowbank. It was deep and cold and he was frozen solid. He could see little snowmen with long carrot noses building an igloo around him, my how pleasant they seemed. . . . "Hey! wait a minute!"

He woke to find himself buried up to the neck in a low mound of dirt near the bank of the stream. The back of his head throbbed as though it had been used as the ball in the Army/Navy football game. He shivered and tried to move. Nothing. He was trapped. It was almost as if the earth had opened up and swallowed him, for there was a smooth carpet of grass all around him, and the soil was not broken.

He craned his head painfully from side to side. No sign of Vaclav or Belphebe. There was the rock he had sat on. There was his club. The book of magic was nowhere to be seen, not that he could see much from his current viewpoint anyway.

Shea yelled for Belphebe and then listened carefully. No answer. After calling a while longer, his head began to pound so horribly that he had to stop. How does one get oneself out of the cold ground? he wondered. He remembered being buried in the sand up at Headlands Beach by Lake Erie in happier times. He had wriggled himself free, but then he had been buried horizontally . . . and in loose sand. He began moving his neck in a circular motion, pushing back a small amount of dirt.

Two minutes and a sore neck later, he stopped and sighed. Practically no progress. At this rate, he would be buried for a very long time.

A stick snapped in the woods nearby. Shea froze. Out of the forest loped a medium-sized gray wolf. It snuffled around in the grass for a moment and then headed straight for him.

So this was it. The great Harold de Shea was about to meet his end, chewed up by a wolf while buried in a dirt pile in the middle of Shakespeare's *The Tempest*. He swore that his ghost would get revenge on a certain Czech!

The wolf trotted up to the strange head rising out of the ground. Shea let out a fierce bark. The animal stopped in its tracks. Shea did not know if he could cast any kind of spell with only the verbal elements at his command, but it was certainly the time to find out. What was it Chalmers had said when he changed Votsy back from a werewolf? Shea began to chant:

"Wolf, oh, wolf. Wolf of the noble Bard,
    Wolf of Shakespeare;
  Now 'tis that I conjure you from beneath the yard;
    Leave me, and disappear!"

Since his hands were not available, Shea gestured wildly in the air with his nose. The animal stared at him for a moment, then turned and trotted off between the trees the way it had come! Shea sighed. Had that really been magic, or only a bored and unhungry wolf? He was glad Chalmers had not been around to witness this particular encounter.

But at least the sudden rush of fear had made him forget how cold he was. Shea resumed his neck motions in an effort to free the top of his body from the earth. At length, his neck hurt so much he gave up struggling and stared miserably up into the trees.

"Harold? Is this you?" Suddenly, before him was a

red-bearded face with eyes where the mouth ought to be. He shook his head and blinked.

"Belphebe! Thank God. Get me out of here!"

The fire crackled pleasantly, but Harold Shea was feeling anything but pleasant. It had taken Belphebe over an hour to dig him out of the ground, and he was just now beginning to warm up. And he had the world's worst headache. Nothing had dug that hole; he had been inserted into the earth magically. He looked at a dirt-encrusted sleeve and frowned. His pin-striped suit would never be the same.

"Be of good cheer, my husband," Belphebe said as she turned a fat rabbit on a stick over the fire. "Our supper is nearly done."

"Vaclav is a mauve Hereford wandering around loose, the book of symbols is gone, our daughter, little Voggie, is home with a babysitter in another universe, and we're lost in a world we know nothing about . . . with no weapons!" grumbled Shea. "Why should I be of good cheer?"

Belphebe touched him on the cheek. "Meseems you do forget, you are not alone, my dearest. Lady Florimel will look after our daughter until our return. Certes you will have us back to Ohio in no time at all. Such is your power, my good husband."

Even without salt, the rabbit was the best meal he had eaten in recent memory. Belphebe was not satisfied with her new bow; but it was good enough, thought Shea. The sun set and the air grew cooler. They dragged several large branches into camp to stoke the fire. Belphebe took the first watch, and Shea was soon asleep with his head in her lap.

Sometime later that night, Shea awoke to the sound of voices. The fire was burning low and he could dimly see Belphebe, but no one else. Vaclav? He sat up abruptly.

"Hello?"

Belphebe answered, "Good morrow, dearest Harold, we are joined by a friend." Directly across from her he could just make out a wispy female form. It was wearing next to nothing, had golden hair . . . and enormous shimmering wings. He leaned forward and squinted for a better view.

"Greetings, good sir," the creature said in a soft voice, "I am called Bitter-Root. Welcome to our island." She extended her hand. Shea reached out and touched it gently.

"Harold Shea at your service." He smiled. "I guess you and Belphebe are acquainted. So where are we? Is this Prospero's Island?"

"I know not of Prospero. This is Setebos' isle, a happy place, once, liv'd in by sprites and spirits and the beasts in peace and harmony. But now we are set upon by the wretched Sycorax, who doth bespoil the trees and the land with pricking-goss and brine pits. . . ."

"Wait a minute!" Shea interrupted. "You mean to say that witch is still alive and kicking?"

"Would that she were perish'd," Bitter Root said with a sigh. "The vile hag hath raised legions of foul goblins and taken our fair Ariel to her dirty service. I fear 'twas Ariel, himself, who stole your book for her. But Belphebe has spoken much of your brave deeds. Surely such a great mage as thyself needs not his library to practice his magicks."

"I wouldn't be too sure of that," Shea said with a wry grin. "So far our magic hasn't been too successful here." He paused a moment and rubbed his chin. "So there's a war between you guys and Sycorax?"

The spirit looked confused. "I know not of war. That Sycorax is evil, there is no doubt. Her storms on the seas bring shipwreck'd sailors. These she turns to stones and plants. Those spirits who refuse her chores are lock'd in the heart of trees to suffer and cry."

Shea looked around into the woods. "Are we safe here, Bitter-Root?"

"Aye, fortune brought you to our side of the island. Her magic is not so strong in these woods. The unicorns hold back the goblins. But now Ariel's her servant, I fear all's lost."

Shea thought about Vaclav. "I don't suppose you've seen a large purple cow wandering around anywhere?"

Belphebe laughed. " 'Twas he who sent Bitter-Root unto us."

"Certes," said the spirit. "We found him near our cell. 'Twas but a simple task to make him right."

Shea mumbled something obscene under his breath. He could just picture Polacek stretched out on his back while a bevy of beautiful half-naked spirits stuffed peeled grapes into his mouth.

Bitter-Root suggested they follow her to her cell, which was not too far away. A unicorn was called to carry Belphebe.

"What about me?" asked Shea. "Don't I get a lift?" The spirit began to explain how unicorns have an intense dislike of men. "Oh, right, I knew that," muttered Shea. There was no candy handy for him to make treats to win this one over to him.

Belphebe patted her mount's ivory haunch and smiled at her husband. "Here's a guide you may hold," she said, indicating the unicorn's tail. "Or would'st conjure yourself a r. . .rynossery as you did in Loselwood?"

Harold winced, recalling the rhino he had accidentally summoned for a mount in Faerie. Quite handy at the time, but this situation didn't really call for a Sherman tank. But if he changed the spell a little bit . . .

"Not a bad idea. Hang on a minute, ladies," said Shea. "I don't intend to stumble around in the dark holding on to a unicorn's tail!" He stepped over to the stream. Using wet sand, he quickly fashioned a crude model of a horse's head, leaving out the stick for a horn that had once brought him a rhino. Shea crouched over his handiwork, gesturing as he recited:

"Oh, steed that feeds on reeds,
    And drinks the whirlpool's surge,
In the name of the horse of Ceres,
    I conjure you now; emerge!

He paused a moment, immersed in deep thought, and then continued:

"Strong, yet of me subservient,
    Bring a horse without a horn,
Up from this small river,
    I conjure you . . . be born!

The model and the stream nearby burst into a cloud of spray and sand. Harold figured the horse of Ceres would have to be some sort of plowhorse. As the spray fell to the ground a deep grunt revealed that his magic had succeeded . . . to a certain degree.

Staring at him blankly from the stream was a small but full-grown hippopotamus!

Belphebe burst into laughter. Shea winced. There was no turning back now. So he'd summoned a hippo; well, he'd ride a hippo! Besides, it was supposed to be subservient. Shea stepped back and leaped onto the animal's back. The enormous creature let out a basso profundo yelp and began waddling rapidly downstream.

Shea bounced around spread-eagled on the broad back and hung on for dear life, the memory of his ride on the bull rhino flashing before his eyes. There must be some way to control this thing!

Belphebe, Bitter-Root, and the fire disappeared behind him. The hippo seemed to be picking up speed. Between its bouncy gait and slippery skin, it was all he could to stay on top. Shea yelled out commands: "Stop! Turn right! Turn left!" He kicked the rotund beast with his heels, but to no avail. The hippo continued its mad, thunderous flight, splashing and jouncing down the stream.

In desperation, Shea grabbed the hippo's head and pulled hard on the right ear. The animal slowed and circled in that direction until it was pointed back upstream. Its manner now docile, it waddled back the way it had come until they reached the dying campfire. Shea pulled hard on both ears and the hippo opened its mouth, belched out a loud grunt, and came to a halt.

"Piece of cake!" Shea said triumphantly. "Any time you're ready, ladies."

His wife chuckled and Bitter-Root shook her head in amazement. Her gossamer wings fluttered silently and she took to the air. Belphebe followed on her unicorn. Now that he was unobserved, Shea breathed a sigh of relief and wiped the sweat from his forehead. He was not sure how to get his bus started again. Cautiously, he kicked the immense creature with his heels. The hippo came to life and plodded slowly after the unicorn.

They were traveling in the dark of early morning, and Shea could barely make out the ghostly forms of his companions in the starlight that filtered through the trees. Fortunately, the hippo seemed to be dogging the unicorn's steps and required no steering at all.

They worked their way uphill, following the stream for some time. At last Belphebe's mount and Bitter-Root stayed alongside the stream. Whenever possible, the hippo preferred to splash noisily through the water, soaking Shea from head to toe.

Just as the purple light of dawn could be seen through the tops of the trees, they turned from the stream and headed into a narrow, tree-covered valley. It was moist and overgrown with ferns, and the air was filled with a pleasant musty odor. Shea noticed that Bitter-Root had been joined by two globes of amber light, floating silently beside her.

The foliage closed in around them, leaving barely enough room on the trail for his wide-bodied mount. Soon, however, the vegetation gave way to rock and the trail widened. The odd procession came to a halt, and the hippo grunted restively.

Bitter-Root was now surrounded by several mysterious floating balls of colored light. She turned and spoke, "Seest thou here, this is the mouth of our cell, and these," indicating the lights, "are my fairy friends. Your animals will come no further. Pray dismount and release them."

Belphebe hopped down in one graceful motion. Shea slid off the hippo clumsily but managed to land on both feet. Belphebe was whispering into the unicorn's ear. Shea slapped his river horse on the rump and said: "Farewell, Horatio!" The beast let out a series of low bleats and waddled off into the morning. The unicorn circled cautiously around Shea and trotted off after the hippo.

III

They entered the mouth of a limestone cavern. More phosphorescent fairies appeared, casting a dim but pleasant glow on the walls of the rock chamber.

"I'll bet this saves on your electric bill," said Shea as they set out again by fairy light. Bitter-Root led them on, escorted by her amber friends. Fairies of several shades of green floated around Belphebe, while Shea's path was lit by a solitary red globe.

"We spirits are not by choice dwellers of the earth," said Bitter-Root. She had turned to face Harold and Belphebe and was flying effortlessly backward into the cave. " 'Tis said Setebos himself liv'd here in times bygone. Yet now we come and are safe from the witch's fury."

The spirit flew up to a ledge above them and tossed down a rope ladder. "I fear you must climb, where I would fly." Shea wondered who needed a rope ladder when all the inhabitants seemed capable of flight. Climbing up the ladder behind his wife, Harold noticed sadly what the short time spent in this world had done to Belphebe's expensive dress. She had tied what little remained of it around her hips.

They walked along the ledge and then turned into a smaller tunnel. This new passage sloped down and was joined by two side tunnels, which branched in from above. Bitter-Root continued on, and soon they found themselves in an enormous room illuminated by hundreds of glowing fairies. The roof was covered by stalactites which merged with stalagmites around the edges to form thick multicolored columns that shimmered in the fairy glow.

As Shea looked about him, he suddenly noticed Polacek on the far side of the room, seated at thick wooden table across from a swarthy, dark-haired man. They were playing a game of chess.

Vaclav spotted the new arrivals, "Hi ya Harold, Belphebe! Welcome to Fairyland." The dark man twisted his thick black beard between his fingers, studying the chessboard intently. "This is Snag, a sailor, late of Naples," Polacek continued. "You'll have to forgive him for not sayin' hello. We're playing timed moves, and there's a hot bet going."

Sitting cross-legged on the table, watching the game, was a male spirit. He motioned to Shea and Belphebe. "Come, be seated and partake of our wine!" Bitter-Root had already drifted over to the table and was filling two goblets. "My name is Moonwort." The male spirit flew up from the table effortlessly and landed in front of Belphebe with a deep bow. "I am blest in your acquaintance." He turned to Shea. "Master Pollychek hath told how you have come from so far to our aid."

Harold shot the Czech a meaningful glare on hearing

this news, but Vaclav quickly averted his eyes. As the
newcomers sat down, Snag made an unintelligible sound,
moved a piece, and turned a small hourglass on the table.
"Your go, Polish." The sailor then turned, grabbed Shea's
hand, and shook it heartily. "All hail, great master. Your
reputation doth precede you. Now shall we make short
work of that miserable Sycorax!" The sailor had paws the
size of baseball mitts.

Bitter-Root passed out the wine and spoke. "Here,
before thee, is the only man we have saved from the
witch. As his ship split upon the rocks, Moonwort and I
carried him off unseen. His companions are all now
stones by the beach."

The wine was light and sweet. Polacek was frowning
at the game. Shea smiled to himself. The Czech was
several pieces down and Snag had accumulated a pile of
American coins.

"Marry, Bitter-Root, is this all your number?" Belphebe asked with concern.

The she-spirit nodded sadly. "Aye, good Quamoclit
stands watch on the hill. With her, we are but three, and
the sailor." A blue fairy danced in front of them. "Yea,
and the fairies . . . and now, ye. Pray, what shall we do?"
the spirit looked into Shea's eyes expectantly.

The wine danced on Shea's empty stomach and made
him light-headed. "How about breakfast, for starters," he
replied. "Then we can make our plans." Snag looked up
from the game and nodded in agreement.

The two spirits vanished immediately. Moments later
they reappeared, each holding a large silver tray laden
with food, which they set before their guests. Harold and
Belphebe helped themselves to bread and cheese and
joints of beef, while the chess game continued. Two more
moves, however, and Vaclav was forced to surrender after
losing his queen and another fifty cents. Snag stuffed his
winnings into a leather pouch and proceeded to devour
an entire roast bird.

Shea leaned back and spoke, "As I see it, we need to

figure out a way to get that book back from Sycorax. We can practice our magic without it," he shot Vaclav a dirty glance, "but I don't want her to have access to the accumulated magical knowledge of six other worlds."

Polacek grimaced. "It may be too late already, Harold; if we can read those symbols, so can she."

The meal continued in a somewhat more somber mood. Looking about, Shea noticed the spirits were not eating. He could not help but wonder if conjured meals had any actual substance to them. Still his hunger had been assuaged, and Snag had finished his meal with several deep, satisfied belches.

After questioning Bitter-Root and Moonwort to some length, Shea learned that Sycorax summoned a storm about every fortnight to blow sailors and their ships to doom. The effort, however, drained the witch so completely that she spent the next day sleeping in her cave to regain her power. That, it seemed, would be the best time to slip in and regain the precious magic book. It was soon ascertained that they had two days before Sycorax could brew up her next batch of meteorological mischief.

That afternoon found the four human beings out in the woods preparing aircraft. Flying broomsticks were a specialty of Shea's. For once, he had time to build them slowly and carefully. High-speed two-seaters were what he had in mind.

Snag and Polacek tramped into the forest and returned with two straight young oak saplings. With some diligent pruning, these were turned into very large broomsticks. Bundles of straw gathered by Quamoclit were tied to the ends. Belphebe and Bitter-Root contributed eagle feathers, which were securely fastened fore and aft. Finally, short crosspieces were attached to the broomsticks, using strong pliant vines.

"Votsy, you and Snag, watch," Shea directed. "Belphebe and I will take one up and show you how it's done." Polacek was noticeably unhappy, but his humbling experience as a purple cow was still fresh in his memory. For the moment he was content to let Harold run the show.

The three spirits hovered overhead as Shea straddled his broom, made mystic passes, and began to recite:

> "Bird of the Aerie, ruler of sky;
>   Lend us your wings, so we too may fly."

The broom jerked in his hands and began to vibrate. Shea looked behind him. Belphebe was astride her end, holding on for dear life.

He looked across to Polacek. "That's just what you say to get the engine warmed up, Votsy," stated Harold. "This next part gets you airborne. Once you're up, use your body to steer." Shea made more passes and chanted:

> "By oak, ash, and maple,
>   The high air through,
> Show me you're able
>   To fly swift and true!"

The broom responded quickly and angled skyward with a rush. Belphebe yelped. Shea leaned to the left and the strange craft circled tightly around the hovering spirits. He pulled back, shifting his weight forward and the broom went into a tight loop.

"Harold!" cried an anguished Belphebe as he leveled off at treetop height. Shea was pleased. This broom was faster and handled better than any he had made before. The double set of eagle feathers probably accounted for the greater speed and maneuverability.

Shea looked down and saw Votsy and Snag in an animated conversation. He eased the broom into a downward spiral, but before he and Belphebe reached the ground, Vaclav straddled his broom and began making magic passes. Snag was gesturing too, but the universal language of his gestures told Shea that Snag was not yet ready to become an aeronaut.

Just as Shea was nosing up to make a soft landing, Vaclav shot into the air at an acute angle.

"We have another wager," yelled Snag, "that he shall not live to touch the earth again!" A desperate scream from above added weight to Snag's conviction. Polacek was hanging by his fingers beneath the broom as it plowed erratically up and down through the treetops.

Belphebe hopped off and Shea took to the air in pursuit of Polacek. Vaclav had somehow managed to regain his seat but was still not in control of his wooden airsteed as Shea approached. Polacek circled left and Shea noted with alarm that they were headed straight at each other on a collision course.

At the last moment, Shea executed a perfect Immelmann and came down on top of the Czech. He then reached down and snatched the feathers from the tail of Polacek's broom and Vaclav nosed up into a stall. While Shea circled effortlessly back to the ground, the Czech came spinning down, landing with an explosion of snapping branches in a clump of juniper bushes.

It took most of the evening to persuade Snag to ride with Polacek. But on his third flight, Votsy performed some complex aerobatics without incident. Even Shea was convinced that the Czech had finally learned to fly the broom.

That night, after another fine spirit-summoned supper, Shea learned that the spirits would not accompany them on their journey to the witch's side of the island. They dared not venture near Sycorax, for fear of being put under a spell, as had happened to Ariel.

They wakened before dawn and assembled at the mouth of the cave. There was ample evidence of the witch's antics. The trees were lashed by wild winds, and rain fell in heavy torrents.

"Can we fly in this weather?" Belphebe asked with concern.

Harold looked up at the darkening sky. "We'll soon find out!"

Bitter-Root fluttered up and handed Shea a lock of her hair tied with a golden thread. "Take thou this," said the spirit, "and if thou seest Ariel, show't. Perchance he will return to us."

Shea stuffed the lock into his breast pocket. Vaclav and Snag had walked their broom out into the rain, which had eased up considerably. They straddled their sapling craft and waved at Shea.

"I'm ready," Belphebe said from behind. Moments later, the two brooms and their passengers spiraled skyward, with the spirits and several colorful fairies flying in company. They rose above the hills till Shea could see great waves covered with whitecaps in the sea around the island.

The rain and wind made the flight uncomfortable, but the brooms handled well. As they flew west, the green forests gave way to an endless vista of lifeless trees. The division between the lands of Sycorax and that of the spirits was very clear indeed.

Shea looked to either side and noticed that the spirits were gone. Vaclav and Snag zoomed across in front of him. The Czech said something and gestured earthward. Shea could not understand a word, but followed Vaclav as he spiraled down. It was raining harder now. The two brooms cruised above the dead treetops and then circled to a landing atop the crown of a high hill.

The wind howled, and large drops of rain drenched them as the four sought cover behind a rock outcrop.

"I saw the witch!" yelled Polacek, as he crouched next to Snag. Shea could just barely hear him through the noise of the storm. "She's over there on the next hill!" Vaclav said, pointing at the rock behind which they were hiding.

As one, they stood up and leaned over the rock hoping

to catch a glimpse of the enemy. The rain had suddenly
let up, but ominous black clouds were scudding overhead, and patches of fog and mist obscured their view.
Just then a frightful bolt of lightning struck the top of
the other hill and Shea was able to make out the figure
of Sycorax, standing atop the summit. Her robe and cloak
were flapping in the wind and she held a long staff in
one of her outstretched hands.

Snag cursed and pointed out at the boiling sea. There
was a ship, its sails torn to rags, tossing about in the
forty-foot waves. It was being blown inexorably toward
the waiting rocks.

They waited and watched the ship meet its doom.
After its keel smashed against a rock, it rolled on its side
and washed up onto the beach. Sycorax vaporized the
bedraggled sailors as they struggled ashore with a
machine-gun-like series of pyrotechnic blasts from the
end of her staff.

"Rocks, all rocks," Snag moaned.

"Well, there's nothing we can do if she's this powerful,
we just have to wait till she hits the sack!" Shea
answered, grimly.

When it was over, Belphebe, her curls matted against
her face from the rain, put her arm around Shea, and
they all sat down to wait. The storm continued in
unabated fury. During the course of the day, two more
hapless ships met their doom. As soon as Sycorax disposed of the crew, antlike swarms of goblins would scurry
out to the remains of the ship and carry back armloads
of cargo, food, and miscellaneous loot. The long lines of
goblins disappeared into the roots of the hill upon which
Sycorax stood. Shea hoped he could find an entrance that
was not quite so well attended.

The rain let up at last, and it was drizzling when they
opened the lunch that Bitter-Root had prepared for
them. Belphebe stood watch over the hill, while Snag

and Polacek made pigs of themselves. Shea rose to give Belphebe an apple; she pointed anxiously.

"Shhh!" she whispered. "Two goblins approach."

Coming through the thorn bushes were two ugly, dark green creatures with heavy clubs resting on their shoulders. They were hotly engaged in discussion, and one seemed ready to use his club on his companion.

Snag appeared at Shea's side. "Let's take them!" he said, a fiery rage burning in his eyes.

Shea nodded in agreement. "It wouldn't hurt to gather a little information. Belphebe," he said softly, "you cover us. We'll wait till they get to that dead tree. Snag, you go around to the right, and stay low. I'll come at them from behind. . . . Votsy!" The Czech was still eating. "Get up here. You're the bait."

"What?" complained Polacek, as he finished the last bottle of wine with a high-pitched hiccup. Snag reached over and grabbed the Czech by his collar, lifted him bodily, and stood him up behind the rock.

Shea continued, pointing out the approaching goblins. "When those birds reach that tree, I want you to rush at them. And make a lot of noise."

"But what if they—"

Belphebe brandished her bow. "Fear not, Vaclav," she said reassuringly. "Dead they shall be ere they can hurt thee."

"Don't kill them unless you have to," cautioned Shea. "I want a prisoner to question!"

Snag had already disappeared down the hillside as Shea circled behind a clump of tall thorn bushes. He crossed a gully on a fallen log and lost sight of the goblins. Just then he heard Polacek screaming, followed by several thumps and the *twunk* of Belphebe's arrow. By the time Shea arrived, one goblin lay dead, and Snag was sitting on top of the other, holding its own club across its neck.

Polacek was sitting on the ground, holding his head in

his hands, moaning. "Where were you?" he complained as Shea walked up.

" 'Twould seem our dead foe struck Vaclav a blow!" Snag said rather cheerfully. "And now I would throttle the other!" He mashed the club down on the goblin's neck and its yellow eyes bulged as it made choking sounds.

Belphebe arrived silently, restrained the sailor, and had him tie the goblin to a tree. However, after much questioning, the creature sullenly refused to talk. Finally, Snag put a knife to its stomach and threatened to disembowel it slowly. The goblin talked; he told of an entrance used only by "employees" that was usually left unguarded. Belphebe managed to keep Snag from killing the hapless goblin, and they left it firmly tied to the tree.

The brooms were stashed under a clump of brown bushes on top of the hill. Harold persuaded Belphebe to leave her longbow as well, as it was unsuited for quick travel in the tight passages of a cave. The storm had mostly passed, though a steamy mist clung to the hillside, and occasional wisps of rainfall still hit them as they made their way in the gathering dusk of evening. The entrance to the cave was hidden at the bottom of a steep valley behind the hill. Polacek happily agreed to stand guard at the exit with Snag while Shea and Belphebe made the attempt to steal the magic book.

"What do we do if you guys don't come out?" asked the Czech.

"We rescue them," Snag said curtly.

"My thoughts, exactly," added Shea. "Give us till morning, then do something if we're not back!"

Belphebe led the way to the low entrance where they found a convenient supply of crude torches. Shea's lighter provided fire, and they set off into the cool darkness. At first the going was easy, as the floor consisted of firmly packed clay. There was little sign of use, and they saw only the occasional goblin footprint. The tunnel suddenly narrowed and then merged with a much larger passage. They turned right and continued downhill.

Every hundred feet or so, a smoldering torch was set into the wall, and a small stream trickled noisily at their side. Belphebe stopped Shea with an outstretched hand. Just to the right of them, barely visible, was a side tunnel. The floor of the passage was heavily scored with footprints leading into the tunnel. Their goblin prisoner had mentioned a wooden door, but, at first glance, Shea had seen none.

He nodded in that direction and Belphebe slipped forward. A low, rotting door stood before them unlocked. The two pulled it open and continued on. The tiny passage led steeply upward for nearly fifty feet then turned left and opened into a room. As Belphebe moved her torch, the light revealed stacks of wooden barrels, chests, and other booty taken from the wrecked ships. The glint of metal caught Shea's eye.

"Over there," he said excitedly. The two of them rushed around a stack of boxes. There on the floor was a pile of swords and other edged weapons. Shea pulled a slender rapier out of the pile.

He smiled as he waved it about, making passes at an invisible enemy. "Almost as good as my saber! Those Italians knew how to make fine weapons."

Belphebe shushed him, taking a small jeweled dagger for herself. "Let's be on with our quest, Harold." A brief search revealed that the only way out was the way they had come. As they descended the steep path, Belphebe stopped Shea again.

"Voices," she whispered. They stood motionless for a long moment. Then Belphebe relaxed, saying: "They have passed." Shea leaned over and kissed her cheek. Her keen hearing came in handy at times like this. But they still walked carefully back into the main passageway.

IV

The two traveled silently on and the passageway
opened into a large, brown-walled chamber. In the distance, Shea could hear the faint drip of water. Just ahead,
there was another torch set into the wall, burning fitfully.
Belphebe turned to make sure Shea was at her side and
took his hand. He thought briefly of Snag and Polacek
and wondered what kind of trouble the Czech would
have gotten them into by now.

They continued deeper into the cave. Belphebe led
the way, almost on tiptoe, being careful not to make a
sound. Shea could see goblin footprints in the mud. They
ducked under a low rock and rounded a corner. Belphebe tugged at his sleeve. There before them, revealed
in the dim yellow light, was a large, iron-bound wooden
door set into the wall.

Upon closer investigation, Shea could make out inter-
locking pentacles lightly painted on the boards. Shea
leaned against the door and shoved. It did not move.
There was no handle nor visible hinges.

"This must be the old witch's room," he whispered to
Belphebe. "Give me a couple strands of your hair." He
knew how to handle a door locked in this fashion.

Reaching into his pocket, Shea produced two flattened
cigarettes and tied them together in the form of a cross

244

with Belphebe's hair. He held this up to the door and tried to remember the proper wording.

> "Pentacles near and pentacles far,
>   Now disappear from where you are!
>   Shemhamporesh!"

The door creaked inward slightly. Just then, however, the sound of bare feet slapping against clay came from all directions. Shea turned to see several yellow-eyed goblins coming toward them out of the darkness.

"Hi, there! We can ex—" But Shea's words were cut off as two of the goblins rushed at him with stout wooden clubs waving and the others headed for Belphebe. Harold pulled out his rapier, dodged the attack, and lunged at the nearest goblin. The blade sank into the creature's chest as it impaled itself with its forward motion. It fell to the ground dropping its club. As Shea bent to remove his weapon, he felt the swish of another club passing over the top of his head. The goblin cursed.

Meanwhile, Belphebe had stuffed the torch in the face of one goblin and was running around the cave with another in hot pursuit. Shea brought his rapier up butt first into the jaw of his adversary. It fell to the ground moaning.

Just then, Shea caught a glancing blow to his shoulder, which spun him around. It was the goblin Belphebe had blinded with the torch. Shea raised his arm and clobbered the monster on top of its head with the hilt of his rapier. The creature dropped to its knees and fell over on its face.

Belphebe ran in front of him with her pursuer hard on her heels. Shea stuck out his foot and tripped the goblin who was trying to club his wife. It snarled, reached over, and pulled Shea's legs out from under him. A wrestling match quickly developed between them, but Harold had the advantage of more than sixty pounds over the monster. They rolled around on the clay floor, grunting and snorting. Shea got his opponent in a vicious full nelson. Suddenly Belphebe was there with another goblin club. She clouted the monster soundly and it slumped in Shea's arms.

Harold looked around, panting. There were no more active goblins. "Nice work, kid!" he said in a breathless whisper to Belphebe.

"Nay, to the hilt end of your blade and to your foot go all the credit, husband!" She bent over him and dabbed at a scrape on his forehead.

They went back to the door and Shea gave it a gentle shove. It swung open.

A dim red light shone out into the cave from within the room. Harold and Belphebe entered, cautiously. Inside, illumination came from a mound of glowing coals, all that remained of a large fire that had been set in the center of the room. Arranged around the edges of the chamber was an assortment of crude wooden furniture, hanging tapestries, some shelves covered with assorted oddities, and a long low bed on which lay—Sycorax. She slept with her mouth open, snoring softly. Shea and Belphebe held their breaths as they edged around the walls of the room past the sleeping witch. Up close, the hag was even uglier than Shea had imagined, and she didn't smell any too good, either. He noticed a smaller, boxlike structure situated near the bed. A strange hissing noise came from within. A quick look inside revealed a disgusting sleeping baby that resembled a dead fish.

"Caliban," Shea whispered to his wife. She nodded her agreement.

They came to the shelves, and Harold examined them carefully, without touching any of the objects they held. The pentagrams were down, but there might easily be other less visible traps guarding the witch's possessions. Belphebe nudged Shea and pointed to Doc Chalmers' books of symbols wedged in between several black leather-bound books. With a careful hand, Shea gently slid the magic book out from between two moldy leather tomes. He opened it briefly; everything appeared to be all right.

Slipping the book into his breast pocket, Shea continued his explorations. Nearby was a small mirror and a small green vial with some writing scratched on the side. At the far side of the shelf, Shea could see Sycorax's red robe, folded neatly, and leaning against it, her long crooked staff.

Beneath the shelves, Harold found a cache of assorted weapons, consisting mostly of daggers, but a large axe with a sharply honed edge lay on top of the pile.

Belphebe spotted the axe and whispered in Shea's ear. "An opportunity to end this struggle once and finally, presents itself, Harold." She picked up the weapon and offered it to her husband.

Shea paused and thought. The witch was dead before Prospero came to the Island in the play. Why shouldn't he be the messenger of her destruction? On the other hand, she was asleep with her baby at her side....

"Harold, if you cannot, I shall do the deed!" Belphebe whispered resolutely. Shea steeled his nerve and grabbed the axe from her hands. If the witch had to be killed, he would not fob the heinous task off on his wife. He tiptoed over to the witch's bed and lifted the heavy blade into the air. He paused again. There was a lump in his throat. This was cold-blooded murder.

Sycorax's eyes flashed open and stared ominously into his. Shea was paralyzed. The witch began to scream in a high-pitched shrill voice. Harold dropped the axe to one side, grabbed Belphebe by the hand, and ran for the entrance. As they passed the large wooden door, he reached out and pulled it shut. It slammed heavily behind them, throwing the cave into almost total darkness.

He paused, shaking with fright. Belphebe pulled him forward, "This way, Harold!" They stumbled along in the dark. She pushed his head down as they ducked under a low rock. Once around the next corner, he could see a dim light ahead. They ran at full speed past some broken statues and then struggled uphill toward the daylight that beckoned ahead.

Belphebe dashed out into the dim light of evening, with Shea right behind her.

"Votsy, Snag!" he yelled, but there was no answer. He could hear a great clamor from the cave behind them. They turned to run up the hill where the brooms were hidden, but the air before them began to blur and a male spirit materialized before their eyes. It spoke two strange words and the ground on which Shea and Belphebe were standing turned to slime. They sank up to their knees, and the spirit laughed. It was the same laugh Shea had heard when he met the harpy.

"Ariel," Shea said quickly, as Sycorax appeared at the entrance of the cave, "you have to let us go!"

"Kill them!" commanded the witch.

Shea reached into his pocket and produced the tiny lock of hair that Bitter-Root had given him. "See this," he said in desperation, "Bitter-Root wants you back. You don't work for this damned witch!"

A look of obvious consternation came over the spirit's face. Suddenly, Shea and Belphebe were once again standing on solid ground. Harold stepped forward and pressed the lock of hair into the spirit's hand.

"C'mon sweetheart, let's scram!" He and Belphebe then raced off into the bushes. The witch issued a volley of curses and shot a lightning bolt at Ariel, who calmly dodged the fiery blast. Amid the turmoil, a crowd of ugly green goblins began pouring out of the mouth of the cave.

"To the brooms!" Shea yelled as he and Belphebe crashed through the thorny bushes to the top of the hill. A small army of goblins followed hot on their heels. At the top of the hill, they found both brooms and Belphebe's bow. But there was no sign of Polacek or Snag. They quickly mounted and Shea hurriedly chanted the flight commands.

The two shot into the air mere seconds ahead of the irate goblins and Shea banked into a slow turn. As they circled overhead, Belphebe put arrow to bow and covered their retreat. Shea searched for Polacek and Snag, but they were nowhere to be seen.

On the next pass over the hilltop, they were met by a shower of rocks, thrown up into the air by the surviving goblins. One rock clipped Harold square on the head. The last thing he heard was Belphebe's shriek.

The next thing Shea knew, he was bound tightly hand and foot and hanging upside down from a long pole, carried by a group of goblins. He craned his aching head for a better look. All he could see was a procession of the green creatures marching along a rocky trail. It still seemed to be evening, and the sky was overcast. There was no sign of Belphebe. His arms were numb, and his head throbbed painfully; this was a fine mess he had gotten himself into!

The goblins marched on in the growing dark, and Shea endured the pain, until at last they stopped for the night. They dropped him, pole and all, roughly onto some wet sod. At least it eased the pressure and allowed a little blood to circulate into his aching extremities.

Shea turned his attention to the camp. There was a good deal of shouting going on. The dispute seemed to be over the lack of fire. Everything was still damp from the storm, and none of the goblins could start a fire.

As Shea struggled to achieve a more comfortable position, his elbow brushed against his pocket. They hadn't taken away his lighter! A plan began to form in his throbbing skull.

"Psst! Hey, you!" Shea called out to a sullen-looking goblin, who had been watching the attempts to make a fire. It ambled toward Shea with a puzzled look on its face. "Yeah, you! I can show you how to make a fire. You'll be a big shot."

The goblin knelt down over Shea. "What wouldst thou, prisoner?" it growled. " 'Tis too damp for fire."

"Maybe for you guys. But I know some magic tricks that'll get you a roaring blaze in no time."

"So show me," the goblin answered.

"You must untie me first, so I can work the spell . . . and don't worry, I won't run away," said Shea.

A little more haggling followed before he could convince the goblin, but finally Shea sat up and sighed with relief as his hands were untied. He gave his lighter to the goblin and showed the creature how it worked. It was enormously pleased and stood up to rush over and show its companions.

Shea grabbed the goblin by the arm and said, "Hey, wait, that's only half the show. Now we'll make some fire-water to go with that. I need a bucket of water and some wood." Shea untied his feet while the goblin hurried off for the water.

The creature returned with a dented pewter bowl, half full of muddy water, and a wet, rotten tree branch. Shea placed the bowl ceremoniously on the ground and dropped in some broken bits of the branch. On a larger piece of wood, he scratched out some letters with a rock:

$$H\ H\ H\ H$$
$$H\ C\ C\ C\ C\ H$$
$$H\ H\ H\ H$$

He thought a while longer. It had been some time since organic chemistry. The stuff he wanted was made of several complex molecules. He scratched out a formula for an isoparaffin, a napthene, and an olefin. Shea began stirring the mixture with the large stick and recited:

"As from the ground comes the bubbling well,
The nectar of Standard and Phillips and Shell,
Internal combustion, petroleum's jewel.
Change now, I command thee, to high octane fuel!"

The color of the liquid suddenly darkened to a deep reddish brown, and other goblins who had wandered over to watch, murmured in awe. Shea sniffed his concoction.

It smelled potent enough. He handed the bowl to the goblin with the lighter.

"Place this on top of your pile of wood over there and do your stuff." He wiggled his thumb at the goblin, and winked. The goblins all walked off to do the deed. Harold began to edge away as inconspicuously as possible, waiting for the fateful click.

Even he did not expect the extent of the explosion, which shook the valley to its roots. The resulting pillar of fire caused quite a stir. Shea slipped quietly off into the bushes and then scooted up and over a gravelly hill, ripping his pants on a thornbush as he ran. He stopped for a moment on the next ridge to listen. He could hear goblins nearby.

There were fewer thornbushes along the top of the hill, and Shea made better progress. Goblins were running below him now, yelling to each other and cursing his very existence. The slope curved sharply upward. Shea found himself rock climbing and his pursuers closing in fast.

Shea stopped and his heart sank. Before him was a thirty-foot drop, and at the bottom were masses of thick brambles. A rock whizzed past his head. He swallowed the lump in his throat, closed his eyes, and leaped over the edge.

v

Shea landed with a crash in the thorny scrub. It was thicker than it looked from above and he plowed through several layers of thornbush. At last his feet hit the ground, and after a struggle he extricated himself from the tangled mass of vegetation. Once free, he took off running again, down the valley. Perspiration stung the numerous tiny cuts made on his hands and cheeks by the thorns.

Harold splashed into a brackish creek and turned upstream, hoping to cover his footprints. He soon slowed to a walk and then to a stagger, as the last glimmer of daylight and his energy simultaneously gave out. Fortunately, he could no longer hear any pursuers; and with the final bit of strength left in his ravaged body, Shea struggled up the bank and into a grassy clearing, where he curled up into a ball in some tall weeds and promptly fell asleep.

The first rays of a sunny morning climbed over a hill and shone cheerfully down on Shea. He opened his eyes with a start, then shivered and remembered where he was. He had been dreaming of an automobile chase. Belphebe was driving their Chevrolet and he was in the backseat while she took corners on two wheels. He'd have to talk to her about that. . . . Belphebe! He had forgotten completely about her. Was she still alive? Desperately, Shea sat up, rubbing his hands together to generate some heat. His muscles ached, and the myriad of cuts and scratches added to his general discomfort. His empty stomach complained, and he crawled slowly down to the creek for a drink. There were brown things floating in the water. He had no idea what they were, and was too thirsty to care; the water tasted good.

Shea stretched his sore limbs and washed his wounds as best he could. As he placed his jacket on the ground it suddenly occurred to him that the magic book was gone from his breast pocket, probably back in the hands of Sycorax. He could only pray that Belphebe had somehow escaped; his multiple knocks to the head wouldn't permit any more complicated thoughts. Soon he set out upstream again. Now that the sun was out, he could tell that he had been traveling north the night before. He stayed in the valley by the creek for over an hour, occasionally climbing a hill to survey his position. There were no goblins to be seen, but neither could he spot the green trees of the land of the spirits.

It was nearly noon when Shea climbed a particularly high brush-covered hill. What he saw made him drop swiftly to the ground. Not fifty yards away were what appeared to be old Roman ruins, consisting of columns, a couple of crumbling buildings, and a large flat tiled floor upon which some goblins were playing what looked like a game of shuffleboard.

Shea watched with detached interest for a while. Then the smell of cooked food attacked his nose, and he began working his way closer by ducking from one bush to the next. Soon he could make out the goblins' conversation—all about their game and the bets they had made on the outcome. He slipped behind a crumbling building. Inside, their meal was cooking in a pot over a small fire—the smell was entrancing, and drove all other thoughts from his mind.

Shea was on the verge of sneaking in when a fight broke out on the shuffleboard court. One of the goblins had been caught cheating, and the others jumped on the villain. The hapless goblin was tied upside down to a column, where it retched and moaned while the game continued. Shea actually began to feel sorry for the creature. A wild idea came to mind.

He mulled it over for a moment and shrugged, thinking: What have I got to lose?

Harold stood up, looked longingly at the stew pot, arranged his ragged suit as best he could, and walked boldly out onto the forum. The two goblins spotted him immediately and one dropped his stick in amazement.

"Good morning, boys," Shea began. "I've been watching your game. You're both pretty talented players. I myself was once the All-Ohio shuffleboard champion." He bent over and picked up the dropped stick. "You see, in Ohio, this game is also known as the national pastime." Shea leaned forward and shoved a rock skillfully across the court. "My name ranks right up there with the all-time greats such as Lou Gehrig, Babe Ruth, and Joe DiMaggio. . . ."

"Loo Gerik?" asked the smaller goblin, its eyes open wide.

The other came to its senses. "Ho, you be the mage sought by the witch. 'Tis a trick!" It nudged its smaller companion.

"Forget the witch. I'll make you a wager," Shea went on. "I'll take on the better of you. If I win, you cut down your noisy companion over there." He pointed at the goblin hanging from the column. "You give me a meal, and I'm gone."

"And if I, Pholantus, win?" the larger goblin asked, defiantly.

"I'm your prisoner."

Pholantus smiled knowingly, baring a misshapen set of brown teeth. The game began. It soon became clear that Shea was up against a master. Each time they shot, Harold's stones were consistently knocked off the mark by those of the goblin. Something was rotten in Denmark. Either this goblin was the best shot in the world, or he was using magic to cheat. Shea wondered just how he could put some subtle magic to use to assist his own cause.

At length, recalling the way Heimdall cheated in the cockroach races back in Surt's stronghold, Harold was fairly certain he could apply the same method to shuffleboard. When the others were admiring a particularly vicious shot of Pholantus', he mumbled discreetly and made passes with his left hand. The goblin's rocks began to consistently slide past the mark, while Shea's stones stopped with mysterious regularity on the highest score. When his total score became larger than that of his opponent, the goblin threw his stick to the deck in anger.

"Damnation! You cozen me and would dance out of your true debt." Pholantus snarled, "Gretio, this sheepbiter needeth thrashing!" He motioned for his smaller companion to attack. But instead, Gretio stood pat. "Nay, I am afeard of this mage!"

The larger goblin growled and strode forward, taking a swing at Shea, who ducked and then put up his dukes. So it was to be a boxing match! Well, boxing was a lot like fencing, just a matter of balance, position, and timing.

Using fancy footwork, he danced around his slow-witted opponent. Shea slipped several punches, adding to the goblin's fury. The other goblin, Gretio, seemed quite content to stay in the background and only once made an effort to trip Harold. Shea laughed, letting his guard down. At that moment, the big one landed a fist square on Shea's jaw, and he staggered backward from the force of the blow.

Now he was angry. Shea recalled the last night he had spent at the fights, and imagined himself the Brown Bomber, Joe Louis. Now he took the fight to the enemy. Harold landed a stiff shot to the goblin's gut and then connected with a left jab followed by a right cross. The goblin wobbled and then crashed to the mat. Shea turned to face Gretio.

"C'mon, bub, you're next!" the champ said defiantly, dancing neatly around in a circle. Rather than fight, however, the little goblin shrieked and ran off into the underbrush. "Hey! What's the matter, you coward?" Shea taunted, shaking a fist at the fleeing foe. He danced around a bit more, shadow boxing, and then came back to reality.

The upside-down goblin hanging from the column was yelling: "Help! Let me down!" Shea walked over to the unfortunate creature.

"If I cut you down, will you promise to help me?"

"Yes, yes! Anything!" So Shea, his head throbbing again, now that the thrill of battle had worn off, loosed the goblin's bindings.

"Many thanks," said the goblin as it fell to the ground, "I'm called Malovio. That was a most impressive display of fisticuffs." It extended a scaly green hand in friendship.

"Harold Shea here," he said as he shook the goblin's hand.

Malovio glanced nervously around and then bent over the unconscious Pholantus. "Methinks we'd best be off before Gretio returns with the sergeant!"

"But I'm hungry," complained Shea, "and they've got a pot of soup on. . . ."

"I, Malovio, can always find sustenance. That cheat Pholantus will wake soon and want revenge. Let us away!" The goblin scooted off into the bushes, and Shea followed.

Malovio led the way through the prickly undergrowth with such speed that Shea was amazed. The little goblin trudged on tirelessly, as though they were being chased by an army. But then, maybe they were being chased by an army. They stopped to drink from a stream.

"Hey, Mal," Shea said, "when are you going to find us that meal?" His empty stomach was tying itself in knots.

"Soon, Harold, I know a secret place." On they went, through endless fields of scrub till they came to a grove of dead trees. There was an eerie look about it. The leafless trees stood like obelisks in a graveyard. Malovio plopped down on a fallen log.

"You, sir, make fire. I shall bring game," said the goblin. "Know ye that I'm a great hunter."

"So what is there to hunt on this island?" asked Shea. "I haven't seen a single animal all day."

Malovio bent down and picked up a pointed stick. "One must know the land to find the game!" he answered casually, and then began walking off. "Make the fire great!" said the goblin as it disappeared behind a bush.

Shea gathered wood for a fire, but with his lighter gone he was afraid he would end up rubbing two sticks together to get it started. At the edge of the grove he stumbled across an old fire pit and carefully laid the wood in the middle. He was also pleased to discover several pieces of flint which somebody, or something, had left behind.

It took him a good bit of smashing stones together to find the right combination, and even longer to persuade a little mound of dry moss to start smoking, but at last he had a fine crackling fire going. Moments later, Malovio came walking proudly back into camp; Harold shuddered when he saw what the goblin had hanging from the stick over his shoulder. A brace of fat rats!

Neither had a knife, so the catch was roasted the way it came, fur and all. Shea was a bit squeamish at first, but the gnawing in his stomach soon took control of his senses.

While supper sizzled, Malovio dug under a pile of branches and produced a small, well-used copper kettle.

"Stew?" asked the goblin.

"Y'know," said Shea, "I'd rather have beer!"

Malovio gave him a puzzled look. "Beer?"

"You'd be surprised what I can do. Fill that thing with water and I'll put my magical powers to work on it. We'll have us some fine brew to go with our supper."

Malovio's eyes lit up. "Most assuredly!"

Shea gathered some grasses that resembled barley and scratched out the formula for alcohol on the end of a stick. He could have made finer stuff with sugar cubes, but one had to make do. He surveyed the sorry pile of ingredients and sighed.

Malovio returned with the kettle full of water, and Shea dumped in the grasses and began to stir it with the stick, chanting:

> "Beer, Beer, beautiful beer,
>   Fill this pot up with it,
>   Clear up to here!"

A corny verse, but it was the best he could come up with after being knocked out so many times. A brown froth began forming in the pot. Shea stuck his finger in the mix. Not bad, he thought to himself. He put the kettle to his lips and took a healthy swig. Then the goblin grabbed it greedily and took a long series of draughts, spilling the dark liquid down from his green lips onto his ragged coat.

"Fair magic," said Malovio, smiling, "thy liquor is unearthly."

Shea thought it had a muddy aftertaste and was very "earthly" indeed, but it did pack a punch. Soon he and the goblin were best of friends, laughing and telling each other inane jokes. The roasted rats tasted as good as gourmet chicken. When the meal was done, the goblin went for more water and insisted Shea brew up a second batch. As night settled in around them, the goblin grew maudlin and Harold began gently to question him for information.

"Before that witch Sycorax, our life on this isle were full-easy. In Firemount we lived, and served the great drake, which was little enough trouble. Yet now we are but stevedores and whipping boys."

"So, you goblins aren't too fond of the witch either," suggested Shea.

"Verily! In defiance now I lead the renegade life, and 'tis not an easy trip," complained Malovio.

"What is this great drake?" asked Shea, sensing a potential ally against the witch.

"At the root of the Firemount now sleeps a mighty drake, once a hot and noisome thing. Yet if we served, it did treat us fairly. Then Sycorax came to our land, accurst the drake, and full seven years hath it slept," Malovio sighed heavily. "And now slaves we are to the witch. The life of a goblin is not easy."

Harold was about to ask more of the drake and if the goblin knew the whereabouts of Belphebe, when Malovio took a long drink from the kettle, grinned, and passed out. Shea poked a stick around in the coals, finished the kettle of earthy beer, and watched the fire die out. He thought wistfully of his wife and determined to set out after her at first light. Then he, too, fell asleep.

It was nearly noon the next day when Harold regained consciousness. His head throbbed. Too much beer, no doubt! Malovio was nowhere to be found. Shea struggled upright and kicked around the smoldering embers on wobbly feet, trying to think what to do next.

It was way past time to continue his search for Belphebe and the spirits. With a sense of urgency, he left the grove and headed for the nearest hill. Some movement caught his attention and he quickly hid behind a tree trunk. It was fortunate he had not slept or delayed any longer, for a party of twenty or more goblins came stomping up and began milling around the fire site. Shea carefully edged away from the camp, putting as much distance as possible between himself and the goblins.

He climbed the next hill, but saw nothing but more bramble bushes and dead trees. The dead zone created by the witch had a queer, depressing effect on Shea. As he wound his way up, down, and around the hilly terrain, not a single living tree could be seen. The only plants were the various brown and olive-drab thorn bushes, and even they seemed only half alive. The overcast sky only added to the general gloom. When he had flown over all this on his broom it has seemed such a short distance.

The day wore on, and Shea stopped for a drink from yet another murky stream. His stomach, empty once again, complained; but he had seen no edible plants, and the rats and lizards he encountered managed to escape his clumsy attempts at capture. At least, he had not met any servants of Sycorax.

Just as he was thinking about how alone he was, Shea climbed to the top of a high hill and saw a view that restored his morale. To the east were the lush green forests of the Spirits, still unspoiled by the witch. He was close! Even as he gazed on the beautiful woodlands, the sun broke through the clouds and shone cheerfully on the living half of the island. Shea sat down to catch his breath.

The moment passed, and the clouds returned. Harold rose wearily to his feet again, and pushed on. Now he was picking his way through the disgusting tangle of thornbushes as best he could and heading generally northeast. He no longer looked back to the dead zone he was leaving behind.

Near sunset, he climbed into a tree near the top of a high hill. By now, the sky was glowing red with twilight, and if Shea had not been tired, hungry, injured, and lost in a strange land, he probably would have enjoyed the sight. He thought how much Belphebe would have enjoyed this with him, then prayed she was safe and vowed that he would find her come hell or high water.

Soon it was too dark to continue. Shea stopped wearily and picked up a small stick. Maybe he could cast a light spell upon it, so he could see his way through the mounting darkness. He spent several frustrating minutes mumbling all sorts of incantations, but none of them sounded very poetic, and what was worse, none of them worked. He threw the stick away in anger and thought of trying to make another flying broom, but, search as he might, he could not find a bird feather in this desolate place.

Pitch-black night came on and a thoroughly discouraged Harold Shea began to clear a sleeping area in a meadow of tall grass. He had just settled down to an uncomfortable night's rest with a rock poking him in the side, when a flash of light suddenly caught the corner of his eye. He shook his head and looked again, and spotted a familiar glowing red ball atop the next hill. It was circling slowly. It was a fairy.

Shea stumbled rapidly up the hill. When he reached the summit, the familiar red fairy who had accompanied him before buzzed excitedly around his head and then started off into the dark. Shea followed, breathless.

The fairy led him along a rough path. After climbing what seemed like an endless procession of low hills, Shea was rewarded by the sight of several more fairies circling in the darkness around two seemingly human forms.

VI

Shea broke into a run crashing through a field of sweet-smelling tall grass. More fairies appeared, hovering close ahead above Bitter-Root and ... Belphebe!

They flew into each other's arms.

"Harold, darling, we have been searching for you, everywhere!"

"I'm mighty glad to see you alive," Shea said and he planted a kiss on her lips.

They returned to the spirit cave on the two-seater broom with Belphebe in the pilot's seat. She had learned how to fly in his absence and handled it with as much élan as she did the Shea Chevrolet. Shea wisely kept his mouth shut.

Shea was in a daze while Belphebe bathed her adventure-scarred husband in a pool inside the cave; the spirits had given him a wine that tingled through his body and restored his strength. Soon the world and its worries faded from view and he slept like a log.

At breakfast, Harold learned that Snag and Votsy were missing, and so was the magic book. He had hardly digested this information when Quamoclit came buzzing in excitedly. The witch and an army of goblins had marched into the spirit lands and had set a great fire which was rolling rapidly toward the spirit cave.

"Damn," Shea said angrily, "Sycorax must be upset over my escape."

"We must do something, Harold," said Belphebe. "Even without the book, you are still a master of magic."

"Against that witch, I wouldn't be too sure," said Shea, "but we'd better have a look. Too much of this island has been laid waste already." Outside they mounted the two-seater broom, and accompanied by the spirits flew off to see what they could do.

Cruising low over the treetops, they soon spotted the fires and landed in the field where Harold, Belphebe, and Polacek had first appeared on the island. It was safe, but the surrounding forests were all ablaze, and in the distance there were hundreds of goblins running to and fro with torches spreading the conflagration.

They made a neat landing in the clearing and Shea dismounted, putting his hand to his head in an effort to remember the spell he had used in the Kalavela to bring rain. Even though in that case it had backfired and brought clouds of soot, he had to try; the forest fire was raging out of control. He made several passes and began to chant a few lines of rather poorly constructed poetry about April showers. He had sung the spell in Finland, but spoken verse seemed to work better in the world of Shakespeare.

Soon, large black clouds boiled overhead. Belphebe shuddered and put her arm around Shea. The air became still and damp and the goblins stopped their work. The crackling forest fire was all that could be heard. Even the witch Sycorax looked warily into the sky. A blinding flash of lightning struck, followed immediately by a deafening clap of thunder.

A fine mist filled the air. That soon turned to rain, which quickly became an unbelievable downpour. It was almost as though they were standing under Niagara Falls. Shea grabbed Belphebe with both arms. He could hardly even see her. The ground on which they were standing became a river, and rushing water swirled around their legs. The spirits arrived and grabbed at Shea and Belphebe, pulling them along to higher ground just as a wall of water, laden with logs and broken trees, washed across the clearing.

Later, after the rain had stopped and the flash flood subsided, a sodden Shea surveyed the desolation below. The forest fire was out all right, and the goblins had been washed away. But so had half the countryside, and the grassy field had turned into a litter-strewn muddy swamp. Bitter-Root and Quamoclit were wringing out what remained of Belphebe's clothes.

"I think I got the decimal point wrong on that one," Shea said humbly.

"Is the fire not drowned, and are not our enemies gone with the flood?" said Quamoclit, turning to him with respect in her eyes.

"Yes, Harold," chimed Belphebe, "the day is ours!"

Shea kept thinking of another line from Shakespeare: "The quality of mercy is not strain'd. . . ." Today it did more than droppeth gently from heaven upon the place beneath . . . and he felt, at the moment, extremely beneath.

Shea waded back into the mud and, with help from his companions, managed to pull his flying broom out of the muck. Most of the feathers were missing, and it was all he could do to get it to limp along a few feet above the ground as they flew slowly back up the stream toward the spirit cave. The flood had certainly done an efficient job of clearing the valley. No help from the witch was even needed.

Belphebe nudged Shea and pointed ahead. Harold could just make out two figures mired in a sea of mud below. He nudged his flying mount closer. The figures turned into Votsy and Snag. The two men in the muck yelled and waved as the broom carrying Harold and Belphebe approached.

"Holy Saint Wenceslaus! You wouldn't believe the storm we just had!" the Czech said excitedly as Shea cautiously landed the broom on the mud and his feet sank into the muck. Polacek was trying to free a log apparatus that looked rather like an oxcart, and was filled with round stones.

Belphebe laughed, "We would believe, Vaclav. Harold summoned the storm to quench a great fire in yon forest."

"Bejesus, Harold, doncha think ya overdid it?" complained Polacek. "It nearly washed us away!"

"So I got the decimal point wrong, as usual. But it had to be done.... Where on earth have you been?" demanded Shea. "You were supposed to wait for us outside the witch's cave!"

The Czech suddenly turned away, shamefaced. "Hey, we waited. Then a bunch of goblins came along and we had to make a strategic retreat before Snag could crack a few heads." The sailor looked up and smiled. "When we came back, all hell had broken loose and the witch's guards were everywhere. So we lay low till dark and then sneaked back to where the broom was hidden."

" 'Twas there Pollychek found the book," added Snag.

"You've got it?" Shea asked excitedly. Nonchalantly the Czech pulled the volume out from under his coat.

"Safe and sound. Your broom was gone, so I figured you and the missus had to be all right. Then I had this idea." Polacek slapped the log device full of rocks proudly. "We've got a whole army here!"

Belphebe's eyes lit up. "You brought back the sailors from the beach!"

"You got it, toots. And this truck used to fly, albeit slowly, till rainmaker Harold washed us out with that biblical flood."

Shea shook his still aching head in disbelief.

They spent the rest of the day, digging the "truck" out of the mire and finally managed to get the load of sailors, in the form of rocks, safely inside the spirit cave. There followed a heated debate between Polacek and Shea as to who would turn the stones back into men, and how.

The spirits, on the sidelines, sadly complained that the power of Sycorax was beyond them; their magic could not help.

At last a course of action was decided upon, much to Polacek's dismay. Shea placed a stone on the center of a table. In very subdued and sonorous tones, he tried the sound magic he once used to raise simulacra. When he had finished there were two rocks on the table, but no sailors. He shook his head in dismay.

Shea let Polacek try next, with one of the spells Chalmers had intended to use to restore Florimel's human form. There was a puff of smoke and his rock turned into a foot-long bullfrog.

Polacek burst out laughing. "A fitting end for a man of the sea!" Snag suddenly appeared and grabbed him by the throat.

"Hey! Hey! Just kidding, just kidding, Snag. It was a joke. Somebody put that frog in a box till I can fix him."

Several hours later, the company went to sleep for the night with a cave still full of rocks.

After a fine conjured spirit breakfast, Shea felt refreshed and restored. He would have to find out just what they did to whip up such refreshing food! His mind turned back to the problem of the stones. Absently he watched Polacek fanning a rasher of bacon that was too hot to eat. Suddenly, Shea stood up with a start:

"Votsy! We were both right! We need to combine the verbal elements of the sound magic with the somatic elements of the spell you used ... and watch the decimal point."

"What?"

Shea quickly placed another stone on the table and began making wild passes with his hands. The Czech finally figured out what he was trying to do and soon they were both making passes and chanting. Their voices reached a crescendo, then,

WHUMP!

A very startled naked man appeared on the tabletop. Belphebe and the spirits cheered. Snag grabbed the Czech and the two danced around the cave. Soon an assembly line was set up. One by one, Shea and Polacek converted the stones back to men, the spirits clothed them, and Snag and Belphebe armed and organized them. By evening the cave was packed with hundreds of ex-rock sailors.

Harold leaned back in his chair and asked, "How many stones did you gather, Votsy?" The spirits arrived with more wine.

"I dunno, maybe a couple thousand."

By the end of the third day, the last stone had been turned. They even restored the bullfrog, who proved to be a businessman from Venice. He was very grateful, just the same. And after that the stone that Harold duplicated produced a pair of twins who had never seen each other before. The crowd had overflowed the spirit cave and a tent city sprang up on the hillside.

In the days that followed, Belphebe sorted out the men most adept at archery, and organized a contingent of missile troops. The rest of the men were armed with assorted spears, swords, clubs, and even rocks. Most of the ships' passengers requested assignment to the ambulance corps.

All seemed well with the world until Ariel returned to the cave for the first time since he had escaped from the service of the witch. He had been keeping an eye on Sycorax, waiting for the right moment to return, he explained. And the news he bore was grave indeed. The witch and her goblins were on the march again, and now there were more goblins than he had ever seen before.

By the time the ragtag sailor army was ready to march, the goblins had already crossed the mudflats and were coming up the valley, heading straight for the spirit cave. Fortunately, the spirits had gathered more eagle feathers and, on a restored two-seater, Shea and Belphebe flew a reconnaissance mission. They, too, were shocked at the number of goblins to be seen in the valley below.

"There must be ten thousand of them down there," Shea complained as they circled back to their own lines.

"Our cause is just, Harold," Belphebe said reassuringly.

The army was deployed in a wide arc across the valley in front of the cave, Belphebe's archers and the best spearmen massed behind the line as a reserve.

As the goblin forces approached, a silence fell over all. Suddenly a bolt of lightning from Sycorax crashed into a tree near Shea and the goblins rushed forward. Just as their ranks reached the spirit army, Belphebe's archers fired a volley into the air. The goblin center disintegrated. On the two flanks, however, the armies came together and were soon locked in fearsome melée.

Shea took Belphebe up on the broom, and he cruised up and down the enemy line while she picked off goblin leaders with well-aimed shots. Sycorax was no dummy however, and soon caught on. Each time they whizzed out from behind the trees she popped lightning bolts at them. A near miss singed the feathers on their tail, rendering the broom sluggish and unresponsive. Shea beat a hasty retreat to the safety of terra firma.

Meanwhile the battle raged and the press of the goblin army was overwhelming. The spirit forces were falling back. At this rate, it was apparent that the witch would soon drive them all into the sea. Shea pulled Belphebe aside and told her to continue the fight; he had a plan and would return. He held her in his arms for a brief parting kiss and then flew off, alone, on his broom.

Shea stayed low, zooming over the treetops till he was out of sight of the goblin army, then turned south for the only smoking volcano on the island. That had to be the Firemount mentioned by Malovio. He was not sure how he would do it, but he intended to enlist the aid of the fire drake. As he cruised in for a landing outside of the volcano, the place seemed mysteriously empty. Small wonder! Every able-bodied goblin had gone to war. A moan caught his ears as he searched the base of the mountain for an entrance.

There on a rope, hanging upside down from a dead tree was none other than Malovio. "You seem to spend a lot of time hanging by your feet. How do you manage to do this?" Shea remarked as he cut the hapless goblin down.

Malovio rubbed his ankles. " 'Tisn't easy, I assure you. Many thanks, Harold. It might well be because I refused to serve."

Shea asked about the way to the fire drake.

" 'Tis on the other side of the mountain," said the goblin, already backing away toward the cover of the undergrowth.

Shea grabbed Malovio by his ragged collar and pulled the monster onto the broom. The goblin eyed it with terror and struggled to escape. "I must away. . . ." But Harold dragged him astride the stick. In a flash he chanted the words and they were airborne. The goblin wailed as they flew rapidly around the base of the mountain. Suddenly Malovio recovered and pointed to the ground. Shea noted a large cave and eased the broom through the dark entrance. They landed and dismounted in silence.

"Thou wouldst strain our friendship!" complained the goblin. "Release me forthwith!"

"I'm sorry, old boy, but this is a life or death emergency; I have to find the fire drake," Shea said as he nudged Malovio with his elbow. The goblin led on, into the cavern. "Say, I thought you said you used to work for this drake?" Malovio grunted noncommittally. "If that's so," Harold continued, "how come you're so afraid to go near him?"

The goblin turned and grinned sheepishly. "Perhaps I portray'd him a bit too fondly. 'Twas the drake's custom to consume a goodly number of our kind upon awakening."

They came upon a deserted guard station, replete with a supply of dusty weapons and torches. Both took a torch and lit it on a burning lamp. Shea pushed his unwilling companion forward. The cavern was wide and tall, large enough, Shea imagined, to let the drake pass. They came to a place where the tunnel split off in two directions.

Malovio became even more nervous, if that was possible, and hopped back and forth from one foot to another. He was obviously going no farther.

"The path to the left!" the goblin cried, as he flung his torch against the wall and ran full speed back the way he had come. Shea started after the rascal, but the peril that Belphebe faced flashed before his eyes and he turned back. There was no time to spare.

Shaking his head over Malovio, Harold hurried along the corridor to the left. The path wound steeply downward. The echoes of his footsteps made him keenly aware of the great size of the tunnel. Some minutes and many tiresome footsteps later, the cave opened into a vast chamber. The torch was too weak to light the far side. Shea cautiously tiptoed as best he could across the room, through a crunchy layer of ashes and cinders.

He blinked. A great black mass loomed in front of him. What he first took to be a rock wall was actually the enormous bulk of the sleeping fire drake. Time for action.

Quietly, Shea backed away, then knelt down and constructed a rough model of the drake out of cinders. In a quiet whisper, he began to chant:

"Great beast of fire, whose council you keep,
        Friend of lord Surt, from under whose eyes,
    I bid thee awaken, from Sycorax's sleep,
            Unto my command, now serve me. . . . Arise!"

Shea fell silent. For a moment, nothing happened, then the great mound that was the fire drake rose and fell in a rumbling deep sigh. Years of accumulated rocks and dust tumbled off the top of the beast. Two glowing orange eyes popped open and stared into Shea's soul.

He fully expected to be roasted by a blast of flame, but the enormous drake rose slowly to its feet amidst a small rockslide, stretched itself interminably, and walked calmly over to its new master.

Shea thanked his stars and hurriedly climbed onto the creature's neck, which was no easy task. He settled comfortably between two large plates on its back, and waited. Nothing happened. Obviously more magic was in order. He recited a further rhyme:

> "Onward, noble steed, to battle we fly,
> For fame and glory, our victory is nigh. . . ."

Before Harold could finish, the drake lurched forward, rose from the cave floor, and sped toward the entrance. Just how the thing flew with its monstrous wings in this confined space was a mystery but somehow it was doing so with alarming speed. Shea hung on for dear life.

Moments later, they flashed out through the opening into the light of day. Shea was temporarily blinded as his eyes adjusted to the light. The great wings of the fire drake now began beating with a low, rhythmic murmur and they rose swiftly above Firemount. Shea was not sure how he controlled the monster, but it was doing exactly what he wanted. Could it be telepathic?

He tested his theory by directing the dragon to make a maneuver it would never do in the natural course of simple flying. Instantly Shea regretted the thought for the drake swirled effortlessly up and over in a tight loop, and for a precarious moment, its rider hung on by his fingernails. Satisfied that he was more or less in control, Harold righted the beast and pointed his juggernaut in the direction of the conflict.

VII

Belphebe cursed as a rock smashed into her shin. Since Harold had departed on his mysterious mission, she, Polacek, and Snag had been in control of the army of spirits, sailors, and fairies, and things were not going any too well. Polacek kept leafing through the magic book and attempting to cast spells which invariably failed, or worse, backfired, wreaking havoc among their own number.

Snag proved to be a natural leader, dividing the forces into platoons of fighting sailors who went into battle with no fear of death. Each time the forces of the witch made a move to outflank, Snag responded by sending in a counterattack which drove her minions back.

Sycorax was persistent, and she coerced her army of goblins forward. Although Belphebe and her archers and Snag and his swordsmen and spearmen took a fearful toll of the enemy, the witch seemed to have an endless supply of dark green, willing-to-die creatures. Snag was forced to give ground once again.

The spirit cave was overwhelmed, and they retreated over the ridge to the next hill ... and then to the next, and then the next. A bolt from the witch struck Quamoclit, and she was pinned to the heart of a pine tree. Belphebe winced as she heard the spirit scream. The sailors retreated at a command from Snag; and all, including Belphebe, ran at full speed over the last hill between them and the sea. The huntress searched the sky in vain for a sign of her husband.

A brief respite was achieved when Polacek cast a spell that actually worked. For several minutes, a large cloud of noxious yellow smoke poured out of a tree stump. As it drifted over the goblins, they reeled back in agony.

"Phosgene," said Polacek, smiling, "it's an old trick of the Huns from the First World War."

Belphebe looked at him with a puzzled expression. Harold had told her of a world war, but she had never heard of magic vapor weapons. But she was more concerned about the fact that there were only seven arrows left in her quiver. The sailors who stood by her side all seemed to have equally low supplies of missiles.

There was a sudden shout, and all faces looked skyward. Coming over the crest of the hill was a monster of enormous proportions. Another of the witch's servants, no doubt. They were surely doomed. Belphebe put her hand to her forehead and groaned.

Polacek began dancing up and down and shook her. "It's Harold," he exclaimed. Belphebe looked up in amazement and awe.

Shea was horrified to see the still vast number of goblins that swarmed over the forests below. His heart sank when he saw the spirit cave overrun. Was he too late? He banked to the left and swooped over the last row of hills.

There they were! He had arrived none too soon. The good guys certainly had their backs to the wall. Well, here was where Harold Shea and his flying fortress saved the day! He put the fire drake into a sharp wingover and thought about a stream of fire.

As his mount swooped in heavily from above, a blast of orange flame shot out of its mouth, engulfing hundreds of unfortunate goblins. Shea hung on tightly as he pulled up and circled for another pass. A few more strikes like that and the witch would be out of business ... and goblins.

He flew low over the army of sailors and could hear a cheer rising up from below. He spotted Belphebe and waved triumphantly. The drake flew out over the sea and then circled back for the next attack. This time, Shea intended to roast Sycorax herself and end the battle once and for all. This pass he caught sight of her red robe and aimed the drake straight at her, thinking flame-thrower thoughts.

Suddenly a bolt of electric blue light rose from where the witch stood and enveloped Shea and his mount. The firedrake shuddered. Its wings stopped beating and it veered off to the left. Shea found himself spiraling to the ground, aboard a dying bomber.

With a dreadful crash, the drake plowed into a mass of trees, snapping them off like matchsticks. Shea was thrown brutally into the side of a sand dune. He lay there, momentarily stunned.

Harold struggled to get his breath. He was still alive, he thought to himself. He rolled dizzily down to the base of the dune and sat, holding his spinning head in his hands, trying to orient himself. At last he saw Belphebe, jumping up and down and motioning to him. Shea struggled to his feet and staggered through a rain of goblin-thrown rocks to reach her side.

Belphebe crushed Harold in her arms. "Oh, dearest, I thought you would be killed," she said breathlessly. "Yet our plight has only grown worse since you arrived. Can you not think of some powerful spell to save us, Harold?"

A goblin spear felled a sailor who stood mere paces away. Shea's mind was a blur. There must be something he could do ... the Dolon Doom spell?

"Could you not summon beasts to our aid?" asked Belphebe, as she fired an arrow at the enemy. That piqued his spirit and Shea made up his mind.

A hail of large stones whizzed overhead and Shea hit

the dirt in the nick of time. A group of sailors nearly ran over him as they charged forward. Shea dashed over to a dead tree, hurriedly gathered some twigs, and then ran to the beach. Oblivious to the battle, he began shaping little forms out of the wet sand and placed two twigs in the nose of each figure. They didn't look much like rhinoceroses, but there was no time to lose.

There was a tremendous crash of thunder and Shea looked up to see the left flank of the sailor army enveloped in flames. He glanced around anxiously till he saw Belphebe and her entourage of archers, still holding their ground. Shea stood back and began making passes over his tiny models, and began to chant rapidly:

"Oh, creatures who feed on dank jungle's weed,
  Rise up from the sand and heed my demand. . . ."

Shea ducked as a long black spear whizzed past his ears. He resumed:

"With tempers most foul, and anger in bowel,
  Arise from the jungle bristling with horn,
  I conjure you now, arise and be born!"

The little images began to blur and a fine spray of sand was thrown up into the air around him. Shea cursed to himself; he had forgotten to invoke a deity . . . yet something was happening. He looked over to Belphebe, who had stopped to watch him. Her jaw dropped open. Just then, something large, brown, cold, and slimy, slapped him in the face and threw him to the sand.

Shea struggled to his knees, and was shocked to see himself surrounded by a herd of enormous twenty-foot lizards, each one with two silly-looking horns sticking out its nose. They began to waddle awkwardly off into the midst of the battle, looking something like iguanas made up to resemble dinosaurs in a low-budget Hollywood movie. Oh well, thought Shea, not exactly rhinos, but they certainly looked fearsome.

He ran back to Belphebe's side.

"Marry, Harold, but those are the strangest creatures you have yet summoned!" she said calmly, as she let loose her last arrow at a retreating goblin. Already the witch's forces were dropping their arms and fleeing in the face of huge horned lizards.

A great cheer rose up from the remnants of the army of sailors as the beasts began choking down incredible numbers of goblins. The tide of battle had indeed turned. Soon a group of goblins came forward waving a shabby white rag on the end of a stick and surrendered to Snag. Sycorax herself disappeared over the hillside under a puff of green smoke. Shea wanted to pursue her, but now there was the problem of how to stop the reptilian eating machines he had set into motion, for the beasts showed no sign of recognizing any sort of armistice or surrender from the goblins. Polacek was at his side.

"Quick, Votsy, find a counterspell in that book. We've got to stop these dinosaurs."

"No problem, chief!" The Czech thumbed quickly to a page and began waving his left hand in a broad series of sweeps while muttering something under his breath. To Harold's amazement, moments later the herd of giant lizards vaporized into clouds of harmless smoke.

Shea slapped his companion on the back. "Hey, well done! Doc Chalmers will be proud of you if we ever figure out how to get back home."

Polacek puffed out his chest proudly then bowed ceremoniously. "Vaclav Polacek, Interplanar Mage, at your service."

The rest of the afternoon was spent rounding up and securing the goblins who had surrendered, tending to the wounded, and burying the dead. Moonwort led Shea and Polacek to the tree to which Quamoclit was pinned. The weapon had missed vital parts, only catching her wing. After several tries, it was the Czech who freed her from

the tree. She was most appreciative and planted a powerful kiss on her rescuer's lips.

"Phew! This is it, Harold, I'm staying here and mar-
rying this babe."

"Forget it, Votsy, you two aren't even the same
species."

"For this I'll forgo offspring!" Quamoclit giggled and
fluttered off into the woods.

"Hey, wait, honey, I meant it! Really!"

By evening, the sailor army and its prisoners marched
back to the spirit cave and the leaders held council. The
sailors and the goblins were all anxious to get off the
island, and the spirits more than willing to be rid of
the lot. Various plans to achieve this were brought to
Shea's attention.

"Thy power of magicks is so great, surely the lot of us
could simply be whisked away to our homes with but a
pass of thy hand." A rich man from Verona was speaking.

"Nix on that option," said Shea flatly. "That's way
beyond our powers. And besides, this island *is* the home
of the goblins."

"No more," growled the one goblin leader who had
been admitted to the conference. "We're worse off with
the damn'd witch than ever we were serving the drake.
Those of us who remain alive are of one mind, and that
is departure by any means."

"This island is still rich with fine tall forests," suggested
Snag, "and among us are many skilled craftsmen. Perchance we might build ships to carry us off." There was
a general murmur of approval at this plan.

"But that could take years!" cried a voice in the back.

A glimmer of an idea came to Shea and he snapped
his fingers. "Maybe not. In my many and varied travels
through different continuua I've had considerable experience conjuring up monsters and the like, as you all may
well have noticed during the recent conflict." The sailors
mumbled approval and the goblin leader spat on the floor

in disgust. "I think that with a bit of help from Master Snag here, I can provide you all with fine ships, ready for you tomorrow, and you may sail them wherever you want." A cheer and applause came from those assembled.

Harold pulled Snag aside before everyone retired and asked if he could carve a small model ship from a bit of wood. The sailor shrugged his shoulders, but agreed willingly. Next morning, Snag delivered the work and Shea carried his tiny hand-carved model down to the beach, with half the sailors in tow. He stopped at the water's edge. The tide was obviously out, for the sand was littered with stranded jellyfish. Harold thanked his lucky stars; that was just what he needed if this scheme was to succeed. He placed the tiny carving that Snag had given him on the wet sand.

Several years back, he had been in Portsmouth, England, and visited HMS *Victory*, Admiral Nelson's flagship at Trafalgar, still preserved in pristine condition. A few copies of the *Victory* ought to be more than enough to ferry the shipwrecked sailors and the displaced goblins away from the island. He began to chant:

"By Nelson, Hardy, Hornblower, and Bush,
    England expects every man to do his duty,
    An hundred *Victories* please come to me now
    To carry the lost ones home beyond the sea."

Shea winced at his terrible blank verse, if that was the word for it, but it was all that came instantly to mind, and hoped that blank verse worked as well as rhyme in this continuum. After all, Shakespeare had written a lot of it. He closed his eyes and began waving his hands in the manner which had once brought forth simulacra in the *Kalevela*.

The earth began to shake, and a blue-gray mist enshrouded the coastline. The sailors fell silent for a moment, then broke out into noisy hurrahs. Shea stood up slowly. There in the water before him were a hundred three-deck ships off the line, identical copies of the HMS *Victory*. Why on earth had he asked for a hundred when ten would have been enough? The damn decimal point again! A fleet this size would have ruled the world had it ever really existed in Napoleon's time. Here in the world of *The Tempest* it would be like a fleet of modern battleships suddenly thrust upon the Phoenicians.

The sailors to a man, including Snag, splashed out into the water and swam for the nearest ship. In no time they had climbed aboard and were lowering boats over the sides. They pulled for shore, and the first one to arrive carried an enthusiastic Snag, who jumped over the gunwale and slapped Harold on the back.

"No finer ships have ere been built by the craft of man! Thou hast given us the dreams upon which a sailor sleeps!" He was grinning from ear to ear.

"I—I'm glad you like them," said Shea, at a loss for words.

"Incredible, Harold," remarked Polacek who was eyeing the mighty fleet in amazement. "But don't you think you overdid it?" A gleam suddenly came to the Czech's eyes. "Ya know, with a fleet like that, we could conquer the world."

"Don't even think about it! Let's hope nobody else thinks of that possibility." There was a lot of firepower afloat out there in those hundred gun ships.

"Seeing as how you conjured that navy up, d'ya think it'll last ... I mean long enough for them to get home?"

"Well, if we can keep the witch away from here, they should be okay. We haven't heard from her since she disappeared in that cloud of smoke, and that worries me."

But the witch did not return, that day or the next, and in that time captains were chosen and crews formed, and a steady stream of small boats ferried men and provisions out to the ships. The goblins were released and given fourteen ships of their own. They disappeared quickly over the horizon soon after they had set sail. Shea wondered how that was managed, since none of the goblins seemed to have had any nautical experience.

The morning of the third day after the battle saw the final boatload of sailors making ready to leave. The spirits, Polacek, Belphebe, and Shea were all there to bid Snag and his companions a final farewell.

"My heart goes out to you, Master Shea, and to you, Pollychek, for all the good you have done these days." There was a tear in the burly sailor's eye. He held Belphebe in his arms and hugged her gently. "Without you, we all had perished, mistress."

"Fair winds, gentle Snag." She kissed him on the cheek. Then the dark man could wait no longer. He tossed a canvas bag into the longboat and pushed it out into the low surf. The men put their backs to the oars, and the boat pulled quickly away. Shea stood with his arm around his wife and watched. The boat pulled up alongside a great ship, the sails filled with the wind, and the ship sped quickly away.

When Snag's vessel had disappeared below the horizon, Belphebe turned to her husband. "Methinks 'tis time we, too, gave thoughts to home and our daughter."

"You're right as usual, darling. And I'm certain we have changed things enough here to satisfy my geas. Votsy, let me have a look at the book." The Czech reached into his coat pocket but stopped with a start. His eyes widened and his jaw fell open and he raised his arm and pointed.

Shea looked around. On the top of the hill stood Sycorax, smiling hideously, holding her crooked staff defiantly in the air.

Harold pulled Belphebe to him. A sudden bolt of lightning from the witch blasted the beach before them, sending up a stinging cloud of sand.

"Hold on to me, Belphebe . . . you too, Votsy," Shea said desperately. "I'm going to try the spell Chalmers gave me to use on Dolon—brace yourselves." He began to gesture wildly with his free hand as he mumbled the dangerous words of the incantation. It had worked before, destroying one of the most powerful magicians in the land of Faerie. It might work now, and destroy the witch ... and possibly the three of them as well.

Shea finished the last words of the incantation, and the world turned gray. More sand stung Harold's face and the entire beach erupted in a terrific explosion.

The smoke cleared, revealing a scene of utter serenity. Gone was Sycorax, gone were the mounds where the bodies had been buried and the carcass of the fire drake. Three bodies were sprawled on the beach behind some clumps of grass. One of them moved.

Shea groaned and pushed himself up on his elbows for a look around. What had happened? He reached over and touched Belphebe, who was just coming around, and saw Polacek, who was flat on his back mumbling something. Why weren't they in Ohio?

Out on the beach he saw a bearded man pulling a small boat ashore. With him was a young girl. The boat crunched into the sand and the man jumped out, lifting his small companion out in one big swoop. The man looked around at the pristine beach and said to the girl: "What quiet and unspoil'd place is this. . . ."

Shea groaned. The man tossed his bundles on the beach and walked inland, holding the girl's hand. Shea nudged Vaclav, who had crawled over to his side and was also watching.

"There's your Miranda, Votsy, a five-year-old! D'you still want to nab her?"

Prospero stopped suddenly and bent down. He picked up a book and leafed through the pages with interest.

"Our book," whispered Vaclav.

Prospero began bobbing back and forth as he read, motioning with his hands. He was reciting something which Shea could not quite understand. Suddenly the world around them turned gray and began to spin.

Pmft!

A whoosh of air made the curtains dance. Shea, Belphebe, and Polacek landed with a thump on the stage at the theater. The lights were dim and the seats were empty save for one man, who began to clap slowly. It was Reed Chalmers. He stopped the sarcastic applause and shook his head sadly.

Shea pulled Belphebe into his arms and swallowed her up in a great big mushy kiss.

"Hey, Doc," said Polacek as he sat up, "I bet you didn't know that one of those books in Prospero's library came from the Garaden Institute, right here in Ohio!"